St. Martin's Paperbacks titles by Jill Jones

My Lady Caroline
Emily's Secret

MY LADY CAROLINE

Jill Jones

St. Martin's Paperbacks

This is a work of fiction based upon the historical facts surrounding the lives of Lord Byron and Lady Caroline Lamb. Other than the historical figures portrayed here, all characters are entirely fictional, and any resemblance to any persons or actual happenings is purely coincidental. Material for the "memoirs" was based upon fact, but the memoirs are entirely fictional.

MY LADY CAROLINE

Copyright © 1996 by Jill Jones.

ISBN: 0-312-95836-6

Printed in the United States of America

St. Martin's Paperbacks edition / June 1996

10 9 8 7 6 5 4 3 2 1

For Brooke,
Erik, and Brad,
who once upon a time were always good
for a ghost story.

ACKNOWLEDGMENTS

I wish to express my heartfelt thanks to Mr. Alistair E. Scott, for his incredible hospitality during my trip to England, for the books and materials he lent me, and for the many unusual doors he opened for my research, particularly a door to the past and a remarkable and timeless love affair. It is almost as if he introduced me to Lady Caroline herself.

My thanks also to Mrs. Margaret Scott, for sharing her home and her wonderful wit.

Inexpressible thanks go to Virginia Murray, archivist at John Murray Publishers, London, who so generously shared her knowledge of Byron and the firm's historical artifacts from the days when her husband's ancestors published the work of Lord Byron.

I also wish to thank Kate Thomas, Conference Coordinator, Brocket Hall, for our tour of Caroline Lamb's favorite residence on the banks of the River Lea in Hertfordshire, and the Canon Fred Green of the Parish Church of St. Mary Magdalene, in Hauknall, near Newstead Abbey, for his kind hospitality as we visited the place where Lord Byron is buried. My thanks also to Gianna Utilini of James Chase Independent Estate Agents, Hertford, for proving that such a property as Dewhurst Manor might exist.

I am grateful to Ann Whisenhunt, Manager of In the Oaks Episcopal Center, Black Mountain, North Carolina, whose tour of this facility gave me many ideas for the fictional country house of Dewhurst Manor.

Thanks to two people who continue to offer excellent

creative advice and strong support, my husband, Jerry Jones, and my editor, Jennifer Enderlin.

And finally, thanks to my good friend, Bonnie Sagan, for accompanying me on my journey into the past, and for putting up with my vagaries along the way.

That beautiful pale face is my destiny.

— Lady Caroline Lamb, from her journal, 1812

⌒ *Prologue* ⌒

"**S**top it! That tickles!"

"Hold still." The handsome but pale young man in the steaming bathtub brushed a dampened lock of curling auburn hair from his forehead and resumed his preoccupied examination of the lady's foot. The water-softened sole of the slender appendage was a maze of lines and creases along which Lord Byron allowed his disturbed imagination to travel. He traced the pattern of interwoven furrows and ridges with his forefinger, lightly at first, then with greater pressure as a strange panic rose in his breast.

He must find a way out.

With every passing day, he felt himself ever more deeply ensnared in a frightful, invisible web being woven around him by the beautiful, erotic, but possessive and demanding Lady Caroline. Even when she was far away, as she was at the moment, he seemed unable to free himself from thoughts of her. She stalked his dreams and tormented his daylight hours. She drew him as if she were an enchantress, her fateful spell one that threatened his very being.

"Whatever are you doing, darling?" Lady Oxford shivered as his touch shifted from gentle to painful.

Byron scowled, wishing she'd bear up in silence rather than interrupt his concentration. But it was, after all, her foot. His lip curled in a mocking grin. "I'm trying to read the future."

"In my foot?"

"Why not?"

Lady Oxford gave a short, derisive laugh. "Byron, my Lord, it's the *hands* the Gypsies tell fortunes from, not the feet."

"I'm not a Gypsy."

Distracted, Byron entwined his fingers with the lady's toes and frowned. There must be a way out. There had to be. But he'd tried everything he could think of to dissuade the lady of her passion, all to no avail. "I suppose I could kill her," he murmured.

Lady Oxford pulled her foot away and sat up in the tub abruptly. Her breasts bobbed like pale pink apples just below the waterline, barely visible beneath the layer of bubbles that floated on the surface. Her face was flushed, and her eyes shone with sudden intrigue. "Did you say kill? Kill who?"

Byron stared at his hands now bereft of their object of meditation. He alone knew the truth behind the rumor that he'd once killed a man in the Orient. He wondered if he could kill someone he knew. "Caro," he replied in a hollow voice.

"Oh, that business again. Why do you continue to bother with that insufferable brat?"

Byron studied the woman whose buttocks he now fondled with his toes. Well into her middle years, Lady Oxford's legendary beauty was beginning to fade. Age was showing in lines around the pale blue eyes, and her generous mouth was likewise scored. Still, she was a master of the art of love, having taken most of England's finest to bed with her, and Byron had to admit he'd enjoyed his turn as her latest paramour. But at her words, his full lips twisted into a cynical smile.

"I thought that 'insufferable brat' was your friend,"

he said scornfully, knowing that Caroline had valued what she perceived to be Lady Oxford's kind regard.

The ease between them that Byron had come to enjoy during his stay at Eywood was suddenly shattered, and the wife of Edward Harley, the fifth Earl of Oxford, raised her sumptuous if well-used body to the edge of the tub and reached for a lace-trimmed towel.

"I suppose she told you that," she replied laconically. Then she laughed, and it was a short, bitter sound that rang of the sort of hypocrisy Byron loathed. "I suppose she actually thought that," Lady Oxford mused, "although our correspondence was more to her benefit than mine. I found it amusing, however," she added, "that she so quickly adopted my ideas. But then she is so . . . young."

Byron watched his mistress-of-the-moment run the towel sensually down her long leg. How could Caro ever have believed her to be a friend? Even though he wanted desperately to rid himself of Lady Caroline's dangerous attention, he felt sorry that she had entrusted her friendship to this woman. He never ceased to marvel at the deceitful nature of the female gender. The sex simply could not be trusted.

"Young, but a determined bitch," Byron replied. "Maybe I should depart for the Continent before she returns from Ireland."

Lady Oxford laughed contemptuously. "Do you really think that would solve your problem?"

Byron stared at her. "What do you mean?"

"You cannot run away from Caroline. She would pursue you across land and sea. She seems not to care what people say, or that she is a married woman."

The truth in her words slammed into him, and Byron slunk down further into the tub of now lukewarm water.

"I must make her hate me then," he growled.

"What, love?" The naked, full-figured woman slipped a petticoat over her head, unmindful of his open observation. There was no reason to mind. They had lain together as lovers for weeks, despite the fact that he was almost young enough to be her son.

"Hate me. I must make her hate me." Byron stood up, dripping from head to toe and shivering slightly in the cool room. He felt the eyes of his experienced mistress travel down his body, which he always believed to be on the verge of corpulence, and he covered himself hastily with a thick towel.

"Why do you bother?" Lady Oxford poured a rich brandy into two crystal glasses that waited on a small nearby table and brought one to Byron.

"If she hates me," Byron replied, slipping into a Turkish dressing robe before taking the proffered glass, "then she will leave me alone. I simply cannot bear another scene on my doorstep like the last."

Lady Oxford laughed. "Caro will never hate you. She is many things, but hateful she is not. It is not in her nature."

It was Byron's turn to scoff. He glanced at his inamorata with a bitter smirk. "Everyone hates, my dear," he said. "It is *human* nature."

The couple, having sated their sexual appetites previous to the bath, now retired to the dining room for tea. The pale late afternoon sunlight strained through the tall windows in a vain attempt to dispel the gloom in the darkly-paneled room. "Let us not speak of that which poisons our peace," Lady Oxford said soothingly, drawing him into the chair next to hers at the head of the long, highly-polished table. "Tell me, my dear Byron," she spoke in a quiet, intimate voice as she traced a nail across the top of his hand, "have we not passed our last month like the gods of Lucretius?"

Byron found he could not disagree. His time spent with the voluptuous Lady Oxford at her husband's country house had indeed been an oasis of calm amidst the turbulence of his existence since he had returned from the Continent. This *belle dame* demanded little and gave much when it came to his pleasure. Besides, among her "Harleian Miscellany," the flock of children sired on her by various liberal leaders in England's House of Lords, were several beautiful young daughters whose charms and open flirtations were not lost on Byron.

"That we have, my dear, but our Olympian pleasure notwithstanding, I must attend to the matter of Lady Caroline. I fear that sweet William will be unable to restrain her for long, and that she will escape from her enforced vacation in Ireland and land back in my lap." He kissed her fingertips, counting on the lady's innately devious nature to help him out. He gave her hand an encouraging squeeze. "You corresponded with her intimately. You know her ways. If she won't hate me, what then, pray tell, will it take to get the woman out of my life once and for all?"

Lady Oxford sighed and withdrew her long, slender fingers from his grasp. She leaned back against the rich damask of her chair, studying him. "It would seem to me, Lord Byron, that your efforts to rid her from your life are predestined to fail."

"Why? What are you saying?"

She shrugged lightly. "I'm saying that I do not believe you really want to be rid of her."

"You're insane! The woman is nothing but a thorn beneath my hide."

"I believe you are still in love with her."

Byron felt his blood beginning to boil. "Nonsense!" he shouted, bolting from the chair and throwing his napkin onto the floor. "Whatever would fill your mind with such rubbish?"

Unruffled, Lady Oxford continued. "I have come to know you well in these last weeks," she said at last. "Although you feign affection for me, your thoughts have never been far from Caroline."

"That's preposterous," Byron thundered.

"Is it?" Lady Oxford twisted her napkin as her lips lifted into a mirthless smile. "Then why must I suffer day and night from your mumblings and rumblings about her?"

Byron was about to deny her allegation again, but stopped abruptly, caught suddenly by the notion that the lady spoke the truth. Not that he was in love with Caroline, but that he was consumed by thoughts of her. Mostly thoughts of how to avoid her, but if he were honest, also thoughts about how her slender, boyish body aroused his passion and how her soft, lisp-laden words managed to slip beyond his normal guard, easing with liquid enchantment into his insecure, love-starved heart.

But did this mean he loved her?

Impossible! Women were a sex he could not love.

Cold perspiration dampened his skin, and he turned to Lady Oxford. "I must escape her. I must!" Byron went to the window and peered into the manicured gardens below. The elegant order that met his eye only heightened his rage. The world did not deserve to be orderly and beautiful when he himself existed in such a state of confused torment. He turned a harsh glare on his mistress. "Think what you will," he snarled, "but I vow to you, I do not, nay never have I, loved Lady Caroline Lamb. And I will be damned if I let her continue to haunt my every waking hour. I will find a way out, if I have to strangle her with these two hands. . . ."

"That . . . won't be necessary." Lady Oxford's voice echoed with cold authority into the dark corners of the room, reminding Byron of his mother. He shuddered and moved to stand behind her chair, wanting to avoid those maternal eyes but waiting eagerly to hear the jealous woman's solution.

"There is more than one way to kill someone," she said at last, steepling her fingertips. "And what I propose is far less messy than murder."

Byron's heart began to pound in his chest. Intrigued, he ran his fingers down the lady's throat and pressed them into the soft flesh of her bosom. "Go on."

Lady Oxford stretched and took one of his hands, drawing him to where she could see his face. She smiled with malevolent satisfaction. "I even believe you will find it amusing, my darling. I daresay I will. It will be like a game, or like playing with a fish on a line. . . ."

⌒ Chapter 1 ⌒

A bell tolled solemnly from somewhere high above, its metallic tone reverberating off the cold stone walls of the cathedral. It sounded unreal and very far away to Alison Crawford Cunningham, daughter of *the* Crawford Cunninghams of Boston, Mass.

Except *the* Crawford Cunninghams were dead.

And Alison sat with a spine of steel in the first pew, staring dry eyed, unbelieving, at the two ornate caskets on the bier in front of her. It seemed impossible. Only last week she had been sunning on the beaches of Cannes. Today, she shivered in the hollow coldness of Trinity Church, listening to the minister conclude the funeral services for her parents. She would never see them again, even in death, for their caskets were closed. The funeral director had said it was best. It had been a horrible crash, with only shards of the small private plane recognizable on the Vermont mountainside.

Not possible, Alison thought, her stomach knotting. This isn't happening to me. Mother and Dad are home, or in Palm Beach, and I'm having a nightmare.

Although Alison had never been close to her parents, had never thought she ranked very high on their priority list, she'd always held out hope that one day, maybe just once, one of them would say, "I love you." Now, she realized with a jolt, that would never, ever happen. She suppressed a dry sob and sighed deeply.

It probably never, ever would have happened anyway.

She felt a hand at her elbow and turned bleakly to the family's attorney, Benjamin Pierce, who indicated that it was time to stand for the closing prayer. Grateful for his quiet support, she managed to rise, but her knees threatened to collapse at any moment.

Afterwards, mourners shuffled quietly toward the rear of the church, speaking in hushed voices. Alison forced a tight smile for the few who came up to her to offer their condolences. They were strangers for the most part. Business acquaintances of her father. Prominent figures in Boston society who comprised her mother's circle of friends. Names she vaguely recognized, but people she didn't know.

There were no family members, because there was no family left.

Only herself.

An unfamiliar ache sliced through her, and Alison feared she might cry. Not that crying was so unusual or out of place at a funeral. But Alison knew that any tears she shed at the moment would not be tears of mourning for her parents, but rather tears of gross self-pity. She wanted to cry for the love she'd craved but never known. She wanted to cry because suddenly she was so alone. And because, whether he loved her or not, her father was no longer there to take care of her every want and need. She had never had to be self-sufficient in her life, and the thought terrified her.

Summoning strength she didn't feel, she veiled her tears and remained outwardly calm, determined not to let anyone see the frightened child she was inside.

Outside in Copley Square, a pale springtime morning greeted them and a late March wind brushed against her cheeks. Scattered clouds skimmed overhead, and a fat-breasted robin hopped among the first crocuses that peeped out at the winter-weary world. It all seemed out of place on this day of death, and Alison wished suddenly and perversely that it was raining.

Gradually, she became aware of the others around her, a sea of black, it seemed, carrion crows standing in small groups, talking quietly, with an occasional nod in her direction. A television crew pointed a camera at her, and she turned away, only to encounter an eager-faced couple, the man and woman who had been seated on the other side of Benjamin inside the church.

"Alison," she heard Benjamin say, "I want you to meet my daughter, Cecelia, and her husband, Drew Hawthorne."

The woman was tall and gaunt, with too-red lips and hollow cheeks. An elegant black woolen cape swirled about her shoulders, topping an expensive black suit. She smiled, but her attempted expression of sympathy stopped somewhere behind cold, marble gray eyes. The man was shorter than his wife, paunchy, with a ruddy complexion and faded blue eyes. His stiffly-moussed brown hair moved as a single mass in the light breeze.

"Hello," Alison murmured. It was all she could summon at the moment.

"I'm afraid I won't be able to accompany you to the cemetery," Benjamin said apologetically. "I have to be in court in less than an hour. But I've asked Drew and Cecelia to go with you. If you need anything, I'm sure you can depend on them."

"Of course, dear." Cecelia spoke in a throaty voice. "We're here for you, poor darling."

Alison shuddered in the cool sunshine. She didn't want to go with these people. She'd counted on Benjamin Pierce to get her through the day. At least his was a familiar face, fatherly, comforting. If he wouldn't go with her, she'd rather be left alone.

Alone.

It struck her again with a vengeance how very alone she really was.

Not watching where she was going, Alison struck the toe of her shoe against the uneven pavement and stumbled. Drew Hawthorne took her elbow and attempted to guide her toward the waiting limousine, but she pulled away from him. She turned to Benjamin to object to his leaving her, but he had disappeared into the crowd of mourners.

Three weeks later, Alison stared out of the window of the giant jetliner as it lowered onto the landing strip of the sunny Florida airport. Palm Beach was a long way from Boston, but as far as Alison was concerned, it couldn't be far enough. She'd had it with the big, cold, lonely mansion in Brookline. With Pierce, Buckner, Fromme, and Withoff, Attorneys-At-Law. With wills and trusts and insurance policies and legal documents she couldn't understand.

And especially with Drew Hawthorne.

She was disappointed that instead of remaining the client of Benjamin Pierce, she'd been shunted off to that idiot. Benjamin Pierce should have been the one to read the will and explain all the complexities to her. After all, he had been her father's attorney for forty years, and she trusted him. But it was obvious that now that her powerful, controlling father was no longer in the picture, the firm had transferred the Cunningham account into the hands of some lesser legal talent than Pierce, his son-in-law Drew Hawthorne. Alison wondered how competent Hawthorne was, if he came by his junior partnership in the firm honestly, or only by marrying that skinny, red-lipped woman.

The plane bumped and squealed as the wheels met the tarmac, and Alison pressed her body into the back of the first-class seat, closing her eyes, feeling the power of the engines slowing the beast down. She tried not to think about how her parents had died, or what their last moments might have been like. If she did, she'd never fly again.

After the chill Boston springtime, Alison welcomed the hot, wet heat that swathed her skin as she exited the plane, and the prospect of seeing her best friend Nicki Carmione bolstered her spirits. The last few weeks had been a living nightmare, and she'd had no one to talk to, no one with which to share her terror.

Nicki was there as promised, waving enthusiastically at Alison from the crowd in the airport. Sudden tears pricked Alison's eyes, and she ran into the sisterly embrace of her tall, dark-haired friend, seeking the comfort no one had afforded her in Boston.

"God, I'm glad to see you," she managed.

"Good to see you, too, Ali," Nicki said, giving her an extra hug. "What a crummy thing to have happen."

Alison drew a deep breath. "You can say that again."

But neither mentioned the tragedy again as they retrieved Alison's luggage, threw it in the trunk of Nicki's convertible, and headed toward the Cunninghams' winter home on the Atlantic shore. It wasn't until they were safely ensconced in her room on the second floor of the sprawling Spanish-style mansion and Alison began unpacking that either dared speak of what both wanted to talk about.

"What are you going to do, Ali?" Nicki asked with her usual forthright approach.

Caught off-guard, Alison dropped the blouse she was unpacking. She bent to pick it up, wishing she wasn't such a klutz. Shrugging with pretended lightheartedness, she hung the garment in the closet and replied, "What I've always done, I guess. Go places. See my friends. Have a party."

A long silence stretched between them. Then Nicki spoke and again cut to the heart of the matter. "Who's taking care of . . . your . . . affairs?"

"You mean my money?" Suddenly angry, Alison turned on her friend. "Well, certainly not me. Those lawyer boys in Boston seem to have everything fairly well in hand. They worked it all out with my father. In fact," she added, unable to hide the bitterness she felt, "they told me not to worry about a thing. I swear to God they treated me like a six-year-old."

Nicki studied her. "It's hard for me to say what I would do if I were in your shoes," she said carefully, "but it would make me real nervous if a lawyer who was in charge of the kind of money in your parents' estate told me not to worry."

Alison slumped onto the bed with a sigh. "I'm sure they have my best interests at heart. Besides, what choice do I have? I don't know beans about finance. Daddy always took care of everything. I never thought . . ."

And then there they were . . . the tears she'd fought every minute of every day for three weeks. Tears for the deaths of her parents, despite their years of estrangement. Tears of frustration at finding herself so unprepared to face the massive responsibilities of her inheritance. Tears of self-pity, self-hatred, anger. "Damnit, why did they have to die and leave me like this?" she sobbed.

Nicki sat down beside her, and Alison felt the warmth of her best friend's arms around her. "I don't think they planned it this way, Ali," she said softly.

Alison took comfort in her friend's embrace and allowed herself to empty her heart of tears. "Oh, Nicki," she moaned at last, hiccuping between spasmodic sobs. "What am I going to do? I was such a dumb-ass not to finish college."

"Can't disagree with you there," her friend replied with an understanding squeeze of her hand. "But you can always go back, you know. You only lack a year."

Alison straightened. She'd never thought of returning

to college. There hadn't been any need to. Her father
paid all her bills, and she only had to show up at Christmas. The rest of the time, the world was her playground.
It hadn't mattered before that her knowledge of high
finance and money management was inadequate to her
position as sole heir to a fortune both old and vast. She
simply hadn't cared. Daddy always took care of everything. In her mind, that somehow proved he loved her,
she guessed, even if he never said it directly.

But sitting across the polished mahogany desk from
Drew Hawthorne as he made his way through the will
and the terms of the Cunningham trust and the foundation her father had established and all the other complexities of the estate, she'd felt like an immature
schoolgirl in the principal's office. She'd understood little of what he'd read, other than that her father had
placed most of her assets in trust, and she couldn't
touch them until she was thirty-five.

Nine years from now.

At first, she had been furious that her father would
have done such a thing. Did he trust her so little? But
then, she thought ruefully, she'd never given him much
to trust in. How could she blame him? What did she
know about money management? Investment strate-
gies? Estate planning? She didn't even know what questions to ask.

For the first time, Alison regretted that she'd chosen
early on to butt heads with her domineering father, doing everything she could to disobey him. For the first
time, she wanted desperately to hear—and heed—his
advice.

However, that, like hearing him say "I love you," was
no longer a possibility.

But perhaps returning to college was. She looked up
at Nicki. "That's a thought," she said. "Maybe I will.
But right now, I just wish I could talk to Daddy."

Nicki stared at her. "That's a switch. But it's a little

late now," she added solemnly. "You'd get more answers from your lawyer."

"Hawthorne's a nerd, and half the time I have no idea
what he's talking about."

"Then fire his ass and get someone you can work
with."

"I wish it was that easy," Alison replied morosely.
"The way it's set up, it looks to me like I'm stuck with
Hawthorne unless his own firm takes him off my ac-
count."

She walked to the window and looked out onto the
lush landscape below. The exotic fuschia blossoms of
ancient bougainvillea vines draped the high walls that
surrounded the estate, and clumps of pink and red and
white impatiens bloomed in profusion at the bases of
the swaying palm trees. She had always loved this place,
but according to what Hawthorne had told her, even
though she was to have free use of it at any time, this
home—*her* home—didn't belong to her. Wouldn't, until
the trust expired in nine years. She swallowed over the
tightness in her throat.

"Oh, Nicki, I have screwed up so royally. I would give
my soul just to have one hour with my father right now."

To her surprise, Nicki smiled. "There might be a
way."

"Get serious," Alison replied bitterly. "Nobody talks
to the dead. I was just wishing out loud."

"I am being serious," Nicki said, astounding Alison
further. Nicki was usually the most down-to-earth one in
the crazy set of friends they ran with.

"I suppose you're going to suggest we have a seance,"
Alison replied dryly.

"You're reading my mind," Nicki said with an encouraging grin. "I'm game if you are."

Twilight strained through the high windows at the man's
back, illuminating dusky dust motes dancing in the day's

waning moments. Outside the old warehouse where he'd just taken delivery of his latest prize, London rushed noisily through crowded streets, straining homeward at the end of the workday. But Jeremy Ryder heard nothing as he ran strong, sure fingers over the wooden surface of the fine old desk, stroking the grain as if it were a lover's skin.

The wood on the underside of the desktop, although smooth, had the uneven texture of a piece that had been planed by hand, and the intricate maze of drawers within could only have been created by a master woodworker in a time when craftsmanship was art. The desk, Jeremy was certain, was a superb specimen from the late eighteenth or early nineteenth century, when George IV was prince regent of England and Napoleon sought to rule the world. This piece, he decided, would stay in his private collection.

Unless, of course, someone came along and offered him enough money for it.

He laid his palm flat against the desktop and closed his eyes, palpating the wood with the expertise of a doctor seeking a patient's pulse. He intentionally had scheduled the desk to arrive after his staff had left for the day, for he had never shared the secret to his meteoric success with anyone.

As a boy Jeremy had learned from his Uncle Clive, an Oriental rug merchant, to respect the antiquities that passed through his hands. Clive had taught him to use his imagination to "listen for," or create if necessary, the history of each piece.

"People want to know something exciting about what they are buying, son," he'd said. "A good story is worth money." Jeremy took his uncle's instruction seriously, as a piece of practical business advice to enhance profits, but he'd found to his astonishment when he'd opened his own business that often he could honestly "feel" the history of an important piece like this. When he took the time to "listen," as he was now, he almost always intuited a history that, if not completely accurate, was realistic and believable, and which satisfied his increasing clientele.

Who was the artisan who built this desk? he wondered, letting his mind go back into his extensive knowledge of English history. Who was the original owner? What stories could it tell, if it could only speak?

This was an aspect of his profession he secretly enjoyed, but rarely these days did he have the opportunity to indulge in its practice. His taste and genuine appreciation for the antique, the elegant, the rare, and beautiful, coupled with a sharply-honed business acumen, had rapidly transformed his small, one-man enterprise into a thriving antiquities dealership with a world-class reputation. But now time constraints prevented him from giving each piece his personal attention, unless he suspected it had unusual potential, like this desk.

He smiled, turning over a small drawer and noting the hand-chamfered wood and carefully carved dovetails, features that made him ever more certain that the desk was manufactured before the invention of machines that stamped out more modern versions like cookie cutters.

Jeremy had come across the desk in a ramshackle junk shop north of London, and from the relatively low price asked for it, he'd realized the owner had no idea of its possible true value. Of course, he wouldn't know for sure until he'd appraised it personally, but he'd felt from the moment he'd first seen it that it was likely an authentic Regency piece, worth far more than the price tag on it.

That's why he'd offered the shopkeeper even less.

"Each party to a negotiation must feel as if he's gotten the best deal possible," he'd once explained to a lovely but naive young woman who expressed her shock over his tactics. "My uncle always told me, if you give in too soon, or don't negotiate at all, the seller believes he didn't ask enough. It makes him very unhappy, you know." And then he'd turned his sexiest smile fully on her, looked deeply into her eyes with an expression that left no question as to what he had on his mind, kissed her lightly along her delectable neck, and added in a sensuous voice, "I never want to make anyone unhappy."

He'd won that negotiation as well.

If only women were as uncomplicated as the exquisite antiquities he bought and sold, he mused absently as he continued to explore the complex network of drawers that had been intriguingly designed into the desk. Jeremy generally liked women, and women definitely liked Jeremy, but he'd managed to stave off any serious involvement for his entire thirty-three years. The women he had dated were like the *objets d'art* in which he dealt —beautiful, exquisite, and expensive—but unlike his beloved antiques, they were not content to be admired and then set aside. He could inquire into the history of a piece like this desk with no further obligation. But if he showed the slightest interest in a woman beyond mere flirtation, he often found later that the lady had set her cap for him and was contriving ways to place his wedding band on her left hand.

That would be one cold day in hell, he laughed to himself. As it was, he had his pick of the beautiful women of London, the Continent even. Why would he want to settle down with only one woman and ruin a perfectly civilized existence?

"Ow!" A splinter from the edge of one of the drawers stabbed Jeremy's finger, and in jerking his hand away, he tore a bit of the thin lining from the wood. He placed his finger in his mouth, frowning, and then looked more closely into the drawer. He spied something white peeking from beneath the faded rust-colored fabric. "What's this?"

With the touch of an expert preservationist, he pulled

gently at the musty lining, which gave way easily, revealing beneath it what appeared to be a letter. Gingerly, not wanting to damage the fragile paper, he slowly unfolded his find. He raised an eyebrow. The desk, it appeared, was going to give up its secrets more easily than he'd expected.

It was indeed a letter, addressed to a Mr. John Pembroke, Esq. of London. The handwriting was faded, almost illegible, but he made out the date to be June 12, 1824.

Jeremy's heart picked up several beats. Quickly, he took the paper into his adjoining office and switched on the high intensity lamp on his desk. With a tingle of anticipation, he settled into the rich, well-worn leather of his favorite chair and began to make his way through the message that was traced on the paper in a fine feminine script.

When he finished, he sat staring at the page, not daring to believe that what he held in his hands could be authentic.

But hoping like hell it was.

⟋ *Chapter 2* ⟍

The last of the men invited to the private meeting had arrived, and John Murray hurriedly ushered them in, locking the door behind them.

"Shall we begin then?" he asked, following the men upstairs and into his large office, where listless, nervous conversation was stirring between the rest of the gentlemen assembled. "We all know we are gathered here to . . . uh, discuss how best to protect the interests of our late friend and respected poet, Lord Byron, God rest his soul."

"His interests, or yours?" growled Thomas Moore, into whose keeping Byron had entrusted a thick sheaf of papers, his personal memoirs, before his death in faraway Greece.

"As you well know, sir, I above all, as his publisher, stand to lose the two thousand guineas I have already paid you for the privilege of publishing his memoirs, not to mention the considerable income they would yield when sold. But after reading them, I have changed my mind. I will never print them. I swear, they must not see the light of another day."

"Preposterous!" Tom Moore glared at Murray. "I will gladly give you back your damned two thousand. Byron was a great poet. A great man. These memoirs belong to the world. If you do not wish them to be published, then they must be stored in a vault somewhere, for posterity."

"They belong to Augusta. As his sister and only adult living relative." This from Wilmot Horton, a slender, balding solicitor who was attending the meeting as Augusta's representative. "And Augusta wishes them destroyed."

"As well they should be," added John Cam Hobhouse in a quiet voice. He paused, then continued. "Long have I been called friend by Lord Byron. Long have I sought to keep the prying public from knowing . . . certain aspects of his behavior lest he be further ostracized. Mr. Moore, even you must agree that our mutual friend had a penchant for . . . shall we say . . . overstatement? Especially when it came to his personal affairs. I have not read the memoirs, but I can imagine they differ little in content from his letters, some of which describe true events whilst others are composed solely and deliberately to shock."

"You mean he fabricated stories that could in the end harm him? Why would he write such things?" asked Colonel Doyle, representative of Lady Annabella Byron, widow of the deceased.

Hobhouse and Moore exchanged a wry glance at the man's ignorance of Byron's peculiarities. "Because he loved to scandalize people," Hobhouse replied. "Whether or not his tales were true was immaterial. He loved to shock." Byron's childhood friend gave a short laugh. "Me most of all."

"I have read the memoirs," Moore stated, knowing he was the only one in the room to have done so, "and I have found nothing, shall we say, surprising about them. He simply tells the truth about his most complex life, a truth that if it were known by all the world, now or at a future time, might explain his actions in a way that would ease the many nasty smears that now beset his reputation."

"How say you that," Hobhouse wanted to know, "if he indeed describes all that I know he was capable of enjoying? And," he added, "how can you be sure what he wrote was the truth? We all know Byron had . . . uh . . . difficulty discerning . . . shall we say, fact from fiction." The room grew quiet at Hobhouse's allegation. Most of those gathered there knew Byron's penchant for lying, but still they were reluctant to speak ill of the dead.

Finally Moore spoke. "Lord Byron may often have . . . uh . . . exaggerated his actions, Hobhouse, but I don't believe he did so here. I think you would find, if you read these," Moore indicated the stack of papers beside him, "that much of what is being bandied about London Society concerning his personal behavior, however scandalous on the surface, might, when seen through Lord Byron's eyes, also be forgivable." He picked up the memoirs and thumbed through the first few pages. "Listen to this, for instance:

" 'Confusion over women remains the cornerstone of my Infamy, and my Longing its Perpetrator. I have longed to make peace with the Fair Sex, but in Truth, the Fair Sex has always confounded me. Women have worshipped at my very feet, (except my sweet Mother, who hated them) and yet I have never been able to truly love any woman, except my Lady Caroline. Although I have known many intimately and taken pleasure in their arms, I find myself afterwards regarding them with the same horror as I did May Gray, that monstrous Composer of the Dance of Longing and Confusion. What my mother began, May Gray concluded.

" 'I see her horrid countenance behind closed

eyelids even now, that vile Destroyer of Innocence. May Gray, my childhood nurse, who preached to me strict Calvinist doctrine and the wages of Sin by day, then came to me in the darkest hours of the night and awakened my sexual appetite at an age when most boys are barely able to think on such things. I hated May Gray, but I was unable to resist the wicked deeds in which she and her lovers enjoined me. Indeed, I often found myself longing for the pleasures she and her libertines inflicted upon me. It was a painful physical longing that turned to confusion when the light of day returned once more and May Gray beat into me the Wickedness of my Soul.

" 'The face of May Gray has haunted all affairs with women ever since, rendering impossible a normal union expected between man and woman. I have loved only one of the female sex, the rare and beautiful Lady C.L., for she is the only one with whom I was not required to perform the Depraved Act.' "

Moore looked around the room at each man in turn. "However despicable Byron's actions might have appeared to outside observers," he said softly, "I believe he had reasons for his behavior few ever suspected or might even understand. But we would be doing him, and history, a grave injustice if we fail to give him the chance to vindicate himself by preserving this, his own account of what transpired in his life."

"Lady Byron objects," Colonel Doyle said, unmoved by what he'd just heard. "She has a strong case that the memoirs belong to her, and she wants them destroyed."

"They belong to Augusta," Horton said, raising his voice.

"They belong to the world," Moore returned heatedly.

"They belong in the fire," Hobhouse concluded, and the others stared at him, knowing that of them all, John Cam had been the closest to Lord Byron. "And everyone but you, Moore, wants it so."

"We're making a mistake," Tom Moore said, exasperated. "We should at least have the consensus of all of those whose lives are described in the memoirs. Like Lady Caroline, for instance. There is no one here to represent her. But I know it to be a fact that she has actually read the thing," he continued hopefully, "and she wrote to me that she sincerely wished the memoirs to be preserved. It certainly sounds, from what I have just read, that perhaps we might learn more about their curious . . . relationship from these papers."

Murray went to stand by the fire, putting his back to the others. "I hesitate to disagree with you, sir," he said, turning at last to face Moore, "but I . . . uh . . . received a letter from her quite recently expressing just the opposite. She insisted they be destroyed."

"Humph," grunted Moore. "She must have decided that day she didn't love him after all."

The men shared a laugh at Caroline's expense, although it was a rather short and sad expression of tasteless humor. All in the room thought Caroline Lamb was mad, and that her feelings for Lord Byron vacillated, not by the day, but by the hour, even by the minute, depending upon how much cognac she had consumed.

"Caroline is Caroline. She could, and would, vote both views," Moore admitted at last. "I am loath to do this, but we must resolve this issue once and for all. Today. We shall put it to a vote. How say ye, Doyle?"

"Destroy the blasted thing and be done with it." He cleared his throat. "That is not necessarily my opinion, by the way. It was a direct quote from Lady Annabella."

"And you, Wilmot?"

He shrugged as if it didn't matter much to him one way or the other. "Augusta says destroy."

"Murray?"

The publisher who had so faithfully brought all of Byron's early poems to the hungry reading public in London and who stood to make a small fortune when the content of the memoirs hit the street stood strangely firm on his position. "I agree. We must destroy them. The poems themselves must speak of the poet. We do not need to drag his sordid personal affairs down into history."

"Sordid affairs! If we destroy these memoirs, we will only imply they were disgraceful and obscene and will be throwing a stigma upon the work which it does not deserve!" Moore was almost beside himself in desperation to save the precious papers. He wished now he had not been so magnanimous in granting the others a vote in the matter. He should have placed them in a vault himself. But now it was too late. "Hobhouse?" he said, his shoulders slumping, acknowledging his defeat in advance.

"Burn them." The words were barely audible.

"I beg your pardon? Speak up, man, unless you know the words you speak are a betrayal of your late friend Lord Byron." Moore could suppress his anger no longer.

Hobhouse glared at Moore, then moved to stand by the window, looking down onto the busy street below. "My late friend," he said, louder than before but still in a hushed tone, "once told me never to take seriously anything he wrote. And certainly never to take his Lordship seriously. That is why, Mr. Moore, I must cast my vote to destroy the memoirs. They are very likely not serious, even though you believe they speak the truth. Don't you see, it would be like him to play the last, really big joke upon us all? In our fervor to sustain his reign as the finest poet of the day, we would be giving the world a sham, a version of his life that might not be true, but written so that Byron might, from the grave, continue to manipulate us all."

The room grew silent as even Tom Moore recognized that Hobhouse's suspicion was a possibility. At any rate, he was completely at odds with the rest, and he knew he'd lost. "Let's be done with it then."

Murray picked up the papers in both hands, giving half to Doyle and half to Horton. "Tear them into small enough pieces that they might go more easily into the flame," he said. Then he took the iron poker from its hook and stirred the fire, adding several lumps of coal for good measure.

Moore could scarcely stand by and watch the representatives of Augusta and Annabella destroy the memoirs, but he couldn't blame the women for wanting to protect their own vulnerable reputations. He felt sick, sensing he was watching an historical mistake, monumental in size, but like a witness to a murder, he could not take his eyes from the proceedings. At last, the shreds began to be consigned to the fire, and he stared wide eyed into the flames.

From across the room, Colonel Doyle addressed Hobhouse, who continued to survey morosely the gathering gloom of the encroaching night. "Mr. Hobhouse, since you were in agreement that these should be destroyed, I would like to share with you the honor of executing their demise."

Slowly, the portly figure of the man who had loved Lord Byron perhaps more than anyone on earth turned to face Doyle. His eyes shone with unshed tears.

"No. No, thank you," he said quietly. "No."

Nicki steered the convertible through the traffic on Florida's Turnpike with the ease of a racing car driver. They were headed north, to a small town outside of Orlando, to a psychic and a seance.

A seance, for God's sake. Alison's cheeks burned a

little at the thought. It was crazy. But then, Nicki had always been a little on the crazy side. It was what Alison liked about her. That, and the fact that her father hadn't liked Nicki. He'd believed she was the daughter of a Mafioso, but Alison had never seen anyone in her friend's family who even remotely resembled the Godfather. They were just another family with a lot of money and a big house in Palm Beach.

Sort of like the Kennedys.

"So how much is your allowance?" Nicki asked offhandedly.

Alison flinched. She hated the word *allowance.* Only children got allowances.

Children. And the very spoiled, very immature grownup children of the very rich.

Trust-fund children.

"Three hundred grand a year." It was a sizeable sum. Her father had been generous, if you could call withholding her total inheritance generous. Generous, especially in light of the fact that she had no expenses or obligations other than to pay any bills she incurred.

"Not bad," Nicki commented. "You can make it on that. You'll just have to be a little careful."

Alison stared at the flat landscape streaking by, wondering if she should tell Nicki the rest. Nicki, who knew how to spend money as well, if not better, than Alison. The two had been best friends since they'd met at boarding school as teenagers, and some of their capers had not exactly been . . . frugal. She wondered if Nicki's reaction to her news would include plans for a major, and likely ill-advised, spending spree.

But they'd never kept secrets from each other, and now was no time to start.

"Well, actually, there's more," Alison said.

Nicki honked her horn as she sped around an elderly couple barely driving the minimum speed limit. "Gotta watch them," she said. "They're as dangerous as people like me. What more?"

"An insurance policy. Hawthorne told me my folks were heavily insured." Alison's throat tightened. "Double indemnity in case of an accident."

"How much?" Nicki never minced words.

Alison paused a moment, considering the bizarre turn of events. It had been her mother, Hawthorne had recounted to her utter amazement, who had insisted on the insurance policy. Her mother, who had always commanded admiration and respect, but from a distance, who had never been one to hold or cuddle or show any real affection for her daughter, and certainly never one to make any special provisions for her. But apparently, her mother and father had not exactly agreed on setting up the trust, and her mother, Hawthorne had assured her, wanted to make sure Alison would have "liquid funds" available to her in case they were no longer there to see to her needs.

"Four million."

Without a flicker of surprise in her expression, Nicki reached for her cigarettes from the console. She shook one in Alison's direction, but Alison declined. After lighting her own, Nicki exhaled a long, gray wisp of smoke. "Four million. Four million dollars?"

"We're not talking pesos."

Nicki gave a short laugh. "And I was beginning to feel sorry for you. What're we doing this seance thing for anyway? With that kind of bread, who needs your father's advice?"

Alison bristled. "This was your idea, not mine, remember? And it's probably a stupid one, too. Let's turn around now and go home."

"Look, I'm sorry," Nicki said, tousling Alison's short, russet hair like the big sister Alison had never had. "So you're rich. Maybe you need to ask Daddy what to do with the money."

Alison swallowed hard. It was exactly what she needed. Hawthorne was after her to put the money in the trust, where it would be safe, for her, and for future generations, as he'd put it.

Although, at the moment, it didn't appear there would be any future generations. There was no man in her life, certainly no one with whom she would consider entering into a serious relationship. Except for occasional friendships, she had never cared much for the fast playboys who ran with her crowd of richer-than-rich young people. For the most part, they'd seemed shallow, superficial, self-absorbed.

Just like me, Alison thought with a cringe.

She'd been attracted to a few other men, including one professor with whom she had fancied herself in love. But once they'd learned her background, they all had seemed suddenly more interested in her money than in her. More than once, she'd been dealt a cruel blow by this realization, and over time she gave up on having a relationship with a man. She'd sometimes wished she could run away and change her name, just so she could be like normal people. Being rich had its downside.

They drove in silence for a long while, listening to Depeche Mode on the CD player. Outside of Orlando, Nicki left the tollway and headed north on I-4, passing up the Magic Kingdom, Universal Studios, and all the other garish tourist attractions, slipping easily through the traffic in Orlando, until once again they'd reached rural Florida.

"How'd you find out about this place?" Alison wanted to know, her misgivings about their little adventure growing with each passing mile. "You been here before?"

"Well, no. But I've heard some stories. The place is supposed to be real spooky." A few miles further on, Nicki wheeled the convertible into the exit lane, around a corner, and down a deserted road. Almost instantly, it seemed as if they were in another world.

"Wow!" Alison peered out at the huge moss-draped oak trees that enshrouded the lonely landscape. "You'd never dream you were close to civilization, would you?"

Nicki slowed the car and put a new CD in the player as she steered up the narrow winding roadway.

"What's that music?" Alison asked, finding her friend's taste a little macabre. It sounded like something right out of a graveyard scene in a horror movie.

"Isn't it great? Mannheim Steamroller. The guy at the music store recommended it. Gives a little atmosphere to the thing."

Alison shivered, not knowing whether to laugh or cry. It was so . . . so Nicki. She always made the most of their escapades. "Are you sure about this, Nicki? I mean, it's ridiculous."

"It may be. It may not be," her friend returned. "All I know is that my friend from Miami, Angela Marie, and some of her buddies came here, and this psychic revealed things about her family that no one could have known."

"I suppose her dead relatives told all," Alison replied sarcastically.

"They did! She said it was the damnedest thing. She didn't understand everything so she took the tape of the reading home and played it for her mother, and her mother started crying because it was about things she'd kept secret from Angela Marie all these years."

Alison considered that a moment. "What things?"

But before Nicki could continue, they topped a hill and saw the first signs of the little town. "I think we're here," Nicki said in a hushed, dramatic voice.

"Here" appeared to be not much of anywhere. There was a small bookstore on the left-hand side of the road, and a green wooden structure across the street that looked like it must have been built in the 1930s. "Spiritualist Camp." Alison read the sign out loud. "What's that?"

"Dunno."

Across the street was a large faded pink structure with the word HOTEL barely distinguishable over the front door. It looked distinctly haunted. "We're not staying there, are we?" Alison asked Nicki.

"Why not? When in Rome . . ."

"This is definitely not Rome. I bet they don't even have a pool."

Not listening to her complaining friend, Nicki pulled into a parking space in front of the hotel and looked up, laughing. "Get that!"

Alison saw the sign her friend was giggling at and relaxed a little. If this place was haunted, at least somebody had a sense of humor about it. The sign was blue, with a white illustration on it that looked like Casper the Friendly Ghost. It read, GHOST PARKING.

"Maybe you'd better find another parking space," she suggested, laughing but still irritated that she'd allowed herself to be talked into this. "What time is our appointment?"

"Appointment? I didn't make one."

Alison groaned. "Then let's split. I mean, this is so . . ."

But Nicki was out of the car and shouldering her designer backpack, headed for the hotel. Alison sighed and looked at her watch. It was almost three o'clock. It had taken over four hours to drive here. Wasted a day. No, two days by the time they got home tomorrow.

Suddenly the crazy caprices she'd shared with Nicki and the others no longer held the appeal they once had. This didn't seem like a very adult way of handling things, and she was sorry she'd agreed to come. Maybe there wouldn't be a psychic available and they could turn around and go home, she thought hopefully. She was willing to drive the full trip if she had to.

But shortly after dark, she and Nicki entered a cramped room in an apartment above a small grocery store. Lit by a bare lightbulb, the tiny space appeared to have been furnished from local garage sales.

"You sure this is the place?" Alison had expected red velvet fleur-de-lys wallpaper and red satin draped on the table. A crystal ball here and there. A crone in full Gypsy regalia.

Instead, there was a raggedy linoleum floor, a table that leaned slightly to one side (too much table tapping?), and a middle-aged woman dressed in beige polyester pants and a man's long-sleeved shirt.

"Is it just the two of you?" the woman asked, obviously disappointed.

"Yes. But we're willing to pay . . ." Nicki began, but the woman shook her head.

"It's not the money, hon. You see, seances work better if there are more people. Brings in more spirits, you see."

"Oh."

"I had enough time to run up to the 7-Eleven and get some flowers, though," she said, arranging a red rose and a pink carnation in a tall glass vase. "The spirits like flowers." She gestured toward the motley arrangement of old chairs and sofas. "Sit down. Make yourselves comfy. We'll get started in a minute."

Alison looked to see which seat was the least grimy and chose an armchair directly in the middle of the room. With a grimace, she sat down, shooting a disparaging glance at Nicki, who sat next to her. She'd have to think of a way to get even.

At least the psychic, whose name was Mary, lit some frankincense. So far, it was the only thing that fulfilled Alison's expectations of what might happen at a seance. Before proceeding further, Mary pulled out a small, battery-operated tape recorder and punched the buttons again and again, testing one-two-three. "Sometimes we can get them on tape, you know," she said, looking up with a gleam in her eye.

"Them?" Alison asked.

"The spirits. They can speak. But only some people, like me, can hear them, and it makes other people, the ones who can't, not believe in them. So I've been experimenting, trying to catch spirit voices on tape. I've done it, too!"

Alison cocked her head to one side. "But when you play the tapes, don't people believe you've made them up?"

Mary only looked at her, then pressed the record button. "Let's get started." She lit two white candles and turned off the bare overhead light. "Let us pray. Oh, Spirit, that greater Spirit than us all, be with us and protect us tonight as we make contact with our loved ones who have passed Beyond. Bring to us those we need to hear from, and open our hearts and minds to receive the messages we need to hear. Amen."

Mary took a seat in an old rocker opposite Alison and Nicki. "Now, girls, if you will, give me something personal, something with your vibrations in it, like a piece of jewelry or clothing you wear often."

Like my diamond pendant? Alison thought cynically. Now it was sounding more like the seance she had expected. Instead, she removed a small gold stud earring and placed it in the psychic's upturned palm. But without batting an eye, Nicki took off her sapphire and diamond dinner ring and gave it to the woman. Alison rolled her eyes behind closed lids.

Mary dealt with sapphires and diamonds first, laying Alison's earring on the table. "You come from a large family," she began. "Many still living. Many are in Spirit. I think not all have died easily."

Alison glanced at Nicki and was surprised to see her fidget uneasily. "Uh, I don't know. . . ."

"Do you want to know?" the psychic asked with surprising bluntness.

But before Nicki could answer, Mary's body stiffened, and she began to sway from side to side. Alarmed, Alison wondered if she was having a heart attack or something. And then she spoke in a voice totally unlike that they'd just heard.

"I thought you would never come," she chided in a high, childish voice, softened with a slight lisp and shadowed by an English accent. "I have been waiting long for you." She looked directly at Alison. "You *will* help me find them."

Alison and Nicki looked at each other, startled. Alison smirked at the farce, but shrugged and decided to play along. At least, theatrically speaking, they might get their money's worth out of this.

"Find what?"

"The memoirs," she replied softly. "And the letters he wrote me." And then Mary leaned back and emitted a sorrowful keening howl, an eerie sound which stiffened the downy hair on Alison's arms. "He loved me," she cried. "He did! I have evidence that his heart was mine!"

Alison's heart pounded. She leaned forward, intrigued. Could this be a message from her own father, somehow distorted through the psychic medium? Was he trying to tell her from the spirit world what he'd never said in the flesh? "Who loved you?" she asked hopefully.

There was a long hesitation, then, "That bastard Byron."

It wasn't at all what either spectator had thought they'd hear in this particular room in this particular part of the world. This woman ought to be on stage, Alison thought, scowling, more than a little abashed at her momentary expectation that this was a message from her deceased father.

"Who's Byron?" Nicki asked, watching the woman curiously.

But Mary, or whoever it was, chose to ignore her question. Slowly, dreamily, she rose from the chair and went to the vase on the table. "She is a wonderful woman, is she not?" the voice continued. "She always places flowers here for me." She touched the petals gently. "A rose and a carnation. Just as Lord Byron sent to me. He said I loved all that was new and rare for a moment." A girlish laugh was followed by an extended sigh. "I have waited long for you to come," she said at last, and turned to again look directly at Alison.

"Me?"

"You are the one who can help me. Now. In this time."

"I . . . I'm afraid I don't understand."

Mary, or whoever she was at the moment, plopped like a sullen schoolgirl back into the rocking chair. "Nobody ever understands," she pouted. "I have tried in the most serious manner, but I cannot get anybody to understand. . . ."

Something in the woman's plaintive lament struck a chord in Alison. No one had ever understood her either.

"I'll try," Alison found herself saying. "What is it you want me to do?"

The woman immediately sat forward on her chair. "You will?" she cried with the eagerness of a child. "You will?"

Alison felt her face growing hot, and she determined that she would convince Nicki later that her interest was only pretended, in order to get the phony seance over with.

"What must I do?" she repeated.

She heard Nicki suppress a laugh and she herself squelched a nervous giggle.

"It is not difficult," the woman replied. "Find the memoirs. I hid them long ago, because no one would have believed me then. But now, now is the time for me to redeem my good name, to reinstate my good reputation, and you are the one who shall help me do it."

"Who are you," Alison asked, "and where are the memoirs you are talking about?"

"He used to call me Caro," she began, but before she uttered another word, Mary began to shake all over. Her face contorted into an angry frown, and she burst from the chair.

"Get away from me!" she screamed, and Alison and Nicki both jumped from their chairs and backed toward the door. "Get away, you crazy girl!" Mary opened her eyes and saw her two clients edging away from her, wide eyed. "Wait!" she cried. "Wait. What happened?"

Alison did not want to insult the psychic, so she pretended to believe the performance they just witnessed. "I . . . I think someone, or something, just possessed you," she said, but she was genuinely nervous.

"Was it that damned Caroline again?" Mary asked crossly. She went to the light switch. "Sorry. I can't do any more. She's ruined it again, like she always does."

Alison sat back down. "What do you mean, like she always does?"

"That woman's spirit has been taking over my seance room for years," Mary complained, snuffing out the candle. She picked up the small tape recorder roughly and punched the rewind button. No one spoke as the tape whirred backwards in the machine. But as agitated as Mary was, she placed the player back on the table and signaled for silence. "Listen. Let's see if she'll let us hear her voice."

Alison heard the sound of their own voices during the early part of the seance over the static of the recorder. But after the "spirit" had taken over the psychic's body, there was only a small, muffled sound, almost inaudible, when the spirit-being spoke. Mary stopped the tape abruptly. "Damnit. She always does that."

"Does what?" Nicki asked, her eyes shining in fascination.

"Covers over her voice."

"But why would she do that?"

Mary shrugged. "Because she's a petulant, spoiled brat. She knows what I'm trying to prove. She messes it up just to spite me." But she pressed the button again.

"Who are you, and where are the memoirs you are talking about?" Alison heard her own voice. And in reply, clear as a soft melody floating through the mist, they heard, "He used to call me Caro."

Chapter 3

The writer of the letter he'd found in the old desk had haunted Jeremy ruthlessly since he'd unearthed the astounding epistle. She had come to him again and again in his dreams, and her image stalked his waking hours as well. He saw in his mind her large, limpid eyes. Her pixielike face. Her russet hair and pale complexion. It was the face of a child in some ways, and yet also the face of a beautiful young woman. A sensuous, desirable woman who knew some rather interesting ways to please a man. He'd awakened on several occasions thoroughly aroused, disconcerted at the vividness of his dreams and his physical reaction to them.

He knew who she was. Lady Caroline Lamb. Caro. He'd seen photos of numerous portraits of her over the past few days as he hastily researched the possibility that she might have been the author of the pathetic little letter he'd found in the old desk.

The letter that could set him up for life.

Maybe that was one explanation for his overpowering desire for the woman in his dreams. He admitted that he lusted after the fortune that would be his if he found the memoirs she claimed to have hidden in the old country house known as Dewhurst Manor.

Jeremy wasn't one to let his imagination run away

with him, however. He felt a little foolish, impulsive even, to be making this trip based on so little research. His friend from Harrow school days, forensic expert Malcomb McTighe, had not yet verified that the letter had been penned by Lady Caroline Lamb. But he'd learned that in this business, the unlikely was sometimes possible and that often treasures were found in the nooks and crannies of antiquities, treasures that had made their way through history heretofore undisturbed. Often, it was the antiquarian who moved quickly who reaped the greatest rewards.

The early morning mist was beginning to rise above the historical section of Hatfield in Hertfordshire as Jeremy carefully squeezed his car into a too-small parking space on a steep slope in front of the estate agent's office. He'd been amazed at his good fortune in locating Dewhurst Manor so quickly, and further amazed that it appeared to be headed for the auction block in the near future. If his luck held and he worked this just right, the letter might prove lucrative in more ways than one.

A small brass bell tinkled as he opened the door to the office, which was located in a cramped building in the heart of the old village. The reception desk stood empty except for a few scattered papers, a telephone, and a bottle of scarlet nail polish, open, its lid tilted to one side. From his pocket, Jeremy retrieved the correspondence which had accompanied the photocopy of the house the agent had sent him, making sure he remembered her name correctly. It was an unusual one for England. Gina. Gina Useppi.

He envisioned her as an aggressive young estate agent, with dark Italian eyes and coal-black hair. Exotic. Sexy even.

Perhaps once this had been an accurate description of Gina Useppi, but the woman who hailed him from another room at the back of the office was at least in her early sixties, maybe older. Her thick, straight hair was shoulder length, salt-and-pepper beneath a black head-band. She wore a black turtleneck topped by a muted orange vest and matching slacks. She came toward him on shining black boots.

"May I help you?" Her voice was throaty, and Jeremy surmised she'd smoked cigarettes for many years. He noted that her lips were recently glossed to match the polished nails.

Well, she was sexy, in her own way, he told himself. "Gina Useppi?" He made sure he admired her openly as she approached. "I'm Jeremy Ryder." A woman's age didn't matter to Jeremy, who knew the value of business flirtations. He saw her hesitate for a slight moment and knew his subtle sexual compliment hadn't been missed.

"That I am, sir. You're here to see Dewhurst Manor?" She made an attempt to appear all business. "How'd you hear about the place?" she asked, taking a seat behind the front desk. "Receptionist is out for the day. Please . . ." She indicated a chair opposite her.

"A . . . um . . . friend told me about it."

"Well, it's been on the market for a long time. The owner wanted too much money for it. But she died a few months back. No heirs. The bank wants us to get a good enough price for it, but between you and me, I think we can get them to take any decent offer."

"What are they asking?"

"Five hundred thousand pounds."

Jeremy didn't flinch. He had to convince her he had a legitimate interest in buying the property. It was critical to his plan that he have a chance to take a look around the house that the author of the old letter had described. He wasn't sure what his next step would be, but he'd think of something. "What bank carries the mortgage?"

"Coutts. In the Strand."

Jeremy nodded. His luck just got better. Another of his old school chums would be able to help him out at the bank. He silently thanked his Uncle Clive for making the sacrifices he had in sending Jeremy to a school like Harrow, where alumni were closer than family. He leaned forward slightly. "Do you suppose, Ms. Useppi, that it would be possible for me to inspect the property right away?" He laid his expensive-looking business card on her desk. "I can assure you I am no curiosity seeker, and I am in a bit of a hurry."

She read his card. "Antiquities, eh? Well, Dewhurst Manor is certainly that. It was built in the late sixteenth century as a rather rustic hunting lodge." She got up and went to the coat rack. "But as you will see, it's been added to in a rather, shall we say, eclectic manner over the centuries. That's why I think it has been so hard to sell. Among other reasons," she added almost under her breath. She slipped a woolen cardigan over her shoulders. "Well?" She turned and looked at him with a smile. "Shall we?"

Dewhurst Manor was set back from the highway, secluded in the woods and accessible by only a small lane that ended in a circle drive at the front of the house. Pale gray sunlight struggled through the canopy of spring leaves overhead, dappling the fanciful timbered walls, charging the very atmosphere with a preternatural glimmer. Jeremy's skin prickled, and he was unable to subdue a slight involuntary shudder.

"Looks haunted," he laughed uncertainly.

"Some people say it is," Gina replied matter-of-factly, getting out from behind the wheel of the large Mercedes. "I admit, it's been a problem in selling it actually."

"Who's the ghost?"

She glanced at him over her shoulder, a wry smile on her red lips. "Do you believe in ghosts, Mr. Ryder?"

Jeremy shrugged. "Well, no. No, I don't. It's just interesting folklore."

Gina inserted the heavy metal key, turned it in the lock, and pushed down on the levered handle. The mas-

sive wooden door creaked open with a groan worthy of
a haunted house, and Jeremy gave another short laugh.
They stepped directly into a large hall with vaulted, timbered ceilings that met at a steep angle high into the
second story. A stone fireplace glowered blackly at the
far end of the room, and a gallery lined with bookshelves and portraits ran the length of one wall at the
upper level. The room was hushed and gloomy, the furniture draped.

"This is ghastly," Gina remarked, going to a panel on
the wall and flipping several switchbreakers with authority. "Thank God the old gal brought in electricity. Think
what this place must have been like with only candlelight to see by. Dark as a dungeon."

But the modern lighting did little to add cheer to the
room. A glow emanated from a single chandelier placed
directly in the middle, a large brass fixture with many
lamps that in a lesser space would have served well but
that in this huge place had little effect. Jeremy looked
around. "Is this part of the original building? From the
sixteenth century? You said there had been additions. . . ."

"Oh, yes, this was the original great hall of the hunting lodge. You can see the windows have been reglazed,
of course, and repairs made here and there. But you can
bet that generation upon generation of families and visitors have warmed themselves by that fireplace."

"Any famous visitors?" Jeremy raised a dustcover and
glanced cursorily at the stately chair beneath. Good
stuff, he could tell immediately.

"Some more famous than others," Gina said. "That
portrait above the fireplace is of old William LaForge,
whose Norman ancestors were granted first title to this
land."

Old William was very old. And that portrait alone was
worth a fortune.

Around him were lamps and clocks and tables and

chairs and tapestries and china and glassware. . . . "Does the place come furnished? I mean, is all this included in the price?"

"No. It's to be sold separately. Except for the title. It comes with the property."

"Title?"

"Yes. Lady Julia borrowed quite heavily trying to keep this place up, you see, and since there were no heirs, the bankers who hold the mortgage want to recover as much of their investment as possible. So they are including the title, 'Lord or Lady of the Manor,' along with the estate . . . as if that would make it more valuable," she added dryly. "Whoever buys it will automatically become the Lord or Lady of Dewhurst, with all duties and privileges thereof." She laughed. "They are touting the title as a good 'investment,' although collecting a pound per telephone pole in revenues is not likely to make it a very lucrative one. It's mainly for prestige. Traditionally, the biggest responsibility of the Lord or Lady of the Manor is to organize and open the village fair."

She led him into the first receiving room, an addition which opened to the left of the great hall. It, too, was filled with covered furniture. "Tell me about some of the visitors," Jeremy probed patiently.

"The house has sixteen bedrooms, ten of which were added to the back of the great hall over two centuries ago," Gina said, pulling open a heavy, dust-incrusted drape to reveal a terrace overlooking what once must have been the gardens. "That leads one to believe there must have been frequent guests in those days. I haven't looked into such things, to be quite frank. I suppose the most famous, or infamous, I should say, visitor that I'm familiar with is Lady Caroline Lamb. She was the wife, you know, of William Lamb, Lord Melbourne, who was Queen Victoria's first prime minister. But that's not what made Caroline famous, as I'm sure you know."

He knew, but he wanted to hear what she would say. "What would that be?"

"Why, her scandalous affair with Lord Byron, of course. When it was over, for him at least, she wouldn't give it up. Followed him everywhere, to everyone's embarrassment, except her own. I guess today they'd call her a stalker and she'd be all over the tabloids."

"I recall now," Jeremy said, thinking of the letter's message, hiding his growing excitement behind measured words. "She visited here?"

"Oh, quite frequently. Brocket Hall is the neighboring estate, you know. She used to ride freely on both properties, and was likely as not to show up at tea unannounced. The fifth Lord Chillingcote was aging at the time, and lonely. Apparently he enjoyed her company, and it seems they both relished the cognac from his well-stocked cellars."

"Drinking pals?" From what he'd read recently of Caroline's later years, Jeremy doubted it not a whit.

"That's how the story goes. Who knows? Would you care to move on?"

Gina led him through the other receiving rooms and the long, darkly-paneled dining hall, past the kitchen and pantry areas, pointing out that part of the newer structure now served as a laundry. They went up a flight of stairs at the rear. "This is the back way to the upper guest rooms so the servants aren't seen in the front of the house with the dirty linens," she explained. "The rooms have been renovated to include baths in most. The property can actually be used as a single residence, or separated into apartments. It's also zoned for use as an elderly persons' home, if you wanted to go that way with it."

"It's . . . not what I had in mind."

The hallway connecting the various rooms was dark and labyrinthine. He could envision smoking rushes choking the air in these close quarters, and he was glad when Gina led them out onto the second floor gallery, overlooking the great hall.

"It's like a maze, isn't it?" she commented. "Although they were probably built in the same century, I think these rooms were actually added at different times to the original Tudor structure." She turned to him and grinned. "The various lords of the manor have adjusted Dewhurst to suit their needs, no matter what it might take away from the integrity of the original hall. Wait until you see the swimming pool."

"Swimming pool?" Jeremy, the purist, frowned at the aberration. A swimming pool in a sixteenth-century Tudor manor house?

"It's in the newest wing, which was built by Lord Charles just after the war."

Jeremy consoled himself that the main part of the house at least appeared to retain its Tudor authenticity. Additions didn't count against the original, he told himself. Gina continued the tour, moving into the rooms at the front of the house. "These are the apartments usually occupied by the Lord and Lady of the Manor," she said, opening doors, blinds, closets. "As you can see, everything has been pretty much updated, as far as creature comforts are concerned. But in all, I think the modernization process has somehow maintained the feel of the way the place has been over time."

"Maybe even the ghost of Caroline Lamb might recognize it?" Jeremy asked with a sardonic smile.

Gina cocked her head slightly and paused, then replied, "I suppose she might."

Jeremy's expert eye told him that the furnishings in each room were worth a good deal of money. Probably as much as the house itself.

The tour wound down the front stairs, through the library and back to the great hall. "Now, we'll take a side trip through the new wing," Gina said, leading him to the other side of the house, where she showed him still more guest rooms, these obviously built in the early part of the twentieth century.

"Hell of a place for a party," he commented.

"And I've saved the best for last," Gina promised mysteriously. "But first, let's take a look at the swimming pool."

The pool was surprisingly large, lighted from beneath, and heated. Oddly, it appeared to be well cared for. "Who uses this?" Jeremy asked, puzzled.

"Swim teams from all over Britain used to come here for competitions until Lady Julia died. It was one of the few philanthropic things the old lady did for anyone. But some people say it wasn't philanthropy, but rather revenge that drove her generosity."

"Revenge?"

Gina laughed. "It seems that Lord Charles tore down Lady Julia's prize rose garden and gazebo to build it. Actually the rumors go even deeper. They say the reason he did that was because he once caught her in the gazebo with a lover. Who knows? But when Charles became an invalid in the eighties, Lady Julia seized the opportunity to strike back. He always valued his privacy, and except for his personal friends, he didn't like strangers on the property. So she opened the place, or the pool at least, to the noisiest segment of the population —teenagers."

"They sound like a fun couple."

"Quite. Now for the grand finale. Follow me."

Retracing their steps into the original structure, they went down still another half flight of stairs into a small chamber located just under the library. It appeared to serve no real purpose. "This is it?" Jeremy asked, looking around.

"Almost." Gina pressed a panel near the center of the far wall, and to Jeremy's surprise, it gave way beneath her touch. She pressed a secret latch, and the middle panel of the wall swung slightly ajar, revealing that it actually was a door.

"In olden days, this served as a secret exit," Gina explained as they passed through the thick portal. "If enemies encroached, the family had an escape route through a tunnel that ran behind the wine cellar and came out on the far side of the hill that overlooks the River Lea. The tunnel has long ago been filled in, but this room," she said with a dramatic flourish of the light switch, "has been a favorite of the men of the house for eons."

A long rustic wooden table and chairs stretched almost the full length of the room in front of a huge hearth, which was covered entirely by Delft tile. "They called it the Dutch room, for obvious reasons." Gina moved to the opposite wall and opened another door. "These stairs lead back up to the kitchen, so meals could be served easily," she explained. "All the Lord Chillingcotes down the centuries have used this as their private gentlemen's party room." Then she dug into her huge handbag and retrieved a key that looked to Jeremy as if it were the original Key to the Kingdom. "And now for the best part."

Jeremy watched, amused at Gina's theatrics, as she placed the key in a heavy, archaic-looking lock and snapped it open. She withdrew the heavy chain from the bolt and opened the door. "The wine cellar."

Jeremy had to crouch slightly to go through the door, but once inside, he saw that dusty bottles of wine still lay in rusted metal holders.

"Any of this still good?" he asked.

"I doubt it." Gina pulled out a bottle which, despite the fact it was still corked, was half empty. "Lady Julia wasn't much of a drinker. I understand she sold off all of Charles's good wines and champagnes shortly after he died."

Too bad, Jeremy thought, taking that possibility off his list of potential profits.

"Well, what do you think?" Gina asked some time later when they pulled up in front of the estate office once again. "Is Dewhurst Manor something you'd be interested in further?"

Jeremy turned an open smile her way, the one the women liked so well. And trusted. "Oh, yes, definitely. But I'm afraid I won't be able to spend more time here today. I'm due in London at a meeting before tea. Would you be so kind as to contact the bank and see if you can find out their absolute bottom line? I have some contacts at Coutts I might query as well." He saw concern in her eyes. "And don't worry. If either of us can make the deal happen, I'll make sure you receive a healthy commission. After all, that was quite the tour."

His meeting before tea actually hadn't been scheduled, but it took place nonetheless in the inner offices of his schoolmate from Harrow, Robert Hadleigh, now an officer of Coutts. At its conclusion, Jeremy Ryder walked out of the building and down the block toward Boodle's, his gentlemen's club, a satisfied smile on his face.

Things were working out as he had hoped.

Better even.

> *Through life's dull road, so dim and dirty,*
> *I have dragg'd to three-and-thirty.*
> *What have these years left to me?*
> *Nothing—except thirty-three.*
> —Lord Byron

I do not know why L.H. is so adamant that I write these memoirs. He deems it important that I tell my story for posterity, but I find it difficult to believe that anyone will give a damn about me when I am gone. Society loathes my

*name in London. Shall they not loathe it as well from
Rome? I care not what they think, those Dandies and Dilettantes. I care only for myself, and thus I shall write this,
neither to Enlighten nor Entertain the perfidious scandalmongers who continue to hound me, but to attempt to
unravel these years of Torment and Discontent. Time is
moving quickly. I surely must be nearing my end, and I
welcome that long dark sleep. As it approaches, however, I
find that it is becoming curiously important to me to sort
out the madness that has been my life. Perhaps I shall do
this best after all with pen in hand. . . .*

*. . . Standing at the Crest of my years, I look into the
Valley behind me, and I watch myself in a pitiful, crippled
dance, a desperate dance—between Longing and Confusion. Aye! How I sought to break the rhythm, but My
mother, God rot her soul, set the Music in sway even before I exited her womb. She longed for the perfect babe, the
Childe who would assuage the treachery of my own derelict Father, but she was confused when I was born lame,
and took every chance to blame me for her mistake in
wearing too tight a corset. She confused me with my father,
hating me for his betrayal, but loving me in his place. Even
now I scarcely know the difference between Love and
Hate, but Hate, when coupled with my mother's memory,
seems the stronger. It is confusing to hate one's mother.*

*Confusion over women remains the cornerstone of my
Infamy, and my longing its Perpetrator. I have longed to
make peace with the Fair Sex, but in Truth, the Fair Sex
has always confounded me. Women have worshipped at
my very feet, (except my sweet Mother, who hated them)
and yet I have never been able to truly love any woman.
Although I have known many intimately and taken pleasure in their arms, I find myself afterwards regarding them
with the same horror as I did May Gray, that monstrous
Composer of the Dance of Longing and Confusion. What
my mother began, May Gray concluded.*

I see her horrid countenance behind closed eyelids even

now, that vile Destroyer of Innocence. May Gray, my childhood nurse, who preached to me strict Calvinist doctrine and the wages of Sin by day, then came to me in the darkest hours of the night and awakened my sexual appetite at an age when most boys are barely able to think on such things. I hated May Gray, but I was unable to resist the wicked deeds in which she and her lovers enjoined me. Indeed, I often found myself longing for the pleasures she and her libertines inflicted upon me. It was a painful physical longing that turned to confusion when the light of day returned once more and May Gray beat into me the Wickedness of my Soul.

The face of May Gray has haunted my affairs with women ever since, rendering impossible a normal union expected between man and woman. I long to love one of the female sex, but I cannot. With women I can only satisfy that Carnal Lust with which I am plagued from time to time. For Love, I must turn to those with whom I am not required to perform the Depraved Act. As a schoolboy at Harrow and later a student at Cambridge, I sought to quench my dire thirst for Love in the company of slender handsome youths, like Clare and Edelston. They were beautiful creatures, not so different from the young girls I longed for but knew I could not love.

It was the resemblance to these slender youths, I am certain, that instantly attracted me to the only woman who ever came close to resolving the unbearable dichotomy of my sexual ways. I speak, of course, of Lady Caroline Lamb.

⌐ Chapter 4 ⌐

*T*he twin beds in the old hotel were covered with cheap yellow chenille spreads. A paint-chipped arch of iron stood at the head of each. Water dripped a rusted pattern on the stained lavatory in the cramped room.

"You sure we want to spend the night here?" Alison asked crossly, plumping her pillow. "It's not too late to find something a little more . . . well, livable."

"You're such a brat," Nicki sighed as she came out of the adjoining closet-sized room that contained both shower and toilet. "Where's your spirit?"

They looked at each other and burst out laughing at the unintentional play on words, releasing the tension that had stretched tightly between them since they'd paid Mary and left her cursing the entity named Caro. "Right here, I imagine," Alison relented, giving up any hope of reposing in greater creature comfort. "What did you think of that psychic? Was she some kind of nut or what? Wonder where she took acting lessons."

"You really think she was acting?"

"Get real. Of course that was all an act." Alison saw the disappointment on her friend's face. "Nicki, you didn't actually think we'd get to talk to my father, did you?"

"I guess not. I guess this *was* a stupid idea. But you were so upset, I just wanted—"

"I know," Alison interrupted with an understanding and grateful smile. "And I appreciate it that you care. No one else seems to. But that's not the point," she went on, quickly passing over the self-pity she'd been wallowing in lately. "We came here. We gave it a shot. It didn't work. No big deal." She sighed. "I guess I'm just going to have to grow up. Get a life."

"Not that!" Nicki replied in mock horror. Then she switched the subject back to the seance. "Why would Mary, a psychic in Florida, bring up Lord Byron? Don't you think that's a little bizarre?"

"I thought the whole thing was bizarre."

"And who do you suppose Caro is?"

Alison turned down the covers and slipped between the sheets, relieved that at least they felt clean. "A little-known fact of my life," she said, yawning, "is that I've read a lot of Regency romances. You know, the lord-and-lady-of-the-manor stories?"

"I always wondered what those little books were that you used to carry on the airplane."

"Well, now you know. The Regencies are all set in the early nineteenth century, in the court of George IV. He wasn't really the king, because his father wasn't dead yet, only crazy. It was during the time Lord Byron was famous, and I think I recall he had an affair with Lady Caroline Lamb. I'm not totally sure, but I think one of her nicknames was Caro."

Nicki considered this for a long moment, then continued. "But we're in Florida, not England. Where do you suppose that woman came up with spirits from nineteenth-century England?"

"I don't know. Maybe she likes Regencies, too. Good night."

Alison was exhausted, physically, mentally, and emotionally, and she desperately needed a good night's sleep. But it wasn't to be. Instead, her dreams were filled with strange shapes, undefined patterns, white wispy images that seemed to beckon her down a lonely country road. Ancient trees stretched gnarled limbs high overhead, their leafy fingers entwining into a heavy canopy that all but shut out the dusky light.

The wraithlike images then somehow coalesced into a single specter, and unable to resist, Alison followed when it beckoned her, fearing where it might lead her but unable to resist its force. Around her she heard faint voices, but she couldn't tell if they were trying to warn her of something, or encourage her to go on. At last, the figure turned a corner and disappeared from sight, leaving Alison standing in front of a large old house of some sort. A country house, maybe in England, the way it looked, with walls of mildew-blackened stucco embellished with a fanciful pattern of peeling brown timbers. A turret above the front entrance reminded her of the fairy tale prison of Rapunzel. In her dream, Alison felt a nudge in the small of her back, impelling her toward the massive wooden door. Mist swirled around the scene, then formed the image of a face, the face of a young woman, with large eyes and a sorrowful mouth.

"Dewhurst," it murmured.

"What?" Alison wasn't sure what she'd heard.

"Dewhurst Manor. This place. Come! It's important." The voice grew louder, more urgent, with each word. Then the mist swirled again, turning into a violent storm, and Alison felt herself lashed suddenly by an ice-cold wind.

"What?" she called again, this time out loud. She jerked violently in her sleep, trying to escape the storm's wrath, and woke up. She sat up abruptly and found to her relief she was still in the small iron bed in the hotel. Dawn was just beginning to show through the yellowed window shade. "Jeez Louise," she muttered under her breath, her heart pounding. You come to a ghost town, she thought, I guess you're going to dream about ghosts.

Then she realized there was a faint odor about the room that hadn't been there when she went to bed. A sweet, intense perfume, like overripe flowers. She turned her head toward the source of the fragrance, then jumped with a scream out of the bed and on top of Nicki.

"What the hell?" Nicki groaned.

"Nicki, damnit. I know you like a good joke, but give me a break," Alison said with genuine wrath. Then she gave a shaky laugh. "How did you do it?"

"Do what?"

"Get those flowers. Did you go back to that seance room?"

"What flowers? What are you talking about?"

Cold prickles chased across Alison's skin suddenly as she realized her friend had no idea what she was talking about. She pointed to her pillow. "Those flowers."

Next to the indentation in the pillow where her head had been lay two flowers, a red rose and a pink carnation.

Alison Crawford Cunningham had never believed in ghosts. Didn't want to believe in them. But the only other explanation she had for what had happened to her in the past week was that she was losing her mind.

Perhaps that was a possibility. People had always considered her flaky. Maybe with all the stress of recent events, she'd slipped over the edge. It seemed more reasonable than conversing with an actual ghost for three nights straight, more reasonable than finding those confounded flowers on her pillow every morning. Was Nicki paying the housekeeper to keep up the joke? She swore not, but if she was, Alison had ceased to find it funny.

The apparition had visited her in dreams at first, like it had the night in the hotel. Then it had become more brazen, rattling around in Alison's room until it woke her, but then disappearing instantly. Then three nights ago, it had made itself fully visible. At first, Alison was startled by the specter's resemblance to herself, and considered that she might be experiencing some sort of weird hallucination which reflected her own image, although she'd never dressed like that. The figure was short, a woman, she thought, although it could have been a teenage boy. Its hair was cropped and curly, but in the gloom of night, she couldn't make out the color. She'd turned on the light, and the ghost had disappeared, leaving her to wonder if she'd seen anything at all. But the moment she'd turned the light off again, the figure had returned. And this time it spoke!

Remembering the scene vividly, Alison fidgeted uncomfortably in the chair in the waiting room at Pierce, Buckner, Fromme, and Withoff, glad that she now had some fourteen hundred miles between her Palm Beach bedroom and here. She might not care for Drew Hawthorne, she might feel inadequate during these trying discussions about her affairs, but anything, anything was better than those conversations she'd held in the dead of night with an apparition.

Alison had told no one, except Nicki of course, about the nightly visits from the spirit who called herself Caro. The shade claimed she was indeed Lady Caroline Lamb, and that she had been bitterly betrayed by her lover, Lord Byron.

And that she could prove it.

And that Alison had to help her.

At first the conversations had been one-sided, with the ghost weeping intermittently, and carrying on so that Alison couldn't have said anything if she had wanted to. But after a few nights, the supernatural encounters, which Alison wasn't sure weren't creations of her own ebbing sanity, began to wear on her nerves, until finally she'd called out to the whatever-it-was, "Get out!"

The ghost had looked up at her with such a pitiful expression, Alison had wanted to cry for being so mean to it. "But you said you would help," it whined.

"How can I help? I can't do anything. I can't even be sure if I'm in my right mind or not." Alison couldn't believe she was actually talking to the thing.

"That is what they said about me," the ghost lamented in empathy. Then it reached small white arms out toward Alison, who in spite of her alarm, felt a distinct twinge of sympathy for the pathetic creature. Perhaps she didn't know how it felt for everyone to think you were crazy, but she certainly could relate to having everyone around her believe her to be incapable of thinking and acting responsibly.

"Please," the ghost wailed, "say you will come to my aid."

Alison dropped her head and shook it from side to side in disbelief at what she knew she was about to do. Then she raised her head again, took a deep breath, and said, "Okay. I'll try. But you'll have to tell me what to do. And," she added in desperation, "you'll have to promise to leave me alone when I find whatever it is you are looking for."

The ghost instantly shifted into the personality of an excited little girl, the same as it had done at the seance. "I felt assured you would agree," it said enthusiastically, trying to clap its little hands. "I knew when we spoke at Mary's that you were the one. It has taken me e'er so long to find you. I have the memoirs, Byron's memoirs, the ones thought to have been burned. But the real ones were not burned. I copied every page when Mr. Moore left them with me. It was the copies that were burned, you see. The real memoirs are at Dewhurst Manor. You must go to Dewhurst and find . . ."

All this in a breathless rush, and then suddenly, nothing. It was as if a light went out in the room, and Alison no longer felt the presence there. Well, maybe it had used up all its ectoplasmic energy and that would be the end, she thought hopefully as she nestled back into bed.

So far, it had been. The ghost of Lady Caroline had stayed safely in the next plane or wherever it is that ghosts reside. And Alison had been able at last to sleep through the night in peace.

She was anything but peaceful this morning, however, and as the minutes ticked by and Drew Hawthorne kept her waiting, her irritation mounted. She picked up a magazine and began turning the pages with a sharp flick of her thumb, not really looking at the four-color spreads flashing by. Not, that is, until she came upon a page with a photo of a place she recognized instantly.

It was in a real estate advertisement. And the photo was of the house she'd seen in her dream the night of the seance. She was certain of it. Same trees. Same stucco and timber facade. All that was missing was the ghost.

She glanced at the name on the ad and was startled to note that it was an estate agent in Hertfordshire, England. She flipped back to the cover and realized she'd picked up a copy of *Country Life,* a magazine printed in Britain, obviously dedicated to the bucolic lifestyle of rural but wealthy Brits. A ruddy-faced Prince Charles laughed at her from the cover photo. Quickly, she found her place again and studied the photograph. Then she read the description, and her heart stood still.

"Dewhurst Manor. Fine sixteenth-century manor house with great hall, three reception rooms, domestic offices, sixteen bedrooms, most updated to include private baths. Twentieth-century additions include new guest quarters and heated swimming pool."

Alison let the magazine drop into her lap and looked

around furtively, as if the ghost might pop out of nowhere. But it didn't need to.

It had made clear where it wanted her to go.

> *I awoke one morning and found myself famous.*
> —Lord Byron, March 1812

*Seeking to behave in a fashion befitting my station in
life, that of the sixth Lord Byron, and anxious to uphold
the rumours that I was indeed my own dark hero, Childe
Harold, upon my return to London from the Orient, I
undertook seriously the conquest of the Ladies of Society.
During those years when I was the literary lion of London,
I managed to set my confusion aside and indulged in a
number of brief affairs, most of which were with women
who sought short, titillating encounters to relieve the bore-
dom of their tiresome marriages. These were, for me, safe
indulgences, for none required that I fall in Love.*

*There was one, however, who was not content with a
brief affair, despite the fact that she was married and in a
position of high rank. She also made that fatal Demand
upon me which I could not, I thought, fulfill—she fell in
love with me, and expected me to reciprocate her devotion.
I did not know these things, however, when I first laid eyes
on the slender, boyish but beautiful Lady Caroline Lamb.
I longed for her instantly, as sore a mistake as ever I could
have made. I had no suspicion that my beautiful seduc-
tress (to whom I fell willingly) would soon become instead
an obsessive huntress aiming for sole possession of my
heart, or that in the effort to free myself, I would seek to
destroy her, only to be destroyed in turn by her.*

*I wish in these memoirs to sort out my life, and there-
fore, I must exact the full Truth of these matters from the
darkest depths of my soul. Ah, but what is the Truth when
it comes to Caroline? How difficult, painful even, it is to
describe what took place during that spurious affair, even
from the distance of my Italian courtyard and of many*

*years. But I must recall it all, and bear the pain, as I drain
the poison from an old wound. And so I begin, from the
outset of that dreadful liaison—*

*I was in my rooms in London, a happy man, or happy
as I can recall ever having been, when the fateful knock fell
upon my door. The year was eighteen and twelve. March, I
believe the month. My valet opened the door to find a page
with a letter for me—not so unusual in the event, but the
epistle was most provocative. It was lengthy and filled with
flattery, written by an unnamed female admirer of* Childe
Harold. *She asked that I not attempt to discover her identity, but she closed the letter with a truly Carolinish touch,
saying that if I wished to, I could easily enough discover
who she was, although she swore that it would be a disappointment to her.*

*I could have left her an unknown Devotee, as intriguing
as I found this note, until a second letter arrived shortly
upon the heels of the first. She again flattered me, telling
me how she admired my superior Mind. I was new to the
business of being Famous, and therefore was on fire to
know the name of this ardent fan. It was not difficult to
discover that the sender was Lady Caroline Lamb.*

*I arranged a meeting at Lady Westmoreland's house,
fully expecting Caro, as she was called by the Devonshire
House girls, to join the throng of other admiring young
beauties that surrounded me in the drawing room that day.
When I saw her, my breath deserted me, for from her appearance alone, I was instantly drawn to her. Caro was
young, and gamine, and gay and beautiful and outrageous
and innocent—a complex creature that immediately capti-
vated my imagination. Perhaps with one such as she, I
thought immediately, I could experience with a woman
what I had heretofore known only from the male of the
species. To my great astonishment and dismay, however,
the moment she saw me, she turned on her heel, as if
piqued by my very existence, and left the room, exclaiming*

that I was mad, bad, and dangerous to know! Ah, Caro, was it me you were describing, or yourself?

Outside, a spring storm raged. Lightning sizzled over the slate rooftop, followed by grinding thunder. Inside, the fire crackled cozily in the grate in the large main bedroom at Dewhurst Manor, and Jeremy Ryder sat opposite on a comfortable sofa, reading once again a photocopy of the incredible letter that had brought him to this place. On a small table in front of him were stacks of books, resource material for his search.

Books about Regency England. And Lord Byron.

And Lady Caroline Lamb.

He folded the paper carefully and slipped it inside the cover of one of the books. He'd subjected the original to McTighe's intense forensic scrutiny, and only a few days ago, he'd received the results—McTighe and his colleagues all agreed: It could have been written by Caroline Lamb.

Armed with that knowledge and a contract he'd negotiated with Coutts to appraise the entire contents of the house, he'd decided immediately to take up temporary residence at Dewhurst Manor. It was the most expedient manner in which he could accomplish his appraisal work, he'd explained to his banker friends, who had been pleased, or rather ecstatic, to learn that they might recover a great deal of their unpaid mortgage from the liquidation of the antiques in the house. Jeremy generously offered his services, at no fee, in return for the contract to dispose of the inventory when it was evaluated and tallied properly. He could achieve this all quickly if he were able to work on the project undisturbed.

He smiled. It was perfect. They had no clue as to the existence of the letter, and Jeremy felt no qualms at withholding that bit of information. After all, it really wasn't any of their business. The letter belonged to him.

And the property described in the letter didn't belong to the bank either, as he saw it. It belonged to Lady Caroline. Or Lord Byron. Or the British Museum. Or . . .

Finders keepers.

Gina Useppi was the only one unhappy with the arrangement. She'd thought he was a legitimate prospect, and when she'd found out that all he wanted was access to the antiquities at Dewhurst, she'd made no attempt to conceal her contempt.

Jeremy, however, deflected her ire, sweetening her disappointment with a large bouquet of deep red roses and an offer of a percentage of the profit after the goods were liquidated. Flowers and money. It was a time-honored tradition for placating women.

So now, he was ensconced comfortably in the master suite of the old Tudor manor house, surrounded by an unprecedented profit potential and an equally tantalizing treasure hunt. The problem he faced at the moment was where to start.

Jeremy thought back to the day Gina had given him a tour of the house, and to the letter's vague description of where Byron's memoirs might have been placed. If I were Lady Caroline looking for a hiding place in this house, where would I go? he asked himself. The place was rich with possibilities. But only one came quickly to mind.

The wine cellar.

Gina had revealed its secret compartments, and of course, he hadn't seen a stash of old papers anywhere. But maybe there were more secret places. If not, he could at least begin his inventory with the dusty bottles that lay in the cool, earthen-walled room. Maybe all the good wines had been sold or otherwise disposed of, but one never knew. . . .

Slipping on a heavy black pullover against the chill he knew lay outside the bedroom door, Jeremy picked up a notebook and pen, determined to go about this in his usual methodic way. Now if he could only remember how to get to the cellar.

The rain had let up, although the sky remained overcast with the promise of more to come as Jeremy crept stealthily toward the cellar. He tried to ignore the eerie feeling that someone was watching his every move, not approving of his intrusion. He knew that was ridiculous, but he thought suddenly of the woman in the recurring erotic dreams he'd been having lately. The woman with the large eyes and seductive manner. Caro. Was Caroline's spirit still around, peering over his shoulder?

Nonsense.

He laughed nervously, then walked straight into a thick curtain of cobwebs that stretched across the gloomy stairwell leading into the cellar that he'd somehow managed to avoid on his earlier visit. "Ugh!" He wiped his face and spit at the cottony fibers that clung to his mouth. Even though he made his living in the trade of things old and rare and often dusty, he despised this aspect of his business.

Reaching the bottom of the stairs, however, he forgot about the cobwebs and the sensuous nightmares and focused on the target of his search. According to the letter, Caroline had purposefully secreted the authentic memoirs of Lord Byron here at Dewhurst Manor. From his studies of her history and personality, no place was more likely for her to be than the wine cellar. Cognac had been a favored and frequent friend after she'd lost Byron's affection.

He groped for the secret panel Gina had shown him, and when it gave way, found the hidden latch and released the door. Inside the Dutch room, he switched on the light, and his heart began to beat harder.

With the chatelaine's key to the wine cellar poised to gain access to the vault, Jeremy paused, certain he'd heard a noise overhead. A thump of sorts. Probably a tree limb hitting the roof, blown down by the storm. He inserted the key and heard the metal grating of the lock.

He heard another thump. Then a series of thumps, somewhat louder. And then the distinct creak of a door opening.

The hair on his arms stood up in spite of his conscious effort to control his unreasonable fear. He didn't believe in ghosts or haunted houses. More than likely, the wind had blown a door open or a shutter loose. But he decided to investigate and put the matter to rest before continuing his quest.

Retracing his steps, he reached the great hall, but found nothing amiss. The front door was closed, and he heard nothing that sounded like shutters flapping in the wind. He let out a deep breath and scolded himself for behaving like a ninny. Get on with it, he thought, stepping backwards, not looking behind him, and running squarely into something that felt far more tangible than a ghost.

"Aiiee!" An ear-splitting shriek echoed into the far corners of the great hall, and Jeremy nearly jumped out of his skin. He whirled around, his muscles tense, ready to flail his assailant, but to his astonishment, instead found his arms around a small, delectably feminine figure, with large—and familiar—golden hazel eyes.

Chapter 5

It was when Childe Harold came out upon Lord Byron's return from Greece that I first had the misfortune to be acquainted with him—at that time I was the happiest and gayest of human beings I do believe without exception. . . .

—Lady Caroline Lamb to biographer
Thomas Medwin

A smarter man would have left it alone after Caroline's rebuff, but I was swept up in the idea that somehow this woman was different from all the rest, and therefore right for my own tormented soul, & so I pressed for a second meeting. I anticipated further Rejection, but my sudden and surprising longing for Caroline Lamb was greater than my fear. I need not have worried, however. When finally I received the touch of her little hand, I said, "This offer was made you the other day. May I ask why you declined it?" With that I turned on her the brooding "under-look" which I had worked to perfect in front of the mirror & which had won the Sympathy of many another young lady. She murmured something indistinguishable, but I noted with great satisfaction that her cheeks, normally pallid, were spotted with high pink. She gave me a slight, wavering smile, her large golden-brown eyes filled with adoration. I felt a swell in my bosom, and Hope knocked upon my heart's door.

The next day, I called upon her at Melbourne house, & found Rogers and Moore at their ease by the fireside, laughing that Lady Caroline, who had been out riding & had been sitting with them in all her dirt had, when I was announced, flown to Beautify herself. The news gladdened me, but I played the Nonchalant, not wishing to reveal the urgency I felt to test my capacity for Love. Indeed, I continued to assure my friends in jest that I was making every effort to be in Love, although it was an impossibility for me.

Within three days, Lady Caroline had proven to be all I had hoped, & more. I was like a man Possess'd. My heart thundered in my breast when she entered the room. Her eyes arrested my gaze so that I saw nothing else. I wanted her with a longing seated deep within my soul, & yet I was seized by a raw Terror, for my feelings for her were as intense and passionate as those I had held for Clare, or Edelston, and I trembled to think I might have fallen in Love—with a woman. I wanted it to be, and yet feared for my life if it were so.

The Dance began again, in greater frenzy than before,
As Longing and Confusion took the floor.

In an effort to assuage my Fear and assure myself that my Desire was but a fleeting folly, I sought to lose myself in wine, in gaming, in pugilism, but alas in vain! The truth was, Caroline had ensnared my heart, in a tender net that I struggled to escape, but only slightly.

As my Desire for Caro increased, a new fear began to plague me. I watched her at Devonshire House where, with forty or fifty other young laughing people, she was whirled about the dance floor in the arms of first one Dandy and then another, whilst I, unable to perform the waltz because

*of my lame foot, sat like a dowager glowering in a corner.
Being insecure in* les affaires de coeur avec les jeune filles,
*I now feared that I might be in her eyes just another trifle.
My well-meaning friends, not knowing the true state of my
longing, had congratulated me on my Forbearance as concerned the Lady, informing me of her fickle ways. I was
nearly sick with anxiety.*

*When next we met, I presented her with a Rose and a
Carnation, telling her, "Your Ladyship I am told likes all
that is new and rare, for a moment." Was I, my Terror
wanted to know, like these flowers, new and rare to her,
only to interest her for the moment?*

Alison had never expected the door to be unlocked.
When she'd been informed by Gina Useppi, the estate
agent, that Dewhurst Manor wasn't available for viewing, she'd first been disappointed. Then she'd been angry. She was tired of being told no. It seemed like the
whole world was suddenly telling her no.

At their last meeting, Drew Hawthorne had refused
point-blank to go over the investments made by the
trust her father had set up, telling her it was a waste of
time for both of them, since she had no idea what it all
meant anyway. He kept telling her to trust him and not
to worry, but Nicki's comment kept ringing in her ears.
Besides, how would she ever learn that stuff if she didn't
know what she was supposed to try to understand?
She'd left the law offices in a fury and gone straight to
see her personal banker, where she'd learned more details about the insurance policy her mother had insisted
upon so long ago.

Four million liquid cash.

In the bank, with only her name on it.

Thank you, Mother!

Alison almost ran down the steps of the old bank
building. That money was her freedom from Hawthorne, et al. She'd use that money responsibly, she

swore, sincerely sorry for her years of rebellion against her parents. She'd use the money wisely, make investments, not squander it, hoping somehow, desperately, to make it up to them. Make it all up.

Unfortunately, she thought with a stab of pure regret, neither one would ever know.

Alison had a plan, or at least the beginning of a plan, but she needed some time to think it over. She knew she had some major life decisions to make, but they were decisions she wanted to contemplate without Hawthorne's interference. He meant well, she supposed, but his condescending attitude annoyed her.

She'd swiped the *Country Life* magazine from the law office, a minor misdeed that gave her immense satisfaction. That night, she'd pored over the photo of Dewhurst Manor, memorizing it in detail—the tall door in front arching to a point just beneath a rounded tower, the half-timbers laid in a patchworklike pattern, the heavy slate roof. The ad said there were sixteen bedrooms, renovated in this century to include private baths in each. Wasn't real estate supposed to be a good investment? Maybe she could search out the memoirs for the ghost of Lady Caroline and make her first investment at the same time. The house looked as if it would make a terrific inn or something.

A call to her travel agent secured a seat on the Concorde flight out of JFK the following day. With eager enthusiasm, she began to pack.

Before drifting off to sleep, Alison invited the ghostly Caro to visit her dreams, hoping to get further, perhaps more detailed, information about Dewhurst Manor and the missing memoirs, but upon awakening, she had no recollection of any dreams at all.

She was on her own, it would seem.

Even Nicki declined to go along. "Maybe I'll meet you there," she'd apologized, explaining that she had promised her handsome Greek boyfriend that she'd spend time aboard his yacht in the Med this summer. Alison couldn't argue with her choice.

Alison knew that Hawthorne would likely be upset when he learned that she was considering buying Dewhurst Manor, because he had decided for her that she should put the insurance money in the trust. Well, it was her money, not his, and she was determined to make her own decisions about how she spent it. In fact, she was making this trip to prove to herself that she was in control of her own life. That she could behave responsibly, make investments on her own, whether Drew Hawthorne and the trustees liked it or not.

She was tired of them telling her no. With the freedom the insurance money gave her, she could ignore the whole bunch of them for nine more years, when the trust expired and she'd have the pleasure of walking into the offices of Pierce, Buckner, Fromme, and Withoff and firing every last one of them if she so chose.

So when Gina Useppi had told her no, that she couldn't see the old manor house, Alison had responded by simply ignoring her as well. She'd hired a taxi to bring her from London to Hatfield. She hired another to take her to Dewhurst Manor. She'd dismissed the driver, instructing him to return in half an hour. She didn't want to have a curious cabbie watching her snoop around property that didn't belong to her.

Yet.

It was a wet and dreary day, and if she couldn't find a way to get inside the old deserted mansion, she'd have only a short wait until he returned, she had reasoned.

Alison had banged loudly on the door, just in case someone was inside, but it appeared that the house was uninhabited. She pounded again for good measure, then tried the front door handle. To her surprise, it gave and the door creaked open. With a smile for her small victory, she pushed it wide enough to step inside. The room was enormous and gloomy and seemed invaded by the chill. Shutting the door behind her, Alison crept across the wide planked flooring to an alcove where she felt safer and could catch her breath and calm her hammering heart. She wanted a chance to quietly survey her surroundings before she began her exploration in earnest. She listened. The rain pattered. Somewhere a clock ticked loudly. But there was something else. It sounded like . . . footsteps. Someone *was* in the house!

Following her first instinct to run, she left the protection of the alcove and darted back toward the front door, but instead of attaining her freedom, she ran squarely into the arms of a man. At least it felt like a man, a tall, muscular, fit man. But the figure, clad in black, was covered with stringy pale webs and dust, as if he had just risen from the grave. Alison screamed.

Her captor tightened his hold on her. "Steady," he commanded. "It's all right. I won't hurt you. Just calm down." His voice was strangely reassuring, easing her tension slightly. When he felt her relax, he let her go, and Alison immediately jumped away from him. "Wh— who are you?" she demanded, ignoring the disturbing effect the brief contact with his body seemed to have had on her.

The man appraised her fiercely, his black eyes smouldering beneath dark brows drawn together into a frown. "Perhaps you should introduce yourself first, madam. And inform me as to what your business is here."

His tone was cold, authoritative, like her father's. Alison suppressed a low growl in the back of her throat. She was trespassing, but it wasn't like she was a thief or anything. She wished she had asked the cab driver to wait.

"I . . . I've made a mistake," she said, straightening to her full five feet two inches and summoning strength

to her voice. "I thought Dewhurst Manor was vacant.
I'm . . . interested in purchasing the property, and the
estate agent was not . . . uh, available today to show it,
and so . . ."

"So you decided to take a look on your own," he
finished for her, a shadow of a grin sliding across his
handsome if somewhat grimy face. "You wouldn't happen to be an American, would you?"

Alison raised her chin. "And what if I am? Why do
you ask?"

He stepped toward the door, as if anxious to usher
her out. "You Yanks seem to think it's just fine to make
your own rules, that's all. The property is *not* available
for viewing at the moment actually," he said, opening
the wide portal. "And when it is ready, it would be best
to go through Gina Useppi." He gave her an aloof
smile, as if he were doing her a favor. "Proper channels,
you know, that sort of thing."

Alison didn't move. There was something fishy about
the situation. Why would an estate agent spend the
money to place a full-page advertisement for this place
in an international publication and then not be willing
to show it? Earlier, she'd figured that Gina Useppi had
pegged her for a curiosity-seeker and hadn't wanted to
waste her time showing the property. She had no way of
knowing that Alison, as young as she looked, was an
heiress with a genuine interest in buying Dewhurst. But
now, Alison wasn't so sure that was the real reason
she'd been turned away. Something inside her suddenly
became deeply protective of the old house, as if she
already owned it. Who was this man, and what was he
doing here?

"You can shut the door, Mr. . . . ?"

After a slight hesitation which registered his surprise
at her determined stance, he introduced himself. "Ryder. Jeremy Ryder." But he made no move toward hos-

pitality. "And I really do think you should be on your way . . . Miss . . . ?"

Her turn. There was no way around it, even though she was uncomfortable giving him her name. "Cunningham. Alison Cunningham. Look," she added irritably, "what's going on here? I've traveled a long way to see this house. I may not look it, but I am a qualified prospect, and I'm sick and tired of the Gina Useppis of the world giving me the brush-off." Alison was gratified to see a slight lift of an eyebrow in the man's otherwise impassive face.

"I'm sure if Ms. Useppi were to know the full picture, she would be more than happy to oblige you, Miss Cunningham, although," he added, "I would caution you to be very careful in considering this place. As you can see—" he gestured into the gloom of the great hall "—it is not in the best shape. I estimate it would take double the asking price to bring it back to its former glory."

"Thanks for the advice, Mr. Ryder," Alison rejoined sarcastically, angry that every man she seemed to encounter lately kept trying to tell her what to do. "But free advice, I've been told, is worth exactly what you paid for it."

Jeremy nodded, appearing unruffled by her outburst. "That is most likely so, madam. However, I am a busy man, and since the place is not vacant at the moment, one must make the usual appointments. Now, I really must insist that you take your leave." He opened the door still wider, and Alison saw that her taxi had arrived and was waiting in the circular drive.

Alison glared at this Jeremy Ryder person, wishing he wasn't so handsome. Wondering who in the hell he was. And what he was doing at Dewhurst. Was he the owner? For some reason, Alison had thought it was the estate of a deceased woman. Without further exchange, she pulled the collar of her knitted jacket closer around her neck and left the house. Whatever his story was, she didn't trust him, and she was glad to be out of his unsettling presence.

Taking a seat in the back of the old black taxi, Alison shivered, dismayed at this turn of events. Maybe she'd been wrong to come here. Maybe this wasn't such a good idea after all. Maybe she should just tell the driver to return to London, and she should get on a plane and go back to the States before this went any further. What did she know, after all, about the investment wisdom of buying a place like Dewhurst Manor?

The car wheeled around the circle and headed back toward the lane, and Alison glanced back one last time.

"Stop!" she cried suddenly, and was thrown forward slightly as the driver responded.

"Wat's the mattah?"

Alison grabbed the handle and wrenched the door open, jumping out onto the rain-soaked roadside. But she was unaware of the weather or the driver or anything else except the strange golden glow she saw emanating from the tower window high above the arching front door. At first she thought the mansion was on fire, but as she gazed at the aura, she saw it swirl and take form. It was the ghost, larger than life, as if projected on the screen of a movie house, beckoning madly with all its spectral energy, drawing Alison back. She took one step, then two—hesitantly—in the direction of Dewhurst, her heart pounding again with inexplicable compassion for both the ghost and the house.

"I'm coming," she uttered aloud, not caring that the driver was staring at her like she was insane. "I'm coming." She started to run, but stopped, blinking in the mist. For as suddenly as it had appeared, the vision dissipated. The tower was once again a dingy gray turret, covered with moss. The clouds seemed as if they hung even lower, obscuring the top of the roof. And there was no sign of the ghost.

Suddenly Alison became acutely and uncomfortably aware that Jeremy Ryder had come out of the house and was standing in the drive with his arms crossed, watching her little drama with a perplexed look. She whirled to find the exact same expression on the face of the taxi driver. Had they seen the ghost? Alison decided not to ask. Instead, she clambered back into the car and instructed the driver to take her back to the office of the estate agent. She turned to look at Dewhurst just as the car rounded the corner and the old country house was obscured by the spring-green boughs whipping in the wind.

I'm coming, Caro, she vowed silently.

I'm coming.

Jeremy Ryder watched the taxi until it disappeared around the corner and behind the stand of trees at the front of the property. He was furious with Gina Useppi for having mishandled the American woman, although he guessed Gina had dismissed her as being too young to possibly have a serious interest in a place like Dewhurst Manor. But he didn't need this kind of interruption.

This kind of distraction, he corrected himself, for not only had his work been interrupted, he found to his consternation that he had become aroused by the gamine presence of Alison Cunningham. Whether she was seriously interested in Dewhurst Manor or had come here on some kind of student bet that she wouldn't stay overnight in a haunted house, that sort of rubbish, didn't matter to Jeremy. What had stirred him was her image—the small slender body, the large hazel eyes flecked with gold, the short, curl-tousled hair.

For it was the exact image of the woman who had visited his dreams before he came to Dewhurst Manor.

The one who looked distinctly like the pictures of Lady Caroline Lamb and who had awakened him nightly from erotic dreams only to disappear in the darkness, leaving him swollen with need. The elfin figure was like a succubus, stealing into his apartments while he slept and awakening in him a deep sexual thirst unlike anything he'd experienced in his entire thirty-three years.

And only moments ago, he'd encountered the succubus in the full light of day. He'd felt the flesh-and-blood presence of the woman in his arms, her lissome figure pressed against his body. His response was the same as to the dream woman, only stronger. Jeremy groaned. What was happening to him?

He turned and went back inside the house. For the moment, he'd lost all enthusiasm for the search for the memoirs that held such tantalizing promise of wealth and fame. He was no more interested in returning to the wine cellar than he was in flying to the moon. What he wanted to do instead was—

Well, that was impossible, since he'd sent the lady on her way.

With heavy steps, he climbed the stairs, his weight causing the old boards to creak in protest. Throwing another log forcefully onto the fire, Jeremy reproached himself. It wasn't like him to lose it like this, especially over a woman. He had to pull himself together. He had to get on with the work at hand, posthaste. He'd seen the look of defiance in Alison Cunningham's eyes. He'd sensed her anger and determination. She would be back.

And when she returned, he knew he was in for trouble.

Jeremy Ryder glanced down at the stack of books and thought about the letter he'd found. Was it true? Were Byron's memoirs stashed somewhere around this gloomy old manor house? Or was he only chasing shadows, allowing his greed to outweigh his business sense?

"Caroline," he said out loud, as if invoking her spirit, "where'd you put the damned things?"

But the silence of the afternoon was broken only by the sound of the wind soughing through the eaves and the rhythm of the rain, which had begun to drum a steady tattoo on the slate roof overhead.

≈ **Chapter 6** ≈

> *Yet feign would I resist the spell,*
> *That would my captive heart retain.*
> *For tell me dearest is this well,*
> *Ah, Caro! do I need the chain?*
> —Lord Byron

My fears concerning the premature forfeiture of Caroline's affections were unfounded, as it soon became apparent to everyone that I was now her Favourite. A part of me rejoiced in this knowledge, but at the same time, Terror continued to devour my Soul. I desperately wanted to know her as I had never before known a woman, with my heart as well as my body, yet I felt threatened, exposed. Whenever I was with her, she consumed my very Being. She was like opium—the more I partook of her essence, the more I wanted, and the greater hold she had upon me. Not soon enough, I discovered that I could not walk away from her as I had the rest.

She presented me with a golden Chain to wear about my neck, an ironic gift which I hesitantly accepted, for I was beginning to suspect that I might now be linked to Lady Caroline by a chain stronger than gold.

* * *

Alison paid the taxi driver and squared her shoulders before entering the estate agent's office. She *would* return to Dewhurst Manor before the day was out, and if Mr. Ryder didn't like it, he would just have to get over it. She would return, even if she had to resort to the old golden rule—the one with the gold makes the rules. She'd invoked it often during her lifetime when she particularly wanted her way because, simply put, bribes worked.

The bell tinkled loudly as she pulled the door open and shut it again firmly behind her, startling the woman behind the front desk.

"May I see Ms. Useppi again?" Alison repeated politely, although the more she considered the earlier brush-off, the more irritated she became.

"Uh, do you have an appointment, Miss . . . ?"

But before Alison could answer the receptionist, the agent, tall and fashionably dressed, strode out of her private office and came down the hall toward Alison. "Miss Cunningham?"

Alison was thrown off guard that the woman knew her name, for they hadn't even gotten that far in their first encounter. "Yes. How did you . . . ?"

"Mr. Ryder rang me up. Said I could expect you. Please, step into my office."

Alison followed Gina Useppi into a cramped, paper-laden office, her suspicions of the pair increasing. "Why would he do that?"

"I suppose, Miss Cunningham, because we have a close working relationship when it comes to Dewhurst Manor. I have promised to protect the property from . . . curious unqualified buyers, you see, a service Mr. Ryder and his colleagues greatly appreciate."

"And I take it you consider me in that category?" Alison said, carefully concealing her rage.

"Well, frankly, you don't exactly look . . ."

"A Mercedes dealer once made that mistake, Ms.

Useppi," Alison interrupted. "Cost him the sale of a bright red little 450SL. And I made sure that when I purchased the car from his rival, I drove it into his lot and suggested that next time, he shouldn't judge the proverbial book by its cover." Alison couldn't believe she was behaving in such a manner, but when arrogant salespeople like the Mercedes dealer punched her buttons, she'd found she could be a real bitch.

Like she was being now.

"I see," Gina Useppi replied without evident emotion, studying Alison at length. "What interests you so much in Dewhurst, Miss Cunningham? I mean, you do seem young to be considering such a property."

Alison took a deep breath. There was no reason to antagonize this woman. In fact, she might be helpful down the line. So she decided to take off her bitch hat and remove the rather large chip from her shoulder. It was, she thought, pleased with herself, an exercise in growing up. She looked directly into Gina's black eyes. "Yes, I am young, Ms. Useppi. But I am also very, well, let's just say I've come into a rather large inheritance. I am looking for a real estate investment, and I believe Dewhurst Manor might be it."

"Dewhurst an investment?"

Alison heard the incredulity in Gina's voice. "Well . . . yes."

The estate agent drummed her pencil lead absently on the desk, and Alison could almost see her thoughts colliding with one another. *She must be wondering if she has a live one on her hands, or some kind of nut case,* Alison thought, suppressing a grin. She wasn't going to make it easy on the woman. She simply waited to see what she said next.

"Dewhurst Manor is a very large estate, Miss Cunningham," she said at last. "The asking price is five hundred thousand pounds. Depending upon what you want to do with it, the renovations will likely run in about the same range. And there is the matter of back taxes. Perhaps before we go further, we should determine if that amount, or somewhere close to it, is . . . within your means."

Alison wasn't sure exactly what the amount Gina estimated translated to in American dollars. Almost a million, she guessed.

But not four million.

Yes, it was within her means, although it was still a large sum for her to put out on her very first venture. But she wasn't going to let this uncompromising agent intimidate her. For a moment, in spite of her own irritation, she fleetingly admired the woman's determination to qualify her buyer.

"I can write you a check for a good faith deposit, if that would help," Alison replied without hesitation. "Say one or two percent of the price. Or," she added in an offhand manner, gazing out the window, "I could make it a personal check, made out to you, not your company, for a thousand pounds, just for showing me the place. I might not even like Dewhurst Manor, but either way, you can keep the money."

"That will certainly not be necessary," the agent sniffed, and Alison knew she had insulted the woman. Well, turnabout, she thought.

"You'll show me the place then?"

Gina scowled at being outmaneuvered. "Well, I suppose there'd be no harm in it, as long as we don't disturb Mr. Ryder."

"I would think," Alison commented dryly, "that if he seriously wants to sell his house, he'd be happy to allow a prospective buyer to examine it."

"His house?" Gina gave a short laugh and pushed her chair away from the desk. "Oh, it's not his house, dear. Dewhurst Manor belongs to the bank. Coutts, in London. Mr. Ryder is friends with the bankers, and they have, in fact, hired him to appraise the contents. The

furniture isn't included in the price of the place, by the
way. Mr. Ryder has convinced the bankers they'll recover a large portion of their losses by liquidating the
contents of the house. It is an enormous job, and one
reason I've promised to . . . show the place only to
. . . qualified prospects."

Alison was stunned. That arrogant jerk! He was nothing more than hired help! "The way he was acting, I
thought he lived there," she remarked with a smirk.

"Oh, he does. At least at the moment. You see, he has
rooms and rooms full of furniture and Victorian bric-a-
brac to appraise, and he generously consented to doing
the work on site rather than have all the pieces hauled
into a warehouse where they might be damaged or
stolen. He has taken up residence at Dewhurst Manor
temporarily, although it must be a considerable inconvenience for him." Gina picked up the phone and dialed a
number.

Inconvenience? Alison thought it sounded a little *too*
convenient. What if he was a thief or something? Nobody was there to watch over his shoulder. He could
make off with anything he wanted and no one would
know the difference. But she kept her opinion to herself. "Why would it be an inconvenience for him to stay
there while he worked?"

"You'll see," Gina said, then spoke into the phone.
"Mr. Ryder? Gina Useppi here. I'm bringing a client
over in a few minutes. I promise we'll not disturb you.
Thanks." She replaced the receiver and stood up, going
for her heavy sweater. "The place is enormous and not
well heated. It hasn't had a good cleaning in years. But
the main inconvenience is that hardly anyone is willing
to come to work there."

"Why not?"

Gina paused, then looked at Alison. "If you are sincere about buying the place, I guess it's only fair to let

you know that most of the locals consider the place to be . . . well . . . haunted."

Jeremy hung up the phone, irritated that Gina hadn't been able to get rid of the American woman. Was, in fact, bringing her back.

This afternoon.

Damn!

Well, he'd try to make himself invisible, taking his appraisal chores to the most obscure room he could find. He didn't want to see the woman again. Even though she was a virtual stranger, she had that same disturbing erotic attraction for him as the dream creature, the allure which left him feeling vulnerable and out of control. It wasn't a position he liked to be in when it came to women.

Surely it wouldn't take long to dampen her enthusiasm for Dewhurst Manor. The place was a dreary, rundown monstrosity. He couldn't imagine what Alison Cunningham, or anyone else for that matter, would want with it. He, and only he, knew about the one remarkable treasure hidden on the premises.

Jeremy picked up his bag of tools, a yellow legal pad, and a calculator and prepared to head back to close up the cellar before starting his search in the wing of bedrooms at the back of the house. Surely he could make himself unobtrusive, if not invisible, in that maze.

As he closed the door to the master suite behind him, he thought he heard a muffled noise coming from the great hall. Were they here already? He hurried along the corridor to the stairway, then paused a moment, listening, not wanting to accidentally encounter the pair.

The sound seemed louder, but he knew intuitively it wasn't Gina or the American woman. But it did sound like a woman—a woman's laughter, or rather a light girlish giggle. He considered for an instant the stories he'd heard about the place being haunted. Maybe he was hearing the resident ghost. Poppycock. His ears were playing tricks on him, the same as his libido had been doing lately. Maybe he needed a thorough physical when he finished here. He made a mental note to set an appointment with his doctor first thing when he got back to London.

And then he heard a sound he recognized as being definitely of this world, the crunch of tires on the pebble drive. Blast! They were here already. There was no time now to get to the cellar or to hurry across the great hall to the rear wing, unless he wanted to crawl down the exposed upper gallery on hands and knees so they wouldn't see him, and his dignity would not allow him to do that. He couldn't go back to his room either. Gina was sure to show the master suite as part of the tour.

Feeling quite the fool, Jeremy opted for a ridiculously Shakespearean hiding place: He slipped behind the heavy Arras tapestry at the end of the corridor, a corner that was without electric lights, enshrouded in shadow. He prayed that Gina would show this part of the house first so he could wait out the rest of their visit in the comfort of his quarters.

And he also hoped they wouldn't notice the unexplained pair of feet that were bound to be visible beneath the bottom edge of the tapestry. He heard the front door open, and the sound of feminine voices.

"This is as far as I got," he heard Alison say, "before Mr. Ryder . . . uh . . . intercepted me. I really hadn't meant to trespass, you know. But I had come so far to see this place, and when you wouldn't show it to me . . ."

"I apologize for that, sincerely," Gina interrupted. "If nothing else comes of this, I will at least have learned your lesson about the red Mercedes."

What the hell was she talking about? Jeremy wondered, alarmed that they sounded so . . . so chummy.

"Oh, wow! This is so cool!" Alison's voice carried

clear and young through the fabric of the tapestry, and
Jeremy winced. Cool? He'd never heard a place like
Dewhurst Manor described as "cool." "It looks like it
must be haunted," she continued enthusiastically. "Who
do you suppose the lucky ghost is?"

Lucky ghost? Wasn't that an oxymoron?

Then Gina's deep mature voice set her straight.
"Now, don't take that haunted house story too seriously.
It's been tossed around for a long time now, but no one
has actually seen the ghost. No one except old Ashley T.
Stone."

"Who's Ashley T. Stone?"

Gina laughed, a throaty sound that ended in a wheez-
ing cough. "Too many cigarettes," she apologized before
continuing. "Oh, he's a local character. He's lived
around here all his life. Must be ninety-something by
now, if he's not a hundred. He seemed like an old man
when I was just a little girl." Another raspy laugh. "It
was Ashley who got the story started in the nineteen
thirties about this place being haunted. Claims he saw
the ghost, right here in the great hall, sitting in a chair, a
young woman holding her arms tightly around herself,
and crying and crying. I can tell you, it's played havoc
with the place's perceived value."

"You mean people believed him, even though nobody
else has seen her? The ghost, I mean."

"Oh, he's not the only one who *claims* to have seen
her, but he's the only one I tend to believe. The rest,
well, who knows? It makes for a good story, you know
what I mean? Let's move along into the receiving
rooms, and I'll fill you in. See those panels? Hand
carved. These rooms were added in the seventeenth
century. . . ."

From his hiding place, Jeremy could no longer hear
their conversation, but his interest was piqued by Gina's
story. A young woman, crying and crying? Lady Caroline Lamb, weeping for her lost love? Of course, the

idea was ludicrous. But it was even more ludicrous that
he was cloaked here behind this curtain like some kind
of thief in the night.

Throwing off the heavy tapestry in self-contempt, he
strode to the stairwell again and made his way into the
great hall. From there, he could hear Gina and Alison
Cunningham moving from the receiving rooms into the
dining hall, still discussing the ghostly aspects of the
property. Just as well, Gina, he encouraged silently.
Maybe a good scare will send her scurrying back to
wherever she came from, and she'll leave me in peace.

Taking his tool bag to a window sill, he brought out a
polishing cloth, a ruler, and a magnifying glass. With a
flourish, he threw back the white shroud that protected
a large piece of furniture in one corner of the drawing
room, revealing a magnificent harpsichord. With a low
whistle, Jeremy ran his fingers lightly across the keyboard and would have tested the instrument except he
did not want to attract the women's attention. He knew
from the woodwork, however, that it was a period piece,
likely from the late eighteenth century. It might have
been crafted around the same time as the old desk that
now stood in Jeremy's London townhouse.

Setting about his work in earnest, Jeremy examined
every inch of the harpsichord, making note of its condition, every flaw or bit of damage that was in evidence.
He carefully searched the inside of the box and the seat
as well, just in case, wondering how thick the sheaf of
memoirs might be, and what size hiding place Lady Caroline would have needed. Surely she would have found
a niche somewhere not quite so apparent as this musical
instrument. Probably high up on a shelf somewhere,
maybe in the library. Perhaps even between the covers
of a book, making it appear as if it were just another
volume on the shelves. The library at Dewhurst Manor
was large, containing thousands of books. That search
would take a while.

Suddenly, he heard Gina's voice again, growing louder as the women reapproached the great hall from another entrance to the rear wing. "So you see, it could make a wonderful inn. With all those bedrooms, you might possibly make a go of it. Perhaps you could turn it into a conference center. That's what they did at Brocket Hall, you know. Lord and Lady Brocket still live on the estate, but the main house is used as an exclusive retreat for private parties and businesses. Who knows, you might even catch their overflow."

For God's sake, Gina, Jeremy thought. Quit selling! But he knew that anyone as committed to a career as an estate agent as Gina Useppi would never deliberately try to lose a sale. He rolled his eyes and moved to a corner of the room where the women were unlikely to be able to see him as they moved from one end of the great hall to the other.

"But wouldn't the rumor that the place is haunted keep people from coming?" Alison asked.

"You could possibly turn that to your advantage, I believe," Gina replied, overcoming a familiar objection. "There is a tour of haunted houses in London. Perhaps you could get on the ghost circuit, you know, attract people who deliberately go out of their way to experience ghostly contact."

"I don't know," Alison replied, and Jeremy was pleased to hear the evident doubt in her voice. "I might end up with a lot of crazies. . . ."

"I suppose that's a possibility," Gina crooned in a voice that made it clear that she thought it unlikely. "Let's go up to the master suite now." The sound of their footsteps echoed on the stairwell, and Jeremy heard a door open. "This is the master bedroom, where Mr. Ryder is staying at the moment, so you must excuse the mess."

Jeremy frowned. He didn't think he'd left the room in much of a mess. But Alison didn't seem to mind.

"I love this!" she enthused. "Look how welcoming the fire is, a perfect place for reading a book on a rainy day." She paused, and her next words made him wish he had straightened the room and put away certain items, including the books on Byron and Caroline Lamb. "Hmmm," Alison remarked. "Interesting reading." But she evidently thought there was nothing unusual in his choice of titles, for she quickly moved on. "From this window, the view is lovely," she said. "It's like looking out over an enchanted woodland or something."

"It is beautiful, isn't it? Now that the rain has stopped and the sun is out. Oh, look," Gina added, "a rainbow. Maybe . . . that's a good sign."

Jeremy heard Alison give a delighted laugh, and he suppressed a groan. Give it up, Gina. . . .

Half an hour later, the tour complete, Gina and Alison returned to the front of the great hall. Jeremy had forced himself to keep to his task, working his way through the furnishings in the first receiving room, finding to his delight some priceless antiques and artwork. His friends at Coutts would be pleased, as would his friends at Sotheby's. Again, he withdrew to remain out of sight, and he listened, appalled, as Gina went in for the kill.

"So, Miss Cunningham, what do you think? Isn't it just perfect for your plans? I mean with the swimming pool and everything?"

"I . . . think it could be," the American woman replied with a surprising note of caution. "Of course, I'll have to get in touch with my bank. How much do you need to hold it for me?"

No. She wasn't for real, was she? Jeremy looked about him in dismay. He'd just begun his search. He knew it would take days, even weeks maybe, to go over this place, unless he got lucky and Caroline hadn't been as crafty as she had believed in selecting her hiding place. But he heard Gina's purring reply.

"Five percent would suffice, I believe. That would be twenty-five thousand pounds."

Jeremy heard the echo of footsteps approaching slowly from the great hall. He thought he was about to be discovered in his little act of eavesdropping, but then the sound stopped.

"There's only one other thing, Gina." Alison Cunningham's voice was sweet and light, very much the innocent ingenue. But her next words seemed calculated to strip Jeremy of any hope he had of continuing the search alone, if at all.

"I want to take possession immediately. Sole possession. Mr. Ryder has got to go."

⌁ *Chapter 7* ⌁

"*T*hat will be impossible, I'm afraid." A deep voice with a stiff British accent echoed through the great hall where Alison stood contemplating the enormity of the decision she was about to make, a decision she would never have considered except for the insistence of one particular little ghost.

But even if she hadn't made a semicommitment to finding the missing memoirs, she was enchanted with Dewhurst Manor and in her mind, as she'd peered through the dust and cobwebs, she had easily envisioned the place filled with people—tourists, visitors, maybe conference attendees, as Gina had suggested. The manor cried out for people, fun-loving, spirited people who would appreciate the idea and the experience of staying in an ancient Tudor mansion. Alison thought back to the many times she and her crowd of international friends had sought out unusual sites for their rendezvous. Dewhurst, with improvements, of course, would be perfect.

But Jeremy Ryder seemed to have other ideas. He had appeared so quickly, almost out of nowhere, that Alison jumped as if he had materialized like Caro's ghost. But he was real, very much in the flesh, and even more handsome than she recalled. "Why would that be,

Mr. Ryder?" she replied, mustering as much indignation as she could and ignoring the way he made her heart beat just a little faster.

"I have only just started this project," he replied, his voice annoyingly aloof. "I don't believe Mr. Peterson at Coutts would appreciate the interruption, and the expense, that would be involved should I be required to move every piece of furniture to my warehouse to continue with the appraisal. My contract clearly states that I will have the right to remain on these premises until I have finished the job."

"I'm certain that something could be worked out . . . ," Gina began, but Alison cut her off.

"No. If I am buying the property, I should have the right to take possession immediately." Alison was used to having her way, and she wasn't above psychologically stomping her foot at the moment to get it.

She wanted that man out.

Now.

It wouldn't do to have him roaming around while she searched for the missing memoirs. He might get suspicious or learn what was going on and decide to help himself to the treasure.

The search for the ghostly memoirs aside, however, Alison was suddenly eager to get going on creating a charming holiday resort from the peeling timbers of Dewhurst Manor, and she didn't want anybody, especially any man, around to tell her what to do.

But at a deeper level, Alison knew that neither of these was the real reason he had to go. The fact was, she simply found his presence too unsettling. When he entered the room, he seemed to fill it up with his dark good looks and his sexy British accent. His six feet or more of broad-chested, square-shouldered masculinity drew her like a magnet.

That, and something else.

Maybe it was his maturity. He was older than most of

the men she'd dated, and she found something about that age difference unutterably compelling. He was without a doubt more of a man than she'd ever encountered before. She suspected that his presence at Dewhurst Manor would throw her off, distract her from what she now considered almost a mission: to invest in and improve this property, and in so doing, to prove to herself she could manage her own business and affairs. If she found the memoirs in the process, so much the better.

That's why she frowned when Gina replied to her rather petulant demand to take immediate and sole possession. "These things do take time, Miss Cunningham. Even if you put earnest money on the property today, it will take a while to set up the closing. You'll have to make arrangements for your money to be transferred, there will be legal aspects to be worked out, that sort of thing. . . ."

Alison could feel her frustration mounting. She was being told no once again. Slowly and with great determination, she said, "This is my offer. I will buy the place. I will pay the asking price. But only if I can take possession now. Today. And Mr. Ryder finds other accommodations." Alison was pleased at her assertiveness, but she wasn't pleased to see Jeremy Ryder make his way to a sofa by the fireplace and nonchalantly, almost lazily, take a seat.

"Have you considered, Miss Cunningham, how very empty this place will be once the furniture is removed? And how difficult it would be for you to replace it with . . . proper furnishings? You might want to reconsider your needs. It's possible that you could work out some kind of arrangement, that is to say, negotiate with the bank, to include some of this," he swept his arm in a gesture that included the total expanse of the great hall, "in the purchase price. It would be foolish not to give it some thought."

Alison's face grew crimson. How she hated it when someone talked down to her like that. Especially when they were right! She clenched her teeth to keep from making an ill-considered response. The man was incorrigible. But he had a good point.

And for once, Alison listened.

"I suppose I should give that some consideration," she said at last. "But . . . I want to stay here, not in some hotel. There is a lot to do, and I want to get started. I'm sure, Mr. Ryder, that you will be gentleman enough to see my point. I'll make you a deal. You can finish your work here in the house, but you must find other lodgings. I mean, we can't both . . ."

Jeremy Ryder stood up again, and Alison could not avoid appraising his long legs and broad shoulders. He was dressed in expensive-looking black slacks and a rich black pullover, clean now of the earlier cobwebs or whatever had been clinging to the wool. His dark hair swept low over his brow, and his eyes gleamed black and impenetrable. When he spoke, his words were measured.

"It would seem to me that you might have a great many arrangements to make in the United States in order to make this move," he said. "Perhaps there is no need for us to dispute who can be on the premises. I am certain, Miss Cunningham, that by the time you return and are truly ready to move in, I shall be quite finished with my assignment here. I would even be most willing to speak to my client in your behalf," he added, turning on her a hint of a smile that she found distressingly appealing, "should you wish to negotiate for some, or all, of the furnishings."

Alison knew she was losing ground, and she found it gratingly difficult to argue with him. But she would have her way.

Or at least part of it.

"Very well, Mr. Ryder, since you seem so determined.

I'm sure your clients would appreciate your loyalty. I will allow you to remain here for now. But you are mistaken in thinking that I need to go back to the States before I close on the house. There is no need whatsoever. It is a matter of a phone call to my banker, you see. He will handle everything for me." She raised her chin slightly and looked from Jeremy to Gina. "However, if you wish to make this sale, my terms stand. I insist on taking possession immediately. I will be staying here tonight. It is a big place. I'm sure Mr. Ryder will find a way to accommodate my wishes."

It was the first time in a long while that Jeremy Ryder had lost a negotiation, especially with a woman. He hadn't in recent memory run across anyone quite so stubborn. Even the brooding half smile hadn't worked. Obviously, if Alison Cunningham had the money to buy a place like Dewhurst Manor on what appeared to him to be nothing more than a whim, she had more money than anyone needed and was accustomed to using it to get her way. He didn't find it admirable, but he didn't think at the moment there was anything he could do about it.

Although he didn't like the idea of her taking up residence at Dewhurst Manor, he had no intention of leaving. He must remain where he had access to all the nooks and crannies where the memoirs might have been hidden. And, he vowed, he would set about that search with renewed vigor immediately, even if he had to do it by flashlight after Alison went to bed. And that thought brought him up short.

Alison in bed.

He wondered suddenly what she looked like naked, how that lithe little body would feel curled up next to him. And then he wondered why he was wondering such a thing. She was everything he despised in the society women who beat a constant path to his door. Rich.

Spoiled. Petulant. She had no idea what it took to build the wealth she so carelessly threw around. The idea of someone paying full price for so overvalued a property as Dewhurst Manor was foreign to every dictum of good business practice in his soul. She was a fool, and as a rule, Jeremy had little sympathy for fools.

And yet, this fool was so young, and pretty. And she had no idea of the enormity of the mistake she was about to make. Perhaps if he were able to soften her inexplicably hostile attitude toward him, he could save her from herself by somehow making her change her mind.

So he changed his tactics.

"I'm certain we can come up with a mutually satisfying arrangement," he said amiably. "Would you ladies be my guests for tea? There is a decent inn nearby that serves a passable fare. Perhaps we could retire there and discuss this thing in a civilized manner."

But he knew the minute the words were out of his mouth, he'd blundered.

"I didn't know we weren't being civilized, Mr. Ryder," Alison said curtly.

But Gina interrupted her before she could go on. "That's a marvelous idea, Jeremy." She turned to Alison. "You must be famished. You've had such a long day. You'll find once you get settled in here that English tea is one of the world's *most* civilized traditions."

Jeremy turned one of his charming smiles on Alison and this time was rewarded with a perplexed look in her eyes that belied her inner conflict.

"Very well," she said at last. "I suppose it wouldn't hurt."

He indicated the front door. "Shall we, then, before it gets any later?" He held the door for the women, noting the light floral fragrance that wafted past him when Alison went by. He smiled. He had, it would seem, won at least a small battle after all.

*"His health being delicate, he liked to read with
me & stay with me out of the crowd. Not but what
we went about everywhere together, and were at last
invited always as if we had been married . . . I
grew to love him better than virtue, Religion—all
prospects here. He broke my heart, & I still love
him."*

—Lady Caroline Lamb to biographer
Thomas Medwin

*Some of Caroline's friends called her pretty little nick-
names like Ariel and Sprite, but others, perhaps those who
knew the other side of her nature, spoke of her as the Little
Savage & the Bat. In Truth, she was both Sprite & Savage,
a combination that continued to attract me. That & the
fact that she did not care a pence for what others thought
of her actions. I found this capacity for Caprice enchanting, at least in the beginning.*

*Her husband, too, seemed not to care that he was cuck-
olded virtually before his very eyes. Caroline told me right
away that although she loved William Lamb, he did not
show her the fiery affection she needed, & in fact encouraged her to find it elsewhere!*

*She desired fiery affection, & my own Passion for the
Sprite was intense, yet our affair sizzled with tension generated by our very abstinence from the act of sex. Ever present was the thought, the desire, the possibility . . . even
the talk of what we might do to one another should we find
ourselves alone in the boudoir, but for all of Caroline's
famous exhibitionism, she was at heart surprisingly naive
& inhibited. She preferred the titillation to be verbal &
theoretical, rather than actual. This discovery came as a
great relief, since my deepest fear had been that in satisfying my carnal desires for her, I would return to that infernal abyss of confusion that forbade me to know both Love
and Sex with a woman.*

I proceeded to court Lady C. throughout the spring of

that fateful year, participating in outrageous, infelicitous behavior that I have long regretted. We were together everywhere. Letters flew between us, sometimes ten times a day! Oh, the Passion that sparked our words in those days—! But our affair did not go unnoticed, and Caroline, not caring what Society thought or said, did nothing to squelch the rumors, in fact, began to flaunt our liaison, ignoring propriety and indulging in scenes that were to become the source of my disillusionment & despair. The Love I had longed for, the Platonic Passion that had fired my imagination, the delicious Wickedness of our illicit Desire soon withered beneath the light of public scrutiny. As I began to lose her to her own impetuosity, I resigned myself to the fact that I was not born to love, in any normal sense, a woman. That I continued to carry tender feelings for Caro for many months I cannot deny. But the Grand Experiment had ended in failure. I had not consummated my Love for her while it endured, and if I fell now to the pleasures of the flesh where Caro was concerned, it would, I was certain, result in the same degradation that I had felt with all the rest.

⌐ *Chapter 8* ⌐

Alison stirred the dregs of the now lukewarm tea in the bottom of her cup, her heart and mind both racing, searching for answers to the dilemma she'd unwittingly created for herself. Jeremy's invitation to go to the inn for tea had been a lifesaver in a way, for she hadn't eaten in hours, and she found she was ravenous by the time the freshly baked scones and clotted cream arrived with the hot pot of tea. But sitting across the table from him in the quaint little inn had also made her realize that she'd erred seriously in giving him permission to remain at Dewhurst Manor.

The man was simply too smooth. Not only was he good looking, he exuded his unquestionable masculinity in an elegant, understated way that threw Alison completely off balance. He was charming. He had ceased to talk down to her.

But his very manner raised her suspicions.

In an effort to get a grip on the situation, Alison averted her eyes from the handsome face and instead focused on her finger as she traced the pattern in the lace tablecloth over and over again. She listened in silence as Jeremy and Gina amiably discussed the possibility of houses being haunted and wondered what they would think if they knew she had arrived on the scene at the invitation of the resident ghost of Dewhurst Manor.

She thought about the ghost's latest appearance, and its urgent, almost desperate appeal to Alison. She thought about the books she'd seen in the master suite, occupied at the moment by Mr. Jeremy Ryder. Why was he reading about Lord Byron and Lady Caroline Lamb? Suddenly she wondered if somehow he had gotten wind that the Byron memoirs were secreted away in the old house. Was that what he was really doing there? Searching for the lost memoirs? Being an antiquities dealer, he would know how very valuable such a find would be, and being in the house alone, he would have every opportunity to find—and steal—the memoirs.

But unless the ghost of Lady Caroline had convinced him, the same as it had her, to come to Dewhurst Manor, Alison could not imagine how he would know about the existence of the papers. And at any rate, he didn't seem the type to fall for the hysterical plea of a pathetic little ghost. He was not nearly as flaky as Alison. No, he was probably reading those books because he was interested in the history of the area as it related to the furnishings he was appraising.

Still, if there was any chance he might be searching for the memoirs, which Alison already considered to be hers—and the ghost's, of course—it was all the more important that he leave.

Immediately.

Her energy restored by the hot tea and succulent scones, Alison pulled herself together and prepared to drop the bad news on him. "I'm sorry, Mr. Ryder, but I've been thinking, and, well, I've changed my mind. . . ."

"Please, call me Jeremy." That devastating smile again. "You've changed your mind? About buying Dewhurst Manor?"

Alison thought he sounded too hopeful. "No. About your remaining on the property."

The smile disappeared instantly. "But I thought we had agreed—" Jeremy began to growl his objection, but Gina interrupted.

"I think we need to put first things first," she insisted, waving her hands in the air as if to calm things down. "We need to get the contract in order before we can proceed with anything. When we're finished here, why don't you come with me, Alison? We'll go to the office, and you can contact your bankers while I draw up the contract. Then you can decide who is going to stay where. By the way, where are your bags?"

Alison had completely forgotten about them. "I left them with the concierge at the Dorchester in London. Guess I need to make arrangements for them to be delivered, although I could probably pick up a few things here in the village in case they don't make it this late in the day. Could I call from your office?"

"Uh, why, of course, my dear. Anything you need."

Alison could tell from Gina Useppi's solicitous smile and eagerness to please that she was beginning to believe that her client actually had the money she claimed and that this sale might go through. Alison suppressed a small grin of satisfaction.

At last she was being told yes.

A glance at Jeremy Ryder told her he was unimpressed by her wealth or anything else. But he was, Alison surmised, beginning to believe he'd better find other lodgings, and he wasn't happy about it. His captivating smile had disappeared, replaced by a scowl darker than the one he'd worn when she'd first encountered him. Even that, she found to her consternation, failed to detract from his handsome features. She was glad he would be gone when she arrived at Dewhurst Manor.

Alison knew she angered him even further when she adamantly refused to let either Jeremy or Gina pay the

bill. It wasn't that she wanted to flaunt her wealth . . .
she'd done that sufficiently already. Rather, she did not
want to owe either of them a debt of loyalty, no matter
how small. Her money was her independence, and she
was fiercely protective of that at the moment.

She opened the door to Gina's car, then paused and
turned to Jeremy, who was standing by the side of his
Porsche, glaring at the two women. "I promise I won't
be hard to get along with, Mr. Ryder," Alison said, forcing a wavering smile onto her lips. "I am certain we can
work out some mutually agreeable way for you to finish
your appraisal work. But you must understand, I need
my privacy. If I have to, I will simply make an offer on
the furnishings, a high offer, and your services will no
longer be necessary."

Jeremy's black eyes were hard as obsidian. "I'm cer-
tain you can arrange anything money can buy, Miss
Cunningham," he said, his tone cold and disdainful.
"Good day."

Dismayed, Alison watched him drive away, the tires
of his car sending an angry spray of gravel over the
parking lot, and for the first time, she felt as if she'd
stepped over the line in exhibiting her financial clout.
Still, if that was what it took to convince him to leave, so
be it.

"He *will* find somewhere else to stay, won't he?" she
asked Gina anxiously as the agent's luxury car roared to
life.

"I don't know him well," Gina said, easing out of the
parking lot. "I would assume he will honor your wishes,
although," she glanced at her young client, "why you
would want that gorgeous man out of your house is beyond me."

Jeremy Ryder had encountered the arrogance of the
very wealthy on many occasions, but this little tart
topped them all. Who was she, and how had she ended

up here? What obsession did she have with Dewhurst
Manor? These and more questions raced through his
mind as he drove the few miles back to the old country
house. He took several deep breaths to calm his rage.
Did she, he wondered, have the money to buy this place
on a moment's notice? And would she, God forbid,
show up on his doorstep later today?

It was *his* doorstep, he thought as he pulled into the
circular driveway and looked up at the old house. His, at
least for the moment. And he wasn't about to relinquish
it to the likes of Alison Cunningham, no matter how
much money she waved under his nose. He surveyed the
house for a long moment before driving on to park in
the adjacent garage. Other than being very old, Dewhurst Manor was not anything particularly spectacular.
There were other houses far more appealing, at far better prices, and not requiring nearly the renovations.
Why had the likes of Alison Cunningham locked onto
this one?

An answer to this last question hovered in a haze at
the back of his mind, but he was unwilling to acknowledge it as a possibility. Did she know about the memoirs? Impossible! He doubted if she knew much about
Lord Byron, and she'd probably never heard of Lady
Caroline. He was just paranoid.

Jeremy eased the car into the garage and turned off
the motor. The sudden quiet was deafening. He got out
and shut the door behind him, then stopped and listened to the small, moist sounds of springtime—water
dripping from the trees, trickling in rivulets down the
sodden lawn to where a small beck flowed at the far side
of the property. The very peace of the place served to
calm his nerves and quench his fury. He could not,
would not, let Alison Cunningham interfere with his
search for the Byron memoirs.

His eyes roamed the rough landscape of the property,
and he envisioned Lady Caroline, miserable in her unre-

quited love, racing across the muddy countryside on horseback and being welcomed by an aging, lonely man who offered her a warm fire, cognac, and a willing ear.

In this very house.

He gazed up at the weathered timbers and the odd turret just above the front door. He thought about the way old pieces of furniture and paintings and other treasures of antiquity had a way of telling him their story. Would Dewhurst Manor do the same, if he took time to listen?

Perhaps he had started his search all wrong. He should begin from the outside. He decided to walk the perimeter of the grounds, despite the mud underfoot. This would give him a clear perspective of the lay of the land. Which way was Brocket Hall from here? Which way would she have come—by carriage down the lane or on horseback over the open field—the day she brought the memoirs to be hidden away for almost two centuries?

The countryside surrounding Dewhurst Manor was overpowering in its greenness. Spring had painted the land with a swash of verdant splendor, and it was difficult for Jeremy to remain in a foul mood despite the fact he was about to be ousted from his search, and his bed, by Alison Cunningham. He forced thoughts of the inexplicably sexy if exasperating young woman from his mind and tried to concentrate on the property and the way the house was situated upon it.

As Gina had explained, the original Tudor structure had been added onto unmercifully over time, with no thought to retaining the integrity of the original architectural style. This fact was painfully evident from the back side of the building, where ten of the sixteen bedrooms had been tacked onto the original structure in such a hodgepodge manner that Jeremy got the impression they had been constructed in a hurry, as if in time for an immediate party.

"The king is coming. Build some more bedrooms for the Court."

Or something like that.

And Jeremy realized with a jolt that Dewhurst Manor had delivered its first message to him.

The grounds had lain unattended since Lady Julia had fallen ill, maybe longer, and Jeremy picked his way slowly through waist-high brambles that snagged the fabric of his expensive slacks and hampered his progress. The ground squished beneath his favorite leather loafers, and he feared with each step that he would end up mired in a bog. The earlier rain now steamed around him in a shallow mist, and his short, rapid breathing echoed in the stillness of the afternoon. The fastidious side of his nature screamed at him to return to the house and change into more suitable attire for a tramp through the mud, but something held him on course in his circumnavigation of the old manor. It was as if he were being drawn inexorably toward . . . what?

He had reached the back of the massive building and could see the new wing with the swimming pool stretching in its incongruous modern, red brick facade, when a sudden whirring at his feet sent adrenaline flooding through his body. A gunshot exploded the cottony quiet of the hazy afternoon, and Jeremy ducked into the tall weeds. What the hell?

Another shot, and the cry of a bird injured by the blast, followed by the excited barking of a dog set on retrieving its quarry. Carefully, Jeremy edged his head above the tops of the weeds, and what he saw almost made his heart stop. It had to be a phantom. The gaunt figure coming toward him was as wispy and gray as the mists that swirled around him. He wore a tattered tweed jacket and an equally disheveled cap set at an angle atop stringy silver hair that hung to his shoulders. The phantom hunter stopped abruptly and raised his gun when he saw Jeremy.

"Who goes there?" he demanded in a voice that quivered with age.

Jeremy decided since the ghostly hunter had a gun, he would oblige with an answer, even if it made no rational sense to be conversing with a specter. "My name is Ryder. And yours, sir?"

The old man squinted, then slowly lowered his rifle. "What're ye doin' round these parts, lad?"

"I . . . live here." Jeremy realized this wasn't quite the truth, but it seemed the most logical explanation to give quickly to the grizzled being who continued to point a gun at him.

"Ye not be a-tellin' me th' truth, lad. Ye don't live here. Nobody lives here, least nobody alive in th' flesh. Hain't since old Lady Julia passed on. Tell me th' truth 'fore I run you in for trespassin'."

The ancient personage that faced him was no ghost, Jeremy realized, but the knowledge provided him only a small degree of relief. He still had the shotgun to contend with. "Sir, I am not trespassing, I can assure you—" he began, but the old man cut him short.

"Seems kind of odd that ye be snoopin' out here in the brambles and all. Who ye be lookin' for? Caroline?"

Jeremy's eyes widened. "Caroline?"

"Yea. Her." He pointed over Jeremy's shoulder toward the house. Jeremy wheeled around and peered through the mist, but there was no one there. He saw nothing except the rear of Dewhurst Manor, in all its scrambled disarray.

"I don't understand," he said, turning back to the hunter. "I don't see anyone."

The old man laughed with a wheeze. "Of course y' don't. Th' ghost only shows herself t' certain folk. But she's there, lad, she's there. She's been gone a long time, and now she's back. I wonder what brought her home?"

The ghost? Jeremy stared at the demented old man,

so ghostlike himself, and realized the spectral hunter was more than likely a poacher. "Who are you?" he demanded suddenly, frowning.

"Stone's the name. Ashley T. Stone."

"Do you have permission to hunt on this land?"

"Don't need no permission," the old one replied defensively. "Been huntin' on this land since I was a boy. Even Lord Charles, rest his soul, told me t' bag a grouse for 'im every now and then. It's th' only decent huntin' grounds left round here, y'know." He bent to take the dead bird from the mouth of the eager retriever. "All th' other estates have been built up into them fancy golf courses and trainin' schools and such. The world's too changed for me. I'll be glad t' be passin' on soon." He glanced up again at the rear of Dewhurst Manor. "Although a lot o' good it did that'n."

Jeremy recalled overhearing Gina tell Alison about an old man named Ashley T. Stone, and how he had created the myth that Dewhurst Manor was haunted by the ghost of a young woman. "How do you know there's a ghost here?" he asked, his curiosity piqued.

"I can see her, plain as day."

"Who is she?"

"That poor Caroline," he said sorrowfully.

"What Caroline? Do you know her last name?"

The old man looked at Jeremy as if he was the one who had lost his mind. "Why, that's th' ghost o' Lady Caroline Lamb," he said, as if it made good sense. "She used t' live in these parts, yonder, in Brocket Hall. She was the wife o' William Lamb, but 'twasn't him she loved. She loved th' wicked Lord Byron, with all her heart, but he didna love her. Some say she went mad with grief and drank herself into her grave. Mad she may have been, but I believe she died of a broken heart, and that's why her spirit still walks. Poor soul! I don't know how she will ever find her peace."

"How do you know all this?"

The old man turned to go. "I used to work at Brocket Hall when I was a lad, for a man who was older than time, like I am now. His father was Lady Caroline's stable boy. He told me all the stories. She was somethin', that one. Byron made a mistake passin' her up."

And with that, Ashley T. Stone disappeared. Just as if he were the ghost Jeremy had thought him to be at first, the gnarled figure seemed to melt into the mist, leaving behind the quiet afternoon, a covey of grouse smaller in number by one, and a very perplexed Jeremy Ryder.

> *Your heart, my poor Caro (what a little volcano!), pours lava through your veins. . . . I have always thought you the cleverest, most agreeable absurd, amiable, perplexing, dangerous, fascinating little being that lives now. I won't talk to you of beauty; I am no judge. But our beauties cease to be so when near you, and therefore you have either some, or something better.*
>
> —Lord Byron to Caroline Lamb

I remind myself again as I put pen to paper that Honesty in my reminiscences is requisite, as difficult as it is to accomplish at times. But only Honesty here shall suffice to soothe my troubled Soul. The night is wild with storms, a good night to continue the tale of my calamitous affair with Lady C.

Just as I determined that I must break it off with Caroline, unable to bear her increasingly public and ofttimes embarrassing displays of affection for me, she made the fatal error that sentenced our Love to its certain demise. In my quarters, both of us having had much red wine and brandy, she shed her clothing and came to me naked, asking with those huge compelling eyes that I teach her those things of which we had until now only spoken of in wicked whispers. Unable to control my Lust, I partook of that forbidden fruit, knowing that on the morrow, I would dwell again in Darkness. When later I awoke by her side, that overwhelming Terror again filled my heart. Looking upon her golden curls, both crowns of them, I knew I had lost not only the Battle but also the War. I could love Caro no more, if indeed I ever did, & I determined on the spot to end it with her immediately.

But Lady Caroline would not hear of a separation between us. She insisted that she loved me & that I loved her, & that she was certain I would not wish to live my life without her. To my Horror, she proceeded to attempt to prove our Love by not letting me out of her sight. She followed me to parties to which she had not been invited, waiting outside with the coachmen like a commoner until I arrived to take her away. She appeared unannounced at my apartments, pleading with poor Fletcher to let her in if I was not at home. She stalked me in the very streets of London, dressed always as a page, but I knew it was she. The more outrageous her behavior, the stronger grew my resolve to rid myself of her forever. I hate beggarly displays of emotion, however, and so I determined to go about it in a gentlemanly manner.

My first ploy was to plead penury. Perhaps the Lady would shun a Pauper, even if he was a Lord. I was indeed in dire need of money at the time, not having retained the copyright to Childe Harold *nor taken any money from its publication. My scheme miscarried, however, as she instantly offered me all her jewels to sell. Caroline was nothing if not generous.*

So I bethought another plot, this one more sinister. It was often said that I was the incarnation of my poetic hero, Childe Harold, the doer of dark unspeakable deeds with exotic characters in mysterious settings. It was not said wrong, for my adventures both in England and afar in those days covered a wide gamut of activities, many of them scandalous, nefarious even, to genteel English ears. I was certain that she would be sufficiently shocked by some of the tales of my Experiences that she would flee from me in disgust. Again, just the opposite happened. At first she was appalled when I told her of the boys I had loved, (and how I had loved them) and about how I had once, while in the Orient, killed a rival unnecessarily, just to see what it felt like to have blood on my hands. But then it was her turn to shock me, first by asking for lurid details and then by suggesting we try some of the—carnal activities—ourselves. Even I, as bold & bad as I pretended to be, was amazed at the woman's fascination with all that is unspeakable in our Society. Instead of sending her safely back into her husband's arms, my efforts only served to tantalize her, driving her to even more desperate designs to hold me to her.

⚘ *Chapter 9* ⚘

"**Y**es, you heard me correctly. Eight hundred thousand dollars. Transfer it immediately, please, into this account." Alison read the name and number of the estate agent's escrow account, her impatience mounting. Sure, it was more than she needed to secure the deal. It was, in fact, enough to pay the full price for Dewhurst Manor. But she was taking no chances. The money in the bank meant Dewhurst was hers. "What do you mean you can't do it? It's my money. I can do anything I want with it."

She tapped her foot and listened to the voice on the other end of the line in Boston. "Let me speak to James Seymour," she demanded curtly. Another long pause. "Mr. Seymour, this is Alison Cunningham. I'm calling from Hatfield, England, where I am buying a house. I wish to have eight hundred thousand dollars transferred immediately into the escrow account of the real estate agency. I gave the woman the information already, but she seemed to have a problem with making the transaction. I'm sure you will have no such problem, will you?"

Alison had not thought it would be so difficult to get her hands on her own money. The blasted bankers were no better than the lawyers. "What? Why would I have to do that?" Alison attempted to keep her temper in check as she listened to her personal banker explain that it was for her own protection that they required the request for the transfer of such a large amount in writing. "Yes, I understand," she said at last, drawing in a deep breath. "But I want the money now. Today." She frowned, then covered the receiver with her hand and turned to Gina Useppi who had heard the entire conversation. "Do you have a fax machine?"

"Of course."

"May I use it to send these idiots my request in writing?"

Gina nodded, her face unreadable. Alison returned to the phone. "Okay. I'll write you a letter and send it to you by fax. You want what? A copy of the contract?" Why the banker would want that, Alison didn't know, but her nerves were on edge, and she just wanted to get on with things. "Oh, all right. Just make sure this happens today, Mr. Seymour. It is only morning in Boston, so you should have plenty of time. Thank you."

She hung up the phone and turned to Gina. "Done."

"And so is the contract. All you need to do is sign on the lines I have marked with an *X,* and write me a check for the earnest money."

"And write a letter and send a fax," Alison groused, picking up a pen and signing the contract without reading it. "I'm exhausted," she said moments later. "I'll be glad to get to Dewhurst Manor and settle in." Then she frowned. "Did you say there were no servants?"

"That's right. Mr. Ryder has only been there two days, and he indicated he didn't want to be bothered with servants, but I can imagine you will want some help. However, there's the slight problem of finding someone who isn't superstitious about the so-called ghost. Suppose I make a few calls for you while you write your letter and get the fax off to Boston?"

Alison smiled. "That would be great. Thanks." Gina settled her in front of a typewriter, gave her a piece of agency letterhead, and showed her where the fax machine was located, then left to make her calls in another room. Only then did Alison slow down enough to glance at the contract. Only then did she question her impulsive decision to buy Dewhurst Manor.

Five hundred thousand pounds. Over three quarters of a million dollars. Was the property worth it? She hadn't asked for an appraisal. She picked up the contract and searched through it for evidence that there had been one, but found herself lost in a maze of legalese. "Gina?" she called.

"Yes, dear?" The agent returned to the doorway.

"Has there been any sort of . . . well, appraisal on the property lately? I mean, could I see some paperwork to back up the price the bank is asking for the place?"

Alison perceived a slight hesitation from the agent. "I don't think there actually has ever been an appraisal on the place since Lady Julia died," she replied slowly. "Of course, Mr. Ryder is there to appraise the contents, but that has nothing to do with the building itself." Gina went to a tall filing cabinet and opened a drawer. "What I can show you is a copy of the mortgage Lady Julia took out on the place, based on its value in the late nineteen eighties."

The mortgage was for five hundred thousand pounds, exactly what the bank was asking. But surely Lady Julia had paid some of it off. And something else didn't feel right to Alison.

"The place has been empty for a long time, hasn't it?" she asked.

"Lady Julia died several months ago, but I'm afraid her long illness resulted in the place being rather neglected over the past few years," Gina admitted. "She kept up only the pool and the few rooms she used. Why?"

"Well, it would seem to me that perhaps the value

could have dropped some because it hasn't been taken care of. . . ." Alison sensed she was right, even though she had no experience at this sort of thing, and one look at Gina's face told her to pursue the issue.

"Well, I suppose that could be the case," the agent said hesitantly, "although with an historical property like Dewhurst Manor, the value doesn't fluctuate a great deal."

Alison picked up the contract and tore it in half. "I should have read this before I signed it," she said, amazing herself. "I still want to buy Dewhurst Manor, and I'm still willing to sign a contract and write you a check this afternoon, but I want a clause in it that provides for a current appraisal, stating that the contract price is contingent upon the appraiser's report."

Gina Useppi stared at Alison for a long moment, and Alison returned her gaze unblinking. "Very well," Gina said. "It's a good idea, actually." Without further conversation, she completed another contract, which this time Alison read carefully before signing. The letter to the bank was written and the paperwork was faxed, Gina got a lead on a housekeeper, and before dark, an exhausted but exhilarated Alison Crawford Cunningham made her way in a rented car to the first investment property in her personal portfolio—a huge dilapidated country house in the middle of England, home to a ghost who claimed to be the spirit of Lady Caroline Lamb.

But hopefully, *not* home to a certain handsome but arrogant antiquities dealer who did funny things to the new owner's heart.

So Ashley T. Stone believes the ghost of Lady Caroline Lamb haunts this old place, Jeremy thought as he walked through the big empty house. What had he meant when he'd said she'd been gone a long time, but now she was back? Do ghosts go on vacation? He laughed to himself. But Jeremy saw no sign that any ghost had returned, nor that Alison Cunningham was going to make good on her threat to stay the night at Dewhurst Manor. It was a good thing, because Jeremy had no intention of packing up his things. He had a contract, a firm agreement, and he would stay put until Coutts asked him to leave.

He had spent the rest of the afternoon exploring the property, "listening" with all of his keen intuition for any other stories the old house might have for him, but he'd had no flashes of inspiration as to the whereabouts of the memoirs. If they were here, they weren't talking.

It was all so bizarre, he considered, going into the library and thumbing through several books at random. First the letter written by Caroline, then the erotic dreams about her, and now, the sighting of what was supposedly her ghost, although Jeremy doubted seriously he would encounter any such spirit in the house. And somewhere amongst all this there was Alison Cunningham. Why here? Why now? This old house had been up for sale for years without a single offer. And the resemblance between Alison and the portraits Jeremy had seen of Caroline Lamb was astonishing. He felt as if they were all characters in a play, with Dewhurst Manor as the stage. What, he wondered, was the plot?

Outside, thunder rumbled as the earlier storms began to build again. The heavy clouds brought on a premature dusk, although the sun wouldn't set until well after eight o'clock. Jeremy turned off the lights in the library, inexplicably restless and uneasy. He realized he was hungry, and he wouldn't mind a drink, either, but he hadn't taken time to stock either the pantry or the bar since his arrival. He looked at his watch. Seven forty. Maybe a hearty meal at the local pub and a tot or two of a good single malt whiskey would put him in better spirits. He donned his raincoat that hung on a hook by the front door, picked up an umbrella, and headed for the garage. He carefully backed the Porsche out of the building and put it in gear, and as he did so, he glanced up at the tower. Lightning flashed, streaking the window panes with electric blue, and in that instant, he caught a glimpse of what appeared to be the outline of a woman's figure in the glass. He drew in a sharp breath.

Another shimmer of lightning, a crack of thunder, and then darkness.

A shiver crawled down his spine. Sitting behind the steering wheel, Jeremy felt his heart pounding heavily. He stared up at the window, trying to convince himself that he had seen nothing. Nothing at all. No ghost. No Lady Caroline. Just a reflection of a stormy night and his own taut nerves.

With a frown, he headed down the darkened lane, suddenly anxious for the warmth of the pub and the burn of strong whiskey against his throat.

It had been a long day. . . .

Alison stopped by a small grocer's shop and bought a few things for her supper. Her luggage would not be delivered until the following day, so she picked up a new toothbrush and toothpaste and purchased an oversized T-shirt from a souvenir shop that was just getting ready to close. It wasn't exactly the designer lingerie she was used to, but it would do to sleep in for one night.

She reached Dewhurst Manor just as the clouds burst, washing the countryside in a deluge. There was no sign of Jeremy Ryder, she noted with relief, although she noticed that someone had left a light on inside the house. Had he actually been that thoughtful? She doubted it sincerely from the way he had glared at her when they parted after tea at the inn. More likely, he probably just forgot. Still, the light was like a welcoming beacon, and Alison decided to brave the storm and make a run for it.

The door was locked, and rain dripped down her neck

as she fumbled with the key, but the latch turned easily, and Alison managed to get herself and all of her shopping bags inside without too much damage. Closing the door behind her, she shivered. The great hall loomed in ominous darkness. The light she'd seen emanated from a fixture on the stairwell to her left.

"Anybody home?" she called, not wanting to have the living daylights scared out of her a second time that day in case Jeremy Ryder had not seen fit to vacate the place like a gentleman.

But there was no reply. Only the sound of the wind and storm outside. "Well," Alison said aloud, just to add some life to the lonely old house, "then let's get settled. You here, Caro?" she added with a nervous laugh as she lugged her parcels upstairs and made her way toward the master bedroom. "You'd better be, sweetheart, and you'd better be ready to show me where you put those memoirs, because I have a feeling I have a lot of other work to do here besides your little errand."

She opened the door to the master suite, half expecting to find Caro's ghost lounging by the fire. Instead, she found to her dismay that all of Jeremy Ryder's belongings remained exactly where they had been. The black sweater lay on the bed, the books about Byron and Caroline Lamb were stacked on the end table, a valise stood in the corner.

"Damn!" she muttered, flinging her bags onto the bed. "Just what I need, another confrontation with that man . . ." And with that, Alison began to gather his things together, determined to move him at least as far away as the great hall. If he returned tonight, which she was certain he would, she would insist that he move to an inn or hotel, someplace, anyplace, other than here.

She reached for the pile of books and accidentally knocked the whole stack off the small table. Cursing her clumsiness, she bent to pick them up, when her eye fell upon a letter that had dropped from between the pages of one of the volumes. She looked around furtively, even though she knew she was alone in the house. It wasn't her habit to read other people's mail, but something about this paper caught her attention. Maybe it was because the handwriting looked so . . . old-fashioned. Or maybe, she admitted to herself, it was because she was curious about Jeremy Ryder.

Placing the books back on the stand, Alison took the letter to the lamplight to examine it better. It was difficult to decipher the writing, and many of the words were spelled in an atrocious manner, but her eyes widened at every sentence she read.

Sir,

With this letter I place into your care certain knowledg which although at the moment is of no value to mend my tarnished reputation, if your firm will follow my instructions exactly, at some distant time in the future, my true situation should become reveald and the action of Lord B. against me exposd to all the world for the dastardly deed it is. I am an innocent victim of his cruelty, and I have the memoirs to prove it. They were not burned, though Moore and Hobhouse would swear it! But should I bring this fact to light now, that what M. and the rest thought destroyed was my careful copy, they would deem it a fraud and a fake and lay more charges on me as to my madness. And so, Sir, it is my humble and sincere request that your firm shall vow to me to keep this secret throughout the next one hundred years, and upon the date of my birth in the year of our Lord nineteen hundred and twenty-four, to go to the estate known as Dewhurst Manor, adjacent to my own dear beloved Brocket, for there I have secretted away the authentic memoirs. It makes me laugh to know I will win out in the end after all. It was a heartless act perpetrated upon me by B. and Lady

*O., my good "friend . . ." Time will vindicate me,
and the world will know from his own hand that he
loved me, and that he never ceasd to love me. Good
sir, I will leave nothing to indicate the location of the
memoirs at Dewhurst Manor, for I do not wish to
risk exposure of them before it is time. A careful
search will reveal their existence, however. I choose
D. over Brocket as my secret hiding place, as D. is
less likely to be visited frequently. I trust you and the
heirs to your firm will follow my orders, as you have
followed those of my beloved W.L. for these many
years. Say nothing of this matter to anyone. It is of
extreme importants that my vengeance be taken only
when the time is right.   C.L.*

Stunned, Alison let the photocopied page drop into her
lap. *C.L.* Caroline Lamb? It had to be! From the con-
tent, what it described, it could be nothing other than a
copy of a letter she must have written long, long ago.
Quickly, she placed the letter back between the pages of
one of the books, her mind racing. He knew! Jeremy
Ryder, the antiquities dealer, knew about the memoirs.
That was why he was so adamant about remaining at
Dewhurst Manor. But where did he obtain this letter?
Was it even real? What she'd just read was a photocopy.
Where was the original?

Another thought suddenly struck her. If Jeremy knew
of the possible existence of the memoirs of Lord Byron,
who else knew as well? Would there be more treasure-
seekers showing up at Dewhurst Manor?

"Oh, Caro," she moaned. "Why didn't you just get
Jeremy Ryder to find your damned memoirs? You could
have saved me a lot of trouble." In truth, Alison suddenly felt that the ghost no longer needed her. With the
expertise of someone like Jeremy behind the search,
surely the papers would be unearthed quickly and the
world would know the truth about the affair between

Byron and Caro. The poor woman's reputation would be saved, and perhaps her spirit could move on to wherever ghosts go when they resolve their problems.

Suddenly, an icy breeze stirred through the room, flickering the embers in the fireplace and raising the hair on Alison's arm. "It's you, isn't it?" she called out, irritated. "Show yourself. Talk to me."

For a change, the capricious spirit did as she was bid. A light mist formed, and then turned a pale shade of gold before forming the figure of a petite woman now dressed in an old-fashioned gown. "He must not be the one to find the memoirs," the ghost warned, a look of serious concern on her face.

"Why not? What difference does it make who finds them, as long as they turn up?"

"Nooo," the ghost wailed. "The world must know. They must be published for all to see. If this man finds them, he will sell them to a private collector, and my reputation will never be vindicated. I can never be free. . . ."

It started to cry, making a plaintive wail loud enough to be heard in the nearby village, Alison was sure. "Quiet down! Let me think," she commanded. She'd found assertiveness to be the best technique for handling the hysterics this specter seemed fond of displaying. "Okay, I'll get them for you. But we're here now, at Dewhurst Manor. Why don't you just tell me where they are, and we'll get it over with?"

At that, the ghost cried even louder.

"What is the matter with you?" Alison shrieked. "Where are the damned memoirs?"

"I . . . I do not know," came its faint reply.

"What do you mean, you don't know?"

"I . . . have rather . . . forgotten where I put them. It has been a very long time," she added with an exaggerated sigh.

"Forgotten?" Alison exploded. "You mean you have

dragged me across an ocean and enticed me into purchasing this monster house so I can help you out, and now you're telling me you can't remember where you put the memoirs?" Alison had never been so frustrated in her life, and she had a good mind to take her leave right then and there. Maybe she could convince Gina to tear up the contract. She could stop payment on the check. Maybe her banker hadn't followed her orders and wired the money into the escrow account. Maybe she could pick up her bags and walk out of Dewhurst Manor and leave the ghost and the memoirs and the whole crazy business to Jeremy Ryder.

She turned to do just that, and jumped when she saw the dark figure of the man in question leaning against the doorway, arms folded, a guarded look on his face. "I . . . thought you said you would leave," she stammered, breathless from her diatribe against the ghost and embarrassed that Jeremy might have witnessed the scene.

He pushed away from the doorsill and came into the room. "Who were you talking to just now?"

"Talking? Who was I talking to? Oh, nobody. I sometimes talk to myself, that's all." She spoke rapidly, in a higher pitch than normal.

Jeremy moved through the room with an air of authority, looking into corners and closets until he seemed satisfied that no one was in the room with them. The ghost, of course, had made a hasty exit, but Alison wondered if Jeremy had seen it.

"I was in the process of gathering your things up so I could get settled in here myself," she began, and then stopped short when she saw the rage in his face.

"I am going nowhere, Miss Moneybags," he said in a deadly quiet voice. He walked to where she stood staring up at him with wide eyes. "I have a contract. I intend to fulfill my part of it by remaining at Dewhurst Manor to finish my work. And I expect the bank to fulfill its part, your little intrusion notwithstanding. I am sure Coutts will be delighted to get your offer, as inflated as it is. But they are also well aware that the value of the furnishings might exceed the value of the estate—the . . . true value, if you understand my meaning. I doubt if they will much want to interrupt my appraisal work until every piece is evaluated for potential sale."

He took another step closer, and Alison shrank away. He was a head taller than she, and far stronger, no doubt. Was he going to hurt her? He was so close she could see the outline of his muscles beneath the knit shirt he wore. She could feel his body heat, and she was reminded of Gina's comment about how handsome he was. She was right; he *was* handsome. A hunk, to be exact. And under other circumstances, maybe Alison wouldn't have wanted him to leave.

But at the moment, she was decidedly sorry she hadn't been more definitive when settling their living arrangements earlier. She *must* convince him to leave. The ghost was right. He was a mercenary. He didn't care a fig about Caroline Lamb's reputation. He would sell the memoirs to the highest bidder, and unless that party was a museum or university, which was unlikely, the memoirs would once again disappear from public sight.

Irrational as it seemed even to her to protect the ghostly interests of Caroline Lamb, Alison could not let that happen. She'd promised, and she planned to deliver. Quickly, she stepped around him and made her way to the other side of the room, putting the barrier of the wide bed between them. "I also have a contract, Mr. Ryder," she said, wishing her voice wasn't so shaky. "One that says I own this place. And as the owner, I demand that you leave. Or else I'll . . . I'll call the police."

To her horror, he followed her across the room. "And what, pray tell, are you going to tell them, Miss Cunningham? That I'm trespassing?" His eyes were mocking. "For you well know I am not. I was here before you arrived. These are my quarters. And it is I who now demand that you take your leave."

Alison's fear turned to fury. The man was abominable! She wished she had something to throw at him. Then suddenly she heard a faint giggle, a light mischievous laugh, and she could tell he heard something too, for he whirled around abruptly, searching for the source of the laughter. When his back was turned, Alison watched in astonishment as a huge feather pillow levitated gently from the head of the bed. She heard a ripping sound, and then more laughter as Jeremy Ryder was dusted from head to toe in white goose feathers.

Alison couldn't help herself. She knew it wasn't a very grown-up thing to do, but by God he deserved it. With a gleeful cry, she split open the other pillow and joined her ghostly companion in the prank, emptying it over his head before he could recover sufficiently from his surprise to do anything about it.

"Be my guest, then, Mr. Ryder," she laughed, grabbing her things from the bed and bolting for the door. "The room is yours, at least for the night. Tomorrow . . . well, we'll see."

⫷ Chapter 10 ⫸

*I never heard of such a thing in my life, taking the
Mothers for confidantes!*

—The Prince of Wales

Desperate to be released from Caroline's snare, I
sought advice from her mother-in-law, Lady Melbourne, and found in her an unlikely ally. She became, in
fact, my best woman Friend & Confidante. Lady M. was
seasoned in the ways of Love, & oddly did not think it
strange that I came to her for advice, I who had been, and
if Caro would have her way, would continue to be, the
lover of her son's wife. In fact, I believe she took a certain
vicarious pleasure in learning the details of what went on
between Caro and I. She had never liked Caroline, a fact
she pointed out on our initial visit, so her complicity in the
matter of orchestrating Caro's downfall gave her untold
pleasure.

When Caro learned of my treachery, that I had shared
with her husband's mother some of her private letters written to me, she was outraged, and threw a tantrum in my
apartment. Well done! I congratulated myself, thinking she
would now revile me. But the tantrum passed, and still she
clung to me, pleading, begging me to love her. It was pathetic, & I was little moved.

*But her insane jealousy of Lady M. gave me an idea of
yet another way of ending our debacle. Jealousy comes
naturally to women, I have learned, & I worked very hard
at filling Caro's heart with jealousy. If she could become
jealous of the attentions I paid to a matron old enough to
be my mother, I reasoned, how would she react if the objects of my adoration were the younger belles dames in
Society?*

*Caroline loved to dance, inviting me often to observe as
she was waltzed about the room by leering, lecherous men,
each touching her porcelain skin in ways that only I should
have been allowed to do. When I fancied myself in love
with her, these parties sent me into a foul disposition. But
now, I plotted to use her dancing parties in the ballroom at
Melbourne House to my advantage, openly flirting with
other young beauties right under her nose, hoping she
would leave me in a fit of jealous rage. But again Caro
defeated me. Noting that I had once been displeased by the
waltz parties, she simply discontinued them.*

Jeremy watched Alison leave the room, too appalled
and stunned by her behavior to follow. Around him,
feathers flew. They nestled on the cashmere of his cardigan and fell in soft clouds at his feet. The room was in
shambles. But that wasn't what disturbed Jeremy at the
moment. What concerned him was that he was under
the same roof as a lunatic. First, he'd come upon Alison
deep into some kind of one-sided conversation which
was obviously making her very angry. And then she'd
attacked him with the feather pillows.

The woman *must* be mad.

But how had she done that so quickly? he mused,
brushing the feathers off his arms. One minute they
were conversing, and in the next instant, it seemed,
when he'd turned his back momentarily, she'd managed
to seize the pillow, rip it open, and dump its contents on
him. He stared at the bed, realizing suddenly that not

one, but two torn pillowcases lay there. Two! The crazy woman was fast as lightning. But what had made him turn his back to her? He'd heard something, he was certain of it. A laugh. A woman's high-pitched laugh.

Was Alison Cunningham a ventriloquist as well?

Jeremy wasn't sure of anything at the moment, except that he was going to close the door and lock it, light a roaring fire, and crack open the bottle of cognac he'd bought in town. That accomplished, he sat down heavily on the sofa and tried to think. This wasn't turning out at all as he had planned.

That's when he noticed his books had been tampered with. "Damn," he swore. He'd been a fool to leave them lying about. Someone like Alison Cunningham would have no qualms, he was certain, about snooping through his things. The letter! he thought suddenly. Had she seen the letter? He reached for the middle book, where he remembered hiding the photocopy, and he felt almost physically ill when he didn't find it there.

But wait. The books were in a different order than he'd left them. Had she dropped them? Hurriedly, he searched through the top book and breathed a long sigh of relief to find the copy of the letter. Had she seen it? he wondered again. Even if she had, he reasoned with himself, he doubted she would be able either to make her way through the difficult handwriting or understand its message. Likely, as scatterbrained as she seemed to be, she would take no note of it in any case.

He tossed back a hefty swig of cognac and felt its comforting tingle all the way down. His nerves were wracked. What had started as a quiet day with the promise of an organized search for the memoirs had turned into something altogether irrational. He'd been intruded upon, threatened, insulted, shot at. He'd thought he'd seen a ghost in the tower window. And now this, he looked around, confounded by the feather-drenched landscape of his room. It looked like an indoor snowstorm.

Maybe it would have been better not to argue with Alison Cunningham, he considered. She appeared to be the type who was used to getting her way, no matter what. And gazing into those large eyes only moments before, Jeremy had almost voluntarily let her have her way. She had seemed in that instant small and vulnerable, and very lovely. He had no wish to harm her. In fact, he'd felt a surprising urge to protect her.

That, and other less surprising, more biological urges.

Those urges had flown with the onset of her outrageous behavior, however. It was not his job to protect her. If she wanted to throw away her money buying Dewhurst Manor, it was none of his business. What *was* his business was the search for the memoirs. And he needed to get on with it. The only problem was how to proceed without her noticing. He decided to keep a low profile; stay out of her way. He couldn't afford to aggravate her further. He had to finish up as quickly as he could. Even if it meant working at night.

Jeremy looked at his watch. Eleven o'clock. It was still early enough to work for a couple of hours. He never went to bed much before one o'clock anyway. Draining his glass, he set it next to the nearly full bottle of cognac on the table near the sofa and went to change his clothes. Feathers puffed around his feet as he pulled off his trousers and put on a pair of old Levis and donned a navy blue long-sleeved jersey. The night was chill, and he pulled on his cardigan over the knit shirt. What a childish prank, he thought, running a brush through his thick hair and surveying the room. He'd call a cleaning service first thing in the morning.

Picking up an electric torch, Jeremy decided to return to the wine cellar, which he still considered to be the most likely hiding place for Caroline Lamb's treasure. Maybe he would get lucky. At any rate, Alison probably would not be able to see the light from the cellar, even if she was sleeping on the couch in the great hall. But he took no chances. Before leaving the room, he turned off all the lights. He crept through the blinding darkness, feeling his way down the stairs, around the corner, past the library, down more stairs, until he reached the small anteroom just outside the cellar door. Only then did he turn on the lantern.

His heart was racing, and he felt like an intruder, even though he had every right to be here. Quickly, he pushed the secret panel that unlatched the door. He ducked inside the darkened party room and closed the door securely behind him before turning on the lights. Now, he thought with a certain satisfaction, maybe he could get something accomplished.

Caroline must have been familiar with this cellar, Jeremy surmised. If she and the old Lord Chillingcote were drinking chums, it was possible they had shared a cup or two in the Dutch room. Surely, if the old man had been proud of his collection of wines, brandies, and cognacs, he might have shown off the cellar to his visitor from Brocket Hall. Taking the large key in hand, Jeremy turned the lock just as Gina had done before, and he heard the metal rasp open. He dragged the heavy chain away and opened the door. The wine storage area was long and narrow, and wound around behind the stairs which led from the Dutch room to the kitchen and the back part of the house. The light from the main room only dimly illuminated the cellar, and Jeremy was glad he'd brought along the hand-held light. He turned it on again and flashed it into the darkened corners. Now, if I were Lady Caroline, wanting to hide the memoirs down here, where would I put them? he asked himself.

Not anyplace obvious, according to her letter. Jeremy ran his hand along the edge of the underside of the stairwell and down the dank wall. His skin crawled at the idea that he might meet a rat or some other unpleasant denizen of this moldering underworld. At the far end of the room, he noted that the wall was covered with metal, rather than carved out of the native stone of the area as were the others.

Hmmm.

He pressed hard on the metal, but it appeared to be a solid wall rather than a door. He ran his fingertips along the joint between the wall and the ceiling, and then down again along the opposite wall. Then he discovered a small indentation and a button of some sort that gave way beneath the pressure of his touch.

Well, well. Where there was one secret latch, there could be more. . . .

The metal wall slid away, revealing a second room. A cavern really. Jeremy could not believe his luck. He directed the beam of light in a broad brush across the room and found to his delight it was filled with rows and rows of bottles. A quick survey told him that, unlike those bottles in the outer room, these were intact and likely still good. He would have to come back at a later time and conduct a careful inventory of what was here.

But what else was here? he wondered. He examined each shelf as best he could in the dim light, looking for a sheaf of old papers, wondering if Caroline had placed them in any kind of protective holder, such as a box. Papers exposed to the air for almost two centuries might have deteriorated beyond recognition. He flashed the light to the floor, but saw no pile of rubble that might once have been the memoirs of the infamous Lord Byron. In fact, he came across nothing that even remotely resembled what he was looking for.

Well, he conceded at last, the memoirs were not here, but at least his nocturnal prowlings had not been in vain. He'd discovered the inner cellar, probably where the latest Lord Chillingcote had kept his "good stuff." He returned to the outer cellar and pressed the button again, and the door closed behind him with a rumble, a louder sound, he thought, than it had made when it opened. But then he heard the noise again after the door had locked itself into place.

Thunder?

It sounded more like the deep bass of a musical instrument. A harpsichord.

Curious, Jeremy hurriedly left the wine cellar, locking it securely behind him. He turned off the light in the Dutch room and crept back up the stairs, following the sound that grew louder as he approached the great hall. Someone, it appeared, was playing the harpsichord he had uncovered earlier.

Alison Cunningham?

What a time to exhibit your musical talents, Jeremy thought cynically. Likely, she was just trying to disturb him as much as she could, hoping to drive him away. He came to the doorway between the great hall and the first reception room, and he stopped in his tracks. The music filled the darkness, one of Chopin's *Nocturnes,* if he wasn't mistaken, but he could see no one.

Scarcely daring to breathe, he thought he caught a glimpse of a faint light approaching from the back of the house. What was going on here? Was he seeing the ghost? he thought wildly, illogically. The light grew brighter, and Jeremy drew in his breath sharply when Alison Cunningham entered the room, clad only in an oversized T-shirt and carrying a dripping candelabra. She was a sexy apparition, hauntingly like the one who had seduced him in his dreams. Jeremy stood spellbound, his body reacting in a most disturbing manner to the sight of the slender figure. Her burnished hair was a tumble of polished copper in the candlelight. Her skin glowed, and the thin fabric of the ludicrously large T-shirt left nothing to his imagination concerning the size and shape of her breasts. He stifled a low growl that erupted unbidden from the depths of his libido. He thought he'd been discovered, for her words, when she spoke, seemed directed at him.

"What the hell are you doing?" she demanded, going to the harpsichord. Seeing she wasn't headed for him, however, Jeremy didn't reply, but kept to the shadows and watched, fascinated. The music stopped abruptly, and Alison spoke again. "I need to get some sleep. What? So you like to play the harpsichord. So what's wrong with the daytime?" She paused, as if listening to a reply from some invisible personage. Then, "You act like you've been drinking." Her words were followed by a thunderous discordant roar from the musical instrument.

"Stop that!" Alison screeched. "Go away! Get out of here, now!"

If there was another person in the room, Jeremy couldn't see him, or her. And yet, he got the distinct impression that a presence of sorts had disappeared, leaving behind only the echo of Chopin, a trembling darkness, and a beautiful woman who seemed the more likely candidate for one who had been drinking. Jeremy hesitated for a moment, trying to get a grasp on what he had just witnessed. Alison Cunningham had obviously been talking to herself again. But the music . . . he could swear it was real, even though no one had sat at the keyboard. How had she done that? Was she some sort of witch? What was her game? He decided to find out.

"That was quite a show, Miss Cunningham," he said, stepping into the circle of light cast by her candles. "Want to tell me how you did it?"

Alison nearly passed out from fright at the sound of Jeremy's voice. She was accustomed by this time to encountering the ghost of Lady Caroline. But the figure that spoke to her out of the darkness was a specter of another kind.

Male.

Handsome.

Hostile.

And very much from this plane of existence.

"I wish you would stop doing that!" she cried angrily, holding the heavy candelabra between them in front of her, ignoring the wax droplets that spilled onto her forearms.

"Doing what?" Jeremy replied, his expression hidden in the flickering shadows. He went to the bench and took a seat at the harpsichord. Looking directly up at Alison, he laid his finger on a key, producing the extended wail of a single note.

His aloof composure infuriated her. "You know very well what. Scaring the hell out of me, that's what."

He turned a cryptic smile on her. "Did I scare you, Miss Cunningham? I thought it was you who seem to be determined to startle me." With that, he played a phantomly flourish on the instrument, and Alison almost expected to see Vincent Price enter stage left. Her skin crawled in spite of her anger.

"Quit that!" she sputtered. "And quit showing up out of nowhere, like . . . like a ghost or something."

Jeremy removed his hands from the keyboard and abruptly turned on the bench to face her. "Do you believe in ghosts, Miss Cunningham?"

Alison glanced around to see if there was any sign that Caro had stuck around after her tipsy performance, but it was hard to tell. "Ghosts? No, I'm not . . . afraid of ghosts."

"I didn't ask you if you were afraid of them," Jeremy pursued. "I asked if you *believed* in them."

Alison saw his gaze travel from her face slowly down her body, her bare legs, and up again. She shivered, but not from the cold. Whether she liked him or not, Jeremy Ryder was a damnably sexy man, and at the moment she was acutely and uncomfortably aware of the closeness between them. She pulled at the hem of her T-shirt, wishing she had put on more clothing. "Believe . . . in ghosts," she stammered. "No, I don't believe in ghosts. That's a childish notion."

The moment the words were out of her mouth, Alison regretted it, for she sensed more than saw what was about to happen. A cold draft swept past her, dousing her candles and plunging the room into darkness. The now familiar swirl of mist began to coalesce as Caroline threatened to prove her existence to them both.

Jeremy bolted from the music bench. "What the hell?"

"Don't!" Alison cried out to the ghost, not wanting it to reveal its identity to Jeremy. "I didn't mean it and you know it. Go away. Go away!"

A light suddenly blazed in the darkness, and Alison watched as Jeremy sent the beam of a powerful flashlight around the room. It traveled over draped chairs and tables, lamps and paintings, all of which appeared ghostly in the gloom, but it revealed no real spirit. Alison let out a sigh.

Jeremy turned the light off again, and Alison could feel his closeness in the dark. And then she felt the touch of his hands on her shoulders. "Are you all right?" he asked, his voice surprisingly gentle.

Alison began to quake in spite of herself. She was cold, scared, and confused by the feelings his touch aroused within her. And she was talking to ghosts. No, she wasn't all right. But he didn't need to know that. "I'm . . . fine."

"You're cold," he replied, and then she felt the welcome warmth of a soft sweater being draped over her shoulders. "Let me take you back to your room," he offered, turning the light on again. "Where did you . . . uh . . . end up for the night?"

Alison felt almost as if she were in a daze. She wasn't sure exactly what room she had been sleeping in. Somewhere in the maze of guest rooms. She didn't want to accept his help, but she was afraid without his flashlight, she might not find her way in the dark back to the warmth and security of her bed.

"Thanks," she mumbled uncertainly. She still carried the candelabra. If he tried to harm her, she could at least defend herself. But she didn't think he meant her any harm. Instead, he seemed strangely protective of her. She pulled his sweater closer about her and caught the scent of a masculine aftershave or cologne, and suddenly, surprisingly, she welcomed his protection.

Together they made their way silently by flashlight through the reception rooms and into the back hall, where Alison quickly recognized the room she had flown to in her earlier rage. She felt his hand at the small of her back, guiding her safely through the midnight dark, and found it disconcertingly reassuring. When they reached the door to her room, she turned to face him.

"Thank you, Mr. Ryder," she murmured, looking up into his dark eyes. He kept the light directed toward the floor, and its beam cast eerie shadows across his face, but she could see clearly that he still had many unanswered questions.

"Please call me Jeremy," he said for the second time that day.

The clock chimed twelve. He said nothing more, but made no move to leave her. They stood as if entranced. Then, to her amazement, he brushed his fingers lightly through her sleep-tousled hair and let his hand come to rest at the back of her neck. Her heart stood still as she watched his head lower and she felt his lips touch hers.

Instead of pulling away and fleeing in panic as she expected she would do if he tried anything, Alison surprised herself and leaned into his embrace, taking pleasure and comfort in the warmth of his arms. She opened her lips and felt his kiss shift from gentle to searching, and her body trembled. Frightened and aroused at the same time, she finally forced herself away. "Please," she said shakily. "I . . . I must go now."

"Yes," he whispered hoarsely. "I think that would be best. Good night."

Alison shut the door behind her and leaned against it, aghast at what she'd just done. She'd kissed Jeremy Ryder, a virtual stranger, a man with whom she was distinctly at odds. And yet, it had felt so right. . . .

From somewhere in the night, Alison thought she heard a ripple of sprightly laughter.

Chapter 11

Much, much later, Jeremy lay wide eyed upon the bed in the master suite, contemplating the incredible chain of events that had taken place in the past twenty-four hours. Who was this hoyden who had shown up on his doorstep like a whirlwind, demanding possession of this house and the very bed he slept in? Who flaunted her wealth and refused to allow him even to buy her tea? Who one moment tried to act the sophisticate and the next emptied feather pillows over his head? Who wandered around in the dark, barefoot and scantily clad, and talked to herself in the most irrational manner?

And who, it would seem, had inexplicably taken over his senses?

Jeremy had no answers for these and a hundred other questions that raced through his mind in the predawn darkness. All he knew was that when he'd collided with Alison Cunningham in the great hall, he'd felt a physical shock charge through him, an almost electric desire that left him tingling still. And only a short time ago, he had done what he'd wanted to do from the start, he'd run his hands through her hair and brought her lips to his. Jeremy groaned and rolled over, recalling the way Alison's supple body had felt next to his, and unbidden, that electric desire recharged itself.

This is crazy, Jeremy muttered, switching on the bedside lamp and going for a shot of cognac to help him get to sleep. He didn't get this way over women. Not once in his life had he felt this . . . force, this unnameable power before which he found himself helpless. Alison Cunningham had cast some kind of a spell over him, an enchantment that left him dazed and out of control.

He didn't like it. He certainly didn't understand it. What was it about her that he found so compelling? Her looks? Certainly that. She was sexy in a fresh faced, youthful way. Her body reminded him of a sprite or fairylike creature, a lovely form he'd seen illustrated in some precious antique lithograph. But he'd known hundreds of beautiful women. What made her beauty so appealingly different?

Aside from her appearance, there was something else about her that called to him—a look of quiet desperation in her large eyes, an unspoken need to defend her actions, a naivete that made him want to hold her in his arms and reassure her. Reassure her? About what? He had no idea what she was really like. What made him think she needed reassurance, from him or anyone else?

Jeremy reached for the glass and the bottle of cognac. It wasn't, he was certain, a need to reassure her that had led him to kiss her as they stood together in the darkness of the old manor house. It was something quite different altogether, something biological over which he seemed to have little control. He had fought the overwhelming urge, that powerful dynamic force that had driven him to taste those full, inviting lips.

Fought it, and lost.

And where, he wondered almost morosely, do we go from here?

Absently, he started to pour a dram of the cognac into the glass. And then he stopped and stared at the bottle. It was empty! Not so much as a drop remained. Jeremy scratched his head. Had he consumed a full bottle of cognac over the course of the evening? He didn't think so. In fact, he recalled he'd had only a single shot before going on his midnight search of the wine cellar.

A single shot.

And now the bottle was empty.

"You act like you've been drinking," Alison had accused her invisible adversary who'd sat at the harpsichord.

It was obvious to Jeremy that *somebody* had been drinking. But who? Had Alison crept up to his room, and finding him gone, helped herself to the rest of his cognac? Maybe she was wandering around Dewhurst Manor under the influence. It would explain her bizarre behavior.

And yet, Jeremy knew she hadn't been drinking. He would have tasted it in her kiss.

That left only one explanation. It must have been the ghost. Ashley T. Stone had insisted that the ghost who supposedly roamed the halls of the gloomy country estate was none other than Caroline Lamb. And Caro's favorite drink was cognac. Jeremy replaced the bottle and glass on the table with a mocking laugh. Right, old boy. It was Caroline's ghost who nipped your liquor.

And Santa Claus is alive and well at the North Pole. . . .

My remaining in town and seeing you thus is sacrificing the last chance I have left. I expose myself to every eye, to every unkind observation. You think me weak and selfish; you think I do not struggle to withstand my own feelings, but indeed it is exacting more than human nature can bear, & when I went out last night, which was of itself an effort, & when I heard your name announced, the moment after I saw nothing more, but seemed in a dream . . . Lady Cahir

said, "You are ill; shall we go away?" which I was
very glad to accept, but we could not get through,
and so I fear it caus'd you pain to see me intrude
again.

—Lady Caroline to Lord Byron

*I have written that I oft found it difficult to know the
difference between Love and Hate, & during this, the Summer of my Greatest Confusion, I both loved & hated Caroline. As odious as I found her behavior, still I was
enchanted by her sprightly manner & found myself longing
for a return to our early days together. It was an impossibility, of course, but when I entered a room & saw her from
afar, with those large, ethereal eyes & slender, supple body,
I ached for what could never be. She tormented me, Body
& Spirit, night and day, until the only relief I found was in
copious amounts of red wine.*

*I contemplated returning permanently to the Continent,
but at that time, I thrived upon the Adoration of London
Society. So I fled instead, temporarily, until Caroline
regained her reason, to the Byron ancestral home, that
ghost-infested mountain of gloom, Newstead Abbey. With
me came Capt. George Byron, my cousin & heir to the
title, & my good friend Hobhouse, all three of us bent on
spending the next fortnight in a delirium of sensuality, myself with the hope of putting all thoughts of Caroline Lamb
from my mind.*

*I had apparently developed something of a reputation
for my peculiar taste in entertainment during an earlier
escapade at the Abbey in which my friends & I dressed up
as monks & drank claret and champagne from the skull-
cup & jested around the house in our friar's garments. So I
laughed when I learned that some of the less brave maid-
servants (& manservants as well) had disappeared upon
hearing of our arrival at Newstead this time!*

*We did nothing to discourage that reputation; rather we
built upon it. Nine days we spent in revelry, nine days of*

wine & good jest—& other things I won't set down here, as they are not pertinent to my story. What is relevant is that when I returned to London, I learned that Caroline had also returned from her too-short stay at Brocket Hall, a stay designed by her family, especially Lady Melbourne, to cool her ardor toward me. But I was met at my doorstep by a page with a letter from her, insisting she must see me again.

I had by this time exhausted all recourse that I could think of to end our affair with Grace and Dignity. I had plead poverty, invoked jealousy, written cruel and hateful letters, spurned her in public, & still she clung to me. When I looked upon that letter, I was filled with fury, & began to contemplate deeds more dreadful than I thought even I might conceive. I would be free of Caroline, no matter what I had to do to achieve it!

The sun was high into the morning sky before Alison became aware of its warmth on her cheek. She opened her eyes and lay still for a long moment, trying to remember where she was. She could hear birds chirping outside the tall, arched window. The room had a musty, unused odor about it. It was chilly. She swung her feet to the floor, gradually recalling her whereabouts. She was in England, in a small town north of London, in a sixteenth-century Tudor mansion she had just bought—probably for too much money.

And she was in the company of two most disturbing guests—a mischievous ghost and an incredibly sexy man who kept emerging from the shadows and scaring the bejeezus out of her.

Jeremy Ryder.

Still exhausted from her long trip and the midnight ramblings around Dewhurst Manor, Alison allowed herself to fall back into bed. She pulled the sheets up to her chin. And only then did she allow herself to consider what had happened when Jeremy Ryder had made his latest appearance from out of nowhere. He'd kissed her!

Surely that hadn't really happened, she thought hopefully. Surely that had been a dream. But then she caught sight of a man's cardigan hanging over a chair in her room, and Alison knew that neither the sweater nor the kiss had been imaginary. In fact, it was so real she could still feel it upon her lips. Her heart skipped at the thought.

Jeremy Ryder.

Who was he? What had he been doing up at that hour of the night? Likely, Caroline's "concert" had awakened him the same as it had her. But he'd been fully dressed. Maybe he'd thrown on those clothes in a hurry, but Alison sensed he hadn't yet been to bed when he came into the parlor last night.

Every ounce of common sense screamed at her not to trust the man. She'd seen the letter he'd tucked into one of his books, and Alison strongly suspected his real motive for being at Dewhurst Manor was not furniture appraisal, but rather to find the Byron memoirs. She wasn't overly familiar with things such as valuable antiquities, but what Caro's ghost had told her made sense. The memoirs would be worth a fortune.

And ripe for the picking by a fortune hunter like Jeremy Ryder.

And yet, she couldn't stop thinking about the gentle way he'd escorted her back to her room last night. He hadn't behaved like the arrogant bastard he'd shown himself to be earlier in the evening, behavior that had led Caro to take it upon herself to cover him with feathers. Alison grinned at the recollection of the look on his face.

Then she sobered again, perplexed by the mixed signals the man had sent her way. What was he up to? Had he decided that since arrogance hadn't driven her from his potential gold mine at Dewhurst Manor, he'd try seduction? Was he just using her, as so many other men had tried to do, to get what he wanted in life? It made sense.

Alison's cheeks burned.

"God, what an idiot I am," she growled, throwing back the covers again and reaching for the pair of slacks she'd worn for too many hours on her journey. She'd kill for a bath and clean clothes. . . . Where was her luggage?

She left the room and made her way toward the great hall. At least it was sunny this morning, and the warm rays glinting through the window panes cheered the old room. Unfortunately, they did little to lift her spirits. Instead, she stood in the center of the room and gazed at her surroundings with deepening apprehension.

What have I done?

She was alone . . . well, almost, in a huge ancient house. Decay was everywhere. Paint peeled from walls. Mildew crept across the plaster. Windows were cracked. Most of the furniture was covered, and those covers were in turn covered with dust. There was no fire in the hearth to warm her, and no wood or other fire-building materials in evidence. She had glanced cursorily into the kitchen and decided to take her carry-out dinner to her room instead. It was obvious no one had been in, or cleaned, the kitchen in many months, perhaps even years. She'd been surprised to find linens on the bed and in the bath of the guest room in which she'd spent the night.

There was so much to do just to exist in this place. She realized now what Gina meant when she'd claimed Jeremy would be inconvenienced by staying here. The logistics were overwhelming. And Gina had also warned her she would have a tough time hiring help, thanks to the ghost tales that surrounded the place.

Her eye caught a welcome sight as her gaze wandered to the front entrance. Her bags were stacked neatly just

inside the door. All seven of them. Somehow, she must
have known she was coming to stay, for she'd brought
anything and everything that she loved with her, including the medals she'd won during her years as a competi-
tive swimmer in high school and college. Awards she'd
never told her parents about, thinking they would belit-
tle them. Just another in a long line of regrets she had
about her relationship with her parents, but it was too
late. At any rate, she was glad Dewhurst had a pool. She
was eager to get back in shape.

But at the moment, she was even more eager to unpack, clean up, and change clothes. Maybe then she'd
feel better and could tackle the next job at hand, getting
some help on board.

But to unpack all this was a major undertaking, one
she didn't want to tackle twice . . . once to move into
the bedroom where she'd just spent the night, and
again, hopefully soon, into the master suite when Jeremy Ryder gave up his claim to her permanent living
quarters.

As she stood trying to decide what to do, the chilly
silence was shattered by the ring of a telephone. It rang
again before Alison realized she didn't know where the
sound was coming from. She followed the ringing into
one of the receiving rooms, but it stopped before she
could answer the phone.

She went to the windows and looked out across the
stone terrace and down into what once must have been
a meticulous English garden. Even with the neglect of
years and a virtual forest of weeds covering the beds,
the eye could still distinguish the symmetrical pathways
and discern a graceful fountain here and there.

What a beautiful place this must have been at one
time, Alison thought, suddenly sad. She wondered what
it had been like in the days when Caroline came to visit.
Had it been well kept? Was it filled with the laughter of
guests enjoying their surroundings and the host's hospi-

tality? Or had it been run-down then too, home to an aging widower whose day was highlighted only by visits from his unpredictable neighbor from Brocket Hall?

She walked to the harpsichord where Caroline's ghost had produced its nocturnal performance. Had the ghost really been playing the music? Or had Alison, in her heavy slumber, only dreamt she heard the sound?

No. The music had been real. And it had been Caro's ghost who produced it. But how could she keep that fact from Jeremy? she wondered. He'd said it was a nice trick. He must have believed she somehow manipulated the instrument to create the music. She must allow him to go on believing that, because if he decided the ghost of Lady Caroline Lamb was in residence, he might try to conjure her up to help him find the letter. Even though Caro's spirit seemed to realize what might happen if her letter was found by the wrong party, Alison had read enough now about Caroline Lamb to believe that even her ghost could be swayed by a handsome face.

She heard footsteps on the stairs and returned to the great hall in time to see that handsome face, and the stunning body that went with it, enter the room. This morning, there was nothing sinister about him. No dark turtleneck jersey, no cobwebs. No sudden entrance from the shadows. He was dressed in a light blue Oxford-cloth shirt, jeans, and Nikes. His hair was freshly styled and he was clean shaven. He looked, in fact, like a typical All-American Male. Except he wasn't American. And his looks, Alison decided, were part of his deceit, designed to encourage her to trust him.

And allow him to remain at Dewhurst Manor.

His eyes remained inscrutable. Enigmatic in their darkness. She could read nothing in them, other than possibly a loss of sleep.

"Good morning, Mr. Ryder," she said stiffly.

"Good morning." His reply was equally as formal. "Your bags were delivered about an hour ago. I didn't know where you wanted them, so I had the driver leave them here."

Didn't know where she wanted them? Was the man daft? She wanted them where they belonged. In the master suite. But she held her tongue. "I assume you paid the driver. How much do I owe you?"

"Forty-five pounds. Not bad for such a large delivery, I'd say."

What was he insinuating by that remark? "I'll write you a check immediately," she snapped. "Tell me, Mr. Ryder, when do you plan to move out? I am anxious to get settled here. I have a lot of work ahead of me."

She saw his gaze travel the circumference of the room. "That's putting it mildly," he said, with a glint of humor in his eyes. "If you will pardon my rudeness, for I know it's none of my business, but what in the name of God are you going to do with a place like this?"

Alison flinched at the criticism in his words. If she'd had a ready answer, perhaps it wouldn't have mattered. But she didn't. Other than having promised a ghost to find some papers that had been missing for some hundred-seventy-odd years or so.

"It *is* none of your business. But," she added, softening, "I don't mind your asking." Alison returned to the window. "I'm . . . thinking of turning it into a resort of some sort. You know, looking out into those gardens, I can almost hear the voices of people who lived here when everything was well kept. Happy people who cared about Dewhurst Manor. This place needs someone who cares about it." She swallowed over an unexpected lump of emotion that had gotten caught in her throat. "It needs laughter once again."

She turned to see an odd look cross his face then disappear instantly. "You do realize that the price you have offered the bank is well over what they would have settled for? If you are planning to run this as a business, don't you think you should get it for as good a price as possible? I mean, you are going to be spending a good deal of money if you hope to renovate this old place into something habitable. Not to mention the overhead you will face."

His words, although not spoken in a patronizing manner, were an echo of others, men, including her father and now Drew Hawthorne, who managed to control her life by controlling her money. Fury flamed through her even as she recognized how much her inexperience with money would probably cost her. "Why do you give a damn what I spend or what I do, Mr. Ryder? You are here to do a job. That's all. And I wish you'd get on with it. You are most definitely intruding, whether you think so or not."

"You can have the room."

"I demand that you find other lodgings. Go to a hotel. A b-and-b. I don't care. I'll even pay for it. Just don't spend another night under this roof." Alison's outburst spilled from her mouth just an instant before his words registered with her. "What did you say?"

"I said you can have the master suite. I apologize for causing you such stress yesterday. I have taken the liberty of calling in a cleaning team." A smile lit momentarily on his lips. "They say cleaning up goose feathers is a bit tricky. But your quarters will be made ready for you shortly."

Alison stared at him, stunned. Why the change of heart? Was he feeling guilty about the stolen kiss at midnight? Or was he sincerely sorry he'd acted like such a jerk? It was Alison, however, who suddenly felt sorry. She knew she'd acted like a brat, too. That was Nicki's favorite name for her when she went too far in demanding her way. Maybe since he seemed willing to accommodate her wishes, she should give in a little as well.

"Thank you very much," she said at last. "I . . . I guess in that case, it would be all right for you to . . . remain at Dewhurst Manor until you are finished with your appraisal work." Now why did I do that? she groaned to herself. His virile presence unnerved her, and she was fairly sure that he was after the same treasure she hoped to find for the ghost. Why hadn't she just sent him packing?

For that she had no answer.

He raised an eyebrow, but no objections, to her offer. "Perhaps we should exchange quarters," he suggested. "Was that room comfortable?"

"I suppose so," she replied, becoming flustered. "I . . . I didn't sleep too well . . . uh, I guess you didn't either, what with that weird noise and all. . . ."

He didn't reply, but his eyes riveted hers and told her that if he hadn't slept well, it wasn't because of Caro's ghostly performance.

Alison suppressed an involuntary shiver. "Well," she said with a rush of breath. "I guess that settles it then. When?"

"I have my things collected already," he replied briskly, going toward the stairwell. "I'll be out of your way in a matter of minutes. I do have a great deal of work to do, and I have already wasted far too much time on the issue of right of habitation."

The arrogant bastard was back. Alison bristled.

"I can assure you that you will be left to your work, and I encourage you to complete it as fast as you can. Now, if you will excuse me, I have some phone calls to make."

Jeremy halted in midstride. "Oh, that reminds me. You received a call just a while ago. From the States." He reached into his jeans pocket and brought out a scrap of paper. "From a chap named Hawthorne. Drew Hawthorne. He wants you to return his call right away. He sounded like it was important."

⌁ *Chapter 12* ⌁

Jeremy didn't mind that his new living quarters were smaller and more cramped than the luxurious suite he'd just voluntarily vacated. His ploy had worked. By being Mr. Nice, he'd managed not to get evicted. And now, he thought, setting the pile of books heavily on an armchair, he'd better get on with it. He'd bought himself some time, but he wasn't sure how much.

He wasn't sure as well that he wanted to spend much more time under the same roof as Alison Cunningham. Whether in his dreams or wandering half naked in the night, her body sent messages to his, dangerous messages, that he neither wanted nor needed. His life was well ordered. He'd worked very hard to build his own small fortune, and even harder to avoid becoming entangled in personal relationships. He'd witnessed his mother's heartbreak when his father had deserted them when he was just a boy, and although as the years passed, he'd ceased to hate the man who had sired him, he'd never fully understood the problems that had existed between his parents.

What he did understand was that it would never happen to him. He'd sworn he would never live in the poverty of his childhood nor experience the pathetic emotional needs of his mother, who had become involved with first one man and then another in a desperate attempt, Jeremy supposed later when he was adult enough to deal with it, to prove she was still desirable.

With the help of his uncle, he'd managed to get an education and had pulled himself into polite society unencumbered by the complexities of life and love that had terrified him as a child.

And he wasn't about to change that now.

Especially not for any rich, crazy American woman, no matter how appealing he found her.

Jeremy did not bother to unpack the valise of its hastily crammed load, but rather picked up his briefcase and made his way back down the hall toward the library, anxious to accomplish the task at hand. Even if everything went well, he figured it would take him at least two weeks to properly appraise the contents of the manor house. Two weeks. Could he avoid Alison for that long? Perhaps it would be better if he moved to a nearby inn.

The doors to the library were carved of dark wood and extended the full length between floor and ceiling. Jeremy pulled on the wooden handle of one and stepped into the hushed, almost reverent atmosphere of the room. Along three walls, from the rich Oriental carpets on the floor to the ornately plastered high ceilings, books were lined up like legions. Jeremy let out a low whistle, impressed at such an enormous private collection. But at the same time, he realized with concern, it might take him two weeks just to make his way through this one room.

Still, his heart beat a little faster in anticipation. If Caro had wanted to hide a sheaf of memoirs, the library seemed the second most logical hiding place she might have chosen.

But where to start? He placed his briefcase on a sheet-enshrouded chair and began a tour of the room. He knew quite a bit about antique books, but he was far from an expert. Perhaps he should call in someone more experienced than he . . . but no. He must not let anyone else near this place until he was satisfied the memoirs weren't here.

In the interest of accomplishing his search as quickly as possible, he opted for a geographical approach, starting at one end and working his way through each book on each shelf until he had searched through every tome in the massive collection. Then he'd call for an expert to appraise it all.

But two hours later, Jeremy realized there was to be no quick way through the library. Each book he examined held a fascination for him. The archives were priceless. He'd come across first editions, rare manuscripts, museum-quality treasures worth a fortune. Whoever had put together the library had known what he was doing.

The collection was arranged, Jeremy discovered, by time period, which enabled him to go immediately to the period of Regency England. Here, halfway up the wall, high on the library ladder, he placed his hands on a thick book bound in leather.

Childe Harold.

Authored by Lord Byron.

With trembling hands he opened the ancient pages. Published by John Murray. London. Eighteen twelve.

He turned the fragile, yellowed pages gingerly, knowing he likely held in his hands one of the first copies of the poem that thrust Lord Byron into the public eye, making him famous almost literally overnight. What a price this piece will bring, he thought, awestruck at his find. Carefully he descended the ladder and took the book to the window. He held it in one hand, and the pages parted of their own accord where a small envelope lay between them.

Scrawled on the outside in a familiar hand were the words, *To Lord Chillingcote.* Jeremy closed the book, which he now assumed had been a gift from Caroline to her neighbor, and placed it carefully upon the window-sill, then unfolded the handmade envelope.

Inside lay a curl of auburn hair.

Caroline's?

With bated breath, Jeremy eased the lock onto the palm of his hand and stood staring at its strawberry sheen glinting in the sunlight. Exchanging locks of hair had been a custom between lovers in the days of Regency England. Had Caroline been Lord Chillingcote's lover? But Gina Useppi had told him that the fifth Lord Chillingcote, the one who had lived at Dewhurst Manor during Caroline's lifetime, was an old man. From what Jeremy had read about Caroline Lamb, he couldn't fathom her being involved with an elderly man, other than perhaps sharing a drink with him on occasion.

He turned the hair over and held it gingerly between his fingers. There must be a way to discern if this was truly Caroline's hair. DNA tests could be run, provided there was another such lock of hair that was known to be hers for comparison. He returned his find to the folded paper and reached for his briefcase. As he bent to unlatch the leather satchel, a sharp cold draft of air struck his face. Startled, Jeremy dropped the envelope. He looked about for the door or window that must have suddenly come open to allow the draft inside, but the room remained as it had been. But there was no denying the chill that now invaded it. He bent to pick up the envelope and noticed that one edge of the paper was unfolded. He peered inside.

The lock of hair was missing. Only a few strands remained, caught in the creases of the wafer-thin paper.

Jeremy dropped to his knees and searched the carpet. It had to be here somewhere. It couldn't have just disappeared into thin air.

But his search produced nothing more than dust balls from beneath a nearby chair.

"Bloody remarkable," he uttered, shaken and unsettled. He returned to where the copy of *Childe Harold* lay on the windowsill, and to his astonishment, saw that it now lay open, exposing the inside of the back cover. Written there, in a different handwriting, was the inscription:

> *For Caro, my love.*
> *B.*

Alison ignored the fact that Jeremy Ryder hadn't had the courtesy to help her move the seven bags up the stairs and into her rooms, as any decent gentleman would have done.

Obviously, he wasn't any decent gentleman.

He was, she suspected, a manipulator, and she'd unwittingly succumbed to his maneuvers for a second time in two days in allowing him to stay in the house. She frowned as she heaved one bag onto the bed and headed back for another.

I can still throw him out, she assured herself, hauling the last heavy suitcase up the stairs and dragging it down the hall. No big deal. But an intriguing thought suddenly occurred to her.

If the letter she'd discovered between the pages of his book was authentic, then he knew of the existence of the memoirs. It followed that perhaps he knew where to look for them. Maybe he had more to go on than the whims of a forgetful ghost. If she allowed him to stay, she would be able to discreetly keep an eye on his activities, see if there was any pattern to his search. If Caroline couldn't remember where she hid the damned things, Alison would have to use other resources, including Jeremy Ryder, to find them.

She was more anxious than ever to uncover them, because now she had other things on her mind more important than a sympathetic quest for a ghost's lost manuscript. She wanted to locate the memoirs, not to please the ghost but rather to get rid of it.

Alison had awakened clear headed, if not somewhat befuddled by her conflicting emotions about Jeremy Ryder. She *was* clear headed, however, that she'd made a very impulsive decision the day before and was determined to rethink that decision rationally to be absolutely sure that she wanted to go through with the transaction. What would her father have thought of her investment strategy? Not much, she admitted with growing trepidation. Jeremy was probably right that she had paid too much for the place. It was a high price for getting her own way. And what in God's name *was* she going to do with it?

Her frown deepened. And then there was the matter of Drew Hawthorne. How had that idiot known where to contact her? She hadn't given anyone her number. She didn't even know it herself. Drew Hawthorne. Thoughts of the irksome man rekindled her determination. She'd find something to do with Dewhurst, if for no other reason than to prove to Hawthorne and the trustees that she could manage her money. She'd rather burn the place down than succumb to Hawthorne's stubborn insistence that she put the insurance money in the trust.

She dug in her purse and came up with Gina Useppi's business card. Going to the bedside phone, she dialed the number.

"Gina. This is Alison Cunningham."

"Well, my dear. Who won?"

Alison was confused. "I'm . . . sorry? What are you talking about?"

Gina laughed lightly. "Who ended up in the master suite? Or," she added with a meaningful tone Alison didn't like, "is it any of my business?"

"Have you talked to someone named Drew Hawthorne?" Alison cut short the woman's snooping questions.

The estate agent's tone immediately became strictly business. "Yes. He called the office a short time ago. He said he was your attorney, and that it was urgent he speak with you. I hope it was all right to give him the number at Dewhurst Manor."

Alison felt her cheeks grow hot. "Actually, it was not all right, but you had no way of knowing that," she replied, trying to remain calm. "Drew Hawthorne represents my parents' estate, not me. I will notify his firm of my new residence as soon as the sale is complete, but until that time, I would appreciate it if you would take messages for me. I . . . have no need to speak with him or anyone else other than my banker at the present time."

The long silence on the other end of the line let Alison know she'd likely offended the estate agent by her terse manner, but at the moment, she simply didn't care. She'd come here to get away from Drew Hawthorne and all the rest of the controlling trustees. She didn't want them interfering, even from afar.

"As you wish," Gina replied at last. "Please forgive my indiscretion."

"As I said, you didn't know to do otherwise." Alison softened her tone. "I wonder how he knew to call your office?"

"Would your banker have notified him when you requested that such a large sum be moved into our escrow account?"

Of course. Nobody, even her personal banker, thought she was capable of making sound financial decisions. Well, to hell with the bankers. And the lawyers. "I suppose," she replied, trying to sound nonchalant. "At any rate, it's not important. There is nothing any of them can do to stop this sale, so don't worry."

Alison hung up the phone, more determined than

ever that Dewhurst Manor would be hers, and that she would make a go of it, if for no other reason than to spite the suits in Boston. She picked up the phone again, and this time dialed the number of the house-keeper Gina had located. Oh, please, she begged silently, say you'll come. . . .

Two hours later, Mrs. Ernestine Beasley knocked at the door, and Alison opened it to find a grandmotherly figure dressed in a black uniform standing staunchly on the front stoop. "Mrs. Beasley?" The woman nodded, and Alison sent up a silent thanks. "Please come in. Oh, thank you so much for taking the position."

"I haven't said I would."

"Oh. I see." Alison motioned Mrs. Beasley inside and watched the elderly woman take in the state of the great hall.

"Not much different than when Lady Julia was alive," she sniffed at last.

"How do you mean?"

"All them covers over everything. Lady Julia did that years ago. Said she didn't like t' have t' take care of such a large house, but everyone knew she didn't have no money to pay for help. She let 'em all go, all except me."

"You worked for Lady Julia?"

"For thirty years."

"Then you must know Dewhurst Manor very well," Alison said, intrigued. Here was someone who could possibly be an invaluable source of information about the history of the place.

Mrs. Beasley took a few tentative steps into the great hall. "Like my own house. Better, maybe. I lived here longer than anywhere else."

"You lived here? You weren't . . . uh, afraid?"

The older woman turned a frown on Alison that made her wish she'd not pressed the issue. "Afraid? What would I be afraid of?"

Alison felt like a fool. "Gina Useppi has told me . . .

that . . . well, some of the local townspeople won't work here because . . . it's haunted."

Mrs. Beasley sniffed. "I never saw no ghost in all my days here. It's the doin' of that old man, Ashley T. Stone, puttin' out the story about the place being haunted." She turned and went to look out the window. "I suspect he keeps that up so he can continue poachin' on this property," she added. "He's tetched, that one. Claims he sees the ghost of Lady Caroline Lamb." She shook her head. "What nonsense."

"Then, if you are not afraid that the house is haunted, what are your concerns about coming back to work here? I will pay you well. What wage are you asking?" Alison had no idea what one paid servants in this part of the world. Or any other part, for that matter. She'd never hired one before.

There was a long silence, then Mrs. Beasley turned to face Alison. "It's not th' wages, madam," she said with a sigh. "I have saved a great deal over th' years, and I have my social pension. It's th' work. I'm not exactly young any more, and I don't know if I want t' work, at least as hard as I used to. I wouldn't want t' take the position and not be able t' care for the place like I did."

Alison panicked. She knew intuitively she needed Mrs. Beasley on her staff.

Staff.

Abruptly, she realized that if she were to accomplish what she was considering, she would need an entire staff, not just a single aging housekeeper.

Employees. She'd never had employees before. She'd never run a business. What was she thinking? She must be crazy.

But Alison swallowed her fear and ignored her pounding pulse. "Of course, I would not expect my senior staff member to actually perform the day-to-day labor," she said with an authority she didn't feel. "I am seeking an experienced person who can supervise others. I would need your help in selecting those who come to work here." She paused in her interview, not wishing to sound too eager. "Do you think you would be . . . qualified for such a job?"

Mrs. Beasley stiffened. "You'll not find another in the area as good for you as myself, madam," she replied.

"Then you'll take the position?"

To Alison's relief, Mrs. Beasley's heretofore guarded expression relaxed into softened wrinkles. "I would be proud to return to Dewhurst Manor," she replied at last. "Only, tell me, madam, what is it you plan to do with the place? It's . . . well, very large. Do you have a big family that would be moving here?"

Her comment shook Alison. Big family?

How about no family?

"No. I'm not sure what I'm going to do with it," she replied tentatively. "I'm thinking of turning it into a resort or something. . . ."

"What about the youngsters?"

"Youngsters? What youngsters?"

"The swimmers. The ones who used to come here and train in the pool. You going to let them take it up again?"

Alison didn't know how to reply. "I . . . haven't decided yet what to do." She gestured around the huge room. "Right now, what I want is to open the house. Get these awful sheets off the furniture. Clean the place up, bring in some flowers. You know, make it livable. I also need estimates on what it would take to make the necessary repairs and renovations, so I can get started as soon as the sale is final."

Mrs. Beasley studied her young employer for a long moment, and Alison knew what she was thinking. Could Alison afford all of her big plans? But that was none of the woman's business, Alison decided. Did she want the job or not?

"May I have my old rooms once again?" Mrs. Beasley asked as if she'd read Alison's mind.

"Of course." Relief washed over Alison. "Will you show me where they are?"

She followed the servant through the winding corridors toward the back of the house. They entered a suite of rooms that was like a small apartment. "This is the administrative office as well as living quarters," Mrs. Beasley explained, then turned and added with a twinkle in her eye. "Maybe this time I'll have somebody to administrate."

> *The spell is broke, the charm is flown!*
> *Thus is it with life's fitful fever:*
> *We madly smile when we should groan:*
> *Delirium is our best deceiver.*
> —Lord Byron

Caroline's rash pursuit continued, driving me to the very threshold of madness. To the ever-prying eyes of London Society, I attempted to maintain an attitude of nonchalance, but my private life was Hell. Her madcap demands upon me culminated in an excruciating encounter one hot day in July, & had it not been for my good friend John Cam, who had vowed to always come to my Rescue should I need him, I might have succumbed in sheer exhaustion to her wiles.

We had heard that Caroline threatened a visit to my apartment in the Albany, & we were just about to make our escape from my quarters around noon when we heard knocks resounding upon my door. Outside, a crowd had gathered, & I groaned as I instantly recognized Caroline, dressed in a strange disguise. It seemed everyone but me knew she had come prepared for an elopement. She ordered poor John Cam away, but he stood staunchly in the doorway & demanded that she change out of her ridiculous attire. She ran into the bedroom & removed her mas-

*querade, only to appear in the sitting room in the dress of a
page. "For God's sake, Caroline," I cried, "for the sake of
decorum in this house, would you please don fitting attire,
even if it is that of a maidservant?" She could see she had
displeased me, whereupon she did as I asked. Upon her
return, Hobhouse begged her in stronger language than I
have ever heard him utter to go away at once. She refused,
in equally strong language. At that point, I was in agony,
for I could not bear such a rude encounter.*

*"We must go off together," I murmured, not knowing
how else to stop Caroline's dogged pursuit. "There is no
alternative." But thankfully, John Cam had a stronger
backbone than I. He became stubborn & said he absolutely would not permit an elopement that day. Caroline
cried, but did not argue. Still she refused to leave, & when
John Cam tried to reason with her, she shouted that blood
would be shed if he made her go. He replied that blood
would be shed if she insisted on staying—her blood, because he would wring her neck! At that, Caro seized a
court sword which was lying on the ottoman & swung it at
him, but I wrested it from her & placed it safely out of her
reach. What a horrid scene! But the outcome was that
Hobhouse saved me from myself that day, for I might indeed have gone through with an elopement. However, I
wonder sometimes now, from the distance of these many
years, if that might not have been a better turn of events
than the Nightmare that followed. . . .*

Chapter 13

Something about the place looked different as Jeremy approached Dewhurst Manor upon his return from London the following afternoon. It appeared less desolate. Less intimidating. Jeremy shook off the notion, knowing nothing could have possibly changed in the short time he'd been gone. Dewhurst Manor was the same wreck of a property. He was just imagining things again. Likely it was just the way the late evening light seemed to enfold the old manor house in a golden aura, shading the mildew lilac and softening the scars left by the peeling paint.

He steered the Porsche around the circle drive and into the garage. He'd spent most of the afternoon in London with his friend, Malcomb McTighe, the forensics expert, who had looked at him as if he were slightly deranged when Jeremy had told him the story of the draft of wind and the missing lock of hair. Luckily, enough strands had remained that a DNA examination would be possible, and surprisingly, Malcomb easily located a lock of Lady Caroline's hair for comparison. Jeremy was anxious to learn the outcome of his enquiry, for if the hair was indeed Caroline's, it would provide strong evidence that she had likely been a visitor at Dewhurst Manor, a visitor on cozy terms with the earl.

Proof of her presence here would validate the letter's claim when he was called on later to prove the memoirs were actually Byron's.

He was equally anxious to return to the library and resume his search. The memoirs had to be there. It was only logical. He'd turn the place upside down if he had to.

Jeremy swung open the heavy front door and stepped inside, then stopped short. Something about the place certainly *had* changed. A fire roared in the grate of the old stone fireplace. The furniture was uncovered and shone with new polish. Flowers stood in tall vases in the window alcoves. Even old William LaForge seemed to exude new life from his vantage point high on the wall of the great hall.

"Good Lord!" Jeremy uttered, amazed. Tempting aromas filled his nostrils, the smell of roasting meat and garlic. His stomach growled an involuntary response.

"Oh, there you are, Mr. Ryder." A familiar feminine voice, suspiciously friendly, met his ears. Jeremy looked to his left and saw Alison Cunningham framed in the doorway to the first reception hall. The impact of her image hit him squarely in the solar plexus. She was dressed in a diaphanous gown, cut extremely low across the swell of her lovely breasts in an empire fashion. Her burnished curls fell forward across her brow, and her eyes shone huge and brightly upon him. He felt something inside his gut contract as desire pumped through every nerve in his body. She was stunning! More beautiful even than the creature of his dreams. But where did she get that dress? It seemed as if it were from another era. Had she found an old wardrobe in the house?

Jeremy didn't really care. He only wanted to let his hungry eyes feast on her beauty. He stood, afraid to move, and gazed at her speechless for a long moment. Then she moved toward him, with a grace and poise he hadn't noticed in Alison before . . . almost as if she were floating.

"You lost this, I believe?" Alison held out her tiny hand. Coiled in her palm was a lock of hair that looked distinctly like the one he'd found in the library.

Jeremy felt the blood drain from his face. "Where . . . did you get that?" he demanded in a guttural voice.

Alison looked at him askance, then let out a light laugh. "Why, *he* gave it to me. It is most valuable. You should not have been so careless."

"Who gave it to you?" Jeremy was convinced that Alison Cunningham had clearly lost her mind.

"My Lord Byron, who else?"

Jeremy was dumbfounded. He watched, appalled, as she moved even closer. He felt a chill surround him. "Hold out your hand," she instructed, and he did as she bade. With a touch light as a feather, she dropped the lock of hair into his upturned palm, then turned a wistful smile on him. "You are a most handsome man. I wish I could have known you then. . . ."

And before he could reply or even pull his wits together, Alison Cunningham disappeared. Vanished. Melted into the gathering shadows of evening, leaving Jeremy shaken, wondering about the state of his own sanity.

He stared at the artifact in his hand. It had to be the one he'd found earlier and then somehow managed to lose. Obviously, Alison and her cleaning people had come across it in the library. But what was going on here? How did she just disappear like that? A shudder crawled along his spine.

Or had that been Alison?

A commotion at the back of the house caught his attention, and he walked through the great hall to the source of the noise. An elderly woman was giving orders in the kitchen where two young people, a boy and a girl,

were banging about, washing pots and pans, stirring
something that boiled on the stove, and in general,
cleaning away the grime of the years. They stopped
what they were doing and grew silent when they saw
him. Then the old woman spoke.

"Who're you?"

"I might ask the same question, madam. I am Jeremy
Ryder. I am staying at Dewhurst Manor temporarily.
And you are . . . ?"

"She's my new head of housekeeping," came a voice
from behind him, and Alison entered the room. She was
dressed in tight jeans and a silken sweater the color of
old gold. She wore short black boots and large brass
earrings. Her curls tumbled in disarray around her face,
just as they had moments before.

Or at least, just as he'd thought they had. But this
woman standing before him was different than the vision he'd seen in the great hall. She was taller, her
hands and feet were larger, her eyes not as ethereal,
although equally as beautiful in their own golden splendor. She looked at him with concern.

"Are you all right, Mr. Ryder?"

Jeremy wasn't sure he was at all. "Were you just . . .
in the great hall?" he managed.

Alison looked at him with a puzzled expression. "I
must have been through there a dozen times this afternoon. It's sort of the crossroads of the house. Why?"

Jeremy closed his fingers around the wisp of hair.
"Oh, nothing. It's . . . nothing . . . well, excuse me. I
must be about my duties."

He moved toward the doorway where Alison stood,
aware that the eyes of all the people in the room followed him. "Excuse me," he said again, brushing against
Alison's slender body as he passed. She smelled of apple
blossoms and fresh air. Her hair was the color of a summer sunset. She was lithe as a reed along the banks of a

lily pond. She was as desirable a woman as he'd ever met.

And she was an enchantress who was playing dangerous games with his mind.

Jeremy hurried along the hallway toward the library, determined to find what he was seeking as fast as he could, if he had to search day and night. Find the memoirs, then get the hell away.

From Dewhurst Manor.

And from Miss Alison Cunningham.

Alison watched the retreating figure of Jeremy Ryder disappear around a corner, curious at his obvious loss of composure. He'd had a wild look in his eye almost. She wondered where he'd been the past day or so, and what had happened to upset his normal equanimity.

"What time will you be serving dinner?" she asked Mrs. Beasley over her shoulder.

"What time do you wish it, madam?" The servant's tone indicated her surprise in being consulted on the matter.

Alison had little experience with the running of a large household, although she'd grown up in homes fully staffed with maids and housekeepers and cooks. Her mother had managed things quietly and efficiently, and she'd never included Alison in the day-to-day affairs of either the Brookline mansion or the Palm Beach estate. Of course, Alison thought, embarrassed, it was up to her to instruct the staff as to her wishes for things like dinner hours. There was so much she didn't know! So much she had always taken for granted.

"Eight o'clock, please. In the dining hall, if it is prepared."

"Thank you, madam. All will be in place by then."

Alison nodded, then made a hasty exit from the kitchen. She wished there was some kind of book she could turn to, like *How To Run A Country House in*

Three Easy Lessons. Despair threatened to envelop her.
She had no business doing this. And with every step she
took, she was getting in deeper and deeper. She knew
nothing about keeping a house, much less running a
resort. She knew nothing about business. Or real estate.
Or investing.

She knew nothing about anything.

Tears stung her eyes by the time she reached the great
hall. And then suddenly, she stopped and looked
around. Gone was the gloom and the dust and the decay
that had earlier begrimed this magnificent room. Everywhere she looked, furniture gleamed. Flowers bright-
ened the room from several large vases, and the fire
took away the chill. She smiled and took a deep breath.
She might not know much about how to run a house,
but she had lucked into finding someone who did.

All it took was money.

And that, she had plenty of.

If her luck held, she would hire more people to restore this home to its former grandeur. Alison wandered
about the room, appreciating it fully for the first time.
Appreciating, too, the fact that it was hers. Not her father's. Not the trust's.

Hers.

She felt again that deep affinity and affection for the
rambling old place. It had been a victim, she felt, of
neglect, of disinterest. No one had loved it in a long
time. A lump of emotion caught in her throat. They
were sort of kindred spirits, she and this old house. And
even though she had no one to love her, perhaps if she
gave her love to Dewhurst Manor, she would be rewarded in turn by the satisfaction she felt at that moment in seeing it regenerated.

It was all the reason she needed to carry on. Cheered,
she went to the enormous inlaid sideboard and opened
the glass-paned doors. A crystal decanter filled with a
deep red liquid invited her to sample, and she poured a

small amount into a wine glass. No telling how long the wine had been there, she considered, sniffing it. She took a tentative sip and discovered to her delight that it was delicious. She filled the glass and turned back to the room.

"To Dewhurst Manor," she murmured, raising the elegant stemware in a toast.

"To Dewhurst Manor," a voice replied in a hollow echo. Alison spun around in time to see the ghost gathering its ectoplasmic energies and materializing before her eyes, and she couldn't resist the temptation to laugh. Only a short time ago she'd been annoyed that she'd followed the whim of this ditzy ghost and come to this lonely, shabby excuse of a country house, but now, she was grateful it had brought her here. "And to you, Lady Caroline," she added.

"May I?" the ghost asked politely, pointing to the wine.

"Of course. Shall I pour?"

"Yes, thank you."

Alison poured a second glass and handed it to the specter, wondering exactly how a ghost digested food and drink. But it seemed to have no trouble consuming the wine. In fact, it drained the glass quickly and handed it to her for a refill.

"So have you remembered where you put the memoirs?" Alison queried, giving her the wine.

"I have been thinking upon it," the ghost replied in its curiously quaint speech. "I visited the wine cellar just now to select this," she said, indicating the decantered liquid. "They might be there, although I found nothing."

"You brought the wine?" Alison squeaked, almost dropping the glass. "But how?"

"Sometimes it is more difficult than others for me to move physical things around," Caro explained. "It is easier when I desire something very much. Like emptying that pillow over the head of that man Ryder." She giggled, and Alison joined in.

"And I suppose you really wanted a drink this evening," Alison replied dryly.

"Yes. I used to enjoy a good claret. I still do, although the taste is not the same."

She sounded wistful, and Alison felt a tug of sympathy. "Please. Try to remember where those memoirs are stashed. I . . . I really want to help you. I think you should be able to . . . go to your rest. You've been wandering for a long time, haven't you?"

Without responding, the ghost handed her half-full glass of wine to Alison, then whispered, "Come." Its light was fading, and as it left the room, it became nothing more than a faint glow. Curious, Alison followed it, feeling the familiar chill air against her skin.

The shade led her to the library and misted right through the closed doors, leaving Alison standing outside, her hands full with the two wine glasses. "Open the door," she commanded. "Or can you do that now?"

She heard footsteps approaching from the other side of the door, and a frown creased her brow. The ghost didn't make any noise when it moved.

But it was no ghost that responded to her demand.

"Is there something I can do for you, Miss Cunningham?" Jeremy Ryder, who opened the library door from inside, appeared to have recovered from whatever had disturbed him earlier, but he was clearly surprised to see her standing there with two glasses of wine.

"I . . . uh, thought perhaps you might like an apéritif," Alison stammered, searching for a logical explanation for the awkward situation she found herself in at the moment. Damn that ghost. "Dinner is at eight, if you would care to join me."

Now what made her do that? Alison could have bit her tongue, but it was too late.

She saw the suspicion on his handsome countenance.

"I thought I was *persona non grata* around here," he said with that smile of his that Alison found so disturbingly sexy. She found all of him sexy, in fact. Way sexy.

"You are," she replied, trying not to appear as shaken as she felt. "But there is no need for us to be enemies. Do you want this or not?"

He nodded his thanks. "Very thoughtful, Miss Cunningham."

She wanted to cry out that thoughtfulness had nothing to do with it, that she'd been set up by the ghost, but of course, that would make no sense to anyone but her. What was that minx Caroline up to? Matchmaking? Or had she seen the ghost at all? Was this predicament of her own making?

Either way, the handsome Jeremy Ryder stood directly in front of her, his dark eyes inscrutable even as they drew her gaze and held it. She felt her stomach take a tumble and her knees turn to jelly. An unfamiliar glow tingled through her, and to her horror, she realized she was hoping he would kiss her again. She could not tear her gaze away from the outline of those lips, nor stop remembering the way they'd felt against hers in the midnight darkness. Her control continued to disintegrate as other sensations stirred from deep within her heart, longings that had been aroused the night before and that didn't seem to have vanished with the morning light.

"What . . . are you finding in here?" she managed at last, forcing her consciousness back into the moment, indicating the library behind him. A queer look lit upon his strong features for a moment, then was quickly covered up. What was that? she wondered. It looked like . . . guilt.

"It's quite a valuable collection," he said, stepping aside to let her pass. "I think it may take days, a week even, to inventory everything in here."

Alison felt his masculine presence in the room. Perhaps because the room itself exuded masculinity. The large wing chairs by the hearth had been uncovered to reveal their dark brown leather upholstery. A stuffed fowl of some sort flew over the rough stone wall above the fireplace. The bookshelves were of a rich dark wood, and the floor was of rough-hewn planks covered by worn but still lovely Persian carpets. The air smelled musty, and there was a lingering odor of tobacco. Had the late Lord Chillingcote smoked a pipe?

She went to where a three-footed stand supported a large, unabridged dictionary. "I wonder what the last owners used this room for?" she asked rhetorically, flipping the pages absently.

"What does anyone use a library for?" Jeremy replied, closing the door behind them and coming into the room. He surveyed one wall of books. "Reading. Writing. Thinking." He pulled a volume from one of the shelves. "But I think whoever put this collection together did it out of love."

What a curious thing for the man to say, Alison thought. He didn't seem the type to be a sentimentalist. "What do you mean?"

"Many of the books here are rare. Very rare," he added for emphasis. "Like this one. A first edition of *Wuthering Heights*. Do you know how difficult it is to come by such an artifact? How much someone would have to pay for it?"

"I would think something like that should belong in a museum or a university," she replied with unveiled disdain, positive that she'd been right in her assessment that he was very much the mercenary. "Private collectors keep so much to themselves that should belong to the public."

"A bleeding heart liberal? I would never have guessed."

"I suppose you don't think it's necessary for the Great

Unwashed to have access to such important historical relics. What would they know about it anyway?"

Alison saw the muscles in his jaw tense. "Is your opinion of private collectors based upon personal experience, Miss Cunningham? Or are you indulging in a romantic stereotype that is sometimes held of the breed of person who has the money, the interest, and yes, the love of the items, to bring them together into such a stupendous collection as this?"

His rebuke stung. She knew no one personally who collected rare and valuable books and manuscripts. She'd been swayed against the idea by Caroline's insistence that her own relic not fall into the hands of a private collector. And in her case, it would be a justifiable point. If the memoirs, wherever they were, proved to be authentic and shed a new light on history, they *did* belong in a museum or university where scholars and historians could study them and glean new, more accurate information about what actually happened between Lord Byron and Lady Caroline Lamb.

But she hadn't considered that a private collector might be motivated by love. She'd figured greed to be the driving force behind wealthy procurements of precious antiquities. And she'd figured men like Jeremy Ryder preyed on that greed to line their own pockets.

Her own attitude astounded her. Maybe she *was* a bleeding heart liberal.

"What value is such a stupendous collection, as you say, if no one gets to enjoy it?"

"How many times have you tried to gain access to very rare documents at a museum or university library, Miss Cunningham? The Great Unwashed, as you say, have little likelihood of enjoying such documents in these places, as access is normally granted only to qualified scholars."

The tone of this entire conversation was another new experience for Alison. Even though they appeared to be at odds over the issue, it pleased her that there *was* an issue. Jeremy Ryder was the first man she'd enjoyed an intelligent exchange with since her college days. He'd disagreed with her, he'd even labeled her, but he hadn't talked down to her.

And yes, she admitted to herself, maybe she had indulged in some elitist stereotyping. But the fact remained, that if and when the memoirs surfaced, they must be brought to the light of day, and not sold off to a private collector, no matter how much the collector might love them.

"Perhaps you are right, Mr. Ryder. But tell me. What will happen to these"—she swept her arm indicating the hundreds, perhaps thousands of books, in the library— "when the bank gets hold of them? Will they be auctioned to the highest bidder?"

Jeremy swirled the wine in his glass. "That could happen. A house such as Sotheby's might place them for the best price. Or . . . other arrangements are often made between the seller and . . . known collectors."

"Who will take the cream before the rest are sent to auction."

Jeremy looked across the room at her with an inexplicable expression. "Yes."

"Then you must admit, Mr. Ryder, that it is possible there are a great many valuable artifacts, items that might even change our view of history, that lie in the vaults of these collectors and that are not available even for scholars to evaluate."

"It is a romantic notion, the part about changing our view of history, but what you say is possible. Not likely, however. Mostly collectors have items like these." He held up the ancient book. "Anyone can read *Wuthering Heights*. You can buy it in soft cover from any good bookstore. It is simply the rarity of one of the original books that gives it its value. Not the content."

Alison nodded, but silently acknowledged that the relic she sought was valuable not only for the rarity, but also, and especially, for its content.

⌒ *Chapter 14* ⌒

*I asked you not to send blood but Yet do—because if
it means love I like to have it. I cut the hair too close
and bled much more than you need—do not you the
same and pray put not the scissors points near where
quei capelli grow—sooner take it from the arm or
wrist—pray be careful. . . . Your wild antelope.*
                            —Lady Caroline Lamb to Lord Byron

As I write these memoirs, I have on my desk the golden
chain given me by Caroline, & I am reminded of the
inventive ways in which she attempted to link us, not all of
which was I able to resist. In August of that same infernal
year, she delivered to me a present so ingenious, so deliciously wicked, it set fire to the darkest corners of my Desire in spite of my growing hatred of the woman. It was a
lock of hair, but taken not from her head, taken instead
from that other crop of curls that adorned her most private
parts.

She begged me to take her to Newstead, where we could
have "lived & died happy," not knowing I had put the
infernal Abbey up for sale to meet my critical need for
cash. Of course, I refused, & attempted again to send her
away. She had a nasty encounter that same day with her
father-in-law, Lord Melbourne, who severely reprimanded

her for her behavior as regards our affair. Her reaction was to run away, but this time not to me. In fact, Lady Bessborough, her mother whom I thoroughly despised, & Lady Melbourne, came to my quarters, alarmed & expecting to find us ready to elope, & were genuinely surprised that I had not seen Caroline on that day. I promised to find her, however, and bribed the coachman who had delivered her latest note, who took me promptly to the home of a surgeon in Kensington wherein Caroline had taken refuge. She'd sold her jewelry for passage out of Portsmouth, where she would have headed had I not intervened. I convinced the good doctor that I was her brother come to fetch her home to her family.

Caro was nearly senseless from hysterics, & I had to carry her off by sheer force. She cried out that no one wanted her, that her love for me was utterly unrequited, & begged me to throw her in the Thames. After some time, I was able to comfort her until she returned to normal. I convinced her that she must return to Melbourne House, that they were all worried about her & would forgive her. I sent her off in a carriage, my heart heavy with guilt and confusion, for I realized then that no matter how poorly I treated her, she would never forswear me. It saddened me to see her thus, yet a part of me wished fervently I had allowed her to make her escape.

Jeremy stood in the shower, wishing the plumbing would provide more than the lukewarm trickle of water that ran down his spine. If Alison Cunningham wanted to turn this place into something hospitable, she would have to spend a fortune on plumbing and wiring, he surmised.

Alison Cunningham.

Who was she? Where did she come from, besides Boston? Her actions indicated that she was wealthy, probably extremely so, but her feelings about historical artifacts belonging to the public seemed to be far from aristocratic. He guessed her to be in her early twenties, although her slight build and carefree ways might make her seem younger than she was.

Alison Cunningham.

A strange, fey creature indeed. Jeremy wasn't sure quite how to deal with the fact that he'd seen her in his highly sensual dreams at least a fortnight before he'd ever laid eyes on her in person. Or what to make of her appearance earlier, or rather he should say, her *disappearance* in the great hall. And what about the wine she'd brought when she'd demanded he open the library door? Had it been meant for him? He wasn't sure, because she seemed genuinely startled to see him. But if not for him, then who?

And he also wasn't sure of the real reason Alison Cunningham was at Dewhurst Manor. A young woman doesn't show up out of nowhere, in a foreign country, and spend half a million pounds for a derelict property without a reason. Jeremy considered that as he dressed for dinner. What possible reason could someone like Alison have for acquiring Dewhurst Manor? But try as he might, he could come up with no logical explanation.

Alison Cunningham.

Another set of questions assaulted him. Why was he so drawn to her? *Drawn,* he decided, was a totally inadequate description of his intense attraction to her. Every time he was in her presence, his feelings spun totally out of control. This was completely out of character for Jeremy Ryder, who always carefully called the shots when it came to women. He was confounded by his reaction to the American woman. Granted, she was very pretty, but then, so were all of the women he had dated.

But it was more than her good looks that seemed to render him witless in her presence. Those wide golden eyes held an appeal that somehow struck his heart. Whether she knew it or not, her expression much of the time seemed to cry out for something . . . someone's help or support, an expression that seemed distinctly at odds with her determined manner. She was a complex, unreadable woman, a tantalizing puzzle Jeremy found too tempting.

Glancing at his image in the mirror, he wondered what the evening would bring. He'd been most surprised when Alison had invited him to join her for dinner, and even more so at his own eager acceptance. He ran a brush through his thick, dark hair and adjusted the collar of the crisp white shirt which he wore open necked under a midnight navy blazer. How would she dress for dinner? he wondered, his breath catching slightly in anticipation that she might appear again in the lovely lowcut gossamer gown he'd seen her in earlier. He frowned at his reflection. *Had* he seen her earlier? She'd given no indication of being in the great hall with him, had not mentioned returning the lock of hair. But if it hadn't been her, what was it he *had* seen? For he was certain his eyes hadn't been playing tricks on him. Somebody, or something, had returned the lock of auburn hair. If it hadn't been Alison, then . . .

Jeremy didn't want to think about it. The lock of hair was safely hidden away in the safe in the library. He wouldn't lose it again.

He looked at his watch, then left the room. On his way toward the dining room, he stopped at a large vase of flowers that stood by a window in the great hall. Fresh from a florist, he surmised, then grinned and selected two flowers from the arrangement.

Didn't a gentleman always bring flowers to a dinner party?

Alison saw the tall square frame silhouetted in the doorway and drew in an involuntary breath as the man entered the room. Jeremy Ryder was devastating. If she'd thought him handsome before, tonight, dressed as he was, he could have been a casual Prince Charming. All of her well-meant determination to stay cool this evening flew out the window. She swallowed hard.

"Uh, hello." She summoned a self-conscious smile. Did he have any idea the effect he was having on her? God, she hoped not.

"I brought you these," he said, handing her the two long-stemmed flowers, a red rose and a pink carnation. "I'm afraid I didn't have time to go to the florist myself, so I took the liberty of . . . borrowing them from one of the arrangements in the great hall."

Alison stared at the flowers. A rose and a carnation. Just as Caro's ghost had kept bringing her. Just as Byron had given Caroline. What was this man up to?

"Is this a joke?" she said, eyeing him with suspicion.

"A joke?" He raised his eyebrows, then his expression grew serious. "I see I have erred, Miss Cunningham. I shall return them to the vase." He turned to go.

"No—it's . . . fine. About the flowers, I mean. It's just . . . what made you pick out those particular ones?"

It was his turn to regard her with curiosity. "I have no idea. They seemed rare and beautiful at the moment. Why do you ask?"

A shiver slithered its way up Alison's spine. How uncanny that his words should so mimic those of Lord Byron when he'd brought Lady Caroline a rose and a carnation at the beginning of their love affair.

At the beginning of their love affair.

"Never mind," she said, not wanting him to press the issue further. "I'll have Mrs. Beasley put them in a vase for our table tonight." She turned and made her way hastily into the kitchen, her cheeks on fire. That man had a way of bringing the most unsettling thoughts to her mind.

Back in the dining room, Alison indicated for Jeremy to take the seat opposite her. On her left, the table stretched the length of the room, with the capacity to seat over thirty people. "I decided if we sat at the head and foot of the table, we'd have to fax our conversation," she said lightly, trying to ignore Jeremy's sexy, clean-shaven appeal and the dark wisps of hair that were just visible beneath his open collar.

"It is a rather stately dining hall," Jeremy remarked, his eyes never leaving hers, and Alison felt his unspoken question: What on Earth are you going to do with such a huge, rambling estate? Fortunately, Mrs. Beasley appeared with the first course, a light vichyssoise prepared by the young chef she had brought in, and Alison shifted the conversation.

"I think I am fortunate to have that woman," she said when the housekeeper had left the room. "She seems very capable, and she's brought in some marvelous help, all in a day's time."

"Yes, quite fortunate. Gina Useppi had given me the impression that the local people were hesitant to work here because of its . . . reputation for being a haunted house." He gave her a small smile that made her heart skip a beat. "Do you think the house is haunted, Miss Cunningham?"

Alison's eyes widened slightly, and she gave Jeremy an odd look. "Shall we suspend formalities, at least for this evening?" she suggested, hoping to avoid his question. "I'm not used to being called Miss Cunningham. I much prefer Alison."

"Alison, then," he said. "Do you?"

"Do I what?"

"Think the house is haunted?"

Why did he insist on pursuing this subject? The last time, Caro's ghost had practically given itself away to him, blowing out the candles and leaving them dangerously close in the night. Would he provoke the ghost again into making an appearance at the dinner table?

But Alison did not have to wait for an answer. A

tremulous glimmer began to light up the chair just next to Jeremy, and Alison drew in her breath sharply.

"No," she commanded the spirit, but to no avail. Caroline's ghost took her place at the table with a slight giggle.

"Do not worry," it said. "He cannot see me. Look at the flowers he brought you. Just like my dear Byron . . ."

"I wish you'd stay out of it," Alison replied, and then realized Jeremy thought she was talking to him.

He raised his brows. "Stay out of it? Out of what? The house? Or conversations about its being haunted?"

"I didn't mean that," Alison said, flustered.

"Isn't he the most exquisitely handsome man?" the ghost commented, turning its large eyes on Jeremy. "I have seen him asleep. He wears no clothing to bed. You would do well to learn more about him, my dear. He is, shall we say, more man than I have ever known."

Alison was shocked at the ghost's words. Shocked, and aroused at the same time. And appalled at the way her dinner party was turning out. She tried to ignore the ghost, but when she focused on Jeremy's handsome features, she realized that she, too, found him to be more man than she'd encountered before. "Talk of ghosts just perpetuates the myth, that's all I meant. I'd . . . I'd really rather talk of other things."

Jeremy finished his soup. "Yes, I suppose that's so. Forgive me if I am being too inquisitive, Alison, but I'm truly curious how you came to Dewhurst Manor. What brought you here, and what are your plans?"

Alison saw the ghost float off its chair and encircle the unsuspecting Jeremy in an ethereal caress. "My God, leave him alone," she uttered.

"I beg your pardon?" Jeremy said, looking bewildered.

"I mean . . . I said, I was looking for a home." Alison's quick recovery amazed her. It sort of sounded like what she'd really said, but she was even more astonished to realize that she'd spoken the truth.

"Oh." He said nothing more as the young male servant, who had been introduced only as Kit, removed their bowls and Mrs. Beasley placed steaming plates of roasted lamb before them. "This is excellent," he said moments later, having tasted the lamb. "You seem to have found quite a talented cook."

The ghost was now seated on the end of the table, its vapory legs crossed. "The evening meal smells divine," it commented in its now-familiar softly lisping voice. "How I have missed those wonderful dinner parties at Devonshire House! My aunt, the Duchess, had an entire kitchen of chefs and servants who did up the most wonderful food, even if we children had to carry our own plates."

Alison could scarcely manage to take a bite. She glared at the specter, but said nothing. An awkward silence grew between her and the slightly befuddled guest at her table, but at last, Jeremy picked up the thread of conversation again.

"You said you were looking for a home?" he ended the statement as a question, encouraging her to continue, and Alison knew she had no choice but to answer if she wasn't to appear totally out of her mind.

"Yes, I suppose that's what brought me here," she said with a sigh, noting that the ghost now crossed its arms, daring Alison to reveal the real reason she'd come to Dewhurst Manor. "You see, I have . . . well, I have other places to live. Nice, large homes. But they . . . they aren't home. My parents died two months ago, and the houses are in trust, so they aren't really mine, either."

"I'm sorry to have brought up such a painful topic," Jeremy said gently.

"No, it's all right. My parents and I . . . were never close, although strangely, now that they're gone, I miss them terribly." Her food caught on a lump in her throat, and she took a sip of wine. "I found Dewhurst Manor quite by . . . chance," she said, shooting the ghost a keep-your-mouth-shut sort of look. "I saw it advertised in a magazine, and something about it just appealed to me."

"Do you have other family? I mean, brothers and sisters who will be living here too?"

Alison shook her head. "Just me." She looked around at the huge room. "It does sort of seem like a waste, doesn't it?"

"I didn't say that."

She smiled at him a little sadly. "You didn't have to. I've said it to myself already. But I find that in the short time I've been here, I have become very fond of this place, and I plan to restore it. Like I said the other day, it needs people here. It needs laughter and life. You may think this sounds crazy," she continued, knowing he likely thought most of what she said sounded that way, "but in a way, I have found Dewhurst Manor to be like the family I've never known. Here, I can be myself, not the daughter of Charles and Elizabeth Cunningham. I can create the warmth in my surroundings that I have always missed. I'm thinking of creating a resort or maybe some sort of retreat. I thought I'd check out what they've done over at Brocket Hall."

She took a small bite of her dinner, then continued, feeling surprisingly comfortable in sharing her thoughts with Jeremy. "I haven't decided exactly what I'm going to do with the place yet. I don't need to just now. First I must close on the sale, don't you think?"

Jeremy nodded. "Of course. When do you think that will be?"

"Gina has lined up an appraisal for early next week. I made the contract contingent upon an official appraised value. If the estimate does not equal the asking price, the contract is void."

"Smart move."

Alison felt a sudden glow at this small indication of his approval, although why she should value his approval escaped her. "I have to admit, Mr. Ry . . . uh, Jeremy, that I haven't much experience in business matters. I . . . my father took care of everything for me, everything in my life, and I just never stopped to consider that I might one day have to fend for myself."

She saw a flicker of sympathy in his eyes and suddenly regretted sharing such intimate details of her life with this virtual stranger. She did not want or need his sympathy. "Please don't think I am totally without resources," she added in a sarcastic tone. "Money, I have found, usually fills in the gaps."

"Sometimes," he said in a strangely quiet voice, and Alison wondered just what he meant. But before she could press him to reciprocate with some details of his own life, the ghost grew tired of being ignored. "Why do you not finish this boring dinner and get on with the evening?" it admonished, then pirouetted across the table top. "I think you should let him kiss you tonight."

"What?" Alison gasped.

"Nothing," Jeremy replied, giving her a quizzical frown. "Are you sure you are all right?"

"I'm fine," she said, willing with all her might for the ghost to return to the ethers. "I'm just anxious to have certain matters taken care of so I can get on with my life. Some people . . . have been rather forgetful lately," she said pointedly to the ghost, who somehow managed to remain invisible to Jeremy.

"Let him kiss you," it said again with a faint trickle of laughter, and then to Alison's great relief, the spirit dissipated into nothingness, leaving behind only a flutter of the flame of the candles on the table. Alison let out a long sigh.

"Would you like to take dessert in the great hall?" she asked, wanting suddenly to be out of the room.

"If you wish," Jeremy said, "although the meal was so excellent, I could do without dessert. I think I will stick with a little port."

He stood and came to help Alison with her chair. So formal, she thought. So British. And yet, she sensed genuine consideration for her behind his polite actions. She stood and took the arm he offered, allowing herself for a fleeting moment to pretend he was *the* man in her life . . . the one who didn't in reality exist. Would she ever have a man, someone she could love and who could love her, with no other strings attached? It was more difficult than she wanted to think about. So many men had tried to assure her they were *the one,* but she'd found it was her money that they were after, not her. This one, she considered, would likely be the same. She already suspected he was a mercenary, a treasure seeker. Was that behind his change of heart about the room, his pleasant company tonight? Had he figured out who she was, and what she was worth? The thought depressed her.

It wasn't easy being an heiress.

They entered the great hall, and Alison saw that the fire had been fed, and that a tray of cheeses and fruit sat on a small table between two large chairs near the hearth, along with a carafe of red wine of some sort. Port? Was Mrs. Beasley psychic? It wouldn't surprise her. These days, nothing surprised Alison.

Alison's fingers were cold when Jeremy laid his hand across hers where she held onto his arm. She was beautiful in the candlelight of the dining room, and even more stunning by firelight. But she remained a most perplexing puzzle. At dinner, Jeremy had seen a glimpse of the real Alison, the one he believed to be far more vulnerable than she let on. The innocent. The ingénue, regardless of her attempt to hide behind her money. He'd felt the pain behind her words when she had told him she was looking for a home and described her estrangement from her parents.

He related to that. He'd spent years after his father deserted him and his mother looking for that feeling called "home," that place where you felt safe and loved and secure. He'd finally decided it was just a fairy-tale place, a myth that didn't exist in an adult world, and he quit looking, settling instead for private, upscale living quarters and an independent lifestyle. That had always been sufficient.

Sufficient, that is, until he'd met Alison Cunningham.

Strangely, she'd somehow managed to open that door again, the one that held back all the longings for home and family.

He wished she hadn't.

He led her to one of the large, tapestry-upholstered chairs by the fireplace, gazing at the exposed flesh of her breasts that was just visible above the fabric of the silken tank top she wore with a light cardigan that matched. Her legs were clad in simple but elegant black trousers, the appeal of which was enhanced by the high heels on her dainty feet.

"May I pour you a glass?" he asked, trying to control the desire he felt building in every nerve of his body.

"Yes, please," she replied demurely. "Look, Jeremy, I didn't mean to get so personal in there."

"What's wrong with that?" he said, handing her a crystal goblet filled with deep red wine. He sensed she was uncomfortable that she'd revealed herself, even so slightly, to him, and he wanted to set her at ease. "I don't bite, you know."

She grinned. "It's just that we barely know one another. Tomorrow, the next day, or next week, you will be finished with your work here, and I'll be getting on with my life. There's no need to unload my problems on you, especially over a casual dinner."

"Is that what we had? Only a casual dinner?" He

came to sit on the arm of the chair. "I'd like to think it was rather more than that. And I'm glad you told me those things." He ran the back of his fingers along her shoulder and felt her shiver slightly. "I wish you'd tell me more."

But she scooted away from his touch. "Please. Don't."

But Jeremy was suddenly beyond don't. He wanted this woman. He wanted to hold her and kiss her and tell her everything would be all right. He wanted to find the devils he suspected were lodged in her soul and help her get rid of them. He knew he shouldn't get involved. Alison Cunningham threatened the very essence of his carefully constructed and controlled lifestyle. He should leave now while he still could.

Instead, he took her hand and pulled her to her feet again. Gently, he removed the glass he'd just handed her and set it on the table. "Who are you, Alison Cunningham?" he whispered, touching her hair lightly and raising her face to his. "What are you all about?"

Her eyes were wide, but he saw neither fear nor resistance in them. He drew her into his arms and held her there gently, then placed a light kiss on the top of her head. "I'd like to get to know you better, Alison. If you'd let me." He lifted her chin with his fingers, hoping she would answer him, but all he read in her eyes was confusion. He was pushing her too hard, he knew. They were still virtual strangers, and yet, he could not let her go. He lowered his lips to hers, tasting again the sweetness he remembered, inhaling the light floral fragrance that surrounded his senses. He pulled her tightly against him, feeling the softness of her breasts against his chest, the curve of her waist beneath his hand. Oh, God, what was he doing? He should release her now. Apologize for his beastly behavior, and get the hell out.

But then he felt her lips open and her body melt against him, and Jeremy Ryder knew he was lost.

☞ *Chapter 15* ☜

> *Do not marry yet, or, if you do, let me know it first. I*
> *shall not suffer, if she you chuse be worth you, but*
> *she will never love you as I did. . . .*
> —Lady Caroline to Lord Byron

*I*t came to me one sleepless night, when my eyes burned
with fatigue & my mind was wracked by dark thoughts
of the destruction of Caroline Lamb, an idea so absurd at
first I laughed aloud. My laughter died, however, as I realized I had come upon possibly the only alternative to this
continuing Hell in which I lived my days. It was an alternative I had never considered seriously in my entire life,
one that chilled my bones to the marrow. Marriage! Surely
if I married another woman, Caroline would at long last
give up on me. With malice behind my actions, hoping she
might divulge the content of my letter to Caroline, I wrote
Lady Melbourne that I would be interested in marrying her
niece, Annabella Milbankes, if she would consider me.
The reason for me to make such a choice escapes me now,
unless it was because she was Caroline's cousin & therefore a choice calculated to inflict as much pain as possible
upon my Tormentor. More likely, it was because Annabella
was the sole heir to her father's substantial assets, and such
a match would allay my dire financial straits.

*Either way, Miss Milbankes was far too good for a fallen
Soul such as myself, a point she was to make to me often
over the coming years. We were never suited, not that I
truly wished to be suited to any woman. Annabella was a
Princess of Parallelograms, a Mathematical thinker, perfectly Precise and precisely Perfect, whilst I was a lowly
Poet, an unmathematical Dreamer and a practised Sinner.
In seeking the hand of Annabella, I was true to my course
—I did not love her, therefore I could consummate the
marriage, and if Disgust set in, well, then, at least I would
have her money.*

The next morning, Alison rose early, not because she
particularly wanted to, but rather because sleep had
eluded her for most of the night. Tossing and turning,
she had edged back and forth over the line of consciousness, always with the face of Jeremy Ryder squarely in
front of her.

Damn him!

She dressed quickly and tried to put last night out of
her mind. Alison was certain that the ghost had somehow cast a spell over her. What other explanation could
there be for her falling so easily for Jeremy's charms,
not once, but twice! Find the damn memoirs, she told
herself. Get rid of the unpredictable ghost, who had
turned out to be quite the trickster. And get rid of Jeremy Ryder as well.

She hurried down the stairs, deeply troubled. She
could blame the ghost all she wanted for getting her into
Jeremy's arms, but how could she explain her reluctance
to leave them? For a brief moment, she'd felt safe there.
Warm and secure.

Harbored.

Home.

It had been a delicious feeling, one that made her
hunger for more, even now. One that had allowed her to
let her guard down, just a little. Her body had warmed

to his embrace, and she'd opened herself to his intimate kiss. It had all seemed so right at the time. He'd been tender, gentle. He'd acted like he truly wanted her, like he cared for her. And then . . .

Her cheeks flamed as she recalled what had happened next. Just as she had more or less invited him with her body language to take the next step, she had felt his body tense, and he'd pulled away from her abruptly. He'd looked at her with that same wild, inexplicable expression she'd seen earlier, then stalked out of the room without a word.

Alison was at a loss for an explanation, except that his caring words, his tender caresses must have all been an act. He hadn't meant any of it. He must have been leading her on, just to see how far she would go.

And she was humiliated that she'd fallen for him like some cheap tramp. Her body had betrayed her twice. It wouldn't, she swore, happen again.

She'd discovered Jeremy in the library late yesterday, when the ghost had led her there. The coincidence made her suspect that the memoirs were close by. It was a logical hiding place, one that Jeremy must also suspect. It was an easy place for him to search, too. He could pretend to be inventorying the valuable book collection while he looked for the real treasure of Dewhurst Manor.

Well, two can play that game, Mr. Ryder, she said to herself, pushing open the library door, determined to find the memoirs before he could make off with them.

"Oh, my God," she cried out, astounded at the scene that met her eyes. The library was in shambles. All the books along one wall had been flung from their shelves in obvious haste and lay in disarray on the furniture and floor. "How dare he?" Alison fumed, appalled and sickened. How could he? She picked her way through the rubble, kneeling to carefully retrieve a particularly twisted volume. It didn't make sense. It didn't compute that Jeremy, who professed to admire and value all things old and rare, would vandalize the contents of the library in such a manner.

And yet, who else could have done this? Jeremy was the last person she'd seen in the library. Had he, in his haste to find the treasure before she learned of his deception, returned to the room after his mysterious and sudden exodus from her presence last night and wreaked this havoc in what she now thought of as *her* library? Her anger mounted with each question.

"Damn!"

She began picking up books but had no idea in what order they had been arranged before being hurled from their shelves. "I ought to kill him," she considered angrily, then stopped suddenly when her eye was caught by the title of a book she'd retrieved from the windowsill, one that looked as if it had been placed deliberately out of the way of the rest of the destruction. It was a very old book, covered with crumbling brown leather. The title was embossed in faded gold leaf.

Childe Harold.

Alison picked up the book and held it with trembling fingers, knowing it was the poem that had made Byron famous, the one that had attracted Lady Caroline in the first place. The publication date was eighteen-twelve. She leafed through the pages tentatively, respectfully, realizing that it might even be one of the first pieces of Byron's work ever to be set in print. Then she came to the back of the book, where her eyes spied the same inscription Jeremy had seen.

For Caro, my love,
B.

"My God," she whispered. "He gave her this very book." She closed the volume gently and held it to her breast, then turned and surveyed again the sad destruction in the room. Alison guessed that when Jeremy had found this book, it had confirmed his suspicions that Byron's memoirs must be nearby. Those memoirs must be very, very valuable, she thought. Incredibly valuable. So valuable that he'd thought nothing of leaving other, priceless books such as the one she held, strewn carelessly about the room.

And why should he care? she argued with herself. They didn't belong to him. They didn't belong to her, either, at least not at the moment.

But they would.

Placing the book back on the windowsill, Alison sighed deeply. Maybe she was being foolish, but she'd made another decision. She was not only going to purchase Dewhurst Manor, she was also going to buy everything in it, lock, stock and barrel. It was one way to get Jeremy out for good—before he could do any more damage or steal what rightfully belonged to her. Or before she had a chance to make a fool of herself in front of him again.

Closing the door behind her, Alison went to find Mrs. Beasley to have someone put the library to rights as quickly as possible. Later, with Jeremy safely out of her way, she would mount a search of the room on her own, a methodical, meticulous inch-by-inch, volume-by-volume crawl through the library in quest of the memoirs. She would find them, if they were there.

If Jeremy Ryder had not already found and made off with them.

Jeremy slept later than usual, but he allowed himself a few moments before getting out of bed to contemplate what had taken place the night before. He'd been pleased when Alison had asked him to dine with her, and even more so when she'd started to open up to him. Jeremy was a born listener, and he'd found he had genuinely wanted to hear more of her story, although he was taking a chance, he knew, that she'd be like all the rest and would jump to the wrong conclusions as soon as he showed an interest in her.

What were the wrong conclusions? Normally, they would include such things as committed relationships. Monogamy. Weddings. Things like that. But with this woman, his feelings didn't seem so clear-cut. She intrigued him. She aroused him. She reached inside and touched something he'd long thought untouchable. He was in deep trouble when it came to Alison Cunningham, and he knew it. So what had possessed him to take her into his arms? She had resisted at first. It would have been easy not to pursue her.

Possessed.

That's it. Maybe he was possessed. He had no other explanation for his actions, or for what had happened next. He had stolen a kiss, and to his surprise, after her initial hesitancy, she hadn't resisted, had in fact given it back fully, even with the promise of passion. That in itself was remarkable, and he'd been poised to make the most of the situation. But when he'd raised his gaze, he'd seen, or thought he'd seen, a reflection of Alison as if in a mirror at the far side of the great hall. She had been wearing the sensuous dress with the daring décolletage, and she'd been staring at him with large, dreamy eyes. His flesh had suddenly crawled, and he'd almost roughly shoved Alison from his embrace, leaving her obviously stunned and perplexed by his behavior.

Well, she could be no more stunned or perplexed than he was. Or embarrassed. When he'd looked back to where the figure had been, the hall was empty except for the flickering firelight. Completely shaken, he'd only glared at Alison before taking his leave. Now, he wished desperately he had demanded an explanation. What was she, some sort of sorceress? How could she project her image, like a hologram, across the room? And what was she up to that she kept playing these tricks on him?

Angrily, he swore he'd find out the next time he saw her, then stopped himself. There wouldn't be a next time, not if he could help it. Whatever her scheme, he didn't need it—or her. He'd come here to find the memoirs. It was his only real interest in hanging around Dewhurst Manor. He would begin his search again immediately, and steer clear of the fey Miss Cunningham. Maybe he'd get lucky. Today. Or tomorrow. As soon as he had his hands on the papers, he'd call the bank and make other arrangements for finishing the appraisal work—off-premises.

He dressed quickly and almost sprinted toward the library. She'd interrupted him there yesterday, just when he was getting his search well organized and under way, and he wanted to sustain the momentum. He could pick up where he'd left off and, if he did not allow the rich treasure trove to distract him, he could finish at least a cursory search by nightfall.

But when he stepped inside the large, gloomy room, he looked around in shock and dismay. What he had left in good order was now in total chaos. Fragile bindings were bent and pages were torn as books more rare than most he'd ever seen had been dashed from the shelves. The room looked as if it had been vandalized. What in the world had gotten into that woman? How could Alison Cunningham treat this property in such a manner, tearing into these treasures like a tornado, with seemingly no respect for either their antiquity or their monetary value? So much for her altruistic notions of protecting historical artifacts for the Great Unwashed, he thought bitterly, a knot forming in his stomach as he surveyed the damage. Anyone who gave a whit about history and the relics such as these books that preserved history would certainly never mishandle the books in the Dewhurst Manor collection as Alison obviously had done.

Trying to overcome his shock and disgust, Jeremy be-

gan picking up the volumes one by one and attempting
to put them back as they had been the day before. It was
a huge job and would probably take him most of the day
—a day that would be lost from the search for Byron's
memoirs. His revulsion turned to fury. What had made
her do this?

The thought he'd been trying to ignore flashed
through his mind like a neon sign. She'd been looking
for something in here. She must have been. What else
could explain the situation? What was she after? Had
she read Caroline's letter after all and been smart
enough to know what it meant? He would never have
thought such an air-head would have the kind of eso-
teric education to understand what the letter was all
about. But what else could she be looking for, if not the
memoirs? What else could she be searching for, the
same as he, only without his scruples and sense of pres-
ervation?

Oh God.

The door opened and a young woman, barely out of
her teens, dressed in a gray and white uniform, peeped
in hesitantly. "Good day, sir," she said.

"What do you want?" he snarled, taking his anger out
on the servant girl.

She shrank from his fury. "Uh . . . Mrs. Beasley
sent me in to straighten the library. She said . . . uh
. . . said that Miss Cunningham told her to have someone clean up the mess." Then her gaze traveled around
the room. "Oh, dear," she murmured, her eyes wide.

"Oh dear is right," Jeremy replied. "Bloody oh dear.
Do you know where Miss Cunningham is at the moment?" He'd a good mind to seek her out and force her
to put the room back together, even if he had to paddle
her pretty little bottom to get her to do it. Imagine,
sending a servant to straighten the mess in the room!
How contemptible!

"She's left for the day, sir."

"Damned good thing," he mumbled under his breath. "I'm sure you have other things to do," he said aloud to the girl. "I'll straighten up in here. I have a lot of work to do in this room anyway. No need for two of us to clean up after Miss Cunningham's madness."

The servant managed to maintain an expressionless face, although Jeremy wondered what must be going through her mind about her new mistress. "That will be all."

"Yes, sir. Good day, sir."

The servant left the library, and as she opened the door, Jeremy thought he heard voices from the front of the house. He paused a moment at the door, listening, then followed the sounds which grew louder as he approached.

"What do you mean, I can't come in?" A man's voice was impatiently insistent. "I'm sure she is expecting me."

"Miss Cunningham did not tell me she was expecting anyone, beg your pardon, sir." Mrs. Beasley's voice was unperturbed, but firm. "If you will leave your card, I will inform her of your visit upon her return."

"Return? Where is she?"

"She's gone . . . out for the day. Who may I tell her has paid a visit?"

"Hawthorne. Drew Hawthorne. I'm her attorney, and I must see her immediately."

> *I shall marry, if I can find any thing inclined to barter money for rank. . . .*
>
> —Lord Byron

Annabella turned me down, saving our Disaster for a later date. Greatly relieved, yet still wishing to escape from Caroline, I turned my attentions to as many other women as my Constitution could sustain, including a scullery maid, an Italian opera singer, a seamstress, my agent's wife, & his daughter, too. I even entertained myself before a picture of Napoleon's wife! In October—only days after Annabella's rejection—I came under the spell of Lady Oxford, that Voluptuous & Virtueless practitioner of the art of Aphrodite. Demanding nothing other than the indulgence in unrelenting Pleasure, she was a kindred spirit, & at once I sought in her the refuge from Caroline I so desperately needed. I spent several delicious weeks at her husband's country estate of Eywood—weeks spent, as she described, "like the gods of Lucretius." But even as I luxuriated in her Lasciviousness, I perversely continued to dwell upon Caro.

It was at Eywood that we contrived the Plan, the wicked, premeditated design against Caroline's already tenuous hold on reality. Drive her mad, advised my aging Paramour. She deemed it far less messy than murder. We plotted together coldly & callously, even placing wagers on how long it might take. It seemed the ideal solution, and I entered into the conspiracy with enthusiasm, not knowing that the trap I was setting would ensnare me as well.

Chapter 16

Is this Guy Fawkes you burn in effigy?
Why bring the traitor here? What is Guy Fawkes
  to me?
Guy Fawkes betrayed his country and his laws,
England revenged the wrong: his was a public
  cause.
But I have private cause to raise this flame,
Burn also these, and be their fate the same,
Rouge, feathers, flowers, and all those tawdry
  things,
Beside those pictures, letters, chains and rings,
All made to lure the mind and please the eye,
And fill the heart with pride and vanity.
Burn, fire, burn, these glittering toys destroy,
While thus we hail the blaze with throats of joy.
Burn, fire, burn, while wondering boys exclaim,
And gold and trinkets glitter in the flame.
Ah, look not thus on me, so grave, so sad,
Shake not your heads, nor say the lady's mad.
Judge not of others, for there is but one
To whom the heart and feelings can be known.
Upon my youthful faults few censures cast,
Look to my future and forgive the past.
London, farewell; vain world, vain life, adieu!

Take the last tears I e're shall shed for you.
Young tho' I seem, I leave the world for ever,
Never to enter it again; no, never, never!
                              —Lady Caroline Lamb

The old man lived in a ramshackle cottage near the river at the edge of the village. The country lane that had once passed at the edge of his dooryard had expanded into a major thoroughfare, coming to within inches of the plastered walls of his house, with cars zooming noisily by. Children laughed and squealed as they played in a public park which lay on the other side of the road. "Used t' be in th' middle o' peace and quiet," he grumbled as he and Alison, along with his aging retriever, sat at the river's edge and ate the sandwiches she had brought.

Wanting to get away from the house until she could regain her composure for the inevitable confrontation with Jeremy Ryder, but not wanting to waste a moment in searching for the missing memoirs, Alison had decided to seek out the person who was responsible for starting the rumor that Dewhurst Manor was haunted. Maybe the old man named Ashley T. Stone could shed some light on Caroline's visits to Dewhurst Manor. Maybe if she got him to talking about his favorite ghost, he would inadvertently give her some clue as to where Lady Caroline might possibly have hidden away the memoirs.

Finding Ashley T. Stone had not been difficult. He was a legend in the small community. Some folk, she discovered, revered him, while others laughed at him, and still others were somewhat afraid of him and his peculiar ways. But everyone knew him. She had stopped in at several shops in the village and put together a lunch in a basket, thinking that if she didn't find him, she would at least spend the day outdoors exploring the verdant countryside of her new homeland while she decided what to do about Jeremy.

Ashley T. Stone peered at her suspiciously when he first answered her knock on the door, and then his face had softened, and he greeted her warmly, almost as if he'd been expecting her.

"I'm Alison Cunningham," she introduced herself.

"Yes. I know. You're th' new mistress of Dewhurst Manor, I hear. Please come in."

"How did you know that?" Alison stepped into a tiny but immaculate kitchen at the front of the cottage. He offered tea, which she accepted politely. If she was going to live in England, she'd have to develop a taste for tea, she could see that right now.

"You look just like 'er," he explained irrationally, banging the tea kettle onto the stove.

Alison frowned. "Look like who?"

"Lady Caroline."

She felt a shot of adrenaline pump into her veins. "Lady Caroline Lamb, you mean?" she replied cautiously.

"Yes, exactly." He turned and squinted at her. "White?"

"I—I'm sorry. I don't understand."

"White. Do you prefer your tea white . . . you know, with milk?"

"Yes. Yes, that will do fine." She watched as he returned to the tea-making ritual. "Actually, the reason I came here is to ask you about Lady Caroline."

"I thought it likely."

"Is it true? That you have seen her ghost at Dewhurst Manor?"

"Oh, many times," he said, glancing over his shoulder at her with his blue eyes twinkling beneath bushy brows. "People round about think I'm just an old fool, but I know what I've seen. And I know it's her."

"I believe you," Alison said, taking the tea cup he proffered. "I've seen her, too."

"T'was it Caro brought you here?"

"Uh-huh," she replied, sipping the whitened tea and finding it delicious. "She appeared to me during a . . . well, a seance." She hoped she didn't sound too crazy, but she'd decided to trust Ashley T. Stone. At least he believed in the ghost, so it was unlikely he would make fun of her.

"Where was that? In London?"

"No. In Florida."

He stared at her. "Florida? Now what would take her to Florida?" He mulled that over for a moment, then shrugged. "Well, she was always one for a good time. Maybe she went on a cruise," he laughed. "I knew she wasn't at Dewhurst Manor. I hadn't seen her in a long time. I know when she's there, you see. The house sort of . . . lights up all around, like it's on fire when she is present. It's been dark for decades."

"She said she'd been searching a long time for someone to help her," Alison went on, encouraged. "She spoke through a medium in a small town that kind of . . . uh . . . specializes in seances and that sort of thing. The medium told us that Caro had often taken over her seances. I guess I was the first one gullible enough to take it seriously."

"What did she want you to help her with?"

Now Alison had to take a giant leap of faith. Should she entrust her secret to this old man she hardly knew? But intuitively, she knew it would be safe with him, and she'd come here, after all, to enlist his help in her search. "She wants me to find the memoirs of Lord Byron, which she claims to have hidden somewhere at Dewhurst Manor."

The old man wheezed. "She what? She hid Byron's memoirs? Preposterous. She burned everything he'd ever given her, right in Brocket Park. One hell of a ceremony. Had all the village girls dressed in white, singing little songs and circling a bonfire, while she burned Byron in effigy." He laughed. "It was one of her more famous stunts. I'm surprised you haven't read about it."

"But I did read about it," Alison replied, disappointed that Stone was proving a less than reliable source. "The biography said, however, that she only burned copies. That it was just a farce."

Ashley T. Stone stopped laughing. "A farce, they called it? Humph! I heard the tale from the son of Caroline's stableboy himself, and he didn't think it was no farce. He was there, watching from behind the trees, and he said she'd never looked more beautiful. Or more insane."

"Her stableboy? You couldn't possibly have talked to Caroline's stableboy."

"No. I said his son, who was an old, old man when he told me when I was just a boy. Still, I believe what he said. We've lost it in these days of computers and instant communication," he added with a sigh.

"Lost what?" Alison found it difficult to switch thoughts as quickly as Ashley T. Stone.

"The art of relating history as it really happened . . . by word of mouth. Nowadays, anybody can write anything and get it in the history books, whether it really happened or not."

Alison grinned, dismissing this tirade as being the ravings of a very old man who had outlived the technology of his day. "Maybe so," she agreed, both to please and encourage him. "In that case, would you tell me what really went on with Lady Caroline Lamb? I brought lunch, and I have all day . . . if I'm not keeping you from your work."

Ashley T. Stone snorted. "Work. Nobody lets an old fool like me work anymore. They put me out to pasture long ago, young lady." He looked at her, and a smile cracked the wrinkled face. "It's been many a day since I had lunch with a lovely such as yerself. What say we go down t' the riverbank where there's a little table under a tree, and I'll tell you all I know about Caroline Lamb."

Several hours, and several pints of ale later, Ashley T. Stone had woven a tale that would have made any professional storyteller proud, giving Alison detailed anecdotes of Lady Caroline's life and peculiarities, although Alison was certain he had many of his facts and dates mixed up. He knew the gist of history, though, and Alison wanted his opinion on a question that had been gnawing at her over the past few days. "Did Byron love Lady Caroline?"

"Who knows the truth about that? Byron was a liar. So was Caroline, for that matter. Neither one could tell the difference between the truth and a lie. They both loved passion and romance and intrigue. From what I heard, which of course was spread by the downstairs help in those days, Caroline, at least, was violently obsessed with Byron, even though she remained also devoted to her husband, William Lamb."

"How could that be?"

He shrugged. "Lamb was good to her. He could, probably should, have thrown her out for everything she did to embarrass him and his family, the Melbournes. But he never did. He remained steadfast, although in the end mostly from a distance, but he was with her when she died."

Alison carefully steered the conversation in another direction. "Tell me about Caroline's visits to Dewhurst Manor."

"Ah, she'd always been a favorite of Lord and Lady Chillingcote when she'd visited as a young woman. And when Lady Chillingcote died, the old Lord was grievously lonely. Caroline was the light of his life after that.

"She loved to ride, and she'd ask her stableboy to make her horse ready, then gallop across the fields and meadows around here . . . a wild thing she was! When she tired, she most often stopped in at Dewhurst Manor, for her riding was thirsty work, don't you know." He winked. "And then they'd break out the bottle and get roaring drunk together, so drunk, he'd often have to send her home in his carriage." He paused and gazed out across the river. "Sad, it was. Those two lonely souls, with only the bottle to ease the pain."

Yes, Alison agreed silently. It was sad. Her own sense of loneliness suddenly tore at her soul. Loneliness and a sense of not being loved . . . these were things she shared in common with Lady Caroline Lamb, it would seem. No wonder she'd agreed to help out the poor little ghost. Alison sighed and forced her thoughts back to the matter at hand.

"Would she always come by horseback?"

"Oh, not always. Sometimes she'd pay a visit by carriage. Or if it was raining, she'd go by way of the tunnel."

"The tunnel?" Alison vaguely remembered Gina making reference to a tunnel.

The huge, brow-incrusted eyes grew solemn. "Oh, yes," he sighed. "There used t' be a tunnel ran between Dewhurst Manor and the river, right near Brocket. A tragedy, it was."

"Tragedy?"

"A terrible tragedy," he said, shaking his head and waiting a long moment for effect before resuming his tale. "Legend has it that the tunnel was built nearly the same time as Dewhurst Manor, in the sixteenth century. In those days, outlaws were common, and a lodge such as Dewhurst Manor, seated in the remote countryside as it was then, was easy prey. The tunnel saved the lives of the early owners more than once. Too bad the same couldn't be said for the children who were killed there in later times."

"Children? What happened?" Alison was mortified at the thought.

"It's been a long time, more than a hundred years, since the accident," he continued. "No one had been in the tunnel for years, in fact, I think most people had forgotten about it when some youngsters discovered the entrance in the bluff over the river not far from here. There's no way to know what really happened that day, but the story goes that the children took a lantern and went deep into the tunnel. Apparently the old pillars and beams that supported it gave way when they got too far in, and they was buried alive, they was. Th' whole thing came a'tumblin' down. Sad, sad thing, it was. There's a memorial to the children in the village church."

A lump had caught securely in Alison's throat as Ashley T. Stone related the tale, and she found herself getting depressed. Time to go. She stood up and extended her hand. "Thank you, Mr. Stone. It's been an interesting visit."

He bestowed a benevolent smile upon her. "Believe me, my dear, the pleasure has been all mine."

Alison made her way back to the street, then turned to her host. "By the way," she said, "you are welcome to hunt on the grounds at Dewhurst Manor, at least for now. But please, just don't get too close to the house."

Ashley T. Stone nodded, but Alison thought his expression was wistful. There wasn't much wild land left, she surmised, for the old-timer's love of the hunt. Civilization had crept to his very doorstep.

And soon, she, too, would restore order to the unkempt grounds of Dewhurst Manor, and the last wilderness in the area would disappear. In a way, she was sorry, but she knew it would enhance the property's value, and she had, after all, bought Dewhurst Manor as an investment. "Goodbye, Mr. Stone," she said, "and thanks again."

Alison hurried back to the street and got into the small rental car. Her visit to the old eccentric had been interesting, although he hadn't told her much she didn't already know. It was fascinating, however, to hear it from his lips, as he'd been told it by someone whose father had actually lived in Caroline's time.

Alison started the car and considered what to do next. She didn't want to go back to Dewhurst. She was in no mood to encounter Jeremy at the moment. Maybe she'd just continue her neighborly visitation.

Next stop, Brocket Hall.

From his vantage point at the library door, Jeremy listened to Mrs. Beasley stand her ground for several minutes, stoutly insisting that the visitor be on his way, but the man was insistent, almost to the point of being rude. "I demand that I be allowed to stay and wait for her here," he said, pushing past the older woman at last and flopping down into a large chair in the great hall. "My business with her is quite urgent."

Jeremy scowled. As angry as he was with Alison at the moment, he could not abide bad manners in anyone. When he reached the great hall, he saw that Mrs. Beasley was uncharacteristically flustered as she stood wringing her apron in her hands. He gave her a slight, reassuring nod, then went over to where a short, chubby man had taken up residence in one of the rare and priceless armchairs. "May I help you, sir?" he said coldly but politely.

Hawthorne sprang from the chair, startled. "Who are you?"

"The name is Ryder. I . . . represent Coutts Bank. How may I assist you, sir?"

The stranger stared at him for a long moment. "Coutts, huh? What's she dragged you guys into the picture for? Is she angry because I've held her money up?"

Jeremy raised an eyebrow. "I beg your pardon?" Hawthorne. The name sounded familiar. This must be the man who'd called the other morning. He understood suddenly why Alison had seemed so upset when he'd given her the telephone message. "Miss Cunningham hasn't mentioned her money being held up . . . or that she was expecting you," he replied, not hiding his instinctive dislike for the man.

Drew Hawthorne sneered. "She's not used to anyone keeping such close tabs on her as I intend to." He laughed. "A young fool like that shouldn't be turned loose in the world with four million dollars jingling in her pockets. My firm is charged with the fiduciary responsibility for her estate. Her father wanted to make damn sure she didn't blow her inheritance on crazy schemes, like"—he gestured around the room—"buying a place like this, for instance. I mean, let's get serious. What's the kid going to do with this Godawful piece of property? She's nuts!" He turned back to Jeremy and sighed. "I didn't know when they assigned me to her account I was going to end up babysitting."

Jeremy could scarcely contain his disgust. "I hardly think Miss Cunningham needs a babysitter," he pointed out. "I'm sure she is of age."

"Twenty-six going on ten. I feel sorry for her in a way, if you can feel sorry for someone as rich as she is. She's never had to make any decisions in her life. Her father was always the one in control. Now that he's gone, she's . . . at risk."

"At risk of what?"

Hawthorne looked at him in disbelief. "Of making some terrible financial decisions. Didn't you say you were with Coutts? Surely you've had trust accounts like this before?"

"I said I *represent* Coutts. The Estate Department. I'm an appraiser, just here on assignment."

He watched in amusement as the supercilious little man realized he'd likely betrayed a client's confidence.

"Well. Never mind about all this. When will she be back?"

"I have no idea."

Hawthorne settled down in the chair once again and looked at his watch. "I guess there's nothing for me to do but wait. Got anything to eat around here? I'm starving."

Jeremy was appalled at the man's behavior, but he opted not to interfere further. He had no right, or reason, to meddle in Alison's affairs. If this offensive man could dissuade her from buying Dewhurst Manor, so much the better. It would solve a lot of problems for Jeremy. He could resume his search at leisure, without hiding his activities. And with her out of the picture, he could reclaim his emotional control and maybe quit seeing voluptuous phantoms in the night.

Still, he was deeply disturbed by what the man had unwittingly divulged. What did he mean, her money had been held up? Knowing nothing of Alison's financial situation, other than that she was a very rich young woman, he had no idea what kind of control Hawthorne and his firm might have over her. But he found it repulsive, as he felt sure Alison must as well, that the likes of that man had any control over her whatsoever.

Stay out of it, he warned himself as he returned to the library. It's none of your business. But it seemed as if he wasn't listening. He'd keep an eye on Hawthorne. Pushing the door open, he stepped inside the library. The room felt cold, as if he'd left the window open, but they were shut tight. He looked to his immediate right, the only shelves of the collection that Alison hadn't destroyed in her rampage of the library, and his heart nearly stopped beating.

The books there were now scattered in the same manner as those he'd discovered earlier. What the hell was going on here? Alison couldn't possibly have done this. She wasn't even at Dewhurst at the moment. He walked toward the newly-disturbed shelves and caught a light fragrance in the air.

The fragrance of flowers.

Of roses. And carnations.

Chapter 17

If by December I do not disenchant Dulcinea, then I must attack the windmills, & leave the land in quest of adventures. In the meantime, I am writing the greatest absurdities to Caro in order to keep her gay, all the more so because in her last letter she reminded me that but eight guineas would bring her back to London.

—Lord Byron to Lady Melbourne

Our Plot was simple. Like playing a fish on a line, Lady O. said. I was to write to Caroline, often & with Passion. In one letter I was to declare my love in so ardent a manner as to titillate the poor woman's hopes, & in the next I was to be Devilishly cruel to her, denying that I had ever loved her, & wishing her in Hell. These conflicting letters I was to send daily, even more than once a day. And I was to write them with such passion and emotion as I had never exercised before in all the billets doux I had written to her. I was to make her laugh, fill her heart with hope and joy, and then crush her like the petals of a rose beneath my feet. With words as our artillery, we set up an offensive campaign as strategically planned as ever Napoleon could have conceived of. It was a campaign to keep *her forever off-balance, tormented, insecure. In short, to drive her mad.*

Caroline was never so complex as to be able to see through such treachery. She was artless & naive. I knew from the start that if anything could send her already delicately balanced mind into the Abyss, such calculated mischief should do it sooner than later. I wrote to Lady Melbourne that I was playing off my new mistress in hopes of getting rid of Lady Caroline, but I never let even her, my closest Confidante, know the extent of my complicity. I knew in the basest levels of my heart the Wickedness of the deed, and in Truth, I must admit to this paper that when I received Caroline's first letters in return, I became ill. "For God's sake, Byron, explain yourself," she wrote. "What have I done—if you are tired of me say so, but do not, do not treat me so!" If Lady Oxford had not been there to steady my determination, I should have been unable to go forward with the plan, but with the fortitude of that good woman, we proceeded with our assault. The irony was that Caroline perceived Lady O. to be her friend and even wrote, beseeching her dearest "Aspasia," as she called Lady O., to intervene with me on her behalf. "Will you write to him, will you tell him I have not done one thing to displease him, & that I am miserable . . . I will write no more—never tease him—never intrude upon him, only do you obtain his forgiveness."

Unable to end the charade now, I conceded to Lady Oxford's wish to compose a reply, which she dictated to me & then posted under her own seal—which Caroline was sure to recognize. "Our affections are not in our power," she wrote through my hand. "Mine are engaged. I love another. . . ."

The letter had exactly the desired effect. When Caro learned that my new mistress was her very own "Aspasia," she flew into a violent rage, screaming & tearing her hair, Lady M. told me later. That letter alone drove her to the point of insanity, from which, in her typical theatrical manner, she threatened to commit suicide, adding a twist we hadn't counted on—that she would murder us as well—which of course, she never did.

Alison wasn't certain what she'd expected Brocket Hall to be, but it was nothing like her own rustic, rambling Dewhurst Manor. Brocket Hall was far larger and grander. Newer, as well, having been built in the neo-Classical style in the eighteenth century. It stood like a red brick sentinel on a rise overlooking the River Lea. It had never occurred to her she wouldn't be able to just drive up to the house, and she was grateful when the voice on the intercom at the electronic gate had been friendly.

"I'm the new owner of Dewhurst Manor. I've come to pay a call on Lord and Lady Brocket," she'd said into the speaker, feeling suddenly very young and very American. But the woman who replied seemed undaunted by either the unannounced arrival or the youthful voice.

"You are welcome to visit the estate," she said, "although I'm afraid you won't be able to see Lord or Lady Brocket at the moment. They're both . . . away for a period. Drive through the gate and over the bridge. There's parking behind the house."

The woman who greeted Alison was nearly her own age, and she smiled broadly, extending her hand. "I'm Kathleen March, coordinator of Brocket Hall's conference center. I apologize that Lord and Lady Brocket are unavailable. Perhaps I could be of service in their absence. I can show you around today, since there are no conference attendees in residence at the moment."

"Conference attendees?" Alison hadn't considered that she might be barging in on someone's meeting.

"Yes. I assumed you knew that Brocket Hall is used as a conference center for corporations and government meetings. It's a splendid environment for such a retreat, don't you agree?"

"Oh, yes, it is. Very definitely. I'm thinking of doing something similar with Dewhurst Manor. Not on such a grand scale, of course," she added when she saw the look of surprise on the woman's face. "And I would love a tour, if it isn't too much of an inconvenience."

"Not at all." Kathleen spoke briefly to a security guard who agreed to answer the phones in her absence, then turned to Alison. "Come along."

Alison had lived among opulent surroundings all her life, but neither the Brookline mansion nor the Palm Beach estate possessed the gentrified grandeur of Brocket Hall. Its very size was formidable, and she had difficulty imagining the lonely, distraught Caro wandering these halls, pining for her lost love.

"There are forty-six bedroom suites for our guests," Kathleen explained, leading Alison along a corridor. "This one"—she opened a door, gesturing for the American visitor to enter the room—"belonged to Lady Melbourne, William Lamb's mother and Caroline's mother-in-law, who according to 'whispered history,' privately entertained the prince regent here." She winked at Alison, who surveyed the sumptuous but tastefully decorated room, appreciating the manner in which it had been restored.

Alison gave a light laugh. "Didn't Lady Melbourne also have an eye for Lord Byron?"

"I'm sure she did. She wasn't the type to let small details get in her way. Things like the fact that Byron was young enough to be her son. Or that he was having an affair with her daughter-in-law. As long as they were discreet about their extramarital affairs, the women of her time could have all the lovers they could attract. That *was* a problem for Caroline Lamb, however." Kathleen closed the door to the Lady Melbourne Room and beckoned Alison to follow down another hallway.

"How so?" Alison looked up in awe at the ornate glass-paned dome which topped the three-storied stairwell in the center of the mansion.

"Discretion was paramount to their clandestine affairs in the Society of the day, but Caroline didn't seem to know the meaning of the word. When she wanted something, she went after it with a vengeance, whether it was a trinket or a man. And usually she didn't care who knew what she did. Lady Melbourne, on the other hand, had far more illicit affairs, but she was smart enough to keep them in the shadows. That's why she chose this room for the prince," she added, escorting Alison into a dazzling suite with a huge scarlet-covered bed and hand-painted Chinese wallpaper. "So he wouldn't have far to go."

Alison was charmed by Kathleen's delightful narrative as she continued the tour. At last they came to a room which overlooked the pebble drive at the front of Brocket Hall. Decorated in a distinctively feminine manner, it was smaller, far less imposing than the rest.

"This was Caroline's room," Kathleen explained. "She loved it here." She went to the window and pulled back the curtain. "From here she could see the river and the park. I think she was more at peace here than at Melbourne House in London, especially," she added with a wry smile, "when her mother-in-law wasn't in residence."

Alison expressed her surprise that Caroline would have been given such a small room, when all the others were so much more opulent, but Kathleen replied, "No, I think she chose this room, probably because it was remote and she could enjoy her privacy here."

That was probably why she had taken refuge frequently at Dewhurst as well, Alison decided. And why she had chosen the old hunting lodge as the hiding place for Byron's memoirs. Remote privacy. At Dewhurst

Manor, her secret would more likely be safe until the time was right for it to be revealed.

At the end of the tour, Alison thanked Kathleen for her time and the colorful stories she'd shared along the way. "Please give Lord and Lady Brocket my regards," she said, shaking Kathleen's hand. "Perhaps we will meet soon."

"I will advise them of your visit," Kathleen replied, an enigmatic look in her eyes, and Alison sensed that the present-day residents of Brocket valued their privacy as much as Caroline had.

Dark clouds had gathered over the peaceful Hertfordshire countryside by the time Alison reached Dewhurst Manor, giving her a strange sense of foreboding. From both of her visits, she'd learned little she didn't already know about Lady Caroline's life and peculiarities, except that it seemed somehow different, more real and alive, having heard the stories from the locals and seen Caro's beloved Brocket Hall with her own eyes. The ghost's pathos was even more poignant now, and Alison was anxious to attempt to call up the shade and try to jog its memory.

A dark and stormy night should do nicely.

She entered the house just as the first heavy drops of rain began to echo against the slate roof. She started to call out to Mrs. Beasley, but decided she'd take a quick look around first, to see if Mr. Jeremy Ryder had wreaked any more havoc in her house. She crept to the library and eased open the door, and through the rain-darkened gloom she saw that some of the books had been reinstated on their shelves, while others had been placed in neat piles on the library table. Well, at least the task had been started. She'd help the servant finish up tomorrow.

She wandered into the great hall, gratified that nothing seemed amiss here. Except . . . what was that? She saw a thick, dark brown briefcase on one of the chairs. Jeremy's? She didn't think it looked like the one she'd seen in his room.

Her curiosity roused, she headed down the twisting, darkened hallway toward Mrs. Beasley's apartment. She heard a toilet flush, and a moment later, a vaguely familiar figure suddenly stepped into the hall in front of her.

"Alison!" A solicitous male voice resounded in her ears. "There you are."

It took only a split second for her to recognize him. "Mr. Hawthorne?" she croaked in surprise. "What are you doing here?" The hall seemed to close in on her, and she found it difficult to breathe. He stepped toward her.

"I came to save you from disaster," he replied cynically, and his tone of voice sent a shiver down Alison's spine. In the clinical atmosphere of his Boston law office, Drew Hawthorne had always treated her with respect, albeit condescending respect. Here, in the darkened hallway of Dewhurst Manor, he seemed like a different person.

"I don't need saving," she replied, gathering her shattered nerves. "And I don't recall having invited you here. So please leave."

"Now is that any way to treat your legal counselor, especially one who has made a very long trip to help you out?"

"You are not my legal counselor, Mr. Hawthorne. You're unfortunately in charge of the Cunningham trust, but you are not in charge of me, and I don't appreciate your barging in on me like this."

He leered at her, looking for all the world like a lecherous old man, and panic burned suddenly at the back of Alison's throat. "I may not be your legal counselor, honey," he replied in a low voice, "but I have a lot more grasp on the world than you do. And as the director of

the Cunningham trust," he added smoothly, "I also have
the power to force you to deal with your affairs in a
responsible manner, whether you like it or not."

"You don't have any power over me other than
manipulating my trust, Mr. Hawthorne. And after this
intrusion, I will find a way to have you removed as director." She was aware that her voice had edged upward a
notch.

"I doubt it, sweetheart. But for now, perhaps we
should get to the business at hand."

"We have no business."

"Oh, but we do. And this is no casual intrusion. Since
you don't seem inclined to return my phone calls, I have
had to travel halfway around the world to let you know
that I have filed an injunction against the release of
funds from your bank to purchase this dreadful place."

"You've what?" Alison eyes widened in outrage. How
could this be? The will had clearly stated that the insurance money was not attached in any way to the trust.
She saw the satisfaction on Hawthorne's face at her reaction.

"It's only a temporary measure, to give you time to
change your mind," he said, his voice now kindly reassuring. Fatherly even. "The trustees have only your best
interest at heart, Alison. It's what your father wanted,
remember that."

Alison was appalled at the man's audacity. He'd
treated her like a child before, even talked down to her,
but she'd never dreamed he would interfere in her life
outside the affairs of the trust. "Are you telling me that
the money hasn't been transferred into the escrow account?"

"That's right." He sounded proud of the fact, as if
he'd done her a big favor. "And if I do my job, it won't
ever leave the safety of your bank in Boston. I'm here,"
he said, lowering his voice and touching her cheek, "to

try to talk some sense into that sweet little head of yours."

She recoiled as if she'd been bitten by a snake. "You're a creep, Hawthorne," she said, resisting the urge to call him something more vulgar, something more suitable to his behavior. "Get out."

"Leave her alone, Hawthorne." A deep voice emanated from the shadows behind the attorney, and Jeremy emerged from the doorway where he'd been listening to the exchange. "She's asked you twice to leave. I suggest you do it."

"Who *is* this guy?" Although he knew full well who Jeremy was, Hawthorne turned a mocking grin to Alison, and added, "Your latest lover?"

The man was insufferable, but Alison's cheeks grew hotter at his insinuation. "It's none of your business who he is. None of this is any of your business."

"You're overwrought," Hawthorne said, suddenly conciliatory. "We'll talk about all this in the morning."

But Jeremy stepped between Hawthorne and Alison and put his arm protectively around her shoulders. "There's no need to talk about any of this, now or in the morning, or ever, if the lady doesn't want to."

Whatever her doubts about Jeremy Ryder, she was utterly grateful to him at the moment. His touch reassured her, gave her strength. She put her hand on his. "I understand you mean well, Mr. Hawthorne, or at least I'm willing to give you the benefit of the doubt. But what I do with that insurance money is out of your hands. You had no right to place an injunction on that transaction. It's illegal as hell, and I'll have you canned for doing it."

He gave her an ingratiating smile. "Your old friend Judge Frieberg handled the request himself. Seems he's known your family a long time. Said he thought a ten-day cooling-off period was a good idea, under the circumstances."

"A cooling-off period? The only thing that needs cooling off at the moment is my temper, Mr. Hawthorne." A flash of angry lightning pierced the blackened sky, and thunder rattled the eaves and shutters. "Do you have a car?"

"No. I came by cab. I figured with all these empty rooms, you would surely put me up while I was here."

"You assumed too much, Mr. Hawthorne," Jeremy said, his voice calm, but Alison felt his hand tighten on her shoulder. Another assault of lightning, followed by ear-splitting thunder.

Alison vacillated for a moment. She wanted Hawthorne out, but at the same time, she couldn't just throw him on the doorstep to spend the night in the storm. And she had no inclination for anyone to get out in the weather to take him to a nearby inn. "I have a rental car. You can take it. Find an inn somewhere for the night, and then get on back to Boston tomorrow. You're not welcome or wanted here."

"I'm not driving anywhere in this storm, especially on the wrong side of the road!" he protested. "No sir. Not me."

"I'll be more than glad to take you, or call you a taxi," Jeremy began, but Alison cut him short with a nudge in his ribs. A slight smile crept over her lips as she saw the ghost signaling to her.

"Let me have at him tonight," it said, mischief lighting up its eager face. "I'll give him a scare that'll send him back to the pigsty he came from."

Of course.

Alison didn't hesitate. "I have decided you can stay, Mr. Hawthorne. But just for one night. Follow me." She ignored Jeremy's protest. He hadn't seen the ghost, and he had no idea what Hawthorne likely had in store for him. Alison was silently and maliciously gleeful as she led the two men back toward the great hall, where Drew Hawthorne retrieved his oversized briefcase in which, he said, he'd packed a few clothes, just in case. She took him down another hall into the new wing where he would be as far from her, and Jeremy, as possible.

"I'll send Mrs. Beasley with something to eat," she said. "Goodnight, Hawthorne."

"Uh, thanks, Alison. You'll see things differently by the light of day, I'm sure of it."

"Don't hold your breath," she said, then added in a warning voice, "By the way, I wouldn't advise wandering about in the night. It's a big place, and some people say it's haunted. Sweet dreams." She relished the startled look on his face before shutting the door to his room firmly between them.

She was about to return to the great hall where she'd left Jeremy scratching his head over her sudden change of heart when her eye fell on the door to the swimming pool. She'd almost forgotten about it. Suddenly, she knew that a swim was just what she needed, as she'd told Hawthorne, to cool her temper.

As an adolescent, swimming had often provided Alison with a way to cope with stress and the runaway emotions of a teenager. She'd started swimming when she'd discovered that it helped her to overcome the loneliness, self-doubt, and the perceived clumsiness that plagued her even today. Over the years, she'd become good at the sport, winning ribbon after ribbon, almost making the Olympic team. Later, as the wealthy jet-setter she'd become, she'd chosen to fly off to places with outstanding aquatic facilities, or the ocean. Perhaps subliminally, it had been the fact that Dewhurst Manor had a pool that had swayed her to buy the place.

With Hawthorne put away for the night, she felt suddenly eager to dive in and feel the familiar delicious coolness of the water soothe her rattled nerves. She hurried back to the great hall and headed for the stairs, the only thought in her mind being which swimsuit to wear, when she heard Jeremy's voice.

"Why did you let him stay?"

She turned to him and saw a look of concern for her in his face. It was nice that he was pretending to care, but she wasn't going to fall for that one again. "Why not? He's a nuisance, but not a threat." She found, to her amazement, she meant it. Hawthorne was a bother, that's all. No longer did he loom as omnipotent over her fate and future. The thought felt good all over. "Tomorrow, I'll call Judge Frieberg and find out what this is all about and get it straight. And I'll insist that Hawthorne leave. Which brings me, Mr. Ryder, to a discussion of a similar nature that we need to have. But not tonight. I'm going for a swim, then I'll have Mrs. Beasley bring dinner to my room. You're on your own tonight. You may dine where you wish, only," she paused and frowned at him slightly, "I would prefer that you stay out of the library from now on."

Before he could reply, she darted up the stairs and out of sight. She might have overcome the threat posed by Drew Hawthorne, but Jeremy Ryder was another matter entirely.

⌒ *Chapter 18* ⌒

*All who hate Lady Oxford—consisting of one half of
the world, & all who abominate me—that is the
other half—will tear the last rag of my tattered reputation into threads, filaments & atoms.*
                    —Lord Byron to Lady Melbourne

The winter was the blackest in my memory, although
    others since have proven even darker. The sale of
Newstead did not go through as planned, & creditors
hounded my heels even as Caroline stalked my every move.
It is good she did not fall into collusion with them, or I
would have been lost for certain!

Society began to grow hostile, partly because of my fla-
grant affair with Lady O., who had many jealous enemies.
Their hatred of me threatened to destroy what little reputation I had left, but as time was to prove, I did not need
their help after all. I was quite capable of destroying that
reputation myself.

I spent most of the spring of eighteen & thirteen in the
arms of Lady Oxford, much of the time at Eywood, where
I also cast eyes upon her daughter, Lady Charlotte Harley.
Lady O. did not find this amusing, especially as she believed ourselves about to become parents of what would be

Charlotte's half-sibling, another child in her Harlean Miscellany. Fortunately, it turned out to be a false alarm.

It was during this time that Caroline apparently perfected her already excellent talent for forging my hand. She became so skilled, in fact, that she fooled even my publisher, John Murray, into giving her a portrait of me, the poor man believing the letter she gave him to have been penned by me. I was, quite naturally, enraged when I heard of this, as was my amoroso of the moment, Lady O., to whom I had promised the picture. I immediately wrote to Caroline demanding that she return the likeness, but her terms were too much for me. She would return the portrait, she informed me, only if I would meet her privately in my quarters. I knew Caroline well—oh so very well—& I knew what would transpire should I capitulate to her desires, not to mention my own! But I was vexed at her blatant blackmail & my patience was sorely tried at this point, so I wrote that I would indeed see her, but only in the presence of Lady Oxford. Of course, Caroline declined.

Throughout this winter, she continued to behave irrationally, & from her letters, the contents of many of which bordered on the incoherent, I took heart, believing our letter-writing campaign, which had continued unabated, was succeeding brilliantly. It was clear to me, & many others, that Caroline could no longer be considered sane, although she had moments of lucid brilliance in her efforts to thwart me. Some of her antics I even found delightfully witty, such as when she had her servants outfitted in uniforms with new buttons engraved with the antithesis of the Byron motto—instead of Crede Byron [Trust Byron], they read Ne Crede Byron! A well-aimed thrust, & well deserved, I allow.

She continued to press for a meeting, threatening to haunt me with her ghost if I refused! I could tell that her harangues were playing havoc with Lady Oxford, whose husband had got wind of our affair & who was being pressured to send me away lest the ire of my former mistress

Lady C. spill over into his arena. It mattered not, it seemed, that I had cuckolded him for months. I suppose he was used to that. It was Caroline's mad behavior—& the accompanying scandal—he wished to avoid.

With reluctance, hoping to end it once & for all, I agreed to a meeting. I had not seen her in months, & I was shaken by her appearance. Those golden eyes were dim & large against her thin pale face. She was wasted in body & so weak she had to be accompanied by her mother & Lady Melbourne, a fact I did not regret, not trusting myself to be alone with her. Still, seeing her so near death brought tears to my eyes, & I knelt and asked her forgiveness. It was a monumental blunder, for she did not, as I had expected, die shortly thereafter.

The underwater lights sent an iridescent glow radiating through the aquamarine waters of the pool, a shimmering light that was accented by an occasional flash of lightning from the storm that still rumbled outside. Enchanted by the ambience, Alison chose not to turn on the overhead lights. She tested the water with her toes. Perfect—tepid, but not too warm. Safely protected from the weather by the thick walls and glass roof of the pool addition, she slipped into the pool at the shallow end and let her body become accustomed to the change in temperature, then pushed off vigorously from the side and began swimming laps with strong, sure strokes.

If she'd had lingering doubts about buying Dewhurst Manor, they melted away with each lap. Swimming was her peace, her meditation, and wherever she lived, she knew she would have a pool. This was divine, she thought, keeping her eyes open as she did the backstroke down the center lane, watching the lightning flicker in the skies high above. More than ever, the old country manor felt like home.

But she hadn't bought Dewhurst as a home, she reminded herself, a momentary frown creasing her brow.

It was supposed to be an investment, and she was still at a loss as to what to do with it that would be profitable.

Outside of Drew Hawthorne, she had no one to ask for advice, and she wasn't about to give that nincompoop any more information about her private affairs than possible. Nor was she sure she would listen if somebody else, no matter who or how well meaning, tried to advise her about what to do with the old manor. This was something she had to work out on her own. Well, she sighed, turning for a lap of the sidestroke, maybe something would come to her.

For the time being, she needed to finish her business with the ghost, and get rid of it, as well as Drew Hawthorne and Jeremy Ryder. Sort of a major housecleaning. Hawthorne was an easy matter. She'd give him the old heave-ho in the morning, with the help of the local constable if necessary. He had absolutely no right to be there.

With Jeremy, it wasn't so easy. He had a contract with the bank.

As she swam, Alison focused her thoughts on Jeremy Ryder. Had his madcap search through the library been successful? Had he found the memoirs? No, she decided, reaching the end of the pool and pushing off for another lap, he must not have uncovered them yet, for she fully expected him to make a hasty exit once he had the treasure in hand. He was probably out there now, snooping around right under her nose, trying to find—and steal—what rightfully belonged to . . . to whom? The ghost? The estate of Julia Chillingcote? Herself? None of the above? Certainly not to Jeremy Ryder, but she had no doubt that if he came across them, possession would be nine-tenths of the law as far as he was concerned.

Jeremy Ryder seemed to be everything Alison had disliked in the men who had professed to care for her, when all they really cared about was her riches. He was a user, of that she was certain. He was using Dewhurst Manor and Lady Julia's estate and Coutts Bank to make money off the sale of the treasures that had accumulated over centuries in the old manor house. He seemed to have no qualms whatsoever about disposing of these antiquities for a tidy gain. He was using Alison, too, knowing that his residency here depended upon his remaining in her good graces.

And yet, she didn't completely distrust him, although she didn't understand exactly why. Was it because she was infatuated with him? She couldn't deny she was physically attracted to him. Her self-control vanished like Caro's ghost when she was in his presence. But that wasn't totally it, she knew. Rather, her feelings for him had something to do with the sweater he'd put around her in the dead of night when he'd felt her chilled skin. The one-on-one discussion in the library, when he'd treated her as if she was an intelligent human being with a point of view to be considered. The way he'd stepped between Drew Hawthorne and her tonight, and put his arm around her, backing her up. It was hard to distrust a man who treated you with respect—like an equal.

Alison hadn't met many men like that before.

And yet, it could all be an act. It certainly seemed that way from his abrupt departure last night. The kisses, the flowers, everything, could all be part of his deliberate design to use her to get at the memoirs. She reached the shallow end and stood up, her muscles twitching slightly from the unaccustomed exercise.

"I declare you have fallen in love with him." The voice echoed hollowly in the cavernous room. Startled, Alison jerked her head around, but saw no one.

"Oh, it's you," she said, watching a mist gather at the edge of the pool. "Have you come for a swim?"

"Ghosts do not swim," it informed her emphatically. "No, I came to tell you something important."

"You remember where you hid the memoirs?" Alison asked hopefully.

The ghost, who now hovered just above the wet deck, sighed pensively. "No, not exactly. I thought perchance they were in the library, but I looked and did not find them."

"You!" Alison hadn't considered that the destruction could be the work of her little ghost. "You're the one who threw all the books around. How could you do such a thing?"

It shrugged, undaunted by Alison's wrath. "It is the only way I could summon sufficient energy for the search. Someone had to do *something*," it added cynically.

"And just what do you mean by that?"

"My dear, you have been here three days now, and I have seen you make no effort to find the memoirs," the ghost chided. "It seems to me you are rather more interested in kissing the enemy."

"Why, you little . . ."

The image of the ghost dissolved into the thick, warm air that surrounded the pool, but Alison knew its presence was still there. "Where are you?" she demanded. "Show yourself. What important thing did you come here to tell me?"

But the only reply was distant laughter. Then, "He is in love with you."

"Who is?"

"Mr. Ryder."

"He is not."

"He is. And you are in love with him in return."

"I am not."

"Then why have you lost interest in the search?" the ghost demanded.

"I haven't," Alison argued, sinking back into the water, trying to calm herself, to keep her thoughts straight. She was surprised at the impact the ghost's words had on her. In love? As the ghost had pointed out, she'd only been here three days. How could she be in love? "It would help matters if you'd try a little harder to remember what you did with the memoirs," she retorted, avoiding any mention of love. "It's not my job to find them, if you'll recall. I'm just your human vehicle to get them to the reading public, remember?"

A violent wind whipped suddenly around the room, although no windows were open. "You vowed you would help me," the ghost whined, winding down somewhat. "I am depending on you."

Alison was disgusted at the ghost's continued petulance. "Maybe you shouldn't," she said, deliberately baiting it. She'd grown tired of its impetuous ways, and she wanted it to go away. "Maybe you should show yourself to Jeremy Ryder and lead him to your precious memoirs, and see where that gets you."

As if on cue, the double door to the pool annex swung open, and Jeremy stepped inside.

"Isn't it dangerous to swim alone?" he asked, frowning at Alison.

She started to point out that she wasn't alone, but thought better of it. "I'm a good swimmer," she replied instead. She saw the ghost taking a long, dreamy-eyed look at Jeremy and wondered just who had fallen in love with whom. Turning her back to Jeremy, Alison goaded the ghost. "Go ahead," she whispered. "Now's your chance. Show yourself to him, get him in on your little caper," she dared, hoping to heckle it into behaving more responsibly. But to her horror, the ghost did as she directed.

The mist swirled, turned to a golden hue, and headed straight for Jeremy, who from the look on his face, clearly saw it coming at him. "What the hell!" he exclaimed just before the spectral energy hit him, knocking him sideways and right into the pool. He hit the water hard, sending a spray almost to the ceiling, while ghostly laughter rang among the metal rafters.

Before he could recover from the shock, Jeremy stood up, soaked, and watched with chlorine-glazed eyes a sound and light show like he'd never witnessed in his life. Hollywood couldn't have staged a better one. Sparks flew around the room like small, golden comets, followed by a woman's laughter. Then a fierce wind blew across the water, strong enough to create waves on the normally serene pool. It was a cold wind, a biting wind. Then the wind and the light seemed to bundle into one essence, a whirling dervish of energy that swept toward him, barely missing the top of his head as it passed over him. Another shrill laugh.

And then, as he watched transfixed, the room grew peaceful, and the sound and lights calmed and melded into a figure he recognized instantly, an unclothed figure, like a statue, of an alluring and beautiful young woman. "You!" he murmured in disbelief. He felt the familiar sexual stirring this particular dream creature had been evoking within him for the past few weeks, and he took a step backward. He turned to Alison, almost expecting her to have vanished, to have somehow become the woman of his erotic dreams, but she stood breast-deep in the water, her eyes reflecting fascination, but not surprise.

"What is going on here?" he managed, shaking the water from his hair and taking a step toward Alison.

"Can't you guess?" Alison asked with an annoying grin on her face.

"I have no idea how you do this kind of thing," he snarled, "but I do not find it funny in the least."

"I can assure you, I had nothing to do with pushing you in the pool," Alison said. "That was the doing of the resident ghost you so fervently don't believe in."

"Ghost!" Jeremy turned to stare at the specter, which

had used up much of its energy and was fading in and out. "You're right. I don't believe in ghosts. But I'll be damned . . ."

"Help me," the weakening voice crooned. "Help me. Find the memoirs. Let the world know the truth. . . ." And then the image faded into nothingness, leaving only the sound of the gentle lapping of the pool water against the cement walls.

When she, or it, had disappeared, Jeremy wasn't certain he'd witnessed anything at all. Maybe his desire for Alison Cunningham was leading him into dangerous erotic hallucinations such as the one he'd just experienced.

From the dim light of the great hall, he'd watched her come back downstairs and head toward the pool, clad only in a T-shirt over what he assumed was a bathing suit. A craving had shot through him, a painful need he deplored and tried unsuccessfully to deny. He'd gone back to his room, then come out again. He'd walked outside along the semiprotected terrace, oblivious to the storm. But nothing would assuage the fire in his belly for the woman, and at last he'd succumbed and followed her into the large, brick structure that housed the swimming pool.

After that, he quite literally did not know what had hit him.

The ghost had disappeared completely now, and Jeremy shivered in the clammy shirt which clung like glue to his body. He stripped it off and sunk neck-deep into the water, which was warmer against his skin than the air. Only then did he turn again to Alison. He let out a deep breath. He wasn't quite sure what he'd just witnessed, if anything, but he *was* sure of one thing—Alison Cunningham knew about the missing memoirs.

He waded over to her and took her wrist, trying to ignore the fact that in her brief bikini, she was next to naked against him. "What kind of game are you playing, Alison?"

He saw fright glimmer for one moment in her eyes, only to be replaced by pure anger. "Game? You think that this is a game?" She wrenched her arm free and swam away from him. "Maybe it seems like a game to you, Mr. Ryder, but that ghost is very real, and she's— it's—tormenting me to find . . . certain valuable papers, which I believe you also know about. No, I can assure you, this is no game."

Jeremy stared at Alison for a long moment, knowing even without believing it fully that she was telling the truth. This was no parlor trick. He had peered through the glass panes in the door to the pool area and had seen her talking and gesturing in another of the inexplicable one-sided conversations he'd witnessed over the past few days. But now, instead of thinking she was crazy, he knew who she'd been talking to.

The ghost of Lady Caroline Lamb.

"The memoirs," he said, grasping to make sense of the totally irrational situation. "They're Byron's, aren't they? That's why you're at Dewhurst Manor." He spoke as if he didn't expect, or need, an answer.

"That makes two of us, I suspect."

Jeremy's eyes narrowed. "What makes you think that?"

"I saw the letter that dropped out of one of your books when I was trying to move you out of my room," she confessed. "Where did you get that? Is it for real?"

Jeremy watched Alison swim gracefully, doing the breaststroke as she talked. She seemed completely at ease in the water, like a sprite, unlike the sometimes insecure, hesitant creature he'd witnessed her to be on dry land. "What difference does it make?" he growled, wishing she didn't have such an erotic effect on him. His soggy jeans were growing increasingly uncomfortable. "I haven't been able to find anything that even remotely resembles any memoirs around here, Byron's or anyone else's."

"But if that letter is authentic, at least I know she—it —the ghost—is telling the truth. I had begun to think perhaps I had lost my mind. I don't normally go around talking to ghosts, you know. Or undertake a project like this search just because a ghost asks me to."

Jeremy wasn't convinced that Alison *hadn't* lost her mind. Even now, having seen the ghost firsthand, he thought it incredible that anyone would believe such a ghostly claim enough to move halfway around the world and buy a place like Dewhurst.

"Why should you have to search for them? Doesn't the ghost know where they are?"

"It forgot."

"Forgot? How could she—it—forget something like that?" The whole thing was getting crazier and crazier.

"How can a ghost do anything?" Alison replied wearily. "I have given up asking those kinds of questions. All I know is that poor woman needs some peace. And so do I. And the only thing that will accomplish both of those ends is to find the damned memoirs and bring them to the public awareness. She says they will 'vindicate her tarnished reputation.'"

"Byron's memoirs," Jeremy mused absently, his concentration focused mostly on the way Alison's breasts bobbed out of the water with each stroke. "They were supposedly burned, you know. Somebody said it was one of the greatest crimes in English literary history. But in Caroline's letter, she says they burned her *copy* of the memoirs. That she'd become good at forging his handwriting, and when she had the chance, she substituted her copy for the real thing. Is that what the ghost told you?"

"Exactly."

Jeremy's words were about the memoirs, but his body was having another kind of conversation altogether as he watched Alison's lithe figure cut through the water, her rounded bottom just breaking the surface. At last he could stand it no longer. He slipped out of his wet jeans, taking care that his boxers remained securely in place. He watched her reaction when he threw the wet pants onto the concrete. Her eyes widened. "What are you doing?"

"Getting comfortable." Their eyes locked as he began swimming toward her, and he saw an expression on her face he hadn't seen before, as if she actually wanted him to pursue her. He strained to keep the subject neutral, not to think about what he'd do if he caught up with her. "Do you have any idea how valuable such a find would be?"

The enchanting invitation left her eyes abruptly, and Alison stopped swimming, putting her feet on the pool floor. "Leave it to you to think about the money."

His momentum brought him to within inches of her face. "What's wrong with that?" he said, his feet also touching bottom.

"What about the fact that the ghost of Lady Caroline Lamb has waited almost two centuries to salvage her reputation? Doesn't honor count for anything?"

She had her back against the side of the pool, and Jeremy could not resist the temptation. He grinned wickedly. "You've never accused me of having any honor. Somehow, you seem to have me pegged for a scoundrel and a thief, although why you should believe such things is beyond me." He put one arm on either side of her, hands gripping the side of the pool, blocking any chance for her escape. "However, if I'm to be accused of such crimes, I think I ought to commit them." He saw her large, golden eyes blink twice as he brought his lips to hers. "And I think," he murmured, "I'll start by stealing a kiss."

⌒ *Chapter 19* ⌒

Not again! Alison had sworn she would not let herself fall under Jeremy's spell again, but here she was, her insides turning to butter as his lips met hers. Her back was, quite literally, to the wall. She had no place to run, no place to hide.

And no desire to do either.

Instead, she closed her eyes and felt the strength in his arms as he drew her against him. She allowed herself to experience those emotions she had hungered for, the feelings of being protected, sheltered, wanted. Those, and the other strange, new sensations he had awakened in her that had no names.

When he'd taken off his wet shirt, it had required all of her concentration just to keep her thoughts straight. The ghost had been right about one thing: He was more of a man than most. Standing waist-deep in the pool, his bare shoulders—broad and square—and his muscular chest and arms were reflected in the water, doubling the pleasurable image before her eyes. His hair was thick and dark, his eyes black as the night sky overhead, his face surpassing handsome.

Alison had wanted him with a primal urge she had never before experienced. In spite of her intentions not to become involved with him, a fire had begun to burn somewhere deep within. Maybe the ghost was right. Maybe she *had* fallen in love.

When he touched her, it set her skin afire. She'd pulled away and started to swim, hoping to squelch those mysterious, deep longings, and she had been relieved that he seemed satisfied just to talk about the ghost and the memoirs. Safe, distant topics.

And then he'd removed his jeans. He'd said he was "getting comfortable." Was that all he had on his mind? And what did he have on his body . . . anything? Her heart had begun to pound, for she knew if he made any overtures toward her, she would be easy prey.

The kiss he stole took away her breath as well. Her breath, and her senses, and any thought she had of resisting. His lips had sought hers with an initial tenderness, but the moment they touched, the lightning outside, or the fury of the sound and light show performed by Caro's ghost, were nothing in comparison to the passion that sparked between them. He tasted her mouth as a hungry man approaches a feast, with an intensity of desire she absorbed into her own being. She opened to his kiss, returning it with a craving for more.

Much more.

She put her arms around his neck and ran her hands through his hair, wanting to know every inch of him. She felt the scratch of his cheeks against her face, and gloried in the maleness of it. She could feel his heart pounding only inches from her own as he held her tightly against him. His hands slipped down her back to cup her bottom, and she gasped as he pulled her against his groin.

More man than most.

Alison didn't have a lot of experience with men in the way of comparison, but she didn't need to at the moment. She knew exactly what Caroline's ghost had meant.

"Oh, my God, Alison," he whispered in her ear. "What are you doing to me?"

"I thought it was you doing the doing," she murmured, breathless, running her hands across the expanse of his shoulders. She felt one of his hands move up the front of her body, slowly grazing her hipbone, her navel, the curve at her waist, and coming to rest upon her breast. She thought she would explode from the ecstasy of the sensations that swirled through her, but he brought her to new heights when he released the scrap of fabric that was the top of her bathing suit and took her nipple gently between his thumb and forefinger and began to love it the way the rest of his body was loving all of her.

Instinctively, she wrapped her legs around him, bringing him as close as she could against her. Never had she felt such a need, a desire for closeness, a desire to become one with a man.

"You'd better not do that," he said raggedly, running his hand along one of her legs. "I'm not responsible for what happens next if you don't move away."

"I want what happens next," Alison replied, wanting it with all her heart as well as with her body. "I'm not a child, Jeremy."

"That you're not." His eyes held hers for a long moment, as if asking permission to proceed, and she smiled and nodded ever so slightly. Then she felt him loosen the string ties of her bikini, felt it fall away from her as he removed his shorts. Her belly contracted with need as the fire grew hotter. She encircled him again with her legs, and with his hands on her hips, he brought her to him.

Alison felt the pressure, the delicious warmth of him penetrate throughout her being. He seemed to fill her every cell and fiber with joy and love, replacing the hollow aching emptiness that had been her life until this moment. She felt for the first time complete, whole.

Wanted.

Home.

And with those thoughts, she allowed Jeremy to take her over the edge and beyond, to where all things are possible, and from where there is no turning back.

Jeremy hadn't meant for this to happen, and the aftershock hit him with all the ramifications of what he'd just done. He'd lost all control, all good sense. He'd used no protection. He'd seduced Alison mercilessly, taken advantage of her naiveté.

And yet, he wasn't sorry. Not if she wasn't.

At the moment, she didn't seem sorry at all. She was curled against him, her legs still tightly around his buttocks, and she was holding on to him as if she never wanted to let him go. He felt her shiver.

"You're cold," he whispered, kissing the top of her head. "Let's find a towel."

She nodded and looked up at him. "On the bench behind me."

She released him and allowed him to pick her up and carry her through the water to the steps at the end of the pool. He set her down gently and reached for one of the two large, fluffy white towels that lay on the bench. He dried her face, her neck, her breasts, her belly, then wrapped the towel around her before things got out of hand again. He saw her glance down at the other towel.

"That's odd," she remarked.

"What?"

"I only brought one towel."

Jeremy picked up the second one and dried off quickly, aware that she was watching with that same hungry look on her face he'd seen in the pool.

"I'm getting used to odd things happening when I'm around you," he said with a grin as he tied the towel around his waist. He picked her up again, though she protested she was perfectly capable of walking. But he wanted her in his arms for as long as he could have her, and he knew once he saw her safely to her room, he would have to leave her. He would leave her, and Dewhurst Manor, and the memoirs, which suddenly no longer seemed important. He would go back to London, and his well-ordered life, escaping by a breath this woman who was unlike all others, who posed a dangerous threat to his autonomy, who awoke in him an essential longing that had lain dormant for many years.

They crept past the doorway behind which Drew Hawthorne had been consigned for the night and down the darkened hallway. "Are you hungry?" Jeremy asked Alison as he carried her up the stairs. "I'll see what Mrs. Beasley has prepared. . . ."

"Ummm," was her sleepy reply. He opened the door and took her to the bed, where he gently laid her on the white windowpane lace coverlet. She was limp in his arms, like she was only half-conscious. He turned down one side of the bed and shifted her there, then unwound the damp towel from her body. She smiled faintly, but did not open her eyes.

Jeremy felt the ache of desire building inside him again as he gazed at her slim body lying against the pure linen sheets. Her skin was pale where she had worn a bikini recently in the sun, darker everywhere else. Her breasts were small but beautifully shaped, her nipples soft and inviting in the moonlight that crept over the windowsill. She was like a child now, not the passionate woman who had loved him with such fire only moments ago. She was soft, and tender, and vulnerable. He wanted with all his soul to lay down beside her and hold her in his arms until dawn, but he knew if he did, everything he had worked to create in his life would be meaningless.

And he'd worked too hard, for too many years. He'd forbidden himself these feelings, these desires for love and a woman who would love him in return. The complexities of love had turned into a nightmare for his own parents, a bad dream in which he had been an unwilling player. He wasn't interested in a possible replay in his adult life.

He stared at her a moment longer, as if memorizing the vision she was lying asleep in the moonlight. Then, with a jagged breath, he covered her gently, tucking the sheets beneath her chin. He could not resist one last kiss, which he placed softly upon her cheek. Her breathing was deep and even. She wouldn't even know when he left her.

Jeremy closed the door behind him, and in so doing, determined to close off his feelings for Alison and get on with his life. He listened to the house, dark now in the early nighttime. Toward the kitchen, he could hear Mrs. Beasley and the two young servants preparing the evening meal, and he knew it was just a matter of minutes before she would come in search of the lady of the house.

He didn't want to be caught standing outside her door, clad only in a towel, nor did he wish to encounter anyone between here and his own room. So he made his way quickly along the upstairs gallery and down one of the two back staircases, arriving at his quarters unnoticed. He dressed in slacks and a pullover, then added his favorite cardigan, for he, too, had become chilled in his near-naked prowlings around Dewhurst Manor.

His stomach growled, and he found suddenly that he was ravenously hungry. Nothing like good sex to work up an appetite, he thought, heading toward the kitchen, but he knew more than just good sex had happened between him and Alison.

"Good evening," he said, startling Mrs. Beasley, but rewarding her with one of his famous grins. "It smells delicious. What are you preparing this evening?"

The elderly woman recovered her composure, but blushed anyway. "It's just a stew, sir, lamb stew. I thought I would make the most of the lamb I served yesterday. I hope y' don't mind that it's the second day of it."

"Mmmm," he sniffed appreciatively. "It will be fine, I am sure, although," he added hesitantly, "I don't believe anyone is going to show up at the table for dinner."

Mrs. Beasley looked crestfallen. "But I thought the Lady wished dinner at eight." She looked at her watch. "It's already quarter past now. Is she ill?"

"No. But she has gone to her room, I suspect for the night. Would you be so kind as to prepare three trays, Mrs. Beasley? Carry one to our uninvited guest, Mr. Hawthorne. He's in the new wing, next to the swimming pool. I'll take one to Miss Cunningham's room and leave it by the fireplace if she's asleep." He didn't miss the raised eyebrow at this, but he went on. "Then, if you please, I'll come for my own tray and dine in my quarters this evening. I have a great deal of work to get done, and I'm hoping to leave in the morning."

"Yes, sir," Mrs. Beasley replied, her voice and expression professionally devoid of comment.

He waited while Alison's tray was prepared, then carried it carefully along the winding passageway and through the great hall, which someone had made ready for the evening with a welcoming fire and lamps lit. He was glad he hadn't run into any servants, especially Mrs. Beasley, when he'd borne Alison back to her room. As it was, he was sure the "downstairs" tongues would be wagging by morning.

But by morning, he'd be gone, and it simply wouldn't matter.

As he'd expected, Alison was sleeping soundly when he knocked lightly and opened her door. He silently laid the silver tray with its covered dishes on the table by the fireplace. Then he stirred the fire, added wood, and watched until it blazed properly. He turned to where

Alison lay on the bed. She hadn't moved an inch from where he'd put her. "Good night, my Lady of Dewhurst," he whispered. "Sleep well."

Back in his own room, Jeremy ate the savory stew in thoughtful silence. He had much to ponder, much to try to assimilate. Like having seen a ghost. Not just having seen one, but having been thrown into the swimming pool by one. He poured himself a goblet of red wine and tasted the excellent bouquet, wondering absently who had selected such a fine wine for dinner. Old Beasley was quite a wonder, and Alison was lucky to have her.

Alison, Lady of Dewhurst.

That is what she would be if she purchased the old manor.

The ghost and the lady.

Quite a pair.

As difficult as it was for Jeremy, normally a sane and conservative man, he at last had to suspend his disbelief in ghosts. He thought back over his short tenure at Dewhurst and realized that the only explanation for the "odd" happenings he'd experienced was the ghost. It must have been Lady Caroline's shade playing the harpsichord that first night Alison had been here. Likely, the ghost *had* drunk his cognac. It had been the ghost who had taken the lock of hair and returned it again, dressed to kill in that ephemeral gown that left nothing to a man's imagination. And it had likely been the ghost who had doused him with the pillow feathers, although Alison had joined in the prank.

He was relieved to know that Alison Cunningham was not insane, as he'd thought her to be when he witnessed her one-sided conversations.

Unless now they were both insane.

He sipped the wine. He thought about Ashley T. Stone's queer statement that Lady Caroline's ghost had been gone a long time, and now it was back. Had it come in Alison's luggage? He wanted to know how Alison had hooked up with the specter to begin with, and what her real motive was for coming to Dewhurst Manor. Was it, as she had claimed so believably, to find a home? Or was it to find Byron's memoirs? If so, was it for the ghost alone? What was it Alison had said about honor? That she had promised the ghost to find the memoirs and bring them to the public, to vindicate Lady Caroline's tarnished reputation . . .

Something like that.

It went against every grain of Jeremy's rational business sense that someone would actually undertake such an endeavor without hope of financial gain. And yet, Alison, it appeared, certainly didn't need the money. Hawthorne had carelessly dropped it that she had four million dollars "jingling in her pockets."

Jeremy suspected that might just be the tip of the iceberg. The rest of her fortune, however large or complex it might be, was in trust. He surmised that Alison had a reputation for just the sort of impulsive behavior that had caused her to come to Dewhurst Manor—no, not just come here. To buy the damned place, to satisfy the whim of a ghost. That's why wealthy parents put things in trust for their overindulged offspring, and hired lawyers like Drew Hawthorne, who was here doing his job, which he'd described as "babysitting."

Very rich. Very beautiful. Passionate.

And spoiled. Indulged. Impulsive.

She's bad news, Jeremy warned himself. Get the hell out while you still have good sense.

He was too much of a professional not to finish the job he'd contracted for, however. He'd promised his friends at the bank he'd give them a full appraisal of everything in the house, and he intended to deliver. He'd finish the job. Somehow. He already had a number of the rooms inventoried and values placed on the furnishings. The library remained his biggest challenge. Perhaps he could have the books shipped to his warehouse in London, where he and an expert on antique books could complete the inventory of the impressive collection. It was possible, but he thought it a shame to take the library apart, when in all likelihood, it would never be put together again with the integrity with which the original owner had created it. Frowning, he sat up on the bed and put the wine glass down heavily on the night stand. Had it been Alison who demolished the library, he wondered suddenly, or had it been the ghost, searching for its lost papers? He chose the latter.

What would he do if he came across the memoirs now? he wondered, crossing the room to peer out into the blackness of the Hertfordshire night. They were no longer his private secret. So there was no way he could "discover" them, prove them authentic, and then sell them for a pretty price to one of the many private collectors he knew would bid well for them. The ghost would get her way on this one. Whether he found them or Alison did no longer mattered. Either way, Jeremy was oddly eager to get them into the hands of experts and restore a part of history that Byron's well-meaning friends had destroyed.

It wasn't in his nature to be so magnanimous about the fate of a treasure such as Byron's memoirs, but something had changed in the short time he had been at Dewhurst. Somehow the urgency of London life had left him. The thrill of the chase of something old and valuable had turned into a desire to see it placed in the right hands.

Jeremy shook his head in disbelief at the turn of his own thoughts. The ghostly sound and light show must have fried his brain. Glancing at his watch, he went to his briefcase and found his phone list. He picked up the phone, intending to call Malcomb McTighe, who always worked late, to see if he had been able to make a positive identification of the lock of hair he'd found in the library as Lady Caroline's. He was about to dial the number when he put the receiver to his ear and heard a man's voice on the line.

"Yeah, I found her. The dumb kid is about to blow some major cash on this decrepit old house in the middle of nowhere. I have no idea what's gotten into her. I thought I had it all handled after our last meeting in Boston."

Another man's voice. "You'd better get it handled, Hawthorne. I have everything in place for the California land deal. I've promised the investment bankers we can get the money. I made that promise," the man said slowly, with unmistakable meaning, "because *you* had assured me everything was in order. Don't screw it up, or it may be the last mistake you ever make."

Jeremy heard Drew Hawthorne's nervous heavy breathing. "I can handle it, Fromme. Get off my case. But it may take me a few days. She seems hell-bent going through with this, but you know how she is. By tomorrow, she may decide a trip to the Riviera is more to her taste."

The other man didn't laugh. "You haven't got much time. And that injunction isn't worth the paper it's printed on. Queer that deal and get the bitch back to Boston where we can keep an eye on her."

A click and the phone went dead, then Jeremy heard Hawthorne hang up on his end. Jeremy replaced his receiver as well.

It wasn't hard to get the picture of what that greasy little man had planned for Alison's four million dollars. A California land deal? Maybe it *was* a better investment, he allowed, but the way it was being handled was not only unprofessional, it was, he suspected, highly underhanded.

Alison Cunningham, artless and naive about her own affairs, was a sitting duck for the wolves who circled about her.

My sister! my sweet sister! if a name
Dearer & purer were, it should be thine.
Mountains & seas divide us, but I claim
No tears, but tenderness to answer mind:
Go where I will, to me thou art the same—
A loved regret which I would not resign,
There yet are two things in my destiny,—
A world to roam through, & a home with thee.
  —From "Epistle to Augusta" by Lord Byron

Caroline recovered & resumed her pursuit, but I withdrew my assault upon her Sanity. Indeed, I withdrew from much during this time. I had grown tired of Lady Oxford. Although I was greatly relieved to learn that I was not about to be a father, at the same time I also found out that I was not her only Paramour, & my Vanity was sorely wounded. By mid-May, we had dissolved plans to travel abroad together, & when she sailed in June, (with her Husband!) I was not sorry to see her go.

Women have always been an anathema to me. Only one, my beloved half sister Augusta, had never disappointed me, although we had seen little of each other in our lives. It was to Augusta that springtime that I turned in sheer exhaustion & desperate need for Love & understanding. I invited her to leave her dreary life in Newmarket for a time & enjoy the Season as my Companion. I hadn't remembered her being so lovely as she was when she arrived on my doorstep. I could see the resemblance between us—the large eyes, the fine nose, the sensuous lips. She aroused in me a startling desire, one deeper & darker than I had ever known—even with Caroline. It was a forbidden desire, & one I was eventually unable to resist.

Augusta, unlike all the others, loved me for my Being alone, & nothing more. She asked nothing from me, demanded nothing. She gave me her Love without question, seeing in me the hunger & desperation of a man who is incapable of Loving. She was the very opposite of Caro-

*line, totally devoid of cunning or spite. She was unlike
Lady O. as well, unsophisticated & simple. To me, she was
the protection of a mother, the understanding of a sister
. . . & the fulfillment of a lover. If Augusta perceived our
actions to be Sinful, she never indicated it to me. We went
everywhere together, as brother & sister, to dances & balls
& the theatre. It was good to see her happy again, away
from her drunken husband & miserable noisy brats. She
deserved to live the life of a fine lady, & for a short while, I
saw to it that she did. Gus, as I called her, & I enjoyed
ourselves the most, however, when we were left alone in the
privacy of my quarters. There we could be as we wished—it
was no longer necessary to play a part—& we wished to
know one another in every way possible. Augusta made me
whole, ended the Longing & the Confusion. I will not try
here to explain the inexplicable, why this one woman, of
them all, the one woman forbidden by all that is deemed
holy, should be the one at last to bring peace to my heart.*

*I have been damned by man for my love of Augusta, but
it is damnation based on their ignorance of the Purity of
our affection for one another. The damnation from Annabella is understandable but hypocritical, since at times
she participated willingly in the same kind of three-sided
affair as Lord & Lady Devonshire enjoyed with Elizabeth
Foster. From Caroline, however, it was a damnation fired
by a desire for revenge even more unholy than the Sin I am
accused of committing with Augusta. But I am getting
ahead of my story. . . .*

⇜ *Chapter 20* ⇝

Alison slept dreamlessly through the night and awoke at greater peace with herself than she would have thought possible under the circumstances. She continued to make mistakes . . . had made a major one last night, and yet as she stretched luxuriously then curled around the pillows, she wasn't one bit sorry. If she never knew another man in her entire life, at least she'd had the best, and he'd taken her for a swim she'd never forget.

Typically irresponsible, she heard her conscience nag.

Shut up, she told it.

But it continued to nag until it managed to erode the last remnants of her morning-after reverie. With a sigh, she threw back the covers and realized she'd slept naked for the first time in her life. Maybe that's why she'd slept so well, she thought with a grin. Then she saw the white towel sprawled on the floor nearby and remembered who had taken her to bed and put her there naked. Had he slept with her as well? She glanced at the other side of the bed, but it was undisturbed. So he'd brought her here, tucked her in, and then left.

What kind of lover would do that?

An indifferent one. A lover who was not above taking advantage of an opportunity when it presented itself in all its sexual fury, as Alison had presented herself to him last night. Oh, God, she moaned, pulling the sheets across her breasts, remembering it was he who had warned her to stop, and she who had insisted that he continue. Her cheeks flamed. How could she face him this morning? He must think her the ultimate little fool.

She forced herself out of bed, noting the tray of food by the now-cold fireplace. She was grateful that Mrs. Beasley had cared enough to bring it to her, even though it had gone untouched. Alison made her way to the shower, hoping the warmth of the spray would bring her out of the stupor in which she found herself. It doesn't matter what he thinks, she decided after some minutes beneath the hot water. The deed was done. She'd have to live with it.

Try as she might, she still couldn't bring herself to regret what had happened with Jeremy last night.

But that was then, and this is now, she reminded herself, struggling to regain reality. So what was she going to do today? Then she remembered her uninvited guest. "Ugh!" she said aloud, and made a face. Why had that idiot barged in on her? He was the last person on Earth she wanted to deal with today.

Then she remembered the ghost's promise to give him a fright in the night. Had it used its spectral bag of tricks to scare the living hell out of the prig and get him on his way? Maybe he was already gone, Alison thought hopefully as she dressed.

She chose a pair of cream-colored silk slacks with a matching blouse that had a large collar and a deep V-neckline. The shoulders were well padded and gave her, Alison thought, added height. She tucked a long aquamarine scarf under the collar and tied it casually just at the juncture of the lapels. She added large pearl earrings and a pair of shoes almost the same color as the scarf. She applied her makeup more carefully than she had in years, then stood back to assess the effect.

Did she look older? Wiser? More able to stand up to Hawthorne?

More able to resist Jeremy?

She went directly to the kitchen, where she found Mrs. Beasley and the young cook making plans for the day's work. "Good morning," Alison said brightly. "Do you have anything for breakfast?"

"Yes, ma'am," said the girl with a smile. "I've made some fresh toast. There's sausage and bacon and eggs and broiled tomatoes and . . ."

Alison's stomach rebelled at the thought of a heavy, full English breakfast, as they called it. "I'll just have some toast," she said, hoping not to offend the obviously eager-to-please young woman. "And some fruit, if there is some."

"Oh, yes, ma'am. Would you like tea?"

"Is there coffee?"

"Of course."

"I'd prefer it in the mornings. Also, I'd like to take breakfast on the terrace, it's such a lovely morning. Is there a table set up?"

"I'll have Kit do it immediately," Mrs. Beasley said. "We put the outside tables away last night before the storm, but it won't take a minute."

"Thanks," Alison smiled. "And thank you for bringing my dinner to me last night, although I was so sound asleep, I never even knew it was there."

She saw Mrs. Beasley shoot a quick glance at the servant girl, then heard the older woman's almost hesitant reply, "You're welcome, ma'am, but t'wasn't me who took it to you. T'was Mr. Ryder carried your tray."

Alison nodded, hoping to maintain a cool demeanor. "Oh. I see. Well, I'll wait on the terrace for breakfast."

So, *he'd* brought her dinner! He hadn't stayed the night, but he had thought to leave her something to eat. Now, an indifferent lover wouldn't have done that, would he? Alison was a jumble of mixed emotions as she stepped onto the terrace. The mist was just beginning to lift from the snarl of brambles that was the garden, but the meadow and forest which lay beyond were still hidden behind the soft gray fog. From somewhere in the moist wet silence, a bird called out. Alison went to the rail and leaned on both arms. It was so beautiful here, so peaceful. She knew this was where she belonged. Perhaps the only place on Earth where she really belonged.

In her mind's eye, she could already see the garden restored to a brilliant splendor. She could hear the drone of the mower as the groundskeeper groomed the immaculate lawn. She could smell the roses, freshly cut each day from the beds she herself tended. How did she suppose she was going to pull that off? She laughed at her own romantic notions. She'd never planted a rose bush in her life.

She heard a noise behind her and turned, expecting to see Kit, the tall young handyman Mrs. Beasley had hired, preparing to set up her breakfast table. Instead, Jeremy stood at the entrance to the terrace. He was dressed in what Alison was coming to recognize as his favorite attire—jeans and a sweater, and she found his body just as enticing fully clothed as completely naked. She felt a stir of desire sweep through her.

"Good morning," he said, his face clouded, she thought. With regret? The idea settled gloomily around her heart.

"Good morning," she replied, forcing cheerfulness. She was determined not to reveal her feelings. "Care to join me for breakfast?"

"Sure." He came to her and took her hand, leading her toward the far end of the terrace with a strange sense of urgency. "Alison, I . . . we need to talk."

"There's no need, Jeremy. What happened, happened. I don't hold you responsible. I expect neither an apology nor an oath of undying loyalty. So let's just—"

"You don't understand. I'm not talking about us."

"Oh." She looked at him curiously, and she could tell something was wrong. Dreadfully wrong. "What is it?"

Kit chose that moment to make his appearance, and neither Alison nor Jeremy spoke while they watched him set the table. "Please tell Mrs. Beasley there will be two for breakfast," she said as he completed his task.

"Make that three," came a voice from the doorway. Drew Hawthorne appeared, dressed in khakis and a plaid shirt, as if he were on vacation. "You don't mind if I join you," he stated.

"Would it make a difference if I did mind?" Alison muttered. The man was such a jerk. No class.

Drew Hawthorne chuckled and settled his considerable weight onto one of the garden chairs that had been placed at the breakfast table. "Now, Ali, don't start in on me. I'm not the enemy, remember?"

"I prefer for you to call me Alison," she said sharply.

"Alison, then. Come. Sit down. Here's the coffee pot."

"You'd think this was your place, not mine," she observed wryly, but took a seat across from him and nodded for Jeremy to sit next to her. She watched as the young serving woman, whose name she'd learned was Kate, poured steaming coffee into three cups from a freshly polished silver service. Drew helped himself to three spoons of sugar before continuing.

"Well, it's not yours either," he said, his voice seeking a humorous note and not quite making it. "Not yet. And I'm here to try to get you to change your mind about buying this . . . dreadful hunk of real estate, Alison."

"You're too late," she said smoothly, although she was trembling with anger. "The contract is signed, the money's in escrow. . . ."

"Wrong, darling. Remember, I told you about that little injunction we placed on the transfer of that money. Just to give you time to rethink—"

"An injunction," Jeremy interjected, "that I believe is
. . . not worth the paper it's printed on." He empha-
sized the last few words, and his inflection seemed to
startle Hawthorne and throw him off-balance.

Alison was curious. What did Jeremy know about all
this?

"You stay out of it," the fat man snapped. "This is
none of your business."

"It would seem, it is none of yours, either."

"Who are you, Ryder? What's your interest in Alison's affairs?"

"Suffice it to say I'm someone who has no intention
of standing by while the likes of you continues to exploit
her inexperience."

"Exploit! You're out of line, Ryder. I have no idea
what you're talking about, and if you keep it up, I'll sue
you for character assassination and slander."

"Are you certain you want to do that, Mr. Hawthorne? Because it would give me great pleasure to turn
over a few of your rocks and see what kind of snakes
crawl out from under them."

Alison watched with growing consternation as the two
men snarled at each other across the table, discussing
her and her affairs as if she wasn't even present.

"Stop it, both of you!" she cried at last. "Mr. Hawthorne, what I am doing here—and what I plan to do
with that insurance money—is out of your hands. You
have made a mistake in coming here. And a mistake in
thinking you could change my mind. You are welcome
to finish your breakfast, then call a cab and get yourself
back to Boston. By the way," she added, amused at the
way his face flushed at her unusually assertive stance,
"how did you sleep last night?"

He frowned at her, confused by her sudden change of
conversation. "Sleep? Why, I slept fine. Why wouldn't
I?"

Alison made a mental note to take it up with the

ghost for failing to keep its rendezvous with Drew Hawthorne. "No reason. I was just hoping you had nightmares," she returned with an icy smile. "Now, since the
two of you have utterly ruined this beautiful morning,
I'm going to excuse myself."

She stood abruptly, knocking the table with her knee
and sloshing coffee onto the white linen cloth. Damn,
couldn't she even make an exit gracefully?

Angry with herself and with the men who continually
seemed to want to run her life, she hurried across the
terrace, ducked through the door and raced to her
room, where she slammed the door behind her and fell
onto the bed, crying with rage.

Damn them!

Damn them all. . . .

> With horn-handled knife,
> To kill a tender lamb as dead as mutton.
> Lord B-n, Lady W-., and Lady C. L-b. were
> among the guests at a recent party. Lord B., it would
> appear, is a favourite with the latter Lady; on this
> occasion, however, he seemed to lavish his attention
> on another fair object. This preference so enraged
> Lady C.L. that, in a paroxysm of jealousy, she took
> up a dessert-knife, and stabbed herself . . . 'Better
> be with the dead than thus,' cries the jealous fair;
> and, casting a languishing look at Lord B—, who,
> Heaven knows, is more like Pan than Apollo, she
> whipt up as pretty a little dessert-knife as a Lady
> could desire to commit suicide with, 'And stuck it in
> her wizzard.'
>
> —society report in *The Satirist*

*Caroline, as I have noted, did not have the grace to die
even as she thought herself to be in her deathbed. Instead,
she allowed herself to be nursed back to full health by
midsummer. I am certain that she knew of Augusta's pres-*

ence in London, but in her naiveté, she did not suspect that she had reason to be jealous of her, at least not then. With Lady O. out of the picture, Caroline seemed to relent in her pursuit, or so I thought until that dreadful incident at Lady Heathcote's.

We met at a small, select party attended by the most elite of the beaux monde of London Society. Had I known she would be there, I would not have gone, & thankfully, I did not bring Augusta with me that evening. The evening began dreadfully & descended shortly into Hell. I arrived late, my damnable lameness causing me pain, & lack of a satisfying meal in recent memory eating a hole in my stomach. When I entered the room, I became aware that a hush fell across the gathering, & I turned to determine its cause. Caroline stood opposite me across the room. She was thin & haggard & yet so exquisitely beautiful, I felt a tremor of those old feelings shiver through me. The guests parted to allow us to approach one another, which we did as if drawn by some unseen force. But before we could speak, the orchestra struck up a waltz, that abominable dance which Caroline held so dear & which I loathed so deeply. Our hostess, meaning well, seized the moment to allay the tension between us, urging Caroline to start the dancing. As she passed by me with her first partner, she hissed, "I conclude I may waltz now," a comment acknowledging our disassociation. But it was also a comment calculated to incur my wrath, recalling other days & other dance parties, when I had sat & watched in agony as she flirted & danced with every man in the room but me. "Dance with everybody in turn, Caro," I returned with a sneer. "You always did it better than anyone. I shall have pleasure in seeing you."

After only a short while, her recent illness claimed her energy, & she stopped dancing & asked to be escorted to the supper room. I entered a few moments later with Lady Rancliffe on my arm. Upon seeing Caroline, I commented with jealous malice, for it still drove me mad to watch her dance, "I have been admiring your dexterity." To my hor-

ror & amazement, her reply was to take up a small knife as
if to attack me. Unable to control my contempt, I contin-
ued to harry her, saying, "Do, my dear. But if you mean to
act a Roman's part, mind which way you strike with your
knife—be it at your own heart, not mine—you have struck
there already." Whereupon she burst into tears & at-
tempted to run out of the room. Lady Rancliffe screamed
that Caro was trying to kill herself, & several guests
crowded around to prevent the deed. In the melee which
ensued, Caroline was indeed cut, but not from trying to
commit suicide. The knife, which was too small to inflict
much damage in any case, scraped her fingers when it was
wrested from her. A few drops of blood trickled onto her
gown, & she was rushed back to Melbourne House & into
the hands of her beloved William, the fool.

I returned to my quarters, & Augusta, & allowed her to
soothe my sullen spirit as only she could.

Jeremy watched Alison flee the nasty little scene which
had erupted between him and Drew Hawthorne. He realized it had been a rude and uncalled-for confrontation, at least from her point of view, because she didn't
know about Hawthorne's plans for her money.

"You'd best do as Miss Cunningham wishes," Jeremy
said at last, drawing on every reserve of politeness he
could muster. "I will be happy to call you a taxi."

Hawthorne appeared unmoved by any of it. "Give her
time," he drawled, taking up a fat sausage on his fork.
"She'll like what I have planned for her, once she understands it." He waved the sausage at Ryder. "You her
lover?"

"I beg your pardon?"

"You and Ali. You know, you got a thing going?"

Jeremy hoped he could conceal his true thoughts on
the subject. "Once again, sir, I believe you are meddling
in things that are none of your business."

"Anything that girl does is my business," he replied,

stuffing his mouth full. He chewed noisily a moment, then washed the remnants down with coffee. "I'm the trustee of her parents' estate, you see." He seemed to expand just at the thought of the control that gave him over his client. "I'm only telling you this because if you do have designs on her, you might as well know that she has absolutely no experience in handling money, that whatever insurance money that is left by now won't be around long the way she goes through it. So if you're going to marry her for her money, you'd better hurry up, unless—" he peered at Jeremy, who sat in appalled silence, "—unless you can help me convince her not to throw her money away on wild schemes like this one."

"You assume far too much, Mr. Hawthorne," Jeremy said, standing to leave. "I have no intention of marrying Alison for her money, I would never collaborate with the likes of you on anything, and"—Jeremy looked around at the beauty of the countryside stretching before him in the warm morning sun—"I'm not sure this is such a wild scheme. Excuse me, but I am going to make arrangements for your taxi."

"Don't bother," he heard Drew Hawthorne call after him. "I'm not going anywhere."

Jeremy stood in the great hall, clenching and unclenching his fists, breathing deeply, trying to regain control. He'd come close to punching out the autocratic asshole. But he knew if he did, it would likely only make matters worse for Alison. He sensed Alison was in danger. Hawthorne, although probably not a physical threat, posed a very real legal and emotional threat that she was going to have to face sooner than later.

He didn't know the structure of the trust, of course, but he had known other instances in which the beneficiary, in this case Alison, had no say over what the trustees did with the money that she would eventually inherit. How could Alison's father ever have trusted the likes of Drew Hawthorne over his own daughter, he wondered, incredulous.

But there was much he didn't know.

What he was certain of at the moment, however, is that he could not leave as he had planned, not until he saw that she was rid of the bullying attorney.

⌒ *Chapter 21* ⌒

*F*irst it had been her father. Then the law firm and that idiot Hawthorne. Now it appeared that Jeremy was just like all the rest . . . well, except in that one department, Alison laughed bitterly to herself as she reached for a tissue. It was several hours later; the storm of tears had run its course, leaving her makeup streaked and her carefully chosen silken attire a rumpled mess.

All the men she'd known in her life, including her father, had wanted to control her, tell her how to live her life, what to think, and especially what to do with her money. Not any had seemed to give a damn what *she* wanted or that she might be capable of handling life for herself. She'd thought she would throw up when she heard Jeremy tell the lawyer that he wasn't going to stand by while Hawthorne took advantage of her inexperience.

Noble gesture.

But what made him think she needed him?

Fury dried her tears. Men. She'd like to pack the whole gender in a spaceship and send them all to Mars. In the meantime, she'd deal with Drew Hawthorne and his gang in the only way she knew how.

She picked up the phone.

First, she called Gina Useppi who, in a nervous voice, verified that the money had not been transferred yet and wanted to know if anything had gone wrong. Assuring her this was only a temporary nuisance, Alison reminded the agent that the appraisal was due the following week.

Then she called Judge Frieberg. It was Thursday, and he was at his golf club in Boston. She knew exactly where to find him because her father had golfed with him every Thursday for years. Benjamin Pierce had been part of the foursome, she remembered, still bitterly angry at the elder attorney who had betrayed her by placing her in the hands of his slimy son-in-law. She caught the judge just before tee time, and twenty minutes later when she called her banker, the money was released. There had been no real injunction, just a fatherly phone call from the judge, urging the bank to use caution. Drew Hawthorne had spun him a story about how weak-willed Alison was and how she had fallen into the hands of a predatory real estate agent in England who was trying to pawn off a derelict, worthless piece of property onto her inexperienced little self.

Alison wanted to scream right through the phone loud enough so that everyone at the bank could hear her wrath. *Get your hands off my money!*

She waited one hour, the time she had given the bank to transfer the money. If it took one second longer, she had warned them, she would file a lawsuit against them, charging them with manipulating her money.

She had no idea if there was such a charge. She'd just made it up, but it must have worked, because one hour later, the British bank had been notified that eight hundred thousand dollars was being wired to the escrow account as it should have been almost a week before.

But Alison wasn't finished. She dialed the estate agent again.

"Gina," she said, gathering courage with each victory

of the day. "Get the contract, and bring along a blank one. We're going to London."

Six hours later, just as the sun was going down, Alison dropped the agent back at her office and headed toward Dewhurst Manor. The smile on her face wouldn't go away. She pulled into the drive and got out, noting that another evening thunderstorm was brewing. Well, it would be nothing compared to the storm she was about to raise inside.

She found both Hawthorne and Jeremy, an odd pair, waiting for her in the great hall.

"Where the hell have you been?" Hawthorne yelled, his face contorted with rage. "I hope you know you've stirred up one hell of a mess at home."

"Yes, I suppose I have," she replied with cyanide sweetness. "I'm glad you are here together, for I want you both to hear what I have to say."

Jeremy watched with a mixture of awe and amusement as Alison Crawford Cunningham showed them both exactly what she was made of. He hadn't known her father, but he was certain if the old man was looking down from the next world, it was with pride for his daughter's quick thinking and determination. He admitted later, he couldn't have negotiated the deal any better himself.

"This solves *your* problem, Hawthorne," she said, waving the papers under his nose. "You no longer have to worry whether or not I will blow that insurance money, because I just have. Or at least a big chunk of it. I have bought this derelict, worthless piece of property, as you described it to the judge, from my 'predatory' real estate agent. It's a done deal, Hawthorne. Signed, sealed, delivered." She threw the contractual agreement on the sideboard.

Hawthorne blanched. "But . . . but that's not possible. It takes time—"

"Get real, Hawthorne. All it takes is money. Connections don't hurt either. So now, you have no reason to remain here one more minute. This is my property, and I want you off it immediately."

Hawthorne looked at Alison with pure hatred on his face. "You little bitch," he said then, his lip curling. "You little rich bitch." He took a step toward her, and Jeremy prepared to intervene, thinking the irate attorney was about to harm her. But Hawthorne held himself in check, the muscles of his jaw twitching with tension. "You're gonna be sorry," he hissed. "You're gonna be real sorry you didn't listen to me, sweetheart." With that, he hurried down the hall toward his room and, Jeremy hoped, into history.

"Well done," Jeremy said, turning with a grin to face her. "My turn."

Her face softened. "Yes. It's your turn. All the way to London, I thought about some of the things you have said to me, that I was paying too much money for the house, that the furnishings were as valuable as the house, that they would be difficult to replace once they left here. So," she drew in a deep breath and let it out again in a satisfied sigh, "I made a deal with the bank."

"Go on," Jeremy said, hardly daring to think what kind of bad deal his pals at the bank were likely to dish out to an innocent like Alison.

"You aren't going to like it, I'm afraid."

"Like you said, it's a done deal. What did you come away with?"

"All of it."

"All?"

"The house. The grounds. The furniture." She laughed. "The title. I'm now officially the Lady of Dewhurst Manor."

Jeremy gave her a slight officious bow. "And at the risk of poking my nose into your business, may I ask at what ransom you came away with all of the above?"

He watched Alison go to the sideboard, where she

picked up the contract and brought it to him. "The same as I was going to pay for the house alone."

A glance at the bottom line told Jeremy she wasn't joking. "That's a real coup, Alison," he said, taking her hands. "Congratulations."

But she pulled away from him. "Thanks. But that means you're through here as well, Jeremy. I own the furnishings, and I'm not planning to sell them, so your job's finished."

"And you want me out, too," he finished her statement.

She nodded. "It's best. If I find the memoirs, I'll let you know. I'll need help in having them published—"

Her sentence was blown apart by an ear-shattering screech that rattled the heavy chandelier overhead and seemed to shake the old house to its very foundation. An explosion sounded somewhere in the vicinity of the kitchen, and Jeremy heard the screams of the servants who rushed panic-stricken into the great hall.

"Th' power's off in th' kitchen, ma'am," Mrs. Beasley said, her eyes wide with fear. "It's like th' electrical box just blew up."

Suddenly things went berserk around them. Books tumbled from the shelves in the second-floor gallery and rained down into the great hall. Old William LaForge flopped on the wall and tilted at a crazy angle. The electric lights in the room flashed off and on until many of the old bulbs burned completely out. A few exploded from the energy surge. Jeremy reached for Alison and pulled her into the protection of his body, wondering if this was an air raid or an earthquake.

"What the hell's going on?" Hawthorne scrambled back to the great hall just in time to receive a knock on the head from a falling book.

Jeremy and Alison looked at each other.

"The ghost has remembered." They spoke their thought at the same time, then burst out laughing, while

Drew Hawthorne, rubbing his bruised and battered forehead, looked on in bewilderment.

Alison hoped Caroline would calm down before she brought the entire house down around their ears. "Okay, okay, we're coming!" she called out. She wished she had a video camera to record the look on Drew Hawthorne's face. The ghost may have missed him last night, but he was getting a full show at the moment. "Which way do we go?"

The familiar mist gathered and hung like golden fog for a moment in the room high above them, then Caro's ghost materialized for all to see. "They're in the cellar," it panted. "Go to the wine cellar."

"But I've already searched there," Jeremy protested.

Alison shot him a glance. "So you *were* after the memoirs!"

He shrugged. "Could be. It doesn't matter now, does it?" He turned to the ghost. "You're sure they're in the cellar?"

Its reply was to dissolve into a flash of brilliant light which swept through the room as it had at the pool the night before. The light dipped and bounced and beckoned, as if it were a young child eagerly tugging on its parents' hands.

"Let's go," Jeremy said.

"Shouldn't you get your flashlight?" Alison asked. The afternoon was waning, and the encroaching storm was already darkening the sky.

"Good idea. Wait here." He dashed down the hall to his room and returned only seconds later. In the meantime, Drew Hawthorne attempted to gather his wits.

"What's going on?" he asked, his face white as a traditional ghost's. "What was that . . . that thing?"

"The ghost," Alison said.

"Ghost. What ghost?"

"I thought I told you the place was haunted."

"Yeah, but . . ."

Jeremy was back with the flashlight. "You stay here," he told Hawthorne.

"B—by myself?"

Alison refrained from snorting at the man's pathetic cowardice. "The ghost is going with *us*. You'll be perfectly safe here."

But Hawthorne, along with the three alarmed but curious servants, followed Jeremy and Alison down the stairs toward the cellar. Jeremy released the secret door latch and opened the door to the Dutch room. Caroline's cometlike shape zoomed past them, made several passes around the room, then began rattling with all its ectoplasmic might the chain that secured the wine cellar.

"Look at that!" Alison laughed. "This proves it. Ghosts really do rattle chains!" But it was more than a ghostly joke that filled her with such joy. It proved once and for all that she wasn't crazy. There *was* a ghost. There *were* memoirs. And they were about to make a discovery that might, as she'd told Jeremy, change the way the English-speaking world viewed a certain period of history.

She hoped so, if only for Caroline's sake. Alison watched as Jeremy struggled to wrest the chain and its huge lock from the ghost. "Let go, for God's sake, or we'll never get in there," he yelled at the ghost, who obeyed immediately but buzzed loudly in anticipation. "Hurry! Hurry!" it said.

Alison heard Hawthorne behind her. "I don't believe this," he muttered.

"Then why don't you leave?" she said crossly. She wished he wasn't here to witness what was about to take place.

At last, Jeremy managed to unlock the door, which he opened as wide as possible. The wine cellar gaped like a huge open mouth. "Turn on the lights in the Dutch room," he instructed one of the servants. He flashed his light into the darkness. "I tell you, I've already been through this place. Caro, if those memoirs are here, you're going to have to show them to us, my dear."

"Follow me," said a hollow voice, and the figure of Caroline Lamb materialized wearing her favorite outfit, a page's uniform. Her eyes were large and dark, serious now, almost sad. She turned and walked through the steel door that Jeremy had discovered.

"Wait a minute," he called after her, quickly fumbling for the secret button. The panel slid aside, and Alison drew in her breath.

"Well, I'll be," she said. "How did you know that was a door?"

"Trial and error," Jeremy replied, his face grim. "But I think the cellar stops here. I went all the way to the back wall. It's solid rock."

"I said follow me," Caro said, stamping her foot.

Jeremy flashed Alison an amused look. "Yes, ma'am," he replied.

Like a small parade, Jeremy, Alison, Drew Hawthorne, Mrs. Beasley, Kit, and Kate tiptoed behind the ghost, who once again disappeared through the far wall.

"We can't go there, Caro," Jeremy called.

"Oh, I see them!" came the ghostly reply. "They are here! They are here!"

Alison tugged on Jeremy's shirt. "That must be the entrance to the old tunnel. Ashley T. Stone told me they filled it in when it caved in on some children at the end of the last century. Do you suppose there's a door behind the rock?"

"I'll need a pick or something to dig with," Jeremy said, rolling up his sleeves. "Here, hold the light."

"Hurry! Hurry!" came an excited squeal from the other side. "You can do it with your hands."

Alison directed the light's strong beam where Jeremy ran his hands over the rock. It was a large boulder, he discovered, not a wall at all. "Here, help me," he signaled to Kit. "Let's see if we can push this to one side." The two men struggled for a few moments and were able to move it out about five inches. "What's behind there?" Alison asked, her heart pounding so hard she thought it might explode.

Jeremy knelt and dug around with his fingers. "I think I feel something like wood." He pulled out a handful of shredded rotten planking. "It must be one of the beams that supported the opening of the tunnel. Come on, Kit. Let's get this rock out of the way."

Alison joined the two men, putting her back against the boulder and pushing with her feet. Drew Hawthorne remained in the shadows. At last, the huge rock gave way, leaving enough room for one person to go inside.

Jeremy looked at Alison. "I know this is your show, but it could be dangerous. That tunnel has been closed off for a long time. Let me go in."

Alison had no desire to go crawling around in the dank darkness of some long ago tunnel, no matter what treasure might be hidden there. "Be my guest," she smiled, glad she hadn't run him off too soon. She was grateful for his help.

They could see Caroline's ghostly light pulsing just on the other side of the entrance. "Come on!" it urged plaintively.

Jeremy squeezed through the small opening, then Alison handed him the flashlight, leaving the rest of them in near darkness.

"This is creepy," Hawthorne complained.

"Nobody invited you," Alison reminded him. "Do you see anything?" she called to Jeremy.

"A lot of debris has fallen around here."

Alison heard the scrabble of what sounded like more falling rock, and terror suddenly spread through her. "Jeremy. Is it caving in? Get out of there!"

"Just a minute.. Wait. What's this?"

"Yes! Yes!" cried the ghost.

More scratching sounds, then silence.

"Jeremy?"

His handsome face appeared suddenly at the entrance to the tunnel. "You called, madam?" he grinned, holding the light up to cast eerie shadows on his face.

"Stop it!" Alison laughed nervously. "You scared me silly. Did you find anything?"

Then, slowly he raised a battered and aged wooden box and handed it to her. "Could be."

He squeezed back through the opening, and put his hand in the small of Alison's back. "Let's get out of here," he said.

The troupe made its way back into the Dutch room, where Alison placed the old box gently on the rustic table. "Where's our ghost?" she asked.

Everybody looked around, expecting another appearance by the dramatically-inclined ghost. But there was nothing. Not a sound. Not a light. Not even a whisper.

"I don't believe this," Jeremy said. "The ghost is going to miss its own party?"

"I think," Alison said, brushing dirt away from the box, "that it sort of runs out of steam. I've seen it happen a lot of times. The ghost comes on real strong, then can't get together enough energy to maintain a presence. Shall we open this without it?"

"What's in there?" Hawthorne wanted to know.

Alison glanced at Jeremy. Maybe they should wait until they were alone to examine the contents. "Maybe nothing," she replied. "Come on. Let's go upstairs and wait until the ghost puts itself back together."

"Wait a minute," the fat man insisted, suddenly brave now that he was back in the light of day, although the day had turned dark with the storm. "I've just risked my life to retrieve that box. I want to know what's in it."

"You did what?" Alison couldn't believe the man's temerity. But she had to admit that she, too, was eager to know what they'd discovered. Still, she felt she owed it to the ghost to wait until it could be present before opening the box.

They went to the library, where Alison placed the filthy container on the long walnut table. "Looks like we could be in for a wait," she said, "so let's be civilized about this. Kit, would you please build a fire? Kate, how about bringing tea? Mrs. Beasley, this thing is dreadfully dirty. Could you bring the vacuum with the hose attachment?"

She caught the look of approval on Jeremy's face.

"You're becoming quite British, you know," he said with a teasing smile. "Tea *is* a civilized tradition, isn't it?"

Alison blushed, recalling her petulant attitude the day —could it have been only a week ago?—that she'd refused to let Jeremy pay for her tea. "Yes. I guess I have a lot to learn," she admitted.

"You seem like a quick study to me." Jeremy took her hand. "You are going to do just fine, Alison Cunningham," he murmured. "Just keep your eyes open and your head on straight."

Hawthorne cleared his throat. "I could use a drink," he complained.

"Me, too," said a small voice from out of nowhere.

Jeremy grinned. "Got any cognac, Alison?"

Alison turned to her housekeeper, who nodded toward the cabinet in the corner. "Lord Charles used to keep a stock in there, ma'am. Want me to check?"

"I'll do it," Hawthorne offered, removing his bulk to the liquor cabinet. "Ah, yes. Here it is. Anyone care to join me?" He turned to the group, and Alison was surprised he'd considered anyone but himself.

"Just be sure you pour a glass for Caro," she told him, ignoring the way he rolled his eyes. She waited and watched him fill two crystal goblets, just to make sure he took her instructions seriously. Then she turned to Jeremy. "The ghost is here," she whispered. "I can feel its presence."

"Yes. And I think it wants us to open this now."

"Let's ask. Caro, can you show yourself?" she called softly, taking the glass of cognac from Hawthorne and holding it up to the empty room. "Here's a drink for you."

"You must keep it for me," the ghost whispered. "I haven't the energy now. But please, get to the memoirs."

Alison smiled at Jeremy. "You're the antiquarian. What do we do next? I mean, if we open that box, are the papers going to shrivel up and disappear, like something out of an Indiana Jones movie?"

Jeremy laughed and pulled out his pocket knife. "Hardly. You want to do the honors?"

"No, you do it."

He stuck the knife blade under the lid, and pried away almost two hundred years' worth of dirt and grime. It fell to the tabletop in rusty hunks. "But if those memoirs are in here, we must handle the paper very carefully. In fact, do you have any gloves? It would be a good idea not to touch the paper with our hands if we can keep from it."

"I know where some clean work gloves are," Kate said, having brought in the tea tray. "I'll go find them. It will only take a second."

Alison felt more than heard the throb of spectral energy that surrounded them all now, filling the room with its essence. "We're getting close, Caro," she said in a low tone. "But you want us to do this right, don't you?"

"He loved me," came the only reply. "You will see. The whole world will see. He did. He loved me."

Alison felt a sharp pain sear her heart. She felt so sorry for the ghost, and for the woman it had once been, because Alison knew firsthand what it was like to crave —and not find—love. She prayed that what they were about to uncover would bring the ghost the peace that had eluded it for so long.

Kate handed them each a pair of white cotton gloves. Then the small group gathered round, eyes expectant, as Jeremy lifted the mud-encrusted lid from the box. Inside lay a dried and withered rose, with a companion carnation.

"Of course," Alison whispered. "What else would she put with the memoirs?"

Jeremy removed the flowers and laid them gently on the table. Next there was a small envelope. "This looks like the one that was in the book," he commented.

"What are you talking about?"

Jeremy gave her an apologetic look. "I'll tell you later." He carefully unfolded the envelope and peered inside. "That's what I thought," he said, showing her a lock of hair. "Odds-on, that used to grow on Byron's head."

"Byron?" Hawthorne interjected. "You talking *the* Byron, as in *Lord* Byron?"

Jeremy nodded. "That's right, old boy. You don't know it, but you're looking at history in the making."

Alison cringed, wishing Jeremy would be more discreet about their find. Her dislike of Hawthorne had turned to distrust as well.

"And now we come to the mother lode," Jeremy said in a hushed voice. Gently, he lifted a sheaf of papers about three inches thick out of the box and laid it on the table. "There they are, Caro," he said. "What story will they tell?"

> *Remember thee: remember thee!*
> *Till Lethe quench life's burning streams*
> *Remorse and shame shall cling to thee*
> *And haunt thee like a feverish dream.*
> *Remember thee! Ay, doubt it not,*
> *Thy husband too shall think of thee,*

By neither shalt thou be forgot,
Thou false to him, thou fiend to me!
                              —Lord Byron

The whole stabbing incident became the talk of London, & even poor Caro realized she had gone too far. As for me, I found myself pitying her, rather than hating her. I realized suddenly how mentally unstable she was, & I felt a certain regret for the part I played in amplifying her weakness. It was out of this pity that I began writing to her again, & this time I did not, at least at first, balance every kind letter with a hateful one as I had done at Lady Oxford's urging, for I had learned the potency of that strategy in undermining Caroline's sanity, & I saw no need at the moment to continue the practice.

When we first resumed correspondence, I was delighted that Caroline seemed calmer than I had ever known her to be. I wrote Lady Melbourne that "C. had been a perfect lake, a mirror of quiet," & that I was answering her letters. I did not wish to see her, however, for I feared that seeing her would start the whole dreadful affair over again. My relative peace concerning Caro was short-lived, however. She paid a visit one day while I was out, & my poor old valet Fletcher, over whom Caroline has always held easy sway, allowed her into my apartments in the Albany. He watched her circle the room, examining whatever lay about with careless abandon. Discovering a copy of Vathek which had been sent me by Murray, she had the audacity to inscribe it—"Remember me." . . . Till Lethe quench life!

I wanted no more of Caroline, well behaved or not. I found comfort in the attentions of Augusta, & filled the gap left in my romantic affairs by the exit of Lady Oxford in a brief affair with the wife of an old friend, Lady Frances Webster. She was simple & innocent, very pretty, & I couldn't resist the temptation to seduce her to test that *appearance of chastity which she portrayed. It was a routine seduction, very successful & satisfying, but not long lived. Rumours of the lady's chastity, incidentally, were proven false—*

⌒ Chapter 22 ⌒

Night had come early with the rattle of thunder and a heavy downpour of rain on the slate roof. The lights flickered after a particularly violent slash of lightning, then went out altogether. "That's why Lady Julia always kept a reserve of candles," Mrs. Beasley commented knowingly and hurried out of the library.

"We'll have to remember that," Alison told the two young servants, whom she had only just learned were twins—Mrs. Beasley's grandchildren—which explained how she had managed to hire more help so easily for a place reputed to be haunted. "In case our guests get plunged into darkness."

"Humph!" Hawthorne snorted. "You won't have any guests if that . . . that ghost keeps showing up."

"We're hoping that after tonight, she'll have no need to stay," Alison said softly, giving a wink to Jeremy, who sat on the edge of the sofa. She knew he was eager to examine the memoirs, but he'd told her it was her show, and he was respecting her desire to include the poor ghost in the discovery.

But the ghost of Lady Caroline, after making a half-hearted effort to rematerialize in the library, had disappeared. Jeremy had laid the contents of the box on the table, but when the ghost did not show, they decided to give it some time. They waited for over an hour. Mrs. Beasley and the young servants lit the candles, which spread a warm and cheery glow around the library, enhancing the gentle flickering of the fire in the hearth.

"I give up," Alison said at last, as eager as Jeremy to see what they'd found. "Let's take a look."

Would the ghostly Caroline's claim be proved with these papers? God, she hoped so, for as fond as she had become of her ethereal housemate, she was ready to send it along to the next world and get on with the resurrection of Dewhurst Manor.

The memoirs were tied in two bundles, each held together with a shred of ribbon that had faded to a splotchy rust color. Alison and Jeremy put on their gloves, and each took a parcel and sat opposite one another on the two side chairs next to the fireplace. Hawthorne, who had continued his visits to the liquor cabinet, was now slightly inebriated, and he sat, listing a little to the left, in the corner of the sofa. The three servants were lined like soldiers behind the back of the couch.

"Read it out loud," Jeremy said to Alison, who had the top bundle on her lap. "Just enough to see if Caroline's been telling us the truth about her lover."

Alison began making her way through the old-fashioned writing, pausing here and there, stumbling over the strange sounding wording. "Wow!" she exclaimed when she'd made her way through the first few pages. "No wonder he was a best-selling author. This stuff's pretty lurid."

"It was a pretty lurid age," Jeremy replied. "But I think we may have discovered more than we bargained for."

"What do you mean?"

"Read that last paragraph again."

" 'Confusion remains the cornerstone of my Infamy, and my longing its Perpetrator,' " Alison read. " 'I have longed to make peace with the Fair Sex, but in Truth, the Fair Sex has always confounded me. Women have worshipped at my very feet, (except my sweet Mother, who hated them) and yet I have never been able to truly love any woman. Although I have known many intimately and taken pleasure in their arms, I find myself afterwards regarding them with the same horror as I did May Gray, that monstrous Composer of the Dance of Longing and Confusion. What my mother began, May Gray concluded.' "

"Stop right there."

"What's the matter?" Alison could see a deep furrow between his brow.

"Listen to this." He began reading from a page in his stack.

" 'Confusion remains the cornerstone of my Infamy, and my longing its Perpetrator. I have longed to make peace with the Fair Sex, but in Truth, the Fair Sex has always confounded me. Women have worshipped at my very feet, (except my sweet Mother, who hated them) and yet I have never been able to truly love any woman.' " Jeremy paused, then continued with emphasis: " 'Except Lady Caroline Lamb.' "

He looked up, frowning. "The rest is the same as what you read."

" 'Except Lady Caroline Lamb,' " Alison whispered, dumbstruck. "You don't suppose . . . ?"

Jeremy thumbed through the pages, taking great care not to bend the brittle papers. "Go to the page that starts with, 'I wish in these memoirs to sort out my life. . . .' "

Alison cleared her throat, her heart pounding. Could it be that Caro had created two versions of the memoirs?

" '. . . And therefore, I must exact the full Truth of these matters from the darkest depths of my soul,' " Alison read, picking up the sentence Jeremy had started. " 'Ah, but what is the Truth when it comes to Caroline? How difficult, painful even, it is to describe what took place during that spurious affair, even from the distance of my Italian courtyard and of many years.' "

"Stop. Here it says 'glorious affair.' "

"Sounds like she wrote her own version of what 'appened," Mrs. Beasley commented.

"It certainly does," Jeremy murmured. "Can you believe it?"

"Of course I can believe it," Alison said, her heart suddenly heavy. "That poor woman was so in love with Byron, she would have done anything to convince herself and others that he loved her in return. Ashley Stone told me that neither Caroline nor Byron could tell the difference between the truth and a lie. My guess is that she wrote this lie, but believed every word of it."

"You're probably right," Jeremy agreed. "But then she forgot to get rid of the original version. The whole thing is so bizarre, I wonder if either of these is authentic at all, or if she made both of them up."

"I don't know," Alison said, stretching, "but the whole thing has given me a headache. I can't read any more it's so dark in here and this writing is so hard to read."

"It's half past seven, ma'am," Mrs. Beasley said. "Should we finish th' supper we were puttin' together when the ghost started all its screamin'?"

"Yes. That would be a good idea. Can you cook by candlelight? Is the stove electric?"

"There is an old woodstove we can use to finish up with. Most of the meal was already boiled."

The servants left the room. "Boiled," Alison said, laughing, "is *not* civilized. But tonight I'll eat whatever she puts in front of me. I'm famished now that I think about it. We didn't stop for lunch in London."

Hawthorne suddenly toppled over on his side and snored loudly.

"I guess we don't have to worry about him tonight." Jeremy laughed.

"How will we get him back to his room?"

"Leave him here," Jeremy said, standing and placing the memoirs back on the table. "He's harmless."

"I suppose." Alison laid her stack next to the one Jeremy had put on the table.

"Just think of it," Jeremy said, staring at the papers. "Not one set of memoirs, but two! I can't wait to see what the experts think. I wonder if Byron actually wrote either of them."

"Time will tell." Alison smiled, and when Jeremy took her in his arms, she didn't resist.

"It hasn't taken much time for me to tell one thing," he murmured, kissing her forehead.

"What's that?" she asked, feeling her pulse rate soar.

"That when I'm around you, anything can happen."

"Now what do you mean by that?"

Jeremy didn't reply. At least not verbally. But his kiss said everything she needed to know.

"You'd do anything to get your bed back, wouldn't you?" Alison teased as Jeremy slid beneath the covers next to her in the large bed in the master suite. They had shared their light supper which, even though it was mostly boiled, had been delicious. But food had not been premier on the minds of either of them.

"I'd do anything to get *you* in bed with me," he corrected her with a lazy smile as he pulled her into his arms. Jeremy felt his entire body catch fire as the silken softness of her breasts nestled against his chest. She was becoming an addiction to him. He knew she was dangerous, that she could undermine the entire structure of his life, and yet, he couldn't do without her. She haunted his every waking thought and continued to seduce him in his dreams. Oh, God, he wished he didn't want her so. He *would* do anything to get her in his bed, and that terrified him.

But at the moment, she was here, and he had only now to fulfill his fantasies. He tasted her lips, ever sweet and sensual, and delighted in the way she kissed him in return, nipping him playfully until the play grew more serious. He wanted their pleasure to last, so he pulled away to slow things down. He lay her against the lace-covered pillows and rested his head on one elbow, feasting his eyes upon her firm, young body. "You are so beautiful," he whispered, stroking her cheek and caressing the edge of her jaw. He continued his exploration, running his hand down her throat, not stopping until he reached the crest of her breast. He heard her sharp intake of breath as he stroked the soft skin there until her nipples stood erect, inviting his kiss.

Leaning over her, he kissed first one and then the other, his passion flaming higher with each taste of her body. He groaned as he felt her nails trace a pattern on the skin of his back. She moved her hips against him, and brought him closer, entwining one leg over his body. Her head moved from side to side, her eyes were closed, a smile played on her full lips, and he knew she was finding the same satisfaction as he.

He was in awe of her, even as his touch traveled to the secret private places he longed to know much, much better. She was so free, so natural, as a lover. Never had a woman pleasured him so sensually while at the same time completely relaxing into her own rhythm of delight. His feelings for her swelled in his own breast, as if she would consume his very soul. "Alison," he whispered. "I want you."

Unable to restrain himself any longer, he found their union, and as she became one with him, he knew he had found home. It was his last conscious thought before the exquisite sensations she aroused in his body joined forces with the essence of his soul, sending his spirit whirling into midnight darkness illuminated by brilliant bursts of life and love.

Some time later, he regained his senses. "Alison?" he called her name softly. She was curled against him, but her quick reply let him know she wasn't sleeping.

"Yes?"

"Are you . . . did you . . . ?"

She raised her head and kissed him with a short laugh. "Did I what?"

"Don't make me say it."

She laughed again, and nudged him playfully. "Okay. So, yeah, it was good for me too." She paused, then added, "It's nice that you care about that."

"I care about that, and everything else that happens to you." He heard her sigh deeply. "What's wrong?" he asked.

"Absolutely nothing. It's just that, well, I've never had anybody that seemed to care much about me, or anything that happened to me. It's a new experience."

"I'm sure there have been lots of people who have cared about you. I can't imagine anyone not falling instantly under your spell."

She laughed again, but now it was an empty, hollow sound. "They fall under the spell of my money."

He lay silent in the darkness for a long moment. "Is that what you think about me?"

It was her turn to remain silent. Then, "I don't know what to think about you."

Jeremy didn't know what to think about him either. Before, when he'd made love to a woman, he'd really only been having sex, he realized with sudden insight. With Alison, everything was different. Was he in love with her? God forbid the thought. And yet . . . he could not deny that his feelings of tenderness, his urge to protect and comfort her, to keep her safe from all the Drew Hawthornes and screeching ghosts in the world had nothing at all to do with sex. He'd said earlier that he would do anything to get her into his bed, and that was true, as far as it went. Now, he realized, he would do anything to make her his.

For life.

But before he could do that, he had to convince her that it wasn't her money that held him spellbound. That wouldn't be an easy task, he thought, considering her previous experience with men. He could only imagine the men who must have eyed her, not with love but rather with greed in their hearts. How many times had she been hurt?

He wanted to hold her and tell her he loved her, for he knew beyond a doubt that he did, but how many men had done just that, men who didn't mean it, men who likely had torn her self-esteem to shreds and left her crushed? Instead, he pulled her gently into the curve of his body, and they lay like two spoons in a drawer. "You'll have to decide for yourself about me, Alison. We can start by being friends if you want. One thing you will find is that I am a good listener. It sounds to me like you might need someone to talk to."

He held her closely, and suddenly he felt the slight convulsion of her sobs as she began to cry. As they lay together on the snow-white linen, he learned that for all her wealth, Alison Cunningham was a pauper when riches were measured in love instead of gold. He heard the aching loneliness behind her words, the self-doubt, the anger, the fear. He also heard her bitter determination to prove to the world she was intelligent, responsible, capable of managing her own life, that she didn't need a man—not her father, not Drew Hawthorne and his entire firm full of lawyers, not Jeremy Ryder—to tell her what to do.

Jeremy knew that loving Alison Cunningham, and convincing her of that love, would be harder than anything he'd attempted in his entire life.

The hardest part would be giving her the time and space to prove those things, not to him, or Hawthorne, or anyone else, but to herself. Because only then would she have room in her heart for the love she craved but continued to deny herself. Only when she loved herself would she be able to let herself love another.

Jeremy was a patient man. He would wait. Even though he wanted her by his side from now through eternity, he knew he must wait and let her deal with the world on her own terms. What would happen after that, he wasn't certain. But he was willing to take the risk.

She had asked him to leave. He would honor her request, although his heart felt as if it had been torn from his chest at the thought.

He held her and listened until the tears had all run dry, and she fell into a deep sleep. And then, he carefully got out of bed, kissed her forehead softly, and whispered, "I love you, Alison Cunningham. And I'm counting on you."

She never heard him, or the drone of the engine of his car, or the sound of the gravel against his tires as he drove away from Dewhurst Manor.

> *This rose to calm my brother's cares,*
> *A message from the Bulbul bears:*
> *It says to-night he will prolong*
> *For Selim's ear his sweetest song; . .*
> *Oh, Selim dear! oh more than dearest!*
> *Say, is it me thou hat'st or fearest?*
> *Come, lay thy head upon my breast,*
> *And I will kiss thee into rest, . . .*
> *I knew our sire at times was stern,*
> *But this from thee had yet to learn:*
> *Too well I know he loves thee not;*
> *But is Zuleika's love forgot?*
>   —from "The Bride of Abydos" by
>   Lord Byron

In spite of the attentions of Caroline, Augusta & Lady Frances, I grew morose in this high summer of eighteen & thirteen. I took to drinking a great deal, & added purgatives & stomach medications to my diet. I became weak in Body & in Spirit. Augusta was my only refuge—Augusta, my sister, whom I loved in ways reserved for mistress or wife. I, descendant of the Wicked Lord Byron, saw our kinship as no obstacle. Others saw it as the ultimate Sin. Augusta, I believe, never understood the Wickedness of our deed, for she knew not that what she did with me was against all moral & civil Law.

From the depths of my dark mood, I found I was not content with having committed the act of incest, I was driven by some inner demon to divulge that Sin to Society. I loathed their self-righteous moral Hypocrisy, & I delighted in the thought of sending many a non-virtuous Lady into a swoon at the idea. Irrationally, I began with Lady Melbourne, who would have defended me to the death for the minor transgression of seduction, for it was acceptable, even expected, in Society. But would she be able to make that leap from acceptable Sin to the most unacceptable? At the time, I never questioned my motive for wishing to expose my dire Depravity. Now, I believe I must have wished for my own downfall, as if I should be punished—as May Gray had always promised I would be —for my Wicked deeds.

I first read to Lady M. a poem I had written, "The Bride of Abydos," in which, until others urged me to make them cousins, the lovers Selim & Zuleika were brother & sister. With a sneer I implied to my Confidante that Selim & Zuleika were in residence at my house. Shrewd & worldly wise as was Lady M., at first she laughed, then an amazed look of comprehension widened her eyes. I was perversely pleased to see the shock & shame registered on her face.

Lady Caroline was next on my list, but with her, my wish was not only to shock, but to repulse. She continued to stalk me, which brought about the very opportunity I

*sought. She stole into my room at the Albany late one hot
summer night, & proceeded to plead with me as always to
take her away. She vowed again her undying love for me,
& swore she would never, ever release me, that she would
haunt me even after her death.*

*I held her & kissed her, depravedly relishing what was to
come. "Poor Caro," I whispered. "If everyone hates me,
you, I see will never change." Then I led her to my bedroom, where I undressed her. Ignoring the flame of desire
she was still able to ignite in me, I asked her if she wanted
to play a game, a secret Lover's game, & of course she was
eager as always. I told her to close her eyes & pretend she
was close to me, close enough to be my Sister. To pretend,
in fact, that she was my Sister. She objected, saying the
very thought was distasteful, which only heightened my anticipation. "You are my sister now," I told her as I took
her. "I love you now as I have loved my own Augusta."
Caroline wriggled away from me & sat up, looking at me
aghast. "You are sick," she told me. Then she gathered her
clothing, dressed quickly, & left without another word.*

*I had in times past attempted to turn her from me by
divulging tales of sexual deviance & even murder, but to no
avail. But this final diabolical behavior succeeded beyond
my wildest expectations. At the time, I laughed out loud.
She was gone, & I held some hope she would stay that
way. But my laughter fell silent, & foreboding crept in to
take its place. I had degraded Caroline, humiliated her in
a way no woman would stand for. The look of loathing in
her eyes held the promise of eventual Revenge. She would
surely tell. And when she did, my already questionable reputation would be dragged deeper into the mire. But then,
isn't that what I wanted? I was a sick & miserable man. I
both loved & hated Caroline. I had committed a grievous
sin against my own sister. And I was about to embark
upon a shameful sham of a marriage because I was in dire
need of money. I didn't deserve to live, much less enjoy the*

respectability of Society. By telling Caro of my sin, & in such a dastardly way, I sought my own destruction & had given Caroline the means—and the desire—to be my Destroyer.

⤏ *Chapter 23* ⤎

Maybe it was the jet lag. Maybe the cognac. Or the fact that Alison Cunningham had in effect cut off his nuts. Seeing a ghost hadn't helped matters. Whatever the cause, Drew Hawthorne awoke with a screaming headache.

"Damned bitch," he swore, holding his head as he eased himself into a sitting position on the sofa. He tried to remember what had been going on before he passed out. Oh, yeah, they were reading those memoirs. Must have been boring stuff to put him to sleep like that.

Memoirs. His fuzzy mind started to clear. They'd said they were Byron's memoirs. Lord Byron's. He stood up on unstable legs and looked around the library. The embers had almost turned to ash in the old stone fireplace, the dying fire barely illuminating the large room. Hawthorne wondered what they'd done with the memoirs. He shuffled toward the door, bumping unceremoniously into furniture on the way, but when he reached the portal, his finger touched a light switch. He flicked it, and several lamps in the room came on. "That's more like it," he mumbled, turning to survey the library. "Quite a place," he said to himself. "Or it would be if it wasn't haunted." He still found it difficult to believe the incredible scene which he had witnessed earlier. Then his eye came to rest upon the long library table and the dirty wooden box and the flowers and the two stacks of papers which lay there.

Drew Hawthorne's fat lips stretched into a broad smile. "Well, well," he murmured, rubbing his hands together. "Got a little careless, did we?" He hurried to the table and picked up the two bundles, then glanced furtively around him. There was no sign of Alison Cunningham. Or Jeremy Ryder. No servants. No one to know what he had on his mind.

"Alison, sweetheart," he said, "you may have just saved my hide. These have gotta be worth something. Maybe I can pull off that deal after all."

He laughed to himself as he returned to the door, flipped off the light, and scurried down the hallway to his room. No one even knew the memoirs existed. How could Alison claim they'd been stolen? he rationalized. He was taking no chances that he'd run into her again. He would leave tonight.

Securing the door to the room behind him, Hawthorne quickly threw his few clothes into the large briefcase, wondering if he remembered how to hot-wire a car. He really wouldn't be stealing the rental car. Alison *had* offered him the use of it, after all.

He felt a gust of cold air rush past him, but he dismissed it as being a draft in an old house. He turned to go, the memoirs under one arm, his bag in the other, when his mouth opened in a voiceless scream. His blood turned to ice water and his knees to jelly.

"My God—"

The specter stretched itself from floor to ceiling, an elongated figure of a woman, its face distorted with rage. It emitted an unholy cry as it swooped toward Hawthorne, knocking him to his knees. "You bastard!" it railed at him, its voice loud enough to rouse any dead that happened to be nearby. "You bastard!" It swirled

around him, spinning him with arms flailing, across the
hardwood floors, sending the papers flying. His skin
burned, like the thing had set him on fire. Drew Hawthorne screamed in terror, but the ghost was relentless.

"Those belong to me," it shrieked, letting loose of the
fat man and sending his porcine body rolling like a
bowling ball down the inner hallway and crashing into a
wall. "Those are mine!"

"Stop! Stop!" Hawthorne struggled to his feet. He
saw the angry creature drawing itself together to come
at him again, and he ran for the window. With a jerk, he
lifted the lever, then leapt into the night, praying that he
wasn't on the second floor and that the whatever-it-was
would not follow. He landed in a bramble bush, but he
was unaware until much later of the scrapes and bruises
he acquired in effecting his escape.

He only knew he had to run or die.

Alison sat up like a shot when the ghostly screams as-
sailed her peaceful slumber. "What the hell?" she said,
jumping from bed. "C'mon, Jeremy. Something's happened."

She was scrambling for her clothing that she'd shed
hurriedly when she and Jeremy had returned to her
room after supper when she became aware of the emptiness of the room. She turned.

"Jeremy?"

But he was gone. His clothing was gone. The presence
of him was gone.

Alison didn't utter a sound. Stunned, she sat back on
the bed, staring at the rumpled sheets. She knew she
wouldn't find that he'd gone to check out whatever the
noise was that continued unabated from somewhere
downstairs. She knew she wouldn't find him at the
breakfast table in the morning. He had left Dewhurst
Manor.

She closed her eyes and bit her lower lip.

Damn.

Another shriek commanded her attention. Caro was full of it now. Alison dressed as quickly as her heavy heart would allow. Her arms and legs felt like lead. "I'm coming, I'm coming," she said, brushing tears from her lashes. "Damnit, I said I'm coming!" she shouted into the hallway as she opened her door.

At first she thought the place was on fire. A bright light emanated from the corridor to the new wing. Was it Hawthorne's room? She hurried down the stairs and ran into Mrs. Beasley and the two young servants who were rushing in their nightclothes to see what was happening.

"Should I call the fire brigade, ma'am?" the old woman wanted to know.

But Alison didn't reply. She ran down the hallway and tried to open Hawthorne's door, but it was locked. "Let me in!" she cried. "Are you all right?"

The four terror-stricken people could hear the most unearthly moans and shrieks coming from behind the door. It sounded as if hell itself had opened its doors and threatened to swallow the entire house. Alison rattled the doorknob. "Caro! Is that you? Stop it this instant!"

Alison thought she heard a man's voice cry out, but she wasn't sure. "Call the police," she said to Kit.

And then, as suddenly as it began, the sound ceased. There was nothing but deathly silence behind the door.

"Do you suppose the ghost killed 'im?" Kate asked.

Alison opened her eyes wide, wondering if a ghost could actually commit murder. "I don't think so," she replied hopefully. "Mrs. Beasley, do you know where there is a key to this room?"

"Yes, ma'am. I'll go get it right away."

"And Kit, forget the police, unless we find him dead. They'd never believe us anyway."

Inside, the suite of rooms looked as if it had been

struck by a tornado. Pictures had been dashed off the walls, lamps were shattered, chairs were toppled, the rug was crushed into a corner, the bedding was stripped, everything was in shambles.

"That Hawthorne fellow must have pissed her off," Kit said crudely but accurately.

"Hawthorne, or Jeremy Ryder?" Alison replied bitterly.

"Ryder? Why would he throw Lady Caro into such a snit?"

Then Alison had a sickening thought. "The memoirs. Where are the memoirs?"

She raced to the library and flicked on the light, and with a glance, her worst fears were confirmed. "He took the memoirs," she murmured. "That bastard."

"You suppose they were in it together?" Kate asked, breathless, relishing the intrigue.

Alison's head jerked around, and she stared at the young woman, stunned. And then the dreadful truth hit her—she'd been set up. Somehow, Hawthorne and Jeremy had conspired to steal the memoirs. Probably while she was in London. She'd returned to find them waiting for her together. Oh, my God, she thought, her stomach turning as the depth of their complicity struck her. Hawthorne had only pretended to fall asleep. Jeremy had suggested they leave him in the library. The memoirs had been left in plain sight. It was so simple. And she'd never suspected a thing.

Jeremy must have been assigned to keep her "busy" while Hawthorne was doing his dirty work, Alison realized with rising nausea. How she had trusted him! He'd been so tender and caring. He'd said he wanted to be her friend. Not only had she had sex with him, she'd opened her heart to him as well, shed much-needed tears, let down her defenses, all the while feeling safe and protected in his arms.

Alison thought she was going to be sick.

Do you remember the first rose I gave you? The first rose you brought me is still in my possession. . . . Now God bless you—may you be very happy. I love and honour you from my heart . . . as a sister feels—as your . . . Augusta feels for you.
 —From Lady Caroline to Lord Byron
 upon his engagement

Society spoke of Augusta & I in hushed tones. The rumours flew! But no one knew the absolute truth except Caroline. The sin was too great for even the most debauched to believe. And when Medora was born, the child of our illicit union, no monster emerged to prove our sin, & perversely, I was somewhat disappointed.

I was listless & out of sorts, writing poorly, worrying about money, drinking excessively, more confused & depressed than ever before. To add to my confusion, the Princess of Parallelograms, Lady Annabella Milbankes, suddenly relented of the cold distance she had maintained between us since rejecting my proposal of marriage the year before. "It is my nature to feel long, deeply & secretly," she wrote to me. The woman was convinced that I had a noble soul & that she could be my Salvation. Although marriage to any woman was an abomination to me, to wed Annabella would solve a number of problems, or so it seemed at the time. I was beginning to regret having blackened Augusta's name & reputation, & my betrothal would go far in stopping the gossip I myself had orchestrated. Also, Caroline would be put off by both the marriage & the choice of bride. Finally, & most importantly, Miss Milbankes being quite wealthy, my financial woes would come to an end. These seemed a fair trade for my name.

☞ **Chapter 24** ☜

Alison slept no more that night. In fact, she could scarcely bring herself to get back into the bed she had shared with her treacherous lover. Her senses were numb, her soul dead. She had encountered conniving men, and women for that matter, who had preyed upon her emotions to get at her wealth. But she'd never been so crassly or coldly used.

It was a lesson she would never forget.

She thought about the memoirs and wondered what the ghost would do now. She wouldn't want to be Jeremy or Hawthorne, if Caro knew they had stolen them. And she felt sorry for the unsuspecting private collector who ended up with them. For Alison had no doubt that the ghost of Lady Caroline would never rest until it had exposed the truth to the world.

But what was the truth? Alison pondered. The little she'd read had revealed that Caroline had made two copies of the famous poet's memoirs, and had doctored one set to tell the story the way she wanted to hear it. Had Byron truly loved Caroline? Or had Caroline been so deluded and obsessed and desperate that she'd created a fantasy about her lover that eventually she came to believe to be the truth?

Is that what I did with Jeremy? she questioned herself

ruthlessly. Was I so desperate for love that I failed to see through him? God, what a little fool I am, she wept into the soft feather pillow. I'm a fool for going to seances and chasing ghosts and making bad investments and falling all over Jeremy Ryder. I wanted to prove to the world I can manage my life, but all I've done is screw it up.

As the first rays of dawn began to turn the morning to a lilac hue, Alison gave up trying to sleep. She put on a bathing suit and threw a towel over her shoulder. Maybe a swim would clear her mind, and she could decide what to do next. She padded down the stairs, shivering in the cool morning air. The house seemed empty . . . and large.

Huge.

And lonely.

Alison heard the clock chime five times as she passed the great hall. She turned down the corridor where the ghost apparently had cornered Drew Hawthorne, and the best Alison could guess was that Hawthorne had had to jump out of the window to escape. If he did indeed escape. The ghost was rather . . . omnipresent. Reaching the swinging doors that led into the pool area, Alison paused, thinking about what had transpired there between her and Jeremy. My God, how could something so good have turned out so bad?

Suddenly, she heard voices coming from the pool. They didn't sound at all ghostly. Rather, they sounded young. She pushed open the door and crept inside and watched, amazed, as Kit stood on the side of the pool with a stopwatch, calling out encouragement to his sister, Kate, who was doing the Australian crawl for all her might down the center lane.

"Go, go, Katie, you can do it! Faster! You've almost got it! There!"

Kate reached the far end of the pool, then grabbed the side and gasped for breath. "Did I make it?"

"By two seconds, on my watch. I'm telling you, Katie, you're going to make the team."

"Olympics, here we come!" the young athlete burst out in glee. Then she saw Alison standing at the pool's edge, and her euphoria turned to a look of horrified dismay. "Oh, no," she groaned. She launched herself up and over the edge and stood up quickly on the wet concrete. "I'm truly sorry, ma'am. I know we shouldn't be here. I didn't think it would harm anything, and it's too early for us to be on duty yet. I didn't know we'd wake you. . . ."

Alison gave the young people a quick, reassuring smile. "You didn't wake me. And I'm happy for you to practice here. I used to be a swimmer myself. I heard you talk about going to the Olympics. Is it true?"

Kate smiled in relief and shot a quick glance at her brother. "Someday if my slave driver here has his way, I think I have a chance to make the British women's team."

Alison recalled what Gina had told her about Lady Julia allowing the youngsters from the area to use the pool for practice, and suddenly it all made sense. Mrs. Beasley had been a loyal servant, and these two treasures were her grandchildren. "Are there others who need to be practicing right now?"

"Our whole swim team," said Kit. "Since Lady Julia died, we haven't had anyplace close by to practice. We have to go into London, to the school where our coach teaches. It's put Kate here very behind in her training. I . . . I know we shouldn't have come here without asking. We just didn't want to bother you after . . . after all that happened last night. We thought you'd probably be sleeping in this morning."

"You may use this pool anytime you need to," Alison said to their obvious delight. "Just don't swim alone. And your friends are welcome. In fact, we should set up a practice schedule." She paused, then added with a grin, "Who knows, maybe I'll even train with you, just for fun. Who's your coach?"

"Alistair Scott. He's the best in the U.K. Teaches at Harrow."

"I'd like to meet him sometime. But for now, I'm going to get in a few laps. You're welcome to stay if you'd like."

"Thank you, ma'am," Kate said, picking up her towel, "but we were just finishing. I need to get dressed and ready to start breakfast."

Another piece fell into place for Alison. "Start breakfast? Are you the one who has been creating such delicious meals around here?"

The girl nodded a little self-consciously. "Yes, ma'am. With Gran's help, of course. Kit cooks too. My father owns a pub nearby. We were brought up in his kitchen. He taught us all his tricks."

Alison heard the pride and love in her voice, and felt a brief pang of . . . not jealousy, exactly, but regret that she'd missed out on the kind of family these kids came from: a grandmother who interceded with her employer to gain a place for the young swimmers to practice, a father who'd included his children in his daily schedule. It was what a family should be, and at the moment, she would have given up her millions to be part of a family like that.

"I'd like to meet him sometime, too," she smiled and waved as they left the pool. Yes, and she'd like someday, somehow, to be that kind of parent, she thought, but the idea brought her back to the source of her present depression.

Jeremy Ryder.

She glanced at the bench where she had laid her towel the night Jeremy had so unexpectedly joined her in the pool, and her face grew warm when she saw his shirt and jeans dried in pancake shapes on the deck of the pool. Had Kit and Kate seen them? she wondered,

embarrassed. And what about her bikini? She'd never
bothered to come back for it. By now, it was probably
sucked up against one of the filters in the pool. She laid
her towel on the bench and dived into the water. Both
pieces, as she suspected, were lodged in one of the filter
intakes. She plucked them from near doom and swam to
the steps, got out of the water, and picked up the now
stiff shirt and pants and rolled the whole thing into a
bundle.

How did one do the laundry around here? she
thought, wondering how she would explain to Mrs.
Beasley about having Jeremy's clothes mixed in with her
own.

And then she remembered with a smile, she didn't
have to explain to Mrs. Beasley.

The shrill ringing of the phone awakened Jeremy from a
fitful, dream-haunted sleep. He groped for the receiver,
trying to clear his head. The sun was already over the
windowsill, and he realized he had overslept.

"Hello."

"Ryder, old chap! You've returned from the hinterlands!" The bright cheery voice of Malcomb McTighe
made Jeremy wince.

"Hatfield is hardly the hinterlands. What's up?"

"I've been working on those strands of hair you
found. I know you were hoping they'd turn out to be
from the fair head of Lady Caroline Lamb. Sorry, but
they're not."

Jeremy was disappointed. "Well, it was worth a shot,"
he replied, taking the cordless phone to the bathroom
and splashing water over his face while he talked. "I
thought since I found them in an old copy, a first edition
maybe, of *Childe Harold,* inscribed from Byron to Caroline, it was possibly her hair." He tried not to think
about the finding, then the losing, of the full lock of

hair, nor the conditions surrounding its return. He heard his friend's voice deliver the verdict.

"Well, it's not hers, but it *is* his."

"His? You mean Byron's?"

McTighe laughed. "Is that so surprising? I mean, in those days they used to cut off locks of hair right and left as a pledge of love. It would make sense that Byron sent a lock of his hair to Caroline, along with the book. That's why I went ahead and checked it out."

Jeremy dried his face. "Yes, it does make sense. Except that on the envelope, somebody, Caroline, I assume, had written 'To Lord Chillingcote.' Why would she be giving him a lock of Byron's hair? You'd think she'd want to keep that, of all things."

"Who knows? Caroline was crazy, you know." Another laugh. "You've heard about the lock of hair she sent Byron, I suppose?"

"You mean the one from her . . ."

"Oh, yes. She clipped that little curling lock, and sent it to Byron and asked that he return her one in kind. I don't think he ever did though. She was outrageous, that woman," he finished with a hearty guffaw. "Any man, even Byron, would have had his hands full with her. Well, I'll let you get about your day. I have the hair samples here at the lab. Stop by, and I'll buy you lunch."

"It's I who will buy you lunch, my friend. Thanks for the sleuthing." Jeremy hung up the phone, considering what his friend had just said. Lady Caroline Lamb *had* been outrageous, and she apparently still was. He'd been trying for the past three days, since his return from Dewhurst Manor, to deal with all that he'd seen of the ghostly version of her.

With Caro's ghost, and her look-alike in the flesh, Alison Cunningham, Lady of Dewhurst.

He'd left Dewhurst Manor with mixed emotions. A part of him conceded that he had fallen in love with Alison and was reluctant to leave her, even if she had expressly told him she wanted to work out her life on her own. She was inexperienced and, Jeremy felt, vulnerable to the likes of Drew Hawthorne. But how could he help her if she didn't want any help? He probably should have left her a note, or at least phoned to explain his hasty departure, but he was afraid if he had any contact, even by long distance, with her, just the sound of her voice would undo his resolve to give her the time she needed to work things out for herself. He imagined she would be hurt and then angry to find he had left without a word. But in the long run, he believed it was for the best.

For both of them.

Once he was out of the sight and sound and taste and feel and smell of Alison Cunningham, however, he had begun to recover his senses. When he returned to the familiar comfort of his townhouse on Hill Street in London's Mayfair, with the city street noises reminding him that *this* was home, not that gloomy ghost-ridden manor, the other part of him, the one that insisted he remain detached from any committed relationship, took over.

The whole incident at Dewhurst Manor was entirely too bizarre for his taste. Although the memoirs were intriguing, and if she asked, he would do his best to put Alison in touch with the experts she'd need to prove their authenticity, he would do so, he'd decided, from a distance. As enchanted as he was with her, Alison was too unsettled in her own life, carried too much unresolved baggage for him. He had a planned and orderly life and lived it in a proper, civilized manner. He had his thriving business to occupy his days, his gentleman's club two nights a week, and a respectably full social calendar. He'd been dazzled by Alison's beauty and passion, but he'd get over it.

Or so he'd thought.

But for three days, he'd found to his distress that she

was with him in his mind's eye every waking hour, and she slept with him in his dreams. He couldn't quit thinking of her, or of the uncanny ghostly encounters he'd witnessed at Dewhurst Manor.

It was all totally irrational . . . the harpsichord concert at midnight that had led him to kiss Alison in the first place, the vision of Alison-Cunningham-who-wasn't-Alison-Cunningham dressed in the provocative, low-cut gown that had so aroused him he had been unable to think of anything at dinner but kissing her again. The spectral push into the pool which had landed him quite literally in Alison's arms where he'd experienced the most incredible lovemaking of his life.

Lovemaking.

It was different from sex.

And he knew that with Alison, he had made love for the first time.

Jeremy sat down heavily on the bed, visualizing what Alison would look like there, dreamy eyed and fresh from sleep. He felt his body respond to the ever-present desire he seemed to carry in his soul for her. What was wrong with him? Had he gone mad?

But he knew he had not. He'd only fallen in love.

And he didn't have a clue what to do about it.

> *After all, we must end in marriage; & I can conceive nothing more delightful than such a state in the country, reading the county newspaper, etc., & kissing one's wife's maid.*
>
> —Lord Byron

I expected the worst from Caroline when she heard of my engagement to her cousin Annabella. Even though I had heard little from her & not seen her since she left my bed—not desiring to be my "sister"—I knew she loved me still, & I fully believed I would be subjected to another of her famous tantrums. But such was not the case, although

*I did blame one unfortunate incident on her which I later
learned was not her fault—The very day after Annabella &
I had announced our engagement, the* Morning Chronicle
*printed an article denying this was the case. This smacked
very much of a Caroline prank, for no one else had the
motive or the malignity to be so petty. Later, I found I had
falsely accused her. But Caroline was so . . . Carolinish
& was famous for such activities. But this time, Caro was
the very opposite. She wrote, congratulating me warmly &
wishing us every good future. I must admit, my Vanity was
somewhat piqued that she should take it all in such good
nature, even sending a wedding present! Where was the
wrath & fire of a woman scorned?! Where was the Caro
who had told John Murray that she would kill herself
should I decide to marry? I rather liked that Caro better.*

*Our marriage took place on 2 January 1815, & it was a
Catastrophe from the outset. I could not find it in my heart
to attempt to love the dowdy-looking woman, & I admit I
was a beast as the wedding day approached. We were married & left for our "treacle-moon"—there being no
"honey" in our relationship—at Halnaby Hall in Yorkshire
without further ado, & we argued the entire trip. Although
I managed to consummate the marriage on the sofa before
dinner, it was my wish that my bride not join me in bed
after, for I have always had an aversion to actually sleeping
with women. However, I gave the new Lady B. her choice,
& she climbed into bed by my side. It was bitterly cold
outside, but a roaring fire in the room kept us warm as we
lay on the four-poster which was surrounded by a curtain
of crimson. Annabella had openly stated that she wanted
to reform me, so it seemed reasonable that first she must
know the depravity & wickedness of which I was capable. I
taught her that night, & to my astonishment found she
actually enjoyed the lascivious acts which I perpetrated
upon her. It was only in the morning, when I awoke thinking the red drape was a curtain of flame & cried out, "My*

God, I think I am in Hell!" that she seemed put off by my behavior.

Scarcely one year later, my wife appeared to have forgotten the pleasure she had obviously taken from the sexual arts we practiced on our wedding night & used the charge of sodomy—indicted me privately to her lawyers only—to achieve a separation from me. But Annabella, if ever you lay eyes upon this Memoir, remember—remember, & acknowledge your pleasure, for to Lie is to Sin, & no one would ever call you a Sinner!

Chapter 25

The day was prettier than it deserved to be, considering Alison's mood. She sat on a grassy knoll by the river, tossing pebbles into the water. Overhead, the late May sun burned warm and golden, but deep within, her heart was as cold and frozen as if it were the dead of winter.

Would the loneliness never end?

Everything, and everybody, was gone.

Alison had searched everywhere for the missing memoirs, to no avail. The ghost had been lying low, if indeed it was still at Dewhurst. Drew Hawthorne seemed to have disappeared off the face of the planet . . . likely with the memoirs in hand and Caro in hot pursuit.

There had been no sign of Jeremy Ryder.

Not that she had expected there to be. He and Hawthorne were likely by now divvying up the profits from the sale of the priceless papers, laughing up their sleeves at her naiveté.

It was more than naiveté they should be laughing at, she thought bitterly.

Stupidité would be more descriptive.

This whole thing had been an exercise in stupidity. She'd come here seeking famous missing papers and a chance to prove to herself she was capable of handling her own affairs. Instead, she'd lost the papers and made a complete fool of herself. She'd bought a huge, run-down property with which she had no idea what to do. She'd wasted almost a million dollars. But worst of all, she'd let down her guard and irretrievably lost her heart to a man who had only used her for his own gain.

Alison didn't know whether to cry or be sick. There seemed to be no other options. She couldn't go to the police and file charges against Jeremy and Hawthorne. She had no proof that the memoirs even existed. How could she charge them with theft? As for the hijacking of her heart, there seemed little she could do about that either, except hope that time would somehow heal the ugly wound without leaving too much scar tissue.

Lost in these and other equally morose thoughts, Alison didn't hear the footsteps approaching her until she was overcome by the wet kisses of a large retriever.

"Hey, hold on, boy," she cried, trying to avoid the eager animal's affectionate greeting. Recognizing the dog as Ashley T. Stone's pet, she looked up and saw the owner silhouetted against the brilliant blue sky, his wispy hair standing away from his head, reminding her of one of those silly troll dolls.

"Are we interruptin' you?" he asked.

"I need interrupting," Alison replied, sniffing away her tears.

"What's th' matter, missy?"

"Just about everything."

"Mind if I sit a spell?" He didn't wait for her reply, but took a seat on a large stone nearby. "Been havin' lots of fireworks up at Dewhurst I see."

"Fireworks?"

"Caroline-type fireworks. Somethin' big must've gone on for what all I saw th' other night. Kept me up most o'th' night."

Alison turned to stare at him. "You saw fireworks? For real, I mean like shooting stars and things?"

"Not real fireworks, although when she gets worked up, the show's almost as good." The ancient one wheezed a laugh through crooked yellow teeth. "What happened?"

Alison, glad to have a confidante, even if it was just the old poacher, smiled. "I'm not totally sure," she explained. "I think I told you, I came here because Caroline needed help in bringing Byron's memoirs to light. You said you thought they'd been burned, but Mr. Stone, I have seen them with my own eyes. Those memoirs were buried at the mouth of the old tunnel. Probably some of the . . . uh . . . fireworks you saw was her rather explosive demonstration when she finally remembered where she put them." Alison laughed at the ghost's antics, and she realized she missed the apparition almost as much as Jeremy.

"Ah, but what was the rest of it about?"

"Some . . . of my erstwhile guests decided they would steal the memoirs once they'd been found. Guess it made her really mad. Neither of the thieves have been seen since." Alison paused. "Well, at least Mr. Hawthorne hasn't shown up back in the States yet. I haven't looked for Mr. Ryder."

"Ryder. He seemed like a nice enough fellow."

"You knew him?"

"Just met him by chance. Come t' think on it, though, he was out snoopin' around the property of Dewhurst. I mistook him for a pheasant in the brush." He laughed. "Good thing I'm a bad shot."

"Maybe not."

"Hey, there, young lady. Now why're y' so gloomy? They were just papers. Y' didna have 'em when y' came here. So what if y' don't have 'em now?"

"It's just that . . . well, I trusted Mr. Ryder, and I shouldn't have, and I feel like a dummy. And now the

ghost is gone, too, and nothing is the same. I'm thinking
of putting Dewhurst back on the market."

"I hope y' put a high price on it again, so's nobody'll
buy it and I can go on enjoyin' my huntin'. But you're
wrong if you think the ghost isn't still there. She's very
much there."

Alison jerked her head up sharply. "How do you
know?"

"I can see the glow from here," he said, gesturing in
the direction of Dewhurst. "My guess is that there must
still be unfinished business over there. She's still wantin'
those memoirs maybe."

"I guess she'll have to go on wanting them," Alison
replied glumly. "There's no telling where they are by
now."

> *Three great men were ruined in eighteen & fifteen*
> *—Brummell, myself & Napoleon.*
> —Lord Byron

That year saw the decimation of my health, my mar-
riage, & my finances. I slept fitfully if at all, my dagger &
pistol by my bed—& a vial of laudanum. I longed for the
freedom that I'd so carelessly tossed away—to think I had
married in part to spite Caroline! I would have been better
off to have eloped with her instead. It is possible I could
have been happy with her, happier than with the dour,
humorless, pious, dog-faced Annabella. I began to dwell
upon Caroline again—in fantasy only, a safer practice
than to resume our affair—& I was delighted when I re-
ceived news that she & her dear William were about to
separate. I never liked the Lamb. But Lady M. squelched
the rumor at once, assuring me that the pair were together
at Brocket Hall & to all appearance like two turtle doves.
Her declaration sent me into an even darker despondency,
which I took out upon Lady B. who was by this time large
with our child.

Other events happened which turned my already Infernal existence into pure Hell. My sick attraction to Caroline led me to write ill-conceived letters to friends, asking of her, & the stories that were related to me only whetted my avaricious appetite for what I could never have. Caro, ever the exhibitionist, continued to outdo herself as she & William traveled from England through the Low Countries to Paris. If I had been present, I would have despised the scenes she excelled in provoking, but from a distance & with an overwrought imagination, every antic, every detail of Caroline's behavior I received through my friends' correspondence titillated me until I thought I might go mad. She became, without ever knowing it, as effective a tormentor from afar as she had ever been when stalking my apartments in London.

Two weeks had passed, and summer was in full dress green, even in the heart of London. Jeremy had managed to keep his vow to stay away from Dewhurst Manor, although thoughts of Alison were never far from the surface of his consciousness. It was for the best, he kept telling himself. She didn't want him interfering in her life, and he had his own life to lead.

But his life, at least, had lost some of its lustre. He seemed to be going about it almost robotically. The enthusiasm for his business had faded, and he found himself snapping at his employees over minor mistakes he once would have ignored. He had turned, he realized grumpily, into something of a misanthrope.

Sunlight streamed through crystal clear windows and onto the snowy linen tablecloth where his housekeeper had laid out a hearty Sunday morning breakfast, with a copy of the *Times* alongside, according to the tradition the two had lived by since Mrs. Fleming had come to work for Jeremy almost five years before. It had seemed like an extravagance at the time to Jeremy, who was then not yet thirty years old. But his lifestyle was fast paced and time intensive, his income was substantial and growing, and his personal tastes required a more orderly household than he was able to maintain by himself. Some men would have looked around for a wife, but Jeremy preferred the detached relationship between employer and employee. It kept things more orderly in every respect.

The bells of the old Wren Church in Piccadilly chimed ten o'clock when Jeremy sat down at the only setting laid at the table. He placed his napkin in his lap and as the matronly Mrs. Fleming poured his first cup of coffee, Jeremy allowed his gaze to survey all that he had brought together, treasures that comprised a most satisfactory lifestyle. The dining table was from the late seventeenth century. He ate from Limoges china. An original Arras tapestry hung upon the wall. The silver service was from the royal court of Russia. Handmade linen napkins were perfectly folded on the inlaid Georgian china cabinet. The Persian carpet had been a gift from his Uncle Clive.

Everything gleamed in orderly profusion, the only way Mrs. Fleming would have it, of course.

It was the gentleman's townhouse Jeremy had dreamed of since he was a boy. Why did it now seem so cheerless?

He sighed and opened the paper, glancing cursorily at the front page, then turning by habit to the classified advertising, a place where he often came across listings of valuable antiques for sale at favorable prices. His eyes scanned the antiques section, then he turned to the estates that were for sale. Lady Julia was not the exception in owning an estate she could not afford to keep up, and such landowners often began to liquidate heirlooms in an effort to pay the heating bills on huge and drafty mansions.

His gaze traveled down the long list, when it caught suddenly on an ad placed by Gina Useppi.

Dewhurst Manor was back on the market.

"What . . . ?" he said aloud, startling Mrs. Fleming, who almost dropped the platter of eggs she was serving.

"Beg pardon, sir?"

"Nothing, it's nothing," Jeremy muttered, scowling. What had happened to all of Alison's big plans for Dewhurst? He recalled how her face had lit up when she talked about renovating the old manor house into a resort, with—how had she put it?—laughing, happy people there. What about her comment that she had found a home at Dewhurst? A sickening thought enveloped him. Drew Hawthorne must have worn her down. Jeremy had never told her about the phone conversation he'd overheard between Hawthorne and somebody named Fromme, who obviously had their own plans for her money.

He had to warn her. He had to keep her from being manipulated by the very attorneys who were supposed to be looking out for her best interests. They might be doing just that, he acknowledged, but intuitively he knew better. He slammed his napkin back onto the table and stood up.

"Sorry, Mrs. Fleming," he apologized for his peculiar behavior. "Something's just come up. I'm going to be leaving for the day. Don't bother about dinner. I'll eat at the club."

"Very good, sir."

Jeremy appreciated Mrs. Fleming's taciturn nature. The woman seemed not to have a nosy bone in her body.

Going into his study, he opened a small drawer in his desk and drew out the envelope that contained the strands of Byron's hair that he'd retrieved from Malcomb McTighe. At one time, he might have been tempted to keep them, since nobody knew he had them. But since his sojourn at Dewhurst, it had never crossed his mind to keep something, even as small as a piece of hair, that belonged in that incredible library. He wondered fleetingly if Alison's servants had been able to put it back together in some kind of reasonable order. He still did not know what to make of the destruction in that room.

The return of a few pieces of hair, the relating of a warning he should have given before now, and nothing else. Those were his reasons, his *only* reasons, for traveling to Dewhurst Manor. But as the Porsche sped northward on the A1, Jeremy felt his entire body infused with new energy. As every mile clicked by on the speedometer, he felt the lethargy and listlessness of the past two weeks lift from his shoulders, replaced by an eagerness he would like to deny but couldn't: a pressing desire to see Alison again.

He left the motorway and drove along the outskirts of Hatfield, where he spotted an old woman sitting beside a cart of flowers along the roadside. He recalled the strange but appreciative look on Alison's face the night he'd given her the two flowers he'd filched from the vase in the great hall. Money and flowers had smoothed Gina's ruffled feathers when she found out he'd used her to get at the antiques at Dewhurst. Alison didn't need money, but maybe flowers might assuage the wrath he expected when he knocked at her door.

He stopped and turned off the ignition, then went to the flower cart and carefully selected the reddest rose he could find. And the pinkest carnation.

Lady Byron could never cohabit with her noble husband again. He has given her cause for separation which can never be revealed; but the honour due to the female sex forbids all further intercourse for ever.

—Opinion of Dr. Lushington
on the Question of Divorce

I traveled with my millstone Annabella to Six Mile Bottom to visit my beloved Augusta. Caroline was safely in Paris, although unexpectedly, she had begun to write again, imploring me to come there & implying she would flee with me to Switzerland where we could abide together in peace & contentment outside the prying eyes of all those in Society. Apparently she had found my Sin forgivable after all. . . .

But I could not bring myself to travel to the city that had so recently been the stronghold of the great Napoleon. Rather I would find some comfort in familiar arms, & dandle my "Godchild" Medora upon my knee, all the while showing the pious Lady B. what a loving relationship could be like. I worked both of the women well, I believe. One evening, for the sport of it, I lay upon the sofa & required each to take turns kissing me. It gave me pleasure to see the outrage on Annabella's face when I reported the results of the test—that Augusta's kiss was far more satisfying.

My life continued just this side of Hell. I was deeply in debt, & returned one morning from a night of gaming at my club to find to my horror that a bailiff had slept overnight at my house so as not to miss me. Utterly debauched, I proceeded to lose myself in dissipation. Caroline was ever in my thoughts, although I was glad enough to be spared her company which would have only made matters worse.

My sole legitimate child, whom I named Augusta Ada, was born on a cold December night, with Annabella upstairs wailing whilst below I drowned my despair in wine & bashed the bottles to shards. I later sought out Susan Boyce, a dull but willing actress with whom I had a liaison during the time of Annabella's encroaching accouchement.

I hated my wife & passed up no opportunity to prove it, even threatening to bring Susan to live with us just after Ada's birth. It should have come as no surprise to me then, when in a fit of melancholy I ordered Annabella to leave

the house & take the child with her. That she did, & chose
never to return.

Annabella was accustomed to my attacks of misan-
thropy, & I fully expected her to return as if nothing unto-
ward had taken place. Indeed, her first correspondence
was pleasant enough, & gave no hint of the vicious plot
which she was setting against me.

It was an ungodly alliance that moved against me from
this time. It started with Annabella, urged on by her righ-
teous parents. I may have hated my wife, but that is not a
strong enough word to describe my feelings against her
mother & father. Lushington & Romilly, despicable law-
yers hired by the Milbankes, connived to spread a cam-
paign of whispers about what abominations I had forced
upon Annabella, without saying exactly what it was I had
done, & this, on top of my reputation for indulging in
incest, proved my final undoing. Once I was the Darling of
London Society, but now, they poised like vultures to de-
vour me. Annabella & her vile copartners were not alone
in plotting my downfall. Innocently, my own beloved Au-
gusta was lured into Annabella's plot, . . . & not so inno-
cently, so was Caroline.

⌐ *Chapter 26* ⌐

Alison sat at the harpsichord in the first receiving room, running her fingers idly over the keyboard, picking out tunes that she vaguely remembered from her days of private music lessons as a child. She was lonelier than she'd ever been in her life. If it hadn't been for Kit and Kate and their rowdy but delightful young friends on the swimming team who had come to practice almost every day in the pool at Dewhurst, Alison thought she might lose her mind.

She hated that she was putting the old place up for sale again, but her earlier enthusiasm for creating a resort had flown with the disappearance of the ghost . . . and Jeremy Ryder. The house was just a big, old empty mansion, no different really from the ones in Boston and Palm Beach. She had no need for such a huge place, no desire any longer to pursue it as a business. In one respect, Drew Hawthorne had been right. It had been a mistake to invest in the derelict property.

But she'd put it on the market at a more reasonable price, and would sell the antiquities separately. The total would add up to a nice profit on her investment, even though guilt nagged at her about separating the house and the furnishings that made it the special place it was. The sale of the books in the library bothered her especially.

She and Kit and Kate had tried to restore order to the havoc wreaked by the ghost, but only the shelves reorganized by Jeremy had made any sense. Books were still stacked along the walls, and Alison had no heart for the task any longer.

Alison had no heart for much of anything. Her life was empty, a frivolous waste, it seemed. She had wanted to control her destiny, but what good was that if her destiny was to live as a rich but lonely brat? She'd wanted her own way, and she'd got it.

If only she knew what to do with it.

The doorbell rang, and she heard Mrs. Beasley open the door. Who would be calling on a Sunday? Alison wondered. Gina would have phoned ahead if she were showing the property. Curious, she scooted off the bench and went to the doorway to the great hall. Her heart lurched when she saw the tall, handsome man who had come to call . . . lurched, and then almost came to a standstill.

Mrs. Beasley was professionally and loyally making her excuses why she could not let him come in, but Alison interrupted her.

"It's okay, Mrs. Beasley," she said, her words catching in her throat. "Please, come in, Mr. Ryder."

The servant left the two of them standing in the cathedral-like ambience of the ancient hall. Alison's pulse raced as emotions swirled through her.

Relief that he'd returned.

Desire. Doubt.

And then anger.

"Where the hell are the damned memoirs?" she demanded immediately. He stared at her, his face carefully void of expression.

"How would I know?"

She laughed derisively. "Because you and that creep

Hawthorne both disappeared like two thieves in the night, along with the memoirs. It wasn't hard to figure out that the pair of you set me up," she added cynically. Her blood was boiling. This man had colossal nerve showing up on her doorstep, with those insipid flowers, for God's sake, like she was some simple little lamebrain who didn't guess what he'd done.

"Set you up?" He said it as if it came as a great surprise.

"Don't play games with me, Jeremy," Alison sneered. "I am capable of putting two and two together."

Suddenly she saw rage on his face, an anger restrained only by a personality that was a master of self-control. "And coming up with five, it would seem," he replied in a voice of steel. "Five, or seven, or ten, or whatever suits you, no matter what the truth is."

"I didn't invite you here, Jeremy," Alison bit back, "and I won't stand by while you insult me."

"I find your accusations *highly* insulting. Why do you think you should have the corner on rudeness?"

Alison wanted to throw something at him. Where was the ghost when she needed it? "You're insufferable. You may think it rude to accuse you of stealing, but from what I know of you, honesty isn't your long suit. You used false pretenses to gain access to Dewhurst in the first place, according to what Gina told me. You were looking all over for the memoirs, and even though I can't prove it, I'd bet money that if you'd found them on your own, you'd have sold them in a heartbeat to some private collector. Too bad you had to share the profits with Hawthorne," she added nastily.

Her breath was coming in sharp, short gasps, and she felt lightheaded. A pain shot through her somewhere near her heart. It hurt to verbalize the agonizing conclusions she had come to after Jeremy had left their shared bed, but she'd been unable to convince herself they weren't true.

Jeremy threw the flowers on the floor and took Alison roughly by the shoulders. "It's about time somebody stood up to your tantrums," he snarled. "You are dead wrong about all this, and you're as big a fool as Hawthorne said if you believe that I had anything to do with the disappearance of those memoirs."

Alison cringed beneath the strength of his hands. She could feel his fury in his powerful clinch. "Then why did you leave?" she said, stifling a sob. "When you and Hawthorne and the memoirs all disappeared conveniently at the same time, what else would I think?"

"I left," Jeremy replied, relaxing his grasp on her shoulders, "because . . . ," he paused as if groping for words, then finished in a voice so low it was barely audible, "I love you."

Alison raised her head abruptly, not believing she'd heard him right. "You what?" She could see in his eyes that he was fighting some kind of inner war that she didn't understand.

"I left you," he said at last, "because you told me you wanted to work out your life on your own, that you resented everyone trying to tell you what to do. I'm the type of man who would likely try to do exactly that, I'm afraid," he said, calmer now. "I've had to fend for myself since I was fourteen, and I'm used to taking charge of things. It seemed to me you had a good idea about turning Dewhurst Manor into a resort, and I thought it best if I gave you that freedom."

Alison guessed she'd heard him wrong. She thought he'd said he loved her, but he didn't repeat that, so she must have misheard him. But what he *had* said went straight to her heart. She would never have dreamed that his leaving her had been a gift, but she saw now that it had been meant that way, and it was a gift she could deeply appreciate. She felt her eyes grow moist. "I mis-understood, obviously," she whispered over a tight throat. "But why did you leave the way you did, in the middle of the night, after . . ."

Jeremy pulled her against him and encircled her with his strong arms. He placed a gentle kiss on the top of her head. "That part isn't so easy to explain," he replied after a moment. She felt his heart beating heavily in his chest, and her own heart echoed its rhythm. The man was an enigma to her, but she yearned for him to offer an explanation that would take away the pain she'd lived with for the past two weeks—the pain of his rejection.

"I'm listening, for a change," she murmured, encouraging him. She felt his short, silent laugh.

"Like I said, I've been on my own since I was a teenager, and I've preferred to keep my distance from others, especially women. I've always believed that . . . permanent relationships usually foul up otherwise perfectly civilized lives. And I've been pretty successful at maintaining my independence—that is, until you came along."

Hope sprang in Alison's heart, but she remained silent, not daring to believe he might actually have said what she thought she'd heard a moment before.

"I left you in that manner because I was afraid," he said at last. "I was afraid if I waited until the light of day, I might never leave. I knew that night, when I held you in my arms, and you talked to me and cried and let me know the real you, that I had fallen in love with you. And yet, because I loved you, I wanted you to have things on your own terms. You needed desperately to do this business with Dewhurst without my interference. And in order to give you that freedom, I knew that I had to leave." He paused, then added, "Maybe it also had something to do with my all-important independence being threatened. Either way, I opted for the coward's way out."

Alison raised her head and looked into his dark eyes, and she saw that he spoke the truth. She saw that it was a difficult truth for him, and she realized that she'd been so self-absorbed that she'd never considered *his* wants or needs. Or anyone else's for that matter. She was exactly what Nicki had called her, she admitted to herself —a brat.

But he loved her anyway.

He loved her!

"Oh, Jeremy," she murmured, a joy unlike anything she'd ever known filling her very being. "How can I ever tell you how sorry I am for accusing you like that?"

Relief etched his handsome features. "Then you're not going to throw me out after all?" he grinned.

"How could I throw out the only man who has ever loved me?"

Jeremy tipped her chin upward with his forefinger. "You do believe me? That it is *you* that I love, not your money?"

Alison swallowed. It was a question that had before posed an insurmountable obstacle between herself and the chance of happiness with a man. One that she may have aggravated unnecessarily in her paranoia and anger against her father.

She considered the two weeks she had just spent, alone and miserable. She had wanted her way. She'd got it. No one had told her what to do. She'd been left to make every choice and decision for herself.

And it was the worst two weeks she'd ever spent in her life.

"I believe you, Jeremy," she said, smiling at him. She splayed her fingers across his broad chest. "I believe everything. And I love you so much."

She ran her hands up his chest and behind his head, and closed her eyes as Jeremy's lips touched hers. Suddenly her world tilted as she let go of the pain and grief and loneliness, the self-doubt, defiance, and anger. Her demons left like ghosts in the night whose spectral energy finally had been exhausted.

> *Go to her whatever the cause, little or great—it must be made up. If you knew what odious reports people circulate when men part from their wives, you would act in this instance prudently . . . I have disbelieved all the reports till now; but I trust they are of far less consequence than some pretend.*
> —Lady Caroline to Lord Byron

I have said of women that they are a sex I could not love. Indeed, I never loved any of them, although I made the show of doing so. It was a lie, & I paid the price, but I am justified in my conviction about the sex, for those I had tried to Love the most—Caroline, Augusta, even Annabella, are those who eventually conspired to destroy me.

The General of the armée fatale was Annabella, upon whom I admit having wrought grievous wrongs, the premiere being that I married her at all. The first recruit in her war of hatred was Augusta—Gus, dear Gus, whose nature was so sanguine & trusting, was unsuspecting when she placed in the hands of the General secrets of our liaison & the truth of Medora's parentage, not knowing that she was actually giving witness against me.

Caroline was an easier recruit. Although in the beginning she pretended to warn me against myself, I believe these warnings were a mere camouflage for the Treachery that followed. I, like many others, believed Caro to be mildly insane & did not deem her capable of thinking clearly enough to pose a threat to me in any way in the nasty affair cooked up by my Princess of Parallelograms. I never realized—until it was far too late—the depth of her wrath or the lucidity of the calculated Revenge she plotted against me.

The fire licked at the logs in the hearth, keeping the chill at bay in the master suite of Dewhurst Manor. Outside, a slow summer rain dripped from the eaves. Alison had given the servants the afternoon off, and she and Jeremy were at last alone.

They lay together naked between crisp linen sheets, their desire satiated, at least for the moment. Alison snuggled closer to Jeremy, allowing herself to get used to the idea that she could be loved by a man. Truly loved. He had spent the afternoon showing her just how much, both in word and deed. She felt languid, fluid, deliciously happy.

"Jeremy?"

"Hmmm?" he replied, nuzzling her ear.

"Should I keep Dewhurst after all?"

"Don't ask me."

"I have put it back up for sale."

"I know. It was the ad in the *Times* that brought me here."

Alison rolled against him, her breasts pressed against his chest. "And all along I thought it was me," she teased.

Jeremy ran his fingers down the silken skin of her back and along the curve of her hips. "Actually, it was Hawthorne," he grinned wickedly.

"Don't bring that bastard into our bed," she cautioned, kissing his neck.

"I came here to warn you that he and somebody named Fromme had plans for your money, once they got you to agree to put the insurance money into the trust."

Alison sat up abruptly. "How do you know about all that stuff?"

Jeremy pulled her back into his arms and held her tightly, and his embrace reassured her that his intentions were good. "Hawthorne told me about the trust. He didn't have much respect for client privilege. The rest I learned when I accidentally picked up the phone while he was talking to Fromme."

Alison sighed. "Too bad he ended up with the memoirs. Since I can't prove they existed, it would be hard for me to file theft charges against him, but I've alerted Benjamin Pierce that I will do whatever it takes, including suing their entire firm, to get him out as the director of the trust." She laughed. "Imagine me telling the formidable Benjamin Pierce what to do."

Jeremy kissed her again. "You still don't realize your own strength, do you?"

"Nobody has ever made me feel very strong. Only incompetent and stubborn and spoiled."

"I'd call you intelligent and capable and assertive."

No one had ever, ever talked to her that way. At the moment, it meant more than even the words *I love you.* Alison's heart was so filled with love and gratitude she thought it would burst. She shifted in his embrace so that her face was above his. "That kind of talk will get you everywhere, mister," she grinned, lowering her lips to his. "Everywhere," she whispered, as she moved to show him just how an intelligent, capable, and assertive woman makes love to a man.

$\backsim$ Chapter 27 $\backsim$

When fortunes changed—and love fled far,
And hatred's shafts flew thick and fast,
Thou were the solitary star
Which rose and set not to the last.
        —Lord Byron, "Stanzas to Augusta"

*C*aroline turned Traitor in the end, betraying the Love she swore she would carry for me into the Hereafter. She went to Annabella loaded with all the ammunition that Dreadful General needed to secure a separation & to destroy what was left of my life. Lady Byron completed her campaign against me as successfully as Wellington conquered Napoleon. I admitted defeat in April, 1816, signed an agreement to our separation, & prepared to go into exile. I was hated by everyone in the canting Beau Monde. Those who had rushed to adore me when I was Childe Harold would not now speak to me on the street. Young women would raise their skirts so as not to sully them if they were forced to pass where I had trod. There was but one, a sycophant named Claire, who offered me solace during those terrible days. In time I came to hate her as much as I now hated Annabella & Caroline. But I will deal with Claire & the offspring of that ill-fated liaison, Allegra, later in these miserable memoirs.

I was rendered penniless & had no choice but to leave England & live in exile for the rest of my days. I left Mayfair just before dawn, mounting my carriage which had been stocked with two bottles of champagne, a cake, & some Jewish pastries for my travels. My good Friend John Cam accompanied me to the quay, & Dr. Polidori. In Dover, a bevy of chambermaids pressed close to get a glimpse of the despicable Lord Byron, some of them strikingly familiar, as if I had been seated across from them at some long distant dinner party in Whitehall.

I see as I review these notes that I have turned churlish. In writing down my memories of what took place in those dreadful years, I sought to resolve my confusion over the whole mad affair with Caroline Lamb, but I believe there can be no resolution. She writes to me still, as if she had nothing to do with my downfall. It is possible that she does not remember. I understand she has taken to heavy drinking & is quite wasted now. She tells me she will Love me through all Eternity, & that if I do not reply, she threatens to haunt me after she is gone. I do not reply. It is only her madness talking, & at any rate, it does not matter any more. Nothing matters. Vanity, vanity, all is vanity. . . .

"I'm famished," Alison said, much, much later as she and Jeremy awoke, entwined in each other's arms as naturally as if they'd been lovers always. Jeremy's hard-fought battle to stay uninvolved was lost, but he no longer cared. There wasn't anything he could do about it now. He *was* involved, and hoped he always would be involved with the copper-haired, golden-eyed sprite with whom he had just spent the most enchanted afternoon of his life.

"Do you suppose Mrs. Beasley would get upset if we broke into her kitchen and raided the refrigerator?" he asked, his own appetite whetted by the energy he'd expended in making love for several hours. "Fleming gets rather agitated by that sort of thing, unless I've asked her to leave me a snack."

"Who's Fleming?"

"My housekeeper." He was amused at the look on Alison's face.

"You have a housekeeper?"

"Who do you think you're looking at? A pauper?"

She laughed and sat up. "More like a prince, I'd say." She cocked an eyebrow. "The question is, Prince Charming or Prince Machiavelli?"

"Maybe a little of both," he laughed, taking in the sight of her slender and yet exquisitely feminine body. It was as if he could not get enough of her. He felt desire flooding to his groin. How long could he endure this powerful, if delicious, passion? He was almost relieved when she got out of bed before he had time to take her back into his arms and ravish her again.

"I'll make you a deal," she said, pulling the bedcover around her modestly. "Let me take the first shower, then I'll make us some supper. That way, I'll bear the brunt of Mrs. Beasley's wrath if she discovers we've invaded her domain."

"Separate showers?" he said, genuinely disappointed, but understanding. For all of her natural passion, he sensed Alison was inexperienced as far as the opposite sex was concerned. He even found her demure attitude toward standing naked before him captivating. He grinned and nodded. "Go ahead. I'll just lie here and dream of my other lover." Alison threw a pillow at him, and they both laughed, remembering the shower of feathers Caro once had rained on him.

But he did have another lover of sorts, he thought after Alison had left the room. Caro. He was certain it had been the ghost of Lady Caroline who somehow had infiltrated his dreams and aroused his passion. But she hadn't shown up since he'd left Dewhurst. Perhaps because dreams of Alison had taken her place.

Where was the ghost now? he wondered. Had it given up after Hawthorne made off with the memoirs? Or had it, he considered with a grin, followed the despicable little man across the ocean? He rather hoped it would stalk Hawthorne until he gave up what was rightfully hers.

Jeremy sincerely regretted the loss of the memoirs, just as the tantalizing puzzle was beginning to come together. The real-life Caroline Lamb must have been either as crazy as they said she was, or so in love and obsessed with Byron that she deluded herself, thinking that by revising his memoirs, she could convince the world that he truly had loved her. That poor, pathetic creature, he thought.

He wondered about Lord Byron himself. Had Byron loved her? Or only led her to believe he loved her? Had he strung her along? Or had he been the innocent victim of an unstable and revengeful Caroline, as most Byron biographers portrayed her? From all that he'd read, Byron's favorite adjective to describe himself—wicked—seemed apropos, and having witnessed the fury of the ghost firsthand, Jeremy could believe that a man with an ego as huge as Byron's could easily and wickedly have played mind games with Lady Caroline Lamb. He sighed.

Too bad the world would never know.

Alison emerged from the steaming bathroom clad in sweats and a heavy pair of socks. She was beautiful even in the baggy sportswear. "I'm going to have a time getting used to this weather," she laughed.

"Then I take it you're staying in England?" Jeremy dared not push her one way or the other, but he was hoping she'd decided to continue with her original plans. She sat down beside him on the bed.

"Yes. I think I'm staying."

He kissed her gently and ran his hand beneath the sweatshirt, discovering that she wore nothing under it.

"I'm glad. Now get out of here before you start something I can't stop."

Half an hour later, Jeremy made his way to the back of Dewhurst Manor and found Alison just finishing the plates she was preparing.

"Not bad, do you think?" she asked. "I found some cold roast beef and fresh baked bread and a potato salad. Even came across some dill pickles."

"Are you craving dill pickles already?" Jeremy laughed and came to stand behind Alison, pulling her gently into his arms, the oddest thought occurring to him.

"What are you talking about?"

"Aren't women who are pregnant always wanting something like that?"

"What makes you think I'm pregnant?"

"I . . . well, we didn't use anything to prevent that condition this afternoon. In fact, we haven't ever, unless you are on the pill or something."

He felt her back straighten slightly. "No. I'm not on the pill. I . . . haven't had the need to be," she said, her voice suddenly uncertain.

"Would it be so bad if you *were* pregnant?" Jeremy murmured, suddenly and surprisingly intrigued with the idea.

Alison turned to face him. "Only if you weren't there to be the daddy." She looked up at him, her face no longer childlike, her eyes searching his anxiously.

"Where else would I be?" He smiled and kissed her. "Alison, I know we haven't known each other long, and this isn't exactly the most romantic place to talk about this, but I—"

His words were interrupted by the sound of a loud, keening wail that came from somewhere in the front of the house.

"Caro!" Jeremy said, grabbing Alison's hand and heading toward the great hall.

* * *

As they entered the immense and gloomy room, Alison saw the figure clearly. The ghost of Lady Caroline was seated at the desk by the window, head bent over what it was reading. It was crying softly now, and holding itself as it occasionally rocked back and forth.

Spread out in front of it were the memoirs.

"So it was you who took them!" Alison exclaimed, stunned.

"They are mine, are they not?" the ghost replied, not looking up.

"Yes," Alison replied softly, feeling a great sense of relief that Hawthorne had not, after all, ended up with the papers. She squeezed Jeremy's hand. "Of course."

Alison sank into a nearby armchair, watching in fascination as the ghost made its way through the papers Caroline had copied so long ago. Jeremy took a seat by Alison's side on the arm of the chair and put his hand on her shoulder. For a long while, they watched in silence as the ghostly figure read, first from one stack, and then the other. It emitted an occasional sob, several short exclamations, and every so often, a loud wail. At last it turned and looked at Alison with large, sad eyes. "There are two copies."

"Yes, we know," Alison replied, surprised that the ghost seemed not to have remembered making a second copy.

"And they are not the same."

Alison nodded again, but didn't reply.

"Which is the real one, the one he wrote?" it cried pitifully.

"Don't you know?" Alison asked.

The ghost returned to its examination. After an extended silence, it heaved a spectral sigh. "Yes. I know. I know which one he wrote, for it describes me wrongfully and cruelly," it cried, its tone changing from grief to anger. "I never thought he really felt that way about me, but treated me as he did because he was under the influence of my mother-in-law, who hated me, and Lady Oxford, whom I once called friend but later traitor."

It wrung its tiny hands as it continued. "But I see now it wasn't as I thought. He played a cruel and cunning game with me. What I took for love was to him only a conquest." Another wail pierced the evening shadows.

A few moments later, the phantom regained its poise and spoke in a quiet voice. "And yet, that is not quite the truth either, for here it says in part that he *did* love me." Now it gave a gentle laugh. "No wonder I went mad," it said ruefully, "what with his pledges of love on one hand and his dastardly schemes against me on the other. In my madness, I must have made the second copy, to portray to the world the way I thought he truly felt. But now, reading them both, I . . . I cannot tell." Its voice faltered. "I cannot tell which is the truth anymore."

Alison remembered Ashley T. Stone's comment that neither Byron nor Caroline could tell the difference between the truth and a lie. It would seem that was still the case, at least where the ghost was concerned.

"He loved me," it moaned at last. "That is the truth of it. I know he loved me. But he would not . . . he could not *let* himself love me."

"Jeremy has friends in London who will read the truth in the memoirs," Alison said gently. "We'll bring your story to the world."

The ghost whirled around in its chair and looked at Alison as if she had said some terrible thing. "No! These memoirs prove nothing," it insisted. "It was all a dream, a terrible nightmare. And it was a lie. He was a lie. *We* were a lie." The shade hung its head and buried its face in its hands, sobbing wildly. "I have waited all these years," it cried in anguish, "for nothing. I was a fool for Byron then, and I have been a fool for him ever since. He never loved me! It says so here. I thought he loved me, but he never did!"

The ghost's contradiction was totally irrational, but Alison was beginning to understand that irrationality must have been part of Caroline's original makeup. Her heart swelled with pity for the poor creature, but she was at a loss as to how to help it.

"What do you want us to do?" she asked in a hushed voice.

But the ghost did not reply. Instead, an icy wind shrieked through the great hall, whipping tapestries and curtains violently. The ghost itself shifted its shape into a ball of fiery light which spun about the desk like a gyroscope, scattering the sheets of paper that it had been reading only moments before. Around and around it swirled, encircling the memoirs, gathering them into its energy.

Alison's eyes grew large, and she clung to Jeremy's arm as she watched, horrified, as the ghost shone brighter and brighter as its energy coalesced into a ball of flame.

"My God!" Jeremy murmured. "She's going to set the place on fire."

They both jumped up, confounded at the incredible scene that was playing out before their eyes. "Call the fire department!" Alison cried out, just before an ear-splitting explosion rocked the room. Jeremy pulled her to the floor and covered her with his own body. She heard the sound of shattering glass and felt the air being sucked out of the room in a sharp draft. Jeremy jumped up and pulled her to her feet, and together they ran to the window. The ball of flame had shot high overhead. It reached an apex and began to fall, when suddenly, it burst into thousands of fiery shards, sparkling down upon the quiet countryside in an incredible fireworks display.

"Holy moly!" Kit yelled, running into the house, with Kate at his heels. "Did you see that?"

Alison was quaking all over. "Yes," she managed, as she felt Jeremy's arm slip around her waist, giving her much-needed support. "Yes, we saw it all." Then she turned and smiled sadly up at Jeremy.

"I just hope Ashley T. Stone was watching."

> *But I have lived, and have not lived in vain:*
> *My mind may lose its force, my blood its fire,*
> *And my frame perish even in conquering pain:*
> *But there is that within me which shall tire*
> *Torture and Time, and breathe when I expire;*
> *Something unearthly, which they deem not of,*
> *Like the remembered tone of a mute lyre,*
> *Shall on their softened spirits sink, and move*
> *In hearts all rocky now the lute remorse of Love.*
> —Lady Caroline Lamb

The drone of lawn-mowing equipment, sounding like so many giant locusts feeding on the grounds of Dewhurst Manor, awakened Alison one morning almost three months after she and Jeremy had witnessed Caro's grand finale. At least, they surmised it was her finale, for the ghost had not been seen nor heard from since. She'd taken the memoirs with her, for not one shred of paper had been found anywhere in the house or the surrounding countryside. Jeremy believed the papers had burned in the intense heat of the energy the ghost had generated.

"It's just as well," Alison had told him, knowing he was deeply distressed at the loss. "Like Ashley Stone told me, we didn't have them when we came here, so what does it matter that we don't have them now?"

"But the historical and literary value they might have had," he had protested, but stopped when he caught Alison's warning look.

"Not to mention their value in pounds sterling," she'd commented dryly. "No, Caro found what she needed to put an end to her torment. Hopefully, she's gone on now to a much-needed rest."

Jeremy had at last agreed, having learned from the change in Alison's life the value of letting go of old anger and pain. He'd learned he could let go of other things as well, such as the profit he would have made if he'd sold the letter he'd found in the antique desk, the one in which Caroline Lamb had indicated that the Byron memoirs were at Dewhurst. It had value as an historical artifact, but bringing it to the public eye might cause some to accuse Alison of planting it to create publicity for her new enterprise. The memoirs no longer existed, so it didn't matter anyway, and Jeremy tucked the little letter away safely in his own private collection.

"What a glorious day!" Alison said, stretching as she gazed out into the courtyard below their bedroom, where roses bloomed in profusion in the cool late summer morning. The fountain had been cleaned and repaired and now trickled merrily in the center of the flagstone patio. From beyond the surrounding wall, she could smell the sweetness of the newly-mown lawn that stretched from the wall down to the river. The sky was a rosy pink without a hint of a cloud.

Jeremy came up behind her and encircled her with his arms. "What else would you expect for our wedding day?"

Alison turned and nestled against him. "You take a chance when you plan a garden party in England, you know."

"I also know that everything you have touched lately seems to have come out a success." He kissed the top of her head, and Alison reveled in both the warmth of his touch and the praise that he never failed to give her.

It still seemed a miracle to her that her life could have changed so much, and so wonderfully, in the short time since her parents had died, and she felt it a shame that it took their tragedy to set her on the right track. She wished her father could have known Jeremy. Even though he wasn't from one of "the" families they had always thought she would marry into, Alison believed Charles Cunningham would have approved of Jeremy, with all his business savvy and experience. She didn't know if her mother would have felt the same, for all those phony society reasons, but she guessed that if Elizabeth Cunningham had been the recipient of one of Jeremy's sexy smiles just once, she would have fallen under his spell.

Alison had thought about her parents a lot over the summer. She'd also thought about the ghost. She was not a religious person, not sure about heaven and hell. But was there, she wondered frequently, a spirit world where her parents now dwelt and from which they could see what was happening in her life? Did Mary, the medium in the Florida spiritualist community, actually talk to the spirits who resided on "the other side"? Again, she had no idea, but having encountered the ghost of Lady Caroline made her believe that it was possible.

The idea gave her great comfort, for she knew that if it were so, then both her father and mother knew that she had loved them in spite of her contrary behavior. She had come to the conclusion as well that, in their own way, they had loved her, too.

She wasn't sure what her father would think of her investment strategy concerning Dewhurst Manor, however, since likely it was not going to show a strong monetary return any time soon. But Jeremy's love and steadfast emotional support had taught her there are more important aspects to life than money.

Things like self-esteem, and pride.

It had been Kate who had given her the answer to her dilemma about what to do with Dewhurst Manor. Sticking to her rigid practice schedule in the pool at Dewhurst, Kate had made the British women's swim team. When Alison saw the pride on the young swimmer's face, she knew immediately what she wanted to do with the old manor house.

With Jeremy's help, and the support of the new director of her trust, her father's old friend Benjamin Pierce,

Alison had used some of the insurance money to endow a foundation that would support a sports training center at Dewhurst Manor, a world-class facility for young athletes, particularly in tennis, swimming, and track-and-field events. Already some of the grounds were being prepared for the special equipment that would be needed. Although she had not sought publicity, Alison Cunningham, the new Lady of Dewhurst, had been the talk of the London press for her philanthropic generosity.

Today, she would likely make the papers again, this time in the society section, which would carry a story about her wedding to Jeremy Ryder.

"The groom's not supposed to see the bride on their wedding day, not until the ceremony," she said, walking her fingers up his chest to his lips, where she playfully received his kisses on her fingertips.

"That would be a little difficult, since the groom has been sleeping with the bride all night."

Alison giggled. "I suppose you have a point. At any rate, we should get downstairs. Our guests will be up and about soon, and I want to make sure everything is in order for this afternoon."

Jeremy watched Alison leave the room, thinking of how she had changed over the course of the summer. No longer was she the angry, sometimes clumsy, defiant, defensive girl he had met so unexpectedly at the front door of Dewhurst late in the spring. She was still stubborn, but no longer willful. She still got her way, but was no longer petulant about it. She was not afraid to ask for help, or to allow herself to receive it. In short, she had changed from an insecure, unhappy girl into a confident, loving woman.

But she wasn't the only one who had changed, he thought with a grin as he stepped into the shower. Who would have guessed three months ago that he, Jeremy

Ryder, the quintessential bachelor, would be getting ready to walk down the aisle? That he would be not only ready, but eager, to tie the knot?

He laughed, thinking of the day he'd taken Alison to meet Mrs. Fleming and had announced their engagement. It was the only time he had ever seen the woman lose her professional demeanor as her brows raised and her mouth dropped in pure astonishment. But she'd quickly recovered, and he had seen the look of sincere approval in her eyes.

Jeremy was somewhat astonished himself at the ease with which he had broken his most inviolate rule never to get seriously involved with a woman. But with Alison, he hadn't had a chance. Whether it had been Caro's ghost who started the whole thing by visiting him in those erotic dreams, or finding Alison, the living image of the ghost, in his arms shortly thereafter, he didn't know. But the spirit of Alison Cunningham somehow had infused his soul. It was as if she were a part of him now, a part that had been missing for all of his life.

A part that made him whole.

He could not imagine life without her. As he dressed, he thought about his mother, and how devastated she had been when his father had left them. Had she loved the man as Jeremy now loved Alison, almost to the point of distraction? If she had, he understood now why she had spent the rest of her short life going from one man to another, trying to fill the void by searching for someone to make her whole again.

Jeremy straightened his tie and ran a brush through his hair. Before leaving the sanctuary of the master suite, he glanced over his shoulder at the rumpled bedcovers and smiled, remembering the tender intimacy he had shared there with Alison and thinking of all the days to come. He knew he would never leave her, and he believed she would never leave him. He silently swore that if they had a family, their children would never suffer the pain each of them had experienced during their own childhoods.

Dewhurst Manor was alive again. Servants bustled to and fro settling wedding guests into the rooms in the rear wing that had lain in disuse for decades. Flowers arrived by the truckload, some ordered by Alison and Mrs. Beasley, who had taken on the wedding plans with gusto, others sent by well-wishers from around the world. Alison was particularly surprised and pleased by a huge, exquisite arrangement sent by Lord and Lady Brocket, who expressed their regrets at being unable to attend.

In the kitchen, Kate was supervising a small army of chefs who were preparing the wedding feast. She personally had baked and decorated the tall wedding cake that stood like a baroque tower on the table in the dining room.

Alison hurried down the stairs, excited as a child at Christmas. She found Mrs. Beasley in her small apartment, going over a list of last-minute preparations. "Did she get here?" Alison asked breathlessly.

"Miss Carmione? Yes, ma'am. Your driver picked her up early this morning. She's in the yellow suite, as you requested."

"Thanks. The place looks great, by the way. What's left to do?"

The older woman smiled up at her in a grandmotherly sort of way, and Alison was struck once again by the lovely sense of family she had been able to enjoy vicariously through Mrs. Beasley and her two grandchildren. "All you have to do, ma'am, is be happy. I'll handle the rest."

Alison wasn't sure what the British protocol was concerning the display of affection toward servants, but she didn't care. She might be the lady of the manor, but she was also unutterably grateful to this woman who had become more to her than a mere employee. "Thanks, Mrs. Beasley," she said, bending to hug the surprised servant. "You've made this day very special for me."

With a little lump of emotion stuck in her throat, Alison left the room and made her way up the back stairs, heading for the rooms she had decided should be called the yellow suite. Not only had the three-room chamber been decorated in shades of lovely pale yellow, accented with white and peach, but they also faced east, their tall windows admitting the early daylight in sunny, yellow rays. Alison had selected the decor for the suite herself, wanting to create a special place for special people to stay, special people like Nicki Carmione, who had arrived just in time to be her maid of honor.

She knew she ought to let Nicki sleep. She'd taken the overnight flight from Miami and would be tired, but she couldn't wait to see her best friend. "Nicki!" she called, pounding on the door. "Nicki! Wake up!" Without thinking, she opened the door, barging in on two sleepy people curled up in the large bed. Nicki sat up and rubbed her eyes.

"It's the brat," she said, smiling. Her bedmate rolled over and groaned something unintelligible in a very masculine voice.

"Oh, God. I'm sorry." Alison flushed bright red. She hadn't known Nicki was bringing Andreas. "Sorry," she said again, backing out the door. But Nicki jumped out of bed and ran to Alison.

"Never mind him. He won't wake up for hours." With a girlish giggle, she dragged Alison into the small sitting room, where the two friends embraced for a long time. "Now, you've got to tell me everything. Absolutely everything," Nicki demanded. "I can't believe how this whole thing turned out. Is the ghost here? Did you find Byron's memoirs? C'mon. Tell all."

Alison rang for coffee and Danish pastries to be sent up to the room, and for the next hour, the two friends caught up with each other's lives. Nicki had a surprise of her own as she flashed her new engagement ring in Alison's face. When her tall Greek fiancé finally made a groggy appearance, Alison gave him a sisterly kiss and left the pair to put themselves together in time for the late afternoon ceremonies.

Back in the great hall, she found Jeremy deep in conversation with Benjamin Pierce. There had been a time, not long ago, when seeing these two particular men in a close dialogue would have raised her defenses, thinking they were conspiring to control her life. But no more. At her own insistence, Benjamin was once again serving as director of the Cunningham trust. He had been appalled at Drew Hawthorne's inept handling of one of the firm's oldest and most valued clients, and he'd apologized profusely and sincerely to Alison for having assigned Hawthorne to her affairs.

Jeremy had remained carefully neutral about Alison's decisions concerning Dewhurst Manor. He'd offered advice only when asked, and then reluctantly.

For her part, Alison had made a conscious effort to grow up. As her self-confidence grew, bolstered greatly by both Jeremy and Benjamin, she had been able to let go of the paranoia that had been eating at her since her parents' deaths. Today, seeing Jeremy with her father's old friend, brought a bittersweet smile to her face.

Benjamin had come to give away the bride.

"Well, you two," she said, taking the hand of each, "what mischief are you cooking up now?"

Jeremy grinned at her. "Benjamin was just filling me in on Drew Hawthorne."

Alison made a face, then apologized. "I'm sorry," she said. "I realize he is your son-in-law."

"Was."

"Oh?"

Jeremy explained with a twinkle in his eye that Hawthorne had returned from his trip to England somewhat mentally unbalanced. "Seems he kept raving about having seen a ghost or something."

"England is full of ghosts, I understand," Alison replied demurely.

"Not only was he blabbering about this ghost, which he said had run him out of Dewhurst Manor, he also claimed some nonsense about finding the memoirs written by Lord Byron," Benjamin continued, shaking his head. "He has really gone off the deep end, and Cecelia just couldn't take any more. She's filed for divorce, and Hawthorne spends most of his days in therapy with his shrink." He squinted at Alison. "There's no ghost here at Dewhurst, is there?"

"Not anymore. Some people used to think the place was haunted, but we haven't seen any ghosts around lately, have we, Jeremy?"

Her husband-to-be shook his head in all seriousness. "Ghosts are just a childish notion," he said, repeating what Alison had told him once. Reflexively, Alison glanced around, half expecting Caro to flex her ectoplasmic muscle, but the great hall remained peaceful.

Other guests had begun to filter in, each with a hug for the bride and congratulations for the groom. Kate and her staff prepared an elegant buffet luncheon, but Alison could scarcely eat a bite as her anticipation grew for the afternoon's events.

"Excuse me," she said at last, giving Jeremy's hand a squeeze. "I'm going to lie down for a while." He gave her a loving kiss on the cheek.

"I'm going to pretend that our wedding day starts the moment you leave this room," he murmured. "I've moved my things to another room. I'll dress there, and leave the bride to herself. After all, it's bad luck for the groom to see the bride before the wedding, didn't you say?"

Removing his things to another room wasn't all Jeremy had done in her absence, Alison discovered. She opened the door to their suite to find a huge bouquet of roses and carnations standing in a tall vase near the window. She smiled and plucked the card from its holder. It read, "For Alison, the most rare and beautiful of them all. I love you, Jeremy."

The servants had made up the room, and on the bed lay a small box and an envelope with her name on it. She sat down on the soft comforter and picked up the envelope. Inside, she found a second envelope, curiously old-fashioned, along with a note, written in a handwriting she didn't recognize. "Lady Caroline wishes to give this, a lock of her own lover's hair, as a wedding gift," she read. "She regrets she is unable to attend the ceremonies." Alison opened the fragile envelope and dropped a curl of auburn hair onto the palm of her hand. Now where had he come up with that? she wondered, loving Jeremy all the more for his thoughtful and creative gifts.

She lay the lock of hair upon the white bedcover and turned her attention to the small box. Carefully, she untied the simple red ribbon and lifted the lid. Inside was a smaller velvet box, which she opened gingerly. Inside that, rubies and diamonds lay in a stunning array in a necklace both exquisite and tasteful. Alison gasped. She'd seen jewels before, but these were more magnificent than anything she'd ever laid eyes on. "Oh, Jeremy," she murmured as she picked up the precious treasure. She saw a small card at the bottom of the box.

"These once belonged to Lady Georgianna, Duchess of Devonshire, Lady Caroline's aunt, who in her time was considered to be the jewel of London Society, but she could never outshine you, my love."

Alison brought the gemstones to her cheek and felt their polished coolness against her skin, appreciating the treasure Jeremy had selected as a wedding present. She thought about the gift she had for him. It was nothing like the rubies and diamonds she held between her fingers, but, she thought with a secret smile, it was a greater treasure by far.

Jeremy stood next to his best man, Malcomb McTighe, watching the procession of Alison's girlhood friends move in time to the music down the aisle to stand beside her as bridesmaids. The afternoon sky was glorious with fluffy white clouds reflecting shades of gold and pink as the sun prepared to bid farewell to Dewhurst Manor and all of its glittering guests. Chairs placed on the terrace were now occupied by over a hundred guests. Music from the harpsichord where Caroline's ghost had performed its nocturnal concert reached beyond the windows of the reception room and filtered into the garden. The grounds were immaculate. The landscape architect had directed Kit and his crew of gardeners who had worked double time to restore the gardens to their very British splendor. There was still much to be done to bring them to the state Alison had in mind, but the symmetry and color of the newly planted flowers and shrubs were impressive.

The harpsichord commanded his attention suddenly, as the musician began *The Wedding March*. Jeremy's eyes were riveted on the vision in white who now emerged from the arched arbor on the arm of Benjamin Pierce. He felt his throat tighten and his heart expand as she walked toward him, her eyes shining large and golden upon him. Her dress was old-fashioned in its style, with a high waist and a modest yet revealing décolletage, much like the empire gown he'd seen on the ghost. The silken fabric was encrusted with tiny seed pearls that shimmered in the last rays of the sun, and the necklace he'd left on the bed for her was a perfect complement at her throat. My God, he thought, I never saw anyone more beautiful.

Jeremy took her arm, and together they turned to the minister who was to perform the ceremony. He felt her shaking slightly, and he covered her hand with his, reassuring her, loving her. Yes, he vowed, he would love her, honor her, cherish her, as long as he lived. Maybe even longer, he thought, considering the ghost.

When it was her turn, Alison repeated her vows, but when asked if she would love, honor, and cherish Jeremy for the rest of her days, she hesitated. She turned to him, lifted her eyes and gave him a curious smile.

"We will."

We? What was that all about? Jeremy wondered. Had her title gone to her head? Was she using the royal "we"? He couldn't imagine his bleeding heart liberal behaving in such a manner. The moment passed, however, and he forgot about it until much, much later, when the party was over and the guests had found their way through the maze to their bedrooms, and Jeremy and Alison lay together on a bed in the Dorchester in London, where they were to spend their first night as husband and wife.

"By the way," she whispered after they had made love for the second time, "thank you for the presents."

"Presents?" he murmured. "I only gave you one. The necklace. But I'm glad you like it. It looked stunning on you, by the way."

He felt Alison move closer and drape an arm around him. "But there was another present on the bed. Don't you remember the lock of Byron's hair?"

Jeremy sat up on one elbow. "Lock of hair? I didn't leave a lock of hair on the bed. I . . . uh . . . put that in the safe in the library."

"What are you talking about?"

Jeremy felt his face grow warm. How could he explain that most inexplicable incident? Even Alison might find it hard to believe that the ghost apparently had taken the lock he'd found in the book in the library, only to return it later, dressed to kill in that diaphanous gown. He decided not to go into detail. "I found a lock of hair

in a copy of *Childe Harold* in the library that was inscribed to Caroline from Lord Byron," he explained. "I
. . . pinched a few strands to give to Malcomb to run a
DNA test on it. I thought the hair might be Caroline's
because it was in an envelope addressed to Lord Chillingcote. Turned out it was Byron's. But I swear, I put
the rest of the lock in the safe in the library."

"And I swear you have larceny in your soul," Alison
laughed. "Then you didn't put the envelope containing
the lock on the bed this afternoon?"

"No. You don't suppose . . . ?"

"I thought she . . . it . . . was gone."

"Hmmm."

They lay in thoughtful silence for a long while, then
Jeremy remembered her odd answer to their wedding
vows.

"What did you mean when you answered the minister
'we will' rather than 'I' will?"

Alison pulled him to her and kissed his lips tenderly.
"Because there was more than one of us answering the
question," she murmured.

Jeremy was puzzled. "I don't understand."

"You don't happen to have any dill pickles around
here, do you?"

$\backsim$ *Epilogue* $\backsim$

The old man stood at the crest of the hill, looking across the newly-groomed landscape of Dewhurst Manor. Beside him, a large dog scratched his ear. The night was illuminated by a full moon which had risen large and golden to shine down upon the guests who had attended the wedding of the Lord and Lady of Dewhurst and who now slept in the many rooms of the old manor house.

Ashley T. Stone smiled. He'd been pleased to be invited, and he'd enjoyed the wedding, watching it from this distant vantage point. He'd never much liked formal affairs, but he'd been there, in his own way. Alison was such a lovely young woman. Looked so much like Lady Caroline, it was a little uncanny, he thought.

He wondered where Caroline's ghost was now. Since the night of the real fireworks, when he'd seen what he thought was a shooting star and had learned later from Alison was the ghost's dramatic exit, the glow had been extinguished from Dewhurst, and Ashley T. Stone figured that the spectacular pyrotechnics had been the final performance of the winsome but volatile specter.

"Come on, boy, it's late," he said to the dog at his side. "Let's go home." He started to leave, but stopped when he saw what he thought was a flicker of light in the tower of Dewhurst. He squinted. Must be mistaken, he thought, knowing that the newlyweds had left already on their honeymoon. But he saw it again, and then realized that a golden aura was slowly illuminating the ancient structure.

He chuckled. "I didn't think you'd stay away long."

BIBLIOGRAPHY

The volume of material that has been written about Lord Byron is enormous, as was the volume of his own correspondence and poetical work. For the purposes of this story, I have used the following books for accounts of Byron's conversations, letters, poetry, and comments of those who knew him:

The Complete Poetical Works of Lord Byron, Houghton Mifflin, Boston, 1933.

The Uninhibited Byron, Bernard Grebanier, Crown Publishers, New York, 1970.

Caro, The Fatal Passion, Henry Blyth, Coward, McCann, & Geohegan, New York, 1973.

The Prince of Pleasure and his Regency, J.B. Priestley, Harper and Row, New York, 1969.

The Essential Byron, Paul Muldoon, Ed., Galahad Books, New York, 1992.

His Very Self and Voice, Collected Conversations of Lord Byron, Ernest J. Lovell, Jr., Ed., Macmillan, New York, 1954.

Byron, A Critical Edition of the Major Works, Jerome J. McGann, Ed., Oxford University Press, Oxford and New York, 1986.

KAT MARTIN

Award-winning author of *Creole Fires*

GYPSY LORD
_____ 92878-5 $5.99 U.S./$6.99 Can.

SWEET VENGEANCE
_____ 95095-0 $4.99 U.S./$5.99 Can.

BOLD ANGEL
_____ 95303-8 $5.99 U.S./$6.99 Can.

DEVIL'S PRIZE
_____ 95478-6 $5.99 U.S./$6.99 Can.

MIDNIGHT RIDER
_____ 95774-2 $5.99 U.S./$6.99 Can.

Alex Hightower, an American professor, has always been fascinated by Emily Brontë and her brief, tragic life. But what were the secrets she took with her to her grave? The answers begin in the village of Haworth, where Emily lived and died, as Alex delves into the past to unlock a hundred-and-fifty-year-old mystery.

Was Emily a lonely spinster of legend? Or a troubled, passionate woman who loved in secret? And who is Selena, the mysterious gypsy beauty Alex meets on Haworth's storm-tossed moors, who speaks of a family curse, and who knows more than she realizes about Emily's secrets?

EMILY'S SECRET

Jill Jones

"Magnificent!"

—*Affaire de Coeur*

It only takes a second filled with the scream of twisting metal and shattering glass—and Chris Copestakes' young life is ending before it really began.

Then, against all odds, Chris wakes up in the hospital and discovers she's been given a second chance. But there's a catch. She's been returned to earth in the body of another woman—Hallie DiBarto, the selfish and beautiful socialite wife of a wealthy California resort-owner.

Suddenly, Chris is thrust into a world of prestige and secrets. As she struggles to hide her identity and make a new life for herself, she learns the terrible truth about Hallie DiBarto. And when she finds herself falling for Jamie DiBarto—a man both husband and stranger—she discovers that miracles really *can* happen.

ON THE WAY TO HEAVEN

TINA WAINSCOTT